ChangelingPress.com

Sarge/Dragon Duet

Harley Wylde

Sarge/Dragon Duet

Harley Wylde

All rights reserved.
Copyright ©2020 Harley Wylde

ISBN: 9798578015816

Publisher:
Changeling Press LLC
315 N. Centre St.
Martinsburg, WV 25404
ChangelingPress.com

Printed in the U.S.A.

Editor: Crystal Esau
Cover Artist: Bryan Keller

The individual stories in this anthology have been previously released in E-Book format.

No part of this publication may be reproduced or shared by any electronic or mechanical means, including but not limited to reprinting, photocopying, or digital reproduction, without prior written permission from Changeling Press LLC.

This book contains sexually explicit scenes and adult language which some may find offensive and which is not appropriate for a young audience. Changeling Press books are for sale to adults, only, as defined by the laws of the country in which you made your purchase.

Table of Contents

Sarge (Dixie Reapers MC 14) 4
   Prologue 5
   Chapter One 8
   Chapter Two 20
   Chapter Three 32
   Chapter Four 47
   Chapter Five 64
   Chapter Six 79
   Chapter Seven 91
   Chapter Eight 101
   Chapter Nine 112
   Chapter Ten 121
   Chapter Eleven 133
   Chapter Twelve 151
   Chapter Thirteen 162
Dragon (Devil's Fury MC 3) 177
   Prologue 178
   Chapter One 186
   Chapter Two 196
   Chapter Three 206
   Chapter Four 218
   Chapter Five 229
   Chapter Six 240
   Chapter Seven 250
   Chapter Eight 262
   Chapter Nine 273
   Chapter Ten 283
   Chapter Eleven 293
   Chapter Twelve 305
   Chapter Thirteen 316
   Chapter Fourteen 330
   Epilogue 339
Harley Wylde 344
Changeling Press E-Books 345

Sarge (Dixie Reapers MC 14)
Harley Wylde

Katya -- I never thought the day would come that my father would sell me to the highest bidder. Oh, he called it marriage, but I knew it was only to advance his rankings in the Bratva. Like I cared about that. But before he ruined my life, I knew I had to get my nephew to safety. My sister had told me of the man who got her pregnant, but not exactly where to find him. With Liliya gone, I needed to get Theo to safety before the shackles on me tightened even more. It never occurred to me the man would be sexy, or so alpha. The bearded beast just made things harder because now I don't want to leave, and I know if I don't that hell will come knocking.

Sarge -- Never knew I had a son, nor did I know his mother had a sister. Seeing her haul back her fist to take down a Prospect was the hottest thing I'd ever watched, and I knew then and there she'd be mine. No matter how much she protests, I'm not letting her go. She might be worried I'll get hurt, but let the Bratva come for her. They're not the Boogeyman, and I'm not scared of them. She's my fierce kitten, and I'll do whatever it takes to drive that home to her, even if I have to tie her to the bed and remind her over and over that she belongs with me.

Prologue

Sarge -- 4 Years Ago

I'd been to the diner so often my brothers were giving me shit about it, but I couldn't seem to help myself. It wasn't the food. It was the waitress. Or rather, the waitress who had vanished after a scorching hot fling. I'd told her I wasn't ready to settle down, didn't want more, but now that she'd disappeared it bothered the shit out of me. Where had she gone? No one seemed to know, or they weren't saying. I'd even asked Wire to look into it, but I hadn't liked what he'd discovered.

The woman I'd been sleeping with two years ago, the one I'd known as Lily Moran, was a ghost. From what Wire had found, Lily hadn't existed before coming to our little Alabama town. Even trying to use facial recognition crap on his computer, he hadn't been able to get any hits on her. Not before she arrived in town and not since she'd left.

I had to wonder if it had been something I said. She kept talking about starting a family, raising kids, and I'd shut that down fast. I already had a daughter, Pepper, who was full-grown and had a kid of her own. Had it really been a deal-breaker that I didn't want rug rats under my feet? I was getting old, dammit, and I deserved to enjoy my life. Hell, Pepper had been a surprise. A pleasant one, but it didn't mean I wanted to start over with a baby.

I was forty-eight years old, and biker years are like dog years. It was more like sixty for the average human. Hardly a young guy ready to change diapers. I did that for my grandson, Reed. And that kid was hell on wheels already. I couldn't handle him for more than an hour or two without feeling like I needed to sleep a damn week. I didn't know how Flicker managed it. I still wasn't overly thrilled he'd claimed my daughter, but she seemed happy, and I had to admit he treated her like a damn queen. He was older than me, but that didn't seem to bother Pepper.

"Sarge, I've told you we don't know where Lily ran off to," Margie said as she set my burger and fries in front of me. "How many times you going to come in here looking for her?"

"I know she's not here, Margie. I guess I just hope that she'll come back one day. Or maybe someone will remember something she said before she took off. Anything that might point me in the right direction."

Margie shook her head. "Listen, I know you and Lily had a thing. She didn't make no secret of it, but maybe it's best you just let this one go. Not like there aren't plenty of girls heading over to that clubhouse of yours all the time. You're not hurting for company."

No, I wasn't. I still wished I knew where Lily had gone, though. I didn't like that she'd run off and I couldn't find her, make sure she was all right. Mostly, I wanted to know if I was responsible for the way she left -- in the middle of the damn night, just snuck out. I'd gone by her place the next morning to find it empty and her car gone. The diner staff had informed me she hadn't shown for her shift, and she'd never been back.

I might be an asshole at least some of the time, but I didn't like the idea she could be in trouble. She'd said she was alone, with no family, and I hated that she might be in need of help and not have anyone to call. If she'd insisted on leaving, I could have at least made sure she knew that I would come get her if need be. What had been so damn important she'd had to take off like that?

Maybe it was the fact Wire said she'd been here under a false name that made my nape prickle. Woman didn't do something like that unless she was hiding. I only hoped that whoever, or whatever, she'd been running from hadn't found her in the last two years. If I never found out what became of her, it might very well haunt me until my dying day.

I finished my food, left some money on the table, and left.

Wherever you are, Lily, I hope you're safe.

There was nothing more I could do, and I knew it. I didn't like to admit defeat, but if the woman didn't want to be found, then that was it. I'd just have to move on and forget about her -- if I could. I hadn't loved her, but we'd had a good time, and I did care what happened to her. If things had been different, if I'd been in love with Lily, then I'd have done whatever it took to keep her by my side. That just hadn't been the case. She'd been sweet but too damn timid.

As my daughter liked to point out, I wasn't getting any younger. The way things were going, I'd be six feet under and still alone. At least I knew Pepper and my grandson would be taken care of, because Flicker would kill anyone who dared to even look at them wrong. With each passing year, I had to admit I wouldn't mind having what they shared. Hell, what half my brothers had for that matter. More and more were settling down, and I was starting to feel old sitting at the clubhouse with all the younger ones.

Time to move on, Sarge.

And that's exactly what I planned to do… just as soon as the right woman came along.

Chapter One

Katya -- Present Day

The more miles I put between myself and my family, the more the knot in my stomach eased. I glanced in my rearview mirror every ten minutes, maybe less, to check on the precious cargo I carried. My sister's child, Theo, slept soundly in his car seat. No one would care that Theo went missing, but my absence would be noticed. With Liliya no longer a viable option, my father would try to pawn me off on one of his friends to strengthen the empire. His words, not mine. The moment my sister had returned, pregnant, I'd known it was only a matter of time. I'd end up marrying the same man she'd been slated to wed.

Until my sister had gone missing about six years ago, I'd been left alone to do my own thing, which had been amazing. Then Liliya had vanished into thin air and my father had put more pressure on me to change and adapt to the way a Voronin should behave. Whatever the fuck that meant. I refused to be the dutiful little girl and marry whatever goon my father sold me to, and that was essentially what it would be. I'd thought about seeking asylum from Viktor Petrov. It was no secret that he looked more kindly on women since marrying, but I didn't know that he would care about my fate. My father was so far down the hierarchy that I was beyond a nobody.

I'd deactivated my GPS on my car, and left my phone at home. I'd grabbed a pay-as-you-go phone so I wouldn't be without a way to call for help should the need arise, but no one knew the number. I'd added any contacts I might need, but hadn't used the phone yet. There was no way they could follow me, but it didn't stop me from checking my mirrors every few miles. I didn't have much to go on. My sister had told me that Theo's father was a guy called Sarge, and he was part of some biker gang or club called the Dixie Reapers down in Alabama. I'd not dared to ask around back home, but I'd hit the road heading south, and stopped when I saw a group of bikers a few hours into my trip. I'd asked if they'd heard of the Dixie Reapers, and they'd pointed me in the right direction.

I only hoped they didn't remember me. If my father sent men in this direction, I didn't want anyone to recall that I'd been there or the questions I'd asked. The last thing I needed was anyone putting my father's guys on my trail. They were like damn bloodhounds already. If they caught a whiff of my trail, it would be a miracle if I reached Alabama before they found me, but I had to try. I owed it to my sister to make sure Theo ended up with his father.

I ached from head to toe by the time I pulled up in front of the gates of the Dixie Reapers' compound. The sun had already risen, and I was so exhausted my eyes hurt. Resting hadn't been an option, so other than breaks to use the bathroom, take care of Theo, or grabbing a bite to eat, I'd pushed through. There was a guy standing guard who eyed my car with a sneer. Great. Already off on the right foot as usual.

Rolling down the window, I peered up at him, hoping my bloodshot eyes didn't make me look like someone trying to find their next fix. It was laughable since I'd never even had a drink or smoked a cigarette, much less done drugs. Not to mention the kid in my back seat, although I supposed if I was hooked on meth or something I wouldn't give a shit if the kid was there or not.

"Whatever you're looking for, you need to find it elsewhere," the man said.

"I need to see Sarge."

He was shaking his head and backing away before I could even explain why. Anger burned hot inside me. I hadn't driven all this way, risking my life and my nephew's, for this asshole to not even let me speak to the guy. I threw open my door and got out, stomping toward him in my Doc Martens. My sister had always called them my badass bitch boots.

"Listen here, you little prick, I need to see Sarge, and I'm not leaving until I do," I said, planting my feet shoulders-width apart and folding my arms over my chest.

He eyed me up and down, then snorted. Yeah, okay, so he was a good foot taller than me. Maybe little hadn't been the right word. Then again. I eyed his crotch so he'd think that's what I meant, and with him being such a dick, maybe he really was overcompensating for something.

"You bitch." He snarled and came after me, but I stood my ground. I saw the fist coming and waited until it was nearly kissing my cheek before I ducked and planted my own against his ribs. *Thank you, self-defense classes!* I was so grateful I'd been sneaking off to a gym between classes.

"Enough!" another man shouted as he approached from inside the gate. "What the fuck is going on, Prospect? We don't hit women. Especially little pixie girls who look like they weigh ninety pounds soaking wet."

"He refuses to let me speak to Sarge," I said.

His gaze sharpened on me. "Russian?"

I bit my lip. The way he said it made me think maybe I wasn't welcome here just because of where my family came from. I'd thought I'd learned to control my accent better, but apparently I was wrong. I knew Liliya had learned to mimic accents from anywhere in the world and had probably passed for one of the regulars around here. I wasn't so lucky.

"Answer me, girl," he demanded, his voice deep and growly.

"Yes, I'm Russian." I tilted my chin up.

His lips twitched like he was fighting not to smile, then he glared at the guy he'd called Prospect. "You get the shit job of cleaning the clubhouse bathrooms for the next week, and those damn things better sparkle regardless of what time of day it is. I don't care if you have to use a fucking toothbrush to get it done. Understood?"

"Yes, sir." The guy's jaw tightened and his face flushed. I could tell he was pissed. I'd probably just made another enemy.

"Let her through." The man looked at me again. "Park in front of the large building right there, and don't wander off or I can promise you won't like the consequences."

Was it wrong that gruff tone paired with his words made my thighs clench and my panties dampen? I'd never been with a man before, but this one was almost enough to make me change my mind. I'd decided long ago they were more trouble than they were worth. Besides, I could get myself off so what was the point of letting some guy sweat all over me?

I got back in my car and pulled through the gate, stopping in front of the building. I left the engine running so the car would be comfortable for Theo, then I got out and shut the door. Leaning against it, I waited for the older man to come over and talk to me. As he drew closer, I looked him over. Tall, far taller than me, and broad but not bulky. He was muscular without looking like he went to a gym for hours every day. Then my gaze landed on the leather covering his shoulders. *Sarge*. Shit. This was the man my sister had slept with?

Sighing, I dropped my gaze. So much for my interest in a man for the first time in my life. Figured it was the guy who broke my sister's heart. Just another reason to stay single. Men were too much trouble.

"What do you want with me?" Sarge asked. He was close enough I could smell his cologne, or whatever he was wearing. It was woodsy, and oh so manly. I licked my lips and crossed my arms, knowing my nipples were hard.

"I came to bring you something."

"Oh, yeah? What's that? Because I've never seen you before, little girl, and I don't have dealings with the Bratva."

My back tensed and I nearly forgot to breathe. How had he known my family was Bratva? My gaze locked with his. "I never said anything about the Bratva."

"You have trouble written all over you. If you're one of their whores, we've already got plenty," he said, waving a hand at the building.

My chest grew tight and my eyes misted with tears. Not for myself, but for poor Liliya. After Theo was born, she'd done what she needed to keep him safe, until her mind had snapped. They'd found her hanging in her room at the Bratva-owned brothel. Thankfully, she'd left Theo somewhere safe, or as safe as he could get, and I'd had access to him. I knew our father had known of his location, but he hadn't bothered with Theo, deeming him beneath his notice.

Didn't mean he wouldn't use my nephew against me if given the chance.

Sarge must have noticed because his stance softened and he came closer, reaching out to run his fingers through my hair. "Easy, sweetheart. I didn't mean to make you cry. Why don't you tell me what's going on?"

"Back seat," I said softly. "Look in the back of the car."

He stepped back and hunkered down, then cursed. "You don't look old enough to have a kid that size."

"I don't. Theo isn't mine. He's my nephew… and your son." I glanced at him to find him watching me like a hawk would a mouse. "My sister was Liliya Voronin, but you knew her as Lily."

He stood, his hands clenched at his sides. "Was? Past tense?"

I gave a jerky nod. "She killed herself. I brought Theo to you so he'd be safe."

"I think you need to follow me to my house. This requires a more lengthy discussion, and not out here in the open. You okay to drive?"

"Yeah. I'm fine." I wasn't, but I'd never admit it. The pain of losing Liliya went deep.

I got back in my car and followed him farther into the little community, or compound. That's how Liliya had referred to it. He stopped in front of a cute house with another one right next door. A little redheaded boy in the other yard went running to him. As he scooped up the kid, I hesitated. Was that his son? What did this mean for Theo?

As I got out, I saw him kiss the boy on the cheek, then set him down. My stomach churned as I opened the back door and woke Theo from his nap. He blinked at me sleepily, then unfastened his safety belt. I helped him from the booster seat and held onto his hand as he climbed out of the car. Sarge stared at him, but Theo didn't seem to notice. He was too busy eyeing the little boy, who looked a bit like him.

"Why don't you let him stay out here with Reed?" Sarge asked. "He'll be safe and he'd probably rather play than listen to us talk."

Theo blinked at me. I asked him in Russian, knowing it would set him at ease, and he gave me a quick nod, then released my hand and wandered over to Reed. They seemed to be close in age. Theo knelt on the grass next to Reed and they started playing with the trucks scattered around. I followed Sarge into the house, and he led me straight to the kitchen, where he pulled a cold beer from the fridge.

"Want anything?" he asked.

"I'm fine."

"That's twice you've said that. I don't believe it any more now than I did then."

"Is that your son?" I asked.

"Reed?" He snorted. "He's my grandson."

Grandson? There was no freakin' way this guy was old enough to have a grandson. Sure, it was obvious he was older than me, but a grandfather? He had to be joking.

"Your son's name is Theo. He's five and should be in school already."

"Should?" Sarge asked.

It seemed we were just jumping right in. There was so much to tell him, and so little time. I couldn't stay for long, not if I wanted to keep Theo's whereabouts a secret. The last thing I wanted was my father getting his hands on my nephew.

"Theo doesn't technically exist. My father made sure of that. He was born at home to a midwife who was more interested in money than doing anything the legal way. There's no birth certificate, no social security card. Even his medical care to this point has been handled under the table, so he doesn't have a shot record either."

Sarge whistled. "So what exactly was Lily hiding from?"

That was a rather complicated question. Or maybe not so much complicated as just... I didn't know where to start. It was clear he'd not known who my sister really was, or where she'd come from. I didn't know how much he knew of the Bratva, or what our lives were like.

"Liliya was groomed all her life to be a trophy, a bargaining chip. An advantageous marriage would mean more power for my father. When she learned who he planned to marry her to, she ran. She was safe while she was here and living under another identity."

He ran a hand through his hair. "It was me, wasn't it? She found out she was pregnant and I was so damn insistent I didn't want a family that she took off."

I nodded. I knew it wasn't what he wanted to hear, but I wouldn't lie. Because of his unwillingness to even consider having a kid, my sister had thought it was better to leave. I thought she'd made a huge mistake. Even before meeting Sarge I'd felt that way. Seeing him with his grandson, I had no doubt that he'd do just fine with Theo. Maybe he wouldn't have married Liliya, but she could have stayed here and let Sarge be a part of Theo's life.

"When she left here, it wasn't but a few months before our father's men found her. They hauled her back home, but she was already showing. It was clear she was pregnant and my father was furious. He'd promised her intended that she was a virgin."

Sarge coughed. "Uh, just to clear the air a bit, I didn't take her virginity. So she'd had some fun somewhere else before coming to me."

That sounded like Liliya. She'd probably rid herself of her innocence the first chance she had, hoping it would change things if she was caught. It had changed everything, all right, but not the way she'd wanted. After Theo was born, our father had shoved her into one of the brothels. She'd taken it as long as she could, but eventually her mind had broken. The Bratva wasn't kind to women. We were possessions and nothing more.

"I need you to take Theo," I said. "He's not safe there anymore, not with Liliya gone. No one cares about Theo, except for whatever use he might be to them." Like using him to make me toe the line.

"Look, I get it. Your sister said he was mine, and I have to admit he resembles me a bit, but I'm going to need more proof than that. You need to stay at least long enough for me to have a DNA test done." Sarge rubbed the back of his neck. "I'll figure out sleeping arrangements for the two of you."

"You don't understand. The longer I'm here, the more danger your club and your son are in. I need to leave, as soon as possible."

Well, that got his attention. That laser-focused gaze landed on me again, pinning me in place. Maybe I should have worded it a little different. To be honest, the way my sister had talked about this guy, I hadn't expected him to be the type to give a shit if I was in trouble or not. She'd made him sound like a first-class asshole, and despite her harsh words I'd brought Theo here anyway, thinking it would still be safer. But I wasn't getting an asshole vibe and more of an overprotective one. Granted, he was guarding himself and his club, but that look… The tone he'd used when I said trouble was on my heels made me wonder if he would be as protective over anyone in trouble.

"Start talking, and start with your name."

I chewed on my lip and wondered if I should tell him anything. The less he knew about me the better. For him and for Theo. My family wouldn't care if my nephew vanished, but I knew they were already searching for me.

Sarge must have sensed my hesitation because he came closer, dropping down into a crouch in front of me. He reached for my hands, which I hadn't even realized I was twisting in my lap. His touch was firm but gentle, if that was even possible. The look in his eyes made my heart hurt. No one had ever looked at me like that.

"Are they going to make you marry someone who will hurt you?" he asked. "Are you in trouble?"

"It's what's expected of me. Since Liliya couldn't fulfill my father's promise, it's left to me."

He reached up and ran his fingers down my cheek. "Such a pretty girl, and too damn young. You even old enough to get married?"

I fought back a smile. I'd heard it often enough, that I didn't look my age. The only reason I'd held off on the marriage for this long was because of my studies. My intended wanted a woman who could impress his colleagues and competitors. My degree would be finished in one more semester, or that had been the plan. Something had changed, though. Maybe it was my sister's death, or perhaps something else was going on. Whatever the case, I was expected to be at a dress fitting in three days.

"I'm twenty-two," I said. "But thank you for calling me pretty. And my name is Katya."

He snorted. "Twenty-two, huh? Still just a baby. My daughter is older than you. Hell, I probably have clothes older than you."

Point made. No matter how attractive I found him, assuming I could get past the whole my-sister-had-him-first thing, he wouldn't be making any advances toward me. I was a kid to him, and maybe that was for the best.

"They'll come for me, if they can find me. I had to stop along the way and ask how to find you."

"And who the hell told you that?" he asked.

"Some bikers. I didn't stop for introductions, but they knew where I could find the Dixie Reapers. If my father sends men for me, and I'm sure he will, and they were to ask around those men could tell them where I was heading. It would lead them straight here. I need to return as soon as possible."

He stood, putting his belt at eye level with me. Or rather, the bulge beneath the belt. Oh, my. I could see why Liliya had wanted to keep him. Was he even hard or was he just that impressive while flaccid? He backed up and I jerked my gaze to his face, only to find him smirking at me.

"You going to be trouble like your sister?" he asked.

"No. I've never been with a man before. I hardly think you want to be the first."

I felt my eyes widen as the bulge in his pants seemed to get bigger. *Holy shit!*

"First off, never tell a man you'd let him be the first in your bed. It gives him ideas. Second..." He sighed. "I need to think about this and figure the best way to handle the situation. I do know one thing. You're not leaving."

Not leaving? What the hell? "You can't keep me here if I don't want to stay."

He arched an eyebrow and straightened to his full height. I had to admit, it was a bit imposing to see him like that. I shrank back in my chair. Standing up to the guy at the gate was one thing, but Sarge was another matter. He was definitely the type who expected to be obeyed or there would be consequences.

Sarge stalked toward me, then caged me between his arms. "Let me tell you something right now, little girl. You *will* stay here, and if you refuse, then I'll spank your ass and tie you to the bed."

My breath caught and my panties got even wetter than before. "Promise?"

I slapped a hand over my mouth. I hadn't meant to say that. The word had just slipped out, but he chuckled, the sound all dark and smoky.

"Oh, yeah, sugar. I sure the fuck promise." He leaned in closer. "And you may very well be naked, but I'm thinking you'll be okay with that."

Oh. My. God. No wonder my sister ended up pregnant. I was about two seconds from combusting and all he'd done was talk to me. I was in so much trouble.

Chapter Two

Sarge

What the fuck are you thinking? She's twenty-two, and Lily's sister. Shit. I had a son I'd never known about. That needed to be first and foremost in my mind right now, not the fact she smelled like goddamn sunshine, or felt like silk. I definitely didn't need to be thinking about how tight her virgin pussy would be, or the fact she seemed just as drawn to me as I was to her.

When I'd seen that little shit at the gate try to hit her, I'd about lost it. He was lucky I hadn't stomped his ass, but Katya had taken care of herself. If it hadn't been for that, we'd have been down a man and Torch would have been pissed. Well, not after I explained *why* we needed a new Prospect. I had no doubt he'd stand by me on that score. No one hurt a woman around here, not without paying the price.

Her little show of defiance, then the way she'd defended herself, had gotten me hard as fuck, even before I'd gotten an up close look at her. After she'd said she was Lily's sister, I could see the resemblance. A little. Maybe. Other than them both being blonde and having blue eyes; that's about where the similarities stopped. This spitfire had something Lily never had. She was a fighter and full of sass. Lily had been quiet and sweet. I'd been intrigued by her, but not in the *I want to keep her* kind of way, not after I discovered she was very timid and meek. We'd had fun, but that was all it had been.

But Katya? Hell. If she were about two decades older, or even just one decade older, then she'd have been exactly the type of woman I wanted and had never found. The age thing was going to cause me problems around here. Not because no one else claimed younger women, but because she was younger than Pepper. My daughter was never going to let me hear the end of this.

I'd put some space between us before I'd done something stupid, like strip her naked and make her come. It was a struggle to maintain control, especially after that softly spoken "*Promise*" had slipped past her lips.

The front door opened and slammed shut, then booted steps headed our way. Flicker had a scowl on his face when he came into the room. "Do you know there's a kid outside playing with my son? Who the fuck is he and where did he come from?"

"Theo is his son," Katya said. "And since you have a kid I'm sure I don't need to tell you where babies come from."

And that was when I knew for damn sure I'd never let her go. Flicker's jaw dropped, then snapped shut as he studied Katya. Then his gaze swung my way, but he still seemed at a loss for words.

"Katya is Lily's sister. It seems when she ran, she took part of me with her."

"So why didn't Lily bring him to you? And why wait all this time?" Flicker asked.

"Because she's dead," Katya said. "I didn't think Theo was safe anymore."

Flicker pulled out a chair and sat, then looked at me expectantly. As an officer of the club, I knew he wanted answers. Even worse, he was my son-in-law, which was all kinds of fucked up with him being older than me. But as long as Pepper was happy, that was all that mattered. I sure the fuck hoped she felt that way about my relationship when I claimed Katya.

"Start talking," Flicker said, his gaze moving to Katya. "How much trouble are you in and who's coming for you?"

Katya sighed. "No one will come here to find me because I'm not staying. I've already accepted my fate, but I needed to make sure Theo was with his father."

Flicker looked my way and mouthed *her fate*? I was done arguing with her. She wasn't going back to the Bratva, and that was final. I needed to officially meet my son, get to know him, figure out what he needed and all that shit. But I also needed to handle Katya, and I had a feeling I was on borrowed time if I didn't tackle that first.

"Watch her," I told Flicker before leaving the room. I heard his muttered *asshole*, and I knew he'd yell at me later for giving him an order. Too fucking bad.

I stepped outside and saw Pepper kneeling with the kids. She stared at me as I walked closer, then looked at Theo, then me. She did that about a dozen times.

"Something I need to know?" she asked.

"Meet your brother, Theo." The kid stopped what he was doing to look at me. "Hey, kid. It seems I'm your dad."

He didn't say anything. I hadn't even considered whether or not he spoke English. I'd heard Katya speak to him in Russian, but she hadn't used English when talking to him, at least not when I was around. Unfortunately, I didn't know any.

"Do you speak English?" I asked him.

He still didn't say anything. Or blink. What the fuck?

"Maybe we need Grimm?" Pepper suggested.

He was the only brother I knew who could speak Russian. I'd ask Katya, but if I brought her out here, I didn't trust her not to try and run. Then again, if she did, I'd have yet another reason to paddle her ass.

"I'll be back," I said, then went to get Katya. She was having a staring contest with Flicker, and it looked like she very well might win. "I need to know if Theo understands or speaks English. He's not responding to me or my daughter."

She snorted, but didn't break Flicker's gaze. "He knows English. Tell him *doveryat'*. It means trust. It's sort of our secret code. If someone tells him that word, he knows it's okay to speak to them."

Smart. I went back to Theo and Pepper, said the magic word, and the little boy relaxed. He gave me a hesitant smile. "You're my dad?"

I nodded. "Yep, it seems that way." He looked at Pepper, his nose scrunched as if he couldn't figure out who she was or why she was there. He had to have heard me tell Pepper that they were brother and sister. Or was he confused because she was an adult? "I had Pepper when I was a lot younger. She's my daughter, which makes the two of you siblings. You've been playing with her son, Reed. My grandson."

"Aunt Kat said that I had to stay here with you now," Theo said.

I was surprised at how clearly he spoke, and how grown-up he sounded. There were times I still had trouble understanding Reed, mostly because he talked so fast it all ran together, but Theo seemed older than his years.

"Yeah, you're going to live here with me," I said. "We'll get everything squared away so you can go to school. Maybe you and Reed will have the same class."

"Aunt Kat taught me when she was around, and other times she made sure I had tutors." He pushed a truck across the grass. "She's always taken care of me. I don't even remember my mom."

Katya had said that Lily was forced into a brothel after Theo was born. It hadn't occurred to me that she'd have hardly ever seen him. Made sense now that I thought about it. It wasn't like she could keep him there with her. But still, Katya was so young. She had to have been in high school when Theo was born. That was a lot of responsibility for a kid to handle.

"Theo, I want to get a chance to learn more about you, and for you to get to know me better too, but first I need to take care of a few things. Like making sure your Aunt Kat is safe. We both want that, right?" I asked.

"If she leaves here, I'll never see her again," he said. "She told me she has to get married and the man isn't nice. I know my grandfather hates me. I ruined his plans for my mom."

The kid knew too much, but I could understand why Katya would explain things to him. The more he knew, the safer he would be. Any other kid wouldn't have these sorts of worries. I didn't think Reed worried about much except whether or not Pepper would force him to eat carrots.

"In order to make sure your Aunt Kat stays here, I need you to go with Pepper for a little while. I'll work on getting a room set up for you, but until then, she'll see that you have anything you need." I glanced at Pepper and she gave me a nod.

"Okay," he said. He hesitated and watched me a moment, and I could see the wheels turning in his head. "If you married Aunt Kat, then she could stay, and she'd be my mom. She acts like a mom already."

I couldn't help but laugh, mostly because that fell perfectly in line with what I wanted. Katya wasn't leaving. If I needed to put a ring on her finger to keep the Bratva away, so be it. Not that I thought for a moment they would care if she was married or not. Whether I married her or just claimed her, she wouldn't be a virgin for much longer, and that's all that seemed to matter to her father. I knew he wouldn't back down easily, but if I made Katya mine, the club would have no choice but to fight for her. With her being my son's aunt, I knew they'd go to bat for her anyway, but I'd never let her know that. I'd take whatever leverage I could get. With me being so much older than she was, I wasn't sure if her attraction was more of the one-night variety or the forever type.

"Marry Aunt Kat, hmm?" Pepper asked.

"Shut it," I told her. "Take care of Theo. I'll send Flicker back out, if he's done trying to stare down Katya."

Theo giggled. "He'll never win."

I had a feeling the kid was right.

When I got back inside, the two of them hadn't moved. Jesus, had neither of them blinked yet? Flicker had narrowed his gaze, but Katya was resting her chin on her fist, looking like she hadn't a care in the world.

"Are the two of you finished acting like kids?" I asked.

Flicker broke first and glanced my way. "She started it."

"I think Reed is rubbing off on you," I said. "Pepper is outside with the kids. Y'all are keeping Theo for a night or two. Not sure what all he needs."

"Almost everything," Katya said. "I grabbed him, his favorite bear, and a few changes of clothes but I had to leave everything else. If it had been noticed I was packing a lot of stuff or filling the trunk of my car, I never would have made it out of town, much less gotten this far. His things are in my back seat."

I'd figured as much. Taking my wallet from my pants, I opened it up and pulled out a few hundreds. Flicker took them and stood. With a nod, he left the room, then the house. I had no doubt he was getting Theo's belongings and would make sure my son had whatever he needed to get by for a few nights.

I eyed Katya, who was staring at me with a hint of defiance in her gaze. Yeah, she was going to be fun to tame. I didn't want to break her spirit, but she needed to learn I was in charge. Moving closer, I waited until I was right next to her chair before I reached for her. I placed my hand on her shoulder and gave it a slight squeeze. As much as I wanted to claim her here and now, I realized there were dark smudges under her eyes, and she looked like she hadn't slept well in a few days.

"Come on, kitten. I think you need to rest."

"Kitten?" she asked. "My name is Katya, but it doesn't mean I'm a cat."

I couldn't help but smile. "That's not why I called you kitten. You look all cute and cuddly, but I've seen that you have claws and a sharp wit."

She relaxed a little, and I could tell she liked the comparison. Made me wonder if anyone had ever given her a pet name before. I urged her up out of the chair and toward my room. I'd renovated my guest room into a play area for Reed, so there wasn't another bed for her to use. There was a third bedroom, but it was currently not designed for company. While she napped, I'd have to come up with a plan for my son to have a space he felt was his own, without leaving Reed out.

Katya froze when we entered my room and she looked around. She tried to take a step back, but I was blocking the doorway. I urged her forward and paused only long enough to open a dresser drawer and pull out one of my softer shirts. I tossed it onto the bed, then folded my arms over my chest and stared her down. She might have tried to win with Flicker, but under my gaze, she submitted, her head bowing.

"You can wear my shirt to sleep in."

"Thought you said you were tying me to the bed," she muttered.

"Maybe later." Her gaze shot up to meet mine. "Right now, you need to sleep. I'll step into the hall to give you some space."

Before I could leave she reached out and grabbed onto my cut. I should have demanded she let go, and with any other woman I would have. Katya was different, and I was going to make her mine, which meant she got certain liberties others didn't. Placing my hand over hers, I waited to see what she wanted or needed.

"Stay," she said.

I lowered my head until our noses nearly touched. "If you want me to stay, then I will, and I will damn sure claim you when you've had some rest, but if you're thinking that baring that hot little body will leave me stupid and give you a chance to escape, I'm just going to go ahead and tell you it won't work."

"You can't claim me," she said. Her eyes turned glassy with unshed tears. "If things were different, I'd love to stay and see where things went between us. I've never been attracted to someone the way I am to you, but I can't risk Theo's safety. Or yours."

It was sweet the way she worried about us. Her fears were unfounded, but she didn't know a damn thing about me or this club. My brothers had my back, and they'd keep Theo safe too. My hands weren't squeaky clean, but I didn't need to tell her that just yet. The last thing I wanted was to send her running scared. Let her think I was better than the men she'd run from. I knew I was just as dirty as they were.

"Kitten, I can take care of myself, and keep my boy safe," I said. "You're not leaving. If you think for one second I'm going to let some Bratva bastard get his hands on you, then you're mistaken. You came here, all full of sass and mother bear instincts, protecting a kid I didn't even know I had, and you think you can just walk away?"

She rubbed at her neck and looked away. I knew she worried that we'd be in danger if she remained here. If the Bratva wanted her back, then they could come and try to take her. They wouldn't win. Once I decided something was mine, I never let it go. Katya made the mistake of catching my attention, far more than a woman ever had before. Sure, I'd had fun with plenty of ladies over the years, but I'd never once thought to keep any of them.

"We'll talk more after you've slept. You're exhausted, kitten. Don't even try to deny it."

Her shoulders slumped and she gave a nod, then reached for the hem of her shirt. I should have walked away, given her some privacy, but the moment the black lace of her bra came into view I was incapable of leaving. She kicked off her shoes and shimmied out of her jeans, then just stood there with a lost look in her eyes. I ran a hand down my face in an effort to knock my brain back on track. I grabbed the shirt I'd pulled out for her, placing it in her hands.

Katya drew it over her head, then reached behind her. Next thing I knew, she was reaching into the arm holes of the shirt and pulling her bra straps off, then the garment fell at her feet. I'd never seen a woman do that before, and it made me wonder what else I'd missed out on by never sticking around longer than it took to get us both off. She kicked the bra away and climbed into bed, pulling the covers up to her shoulders.

I wasn't about to take a chance on her attempting an escape. I held out my hand. "Panties too."

Her eyes went wide, but she obeyed, sliding them off under the covers and giving them to me. I gathered her clothes and walked out. She gasped behind me, but I just smiled and kept going. Not only did I want to make sure she didn't try to sneak away, but it didn't seem like she had anything else with her. She'd want clean clothes until I could take her shopping for a few more things. Our small town didn't boast a lot of the nicer stores, but if she got a few days' worth of items, then I could order more online and have it delivered.

I dumped everything into the washer and got it going, then went back to the bedroom. She still looked a little shocked I'd taken her clothes.

"I'm going to wash your things. I'm assuming you didn't stop to pack, since you said you were trying not to draw attention."

"I don't have anything else," she said.

"After you've gotten a little sleep, I'll take you out to eat and pick up the essentials you'll need. We can order more later."

Her brow furrowed and I knew she was about to argue, tell me that she wasn't staying. I had news for her. She was most definitely staying, even if I really did have to tie her to the damn bed.

I pulled off my boots, set my cut on the dresser, and yanked my shirt over my head. I pulled my belt free and let it fall to the floor. Katya squirmed, but she didn't bolt from the bed, which was surprising. I'd half-expected her to take off when I started getting undressed. I wasn't removing anything else, but she wouldn't know that until I got into the bed with her.

"Think I'll just lie right there with you. Make sure you sleep like you're supposed to."

"I'm not a child," she said.

I chuckled and eyed her curves that I could still plainly see under the blankets. "No, kitten, you definitely aren't a child. What you are is a stubborn woman who refuses to do what's best for her. So you know what that means?"

She shook her head as I approached and slid into the bed next to her. "It means I'm going to take care of you, since you won't take care of yourself."

Her gaze softened and she closed her eyes, a sigh slipping past her lips. "You're biting off more than you can chew."

"You let me worry about that. Sleep, kitten. All your troubles can be dealt with better once you've gotten some rest. I'm betting you've been going non-stop for twenty-four hours, if not longer. You're going to get sick, Katya."

She huffed but her body slowly started to relax. After a few minutes, I reached over and pulled her against my side. She snuggled closer, but didn't wake. While there were things I could be doing right now, I could plan just as easily in this bed as I could pacing my damn kitchen. I'd have to let the others know I had a guest and that she'd brought my son with her, and possibly a bit of trouble, but that could wait. Flicker already knew what was going on. As the club treasurer, I knew he'd tell the others if he thought it was necessary.

A soft snore escaped Katya and I bit my lip so I wouldn't laugh. It was pretty damn cute, but then so was she. Those flashing eyes, sassy attitude, and smart mouth might run off a lesser man. For me, she was absolutely perfect. I closed my eyes a moment as a wave of sorrow hit me, knowing the only reason I'd ever found her was because Lily had died. I might not have loved her, or wanted her long-term, but I'd never wished her harm. I'd hoped that she'd started a new life somewhere, found someone to make her happy. It hadn't seemed likely with the way she vanished, but part of me had wanted to be wrong. I hadn't wanted trouble to find her, even though Wire had said it seemed she was on the run. If only she'd told me about Theo. I wouldn't have married her, or claimed her, but I'd have kept the both of them safe.

Whatever it took, I'd make sure the men who hurt her paid the price. A father was supposed to love and protect his kids, not whore them out. The fucker was dead if he ever showed his face here.

Chapter Three

Katya

When Sarge had said he was taking me to eat and buying me some things, I'd thought he meant fast food and a discount shop. I'd been so very wrong. The restaurant was deceiving on the outside. It looked plain and like they would serve cheap food. My eyes nearly popped out of my head when I saw the prices, but Sarge insisted they had the best steaks for miles. Had my father been paying, I wouldn't have thought twice about my order. I didn't know enough about Sarge to splurge on a thirty-dollar steak.

He yanked the menu from my hands and glowered. "Do you like steak?"

"Yes."

"Baked potatoes or baked sweet potatoes?"

I cocked my head, wondering where this was going. "Either."

"How do you eat your steak? Well done?"

My nose wrinkled. "What heathen would ever do that to a steak?"

His lips twitched like he was fighting back a smile. "Good girl. You just sit there being pretty and I'll order our food. And don't even think of arguing with me."

I wasn't sure if I was flattered or insulted by his demand. While I loved that he thought I was pretty, and he'd told me so before, the other part wanted to snarl and tell him I had a brain and could order my own damn food. I'd always thought the Bratva was bad about domineering men, but I had to wonder if it wasn't just the male species as a whole. Did they all get the Neanderthal you-woman-me-man gene?

"You look both irate and happy at the same time," he said. "It's an interesting expression, even if I'm not sure how you're pulling it off."

Before I could think better of it, I flipped him off. Sarge snorted and then laughed. It was a good look on him. I wondered how often he smiled. He hadn't done a lot of it in the very short amount of time I'd known him. Lily hadn't talked much about him, not anything specific. She'd called him an asshole several times, but other than to tell me he hadn't wanted kids, or her, she'd not said a lot. It felt wrong, being so attracted to him, and knowing he wanted me in return. He'd been Lily's first. Or maybe not, since he'd said he'd never wanted to keep her. It made me wonder if she'd known going in that he wasn't in it for the long haul, or had she thought she would tame him anyway?

Now that was laughable. I could tell already that he wasn't the type to be tamed. Oh, he might let a woman catch him, but he'd still call all the shots. Sarge wasn't the type to roll over and let his woman handle things. I'd been strong all my life, by necessity. My father and his men had let me be for the most part, until the time came for me to replace Lily in his plans. That taste of what my life would be like had been enough to send a spike of fear through me. Sarge called me mouthy, and he wasn't wrong. Women like me didn't fare well with the Bratva.

He said he was keeping me. I would certainly prefer being his than going back home, but I couldn't help worrying over his safety, or Theo's. By me staying, I was bringing trouble their way, and my father would stop at nothing to get me back. It seemed unfair that I finally found a man who interested me, one who made me tingle in all the right spots, and I knew I should walk away from him.

"You're thinking too hard, kitten," he said.

"I just..." I clamped my lips together, not really knowing what to say.

His phone jingled and he glanced at the screen, his lips tipped down in a frown. "I should know this already since he's my son, but is Theo his full name?"

I blinked, trying to catch up to the quick subject change. Had someone texted him about Theo? Was he all right? The man called Flicker had said he'd watch him, and Sarge assured me Theo was safe, but what if he wasn't?

Sarge stared at me, waiting patiently.

"Just Theo. Since he doesn't have a birth certificate, he doesn't really have a last name."

Sarge scowled. "Oh, he sure the fuck does. Mine! And hopefully within the hour, Wire will fix it so that Theo is mine legally in every way possible. There will be a paper trail your father won't be able to refute, and the boy will be safe from the Bratva."

I didn't see how. If they put my sister down as the mother, then my father could still try to get his hands on Theo. I knew he wouldn't really want him, except to use as leverage against me. It was a large part of why I'd brought Theo here. I'd hoped his father would keep him safe from mine. It would have been too easy for Theo to vanish, either sold or left in a dumpster. It was what my father had threatened to do if I didn't bow to his demands, and I had no doubt that he and my future husband would hold Theo over me the rest of my life. One slipup, and my nephew's life would be over.

A server appeared and Sarge placed our order. As he messaged whoever was on the other end of his texts, I nibbled on a roll. My stomach growled, reminding me that I'd eaten mostly junk food for over twenty-four hours in my mad dash to get Theo to safety. He muttered under his breath a few times, but finally he set the phone aside and gave me his attention once more.

"Sorry about that. I had planned to tackle all that after I had you a bit more sorted out, but it seems Flicker already told everyone about Theo. They wanted to make sure he was documented as my son."

It was nice that he had people to help, people who cared. I couldn't remember ever having that in my life. Liliya had cared to a point. Not enough to remain at home, but when I was younger, I'd gotten lots of hugs from her. After she left, there was no one who cared. Our mother had died shortly after I was born, and our father only cared about what he could gain from using us as pawns.

"Understandable." I toyed with the rest of my roll. "Look, now that Theo is safe, I should really --" He reached over and covered my lips with his finger.

"Don't even finish that fucking sentence, kitten. I'd hate to take you over my knee and spank that sexy ass right here in the middle of the restaurant."

My pulse raced at the thought of him doing such a thing. Maybe I'd read too many books in my spare time. The thought of him spanking me shouldn't be such a turn on, should it? I could even feel my nipples getting hard, and hoped like hell he didn't notice. It wasn't that I feared he'd take advantage, but more that I'd crawl onto his lap and beg him to do all sorts of naughty things to me.

His lips tipped up on one corner and laughter danced in his eyes. "Or maybe you like that idea. Something I'll have to keep in mind."

"I won't be here," I murmured around the finger pressed to my lips.

He simply arched an eyebrow with a look that clearly said he disagreed. The man was stubborn as hell, but it made me all warm inside that he wanted me to stay. Sarge pulled back and I licked my lips. His eyes darkened as he watched, and it made me want to flick my tongue over my lips again, just to see what he'd do. I knew I was playing with fire, but at the moment I didn't much care.

Our food arrived and I tried to eat and just enjoy his company without thinking too much about what lay ahead. One way or another, I needed to get back on the road and go home. I didn't know how to make him understand. He'd never dealt with my father, didn't know how treacherous he could be. I'd done my duty to my sister and delivered Theo to his father, making sure my nephew had a chance at a decent life. Now it was time to honor my promise to my father. Well, maybe not so much a promise, but more of an understanding. I obeyed and he didn't lash out by hurting anyone he perceived might be a friend. Too many innocent lives were at stake if I didn't go back.

"Why is your accent so faint?" Sarge asked. "I've only heard you use Russian with Theo, and even then, you didn't say a lot."

That was easy enough to explain. Although, until this trip, I'd honestly thought I'd killed enough of my accent that it wasn't noticeable. It seemed I'd been wrong all this time. No one else had ever asked if I was Russian. I'd thought perhaps I'd picked up my sister's ability to blend in. If she hadn't gotten pregnant with Theo, she could have easily stayed hidden here, off our father's radar. For a while at any rate. After all, I'd been there as a backup if he could never find her.

It hurt that Liliya had never once thought of the consequences of her actions impacting anyone but herself. I knew she had come across as sweet and shy to other people. She *could* be sweet, but I also knew that when it came down to it, she'd have done whatever it took to keep herself safe. It's what puzzled me so much about her leaving this place instead of just telling Sarge about the baby. Had she actually loved him? It didn't seem possible, since I'd never known my sister to love anyone. Not even me. She'd shown me signs of affection over the years, but as I'd gotten older, I'd realized she'd done it so I'd be willing to keep her secrets.

My sister was a selfish bitch deep down, but no one else ever saw that side of her. I hoped that Sarge never found out who she truly was and could continue to remember her as someone timid. She'd suffered enough at the end, and despite her faults, I'd loved her.

"You noticed Liliya sounded like she was from here. It's because she had a gift. I've worked hard to hide my accent, but I guess not hard enough. We came to the US when I was four. My accent might have died completely had I not been surrounded by the Bratva and their families my entire life. It wasn't until college that I was able to immerse myself in a different type of life. One I enjoyed and had hoped to continue." My lips twisted. Until Liliya came back pregnant.

"If your father is so horrible, why didn't your sister take you with her when she ran?" he asked.

Damn. I'd really hoped he would leave it alone. Thinking ill thoughts of Liliya was one thing. I didn't want to speak them aloud, especially to the man who had fathered her child. It seemed wrong on so many levels.

"I was still young when Liliya ran off. When I got older, I'd been permitted to attend a nearby college, with the thought my father would eventually catch my sister and bring her home. When he found her, everything changed. She could no longer be his bargaining chip."

Sarge leaned closer. "In other words, she fucked you over."

I winced, but nodded. "Yes. I know she didn't intend to get pregnant with Theo, and I love him so much, but her no longer being a virgin or at least being capable of pretending to be one derailed my plans. And ultimately, she paid too high a price."

Sarge didn't say anything for several minutes. We ate in silence, but I could tell he was gathering his thoughts. He'd pause now and then, as if he wanted to say something, then changed his mind. I liked that he took the time to contemplate something as simple as a conversation. It meant that he'd do the same when it came to caring for Theo. I was certain I'd made the right decision in bringing my nephew to his father.

"Your sister pretended to be something she wasn't. I didn't love her, couldn't love her for that matter. She was weak and too fucking quiet. Knowing what she did to you just pisses me off even more. It takes a truly spineless person to run off and leave an innocent behind, and don't try to tell me that she didn't realize you'd likely have to take her place. She was a selfish bitch for what she did, and I'm glad I didn't claim her."

I blinked, not sure what to say to that. No one ever saw Liliya that clearly. They all saw blonde perfection. Honestly, she'd have been an amazing Bratva wife. She could be just as cold and calculating as the men, and would have been an asset. I, on the other hand, was the total opposite. I'd fight tooth and nail to prevent an injustice from happening, but I knew if I went back and didn't toe the line my father would find a way to hurt others in retaliation. He'd make me pay over and over again, and my husband possibly would too. I'd heard stories of wives being passed off to multiple men in a single night when they fucked up.

I dropped my gaze to my now empty plate and almost missed him laying down a wad of cash on the table. He stood and reached for my hand, lifting me from the chair. I followed him from the restaurant, unsure how he'd known how much to leave but not wanting to question him. When we got outside, he helped me into the truck that he'd borrowed from the club, insisting his saddlebags wouldn't hold everything we needed. It seemed I was being held prisoner a bit longer. Secretly, I loved it and wished I never had to leave. Being with Sarge was easy. I didn't have to watch what I said because he seemed to like my attitude just fine.

He pulled into a strip mall, and we started at one end and worked our way down to the other. I kept arguing that I only needed a change of clothes, but he'd ignore me and add more to our purchases. Or rather *my* purchases that he insisted on paying for. By the time we got back into the truck, my feet ached and the back seat was full of sacks from multiple shops.

"Grocery store, then home," he said. "And if you even try to get in your car when we get to the house, I'll tie you to the bed."

"You know, that's not the first time you've threatened to tie me down. I'm starting to think you have a fascination with tying up women."

He cut his gaze my way and I felt my cheeks warm. It seemed that maybe I was right, and oddly, it turned me on. A lot. I squirmed in my seat and pressed my thighs together. Sarge jerked the wheel, turning off down another road, almost as if he'd not intended to go this way. He didn't so much as look at me as he pulled into a parking space in front of a shop that said Sensual Delights. The windows were so dark I couldn't see inside.

"Don't fucking move from that spot," he said, pointing a finger at me. "Because if you do, you'll get that spanking right here and now, and possibly a lot more. Understood?"

I nodded, but in my heart I knew that the second I thought he wasn't looking, I'd bolt. Even if I had to leave my car behind, I'd find a way home without it. He gave me a stern look before getting out and walking into the shop. I still couldn't tell what type of place it was, but I counted to ten, my heart slamming against my ribs. When I thought the coast might be clear, I unbuckled my seat belt, opened the door, and took off running.

I only made it half a block before arms banded around my waist and I was hauled back against a hard chest. A growl near my ear sent shivers down my spine. Just by the scent alone, I knew Sarge had caught me.

"I warned you, baby girl. You didn't listen, and now you'll pay the price."

"Please, Sarge. You know I'm right. You know I need to leave."

He started stomping back down the sidewalk to the shop. He pushed the door open and barely gave me a second to look around before he went through a beaded curtain at the back and slammed through a door, shutting and locking it behind him. I looked around, my hands clenching at my sides. The place looked… My breath caught.

"Is this a dungeon?" I asked.

"What do you know about places like this?" he asked, prowling closer, a dangerous glint in his eye.

I licked my lips and looked around again. "Only what I've seen in porn."

That made him pause, mid-step. He stared at me a moment before giving me a faint smile that only lasted a second. Then he was on me, dragging me across the room to a chair. He sat, then popped the button on my jeans, slid the zipper down, and yanked my pants and panties around my knees so fast I didn't have time to stop him. Then I was over his lap, and holy hell! The bulge pressing against me made me wish I'd been bad before this.

His hand cracked against my ass cheek, the sound loud in the small room. I gasped and kicked my feet, but he banded his arm across my lower back to hold me in place. He spanked me again and again. My ass started to burn, but even more embarrassing was the fact I was getting wet. Like really, really wet.

"I told you if you disobeyed you'd pay for it." *Smack. Smack.* Then he let his fingers dip between my legs and he stroked my pussy. He chuckled softly. "Seems my baby girl likes her punishment."

Talk about being mortified! My cheeks were burning as much as my ass and I refused to look at him. *Smack. Smack. Smack.* I moaned and squirmed on his lap.

"Anyone ever made you come?" he asked.

I shook my head so hard my neck nearly cracked.

He spread my pussy open, then teased my clit with his finger. It was almost too much and I sucked in a breath, so close to coming that I wanted to cry out in frustration. He rubbed a little harder and as I started to come, he sank his finger into me, stroking slowly.

"Sarge." I breathed his name like a prayer.

"Right now, I'm not Sarge. When my fingers, or my dick, are in your pussy, you call me Lance."

He plunged his fingers in deeper, curling them slightly and I came so hard I saw stars. I burned from him stretching me, but I welcomed it. I knew in that moment, he'd already ruined me for any other man. No one would ever compare.

His fingers slid from my pussy and he smacked my ass again, then stood me upright. I started to reach for my pants, but he reached down and pulled off my shoes, then removed my jeans and panties completely. My eyes went wide as I stared at him, not certain what he was about to do, but fearing he was about to make a huge mistake.

"Not going to have you run again," he said, reaching for his belt.

He unbuckled it, then unfastened his pants, pushing them down. His cock was hard and pointing straight up. The bead of moisture on the tip made me want to lick it. Would he taste salty? Sarge gripped my hips, lifting me up and setting me down in a... I glanced up and saw chains that slightly rattled. He'd put me in a sex swing? My gaze jerked back to him. He reached for an ankle, slipping a Velcro cuff around it, then did the same to the other, holding me open.

"Wh-what are you doing?" I stammered.

"Sorry, baby girl. I'd have done this different if you weren't so damn stubborn." He stroked his cock and I eyed it with a hunger I'd never felt before. I wanted it. In my mouth. In my pussy. I wanted Sarge more than I'd ever wanted anything, but I knew I should tell him no. He cocked his head to the side as he kept tugging on his shaft. "You going to lie and say you don't want me? That you don't ache to have me balls-deep inside you?"

I opened and shut my mouth, decided to shake my head. No, I couldn't lie and tell him I didn't want those things. But I *shouldn't* want them.

"Never took a woman by force and don't want to start now," he said, coming closer. "But, kitten, you're mine and if this is what it takes to drive that home, then I will fuck you all day and all night. Fill you so full of my cum that there will be no doubt who you belong to."

My lips parted and I felt myself get even wetter. *Holy shit!* My nipples hardened almost to the point of pain. I should tell him to stop. I should. But I wouldn't. The way he was talking to me, just flat out staking his claim, was probably the hottest thing I'd ever heard. I loved every word falling from his tongue.

He smirked. "I think you liked that, didn't you? That it? You want me to talk dirty to you?"

"I... Maybe?"

He gripped the swing and used it to line me up right where he wanted me. I felt the head of his cock brush against me, then he was slowly sinking inside. If I'd thought his fingers made me burn, this was altogether different. I nearly panicked, thinking he wouldn't fit, or that he'd split me in two. Sarge seemed to read my fears and reached down to rub my clit. The pleasure that spiraled through me soon outweighed the pain of him taking my innocence. It wasn't all that painful in all honesty. More like a rug burn.

"Come for me, kitten. Show me how much you want this big cock." He circled my clit before pinching it. "Tell me how much you want my cum."

I threw my head back and tried to focus on the intense sensations that seemed to flow through me. I was close. So very close.

"And after I've filled up this pussy, made it mine enough times there will never be any doubt, I'm going to claim that tight little ass of yours too." I gasped and my gaze flew to his. He shifted and I felt his finger stroke over the spot I'd always thought of as taboo when it came to sex. Sarge seemed to have other ideas. "That's right. I'll wear out your pussy, make you come so many times you lose your voice, then I'll work my cock into this tight little hole and give you a good, hard fucking."

I didn't know if he actually meant any of that, but his words were enough to send me flying. He pressed his finger there as he drove into me, his cock filling every inch of my pussy. When he came, I felt the hot spurts of his release. He didn't stop, didn't slow down. I realized his cock wasn't getting any softer or smaller. I'd always thought only porn stars went more than once, but it seemed I'd been wrong about another thing.

Sarge worked his hand under my shirt and reached up to cup my breast. He pinched my nipple through my bra.

"Please. Please. Please."

"Please what, kitten?"

"I want to come."

"So very, very bad." I knew I was whining and begging, but I didn't care. He'd made me feel things I'd never experienced before and I wanted more. I never wanted it to stop.

He worked my body like a pro and had me screaming out two more orgasms before he came again. This time, he pulled out. A grin crossed his face as he stared at my extremely sore pussy. The bastard even winked at me as I felt his release sliding out of me.

"I think I hate you right now," I said. "No one will ever be able to top that."

He released my ankles, then helped me from the swing. I eyed the contraption and realized there were restraints hanging from the ceiling on the other end too. He could have easily locked my hands in place as well, but he hadn't.

Sarge pulled me closer, then kissed the hell out of me. His tongue tangled with mine, and he gripped my hair so tight I couldn't have escaped. Not that I wanted to. My toes curled and I leaned into him.

"Mine," he said, his voice nearly a growly. "My woman. No one will ever take you from me."

"Lance." I bit my lip. "Or am I back to Sarge?"

A soft smile tipped his lips up at the corners. "Whenever we're alone, you can call me Lance. The rest of the time it's Sarge."

"You've brought hell to your doorstep, but… no one has ever made me feel as wanted as you have. Even when I ran, I wanted to stay."

He pressed a quick kiss to my lips again. "You're not going anywhere, kitten. Next time your punishment will be even worse."

His words made my pussy tingle. If he thought that was a deterrent, he was so very wrong. All he'd done was make me want to misbehave so we could have some more fun. I wondered what he'd try next time.

His lips brushed my ear as he crowded me. "Do you have any idea how fucking hot it is that you weren't some shy little virgin? No, not my kitten. Innocent, yes. Shy? Fuck no. You came on my cock like you were meant for it."

My brow furrowed and I pulled back to glare at him. "Did you just call me a whore?"

The slap to my ass made me squeak in surprise. "Only if you're my whore. Anyone else touches you, looks at you with lust in their eyes, or dares to put their cock in you, and I will fucking end them."

And that was the moment I started to fall for the big, sexy beast. Maybe I was just as crazy as him. I didn't think normal people would react the way I had, but then, normal was highly overrated.

Chapter Four

Sarge

What the fuck had I done? I'd taken her in there to spank her, sure, but I'd never intended to take her virginity in the back room of Sensual Delights. It made me feel like a monster. She should have had a soft bed, candlelight, and I should have taken my fucking time. Instead, I'd tied her legs apart and taken her like some goddamn caveman. Even though she'd seemed to like it well enough, it didn't make me feel any better about my behavior.

Every time she shifted and winced, I felt a little lower. I'd hurt her, even if she didn't say so. Dammit! I knew I wasn't exactly small, even though I didn't have a twelve-inch dick either. Still, eight inches in a pussy that had never had something in it before had to hurt. I'd make it right. Somehow.

At the grocery store, I'd tossed in enough food to keep us going for at least a few days, and made sure she got whatever drinks or snacks she preferred. I saw her eyeing the section for feminine hygiene and wondered if it was about that time of month. I led her over and waited. Her cheeks flushed as she grabbed a box of tampons and put them in the cart, under the boxes of macaroni.

Now that was fucking cute. Screaming as she came in a sex toy store and she'd walked out calm as could be, but buying tampons made her blush. She wouldn't look me in the eye as we headed toward the front, but I paused when I saw the hairbrushes and other girly shit. I didn't remember her buying any of that type of thing when I'd taken her shopping at the strip mall. Pushing the cart down the aisle, I waved a hand at the stuff and waited for her to make a selection. She put a brush and small package of elastic bands into the cart.

"Katya, you can get more. Pick out whatever you need. This isn't going to break my bank account." I leaned on the cart handle. "Kitten, you're starting over. I'm expecting you to need a lot of shit right now, and it's fine."

She leaned in closer and dropped her voice. "I've seen your house. I know you aren't as wealthy as my father, and I don't care, but I won't spend money if I don't have to."

I blinked at her a few times. Well, that was... interesting. Any other woman would have gone wild and started shoving all sorts of shit into the cart, or at least the women I'd known. And here she was, all worried that she'd spend too much. It almost made me want to show her my bank account. I wasn't as wealthy as the Pres or VP, but I hadn't spent my money on much either, except spoiling my grandson. I figured Flicker was taking good enough care of Pepper that I only gave her stuff for special occasions like her birthday and holidays. Other than picking up a new gun here and there, most of my money sat untouched.

I'd seen Katya eyeing a few other things so I grabbed them and tossed them into the cart before going to the next aisle. By the time we were done, she had things she hadn't asked for, and the expression on her face was becoming more and more irate. But I was having fun. Not just getting stuff I knew she wanted or needed, but it was entertaining as hell to watch as the storm built inside her. I had no doubt at some point she'd erupt. Then I'd get to spank that sexy ass of hers again.

I tried to distract her while the cashier rang up the purchases because I had no doubt she'd freak out over the total. It wasn't like I spent six hundred dollars in one spot all the time so I wasn't worried about it. If it got to be a habit, then I'd need to ask about taking on extra jobs at some point, but for now we were fine. And yes, it was *we* because my money was now her money. Sort of. I wasn't giving her free rein with the account -- not right away -- but I didn't see the harm in giving her some cash every week in case she wanted to go shopping or out to eat.

I loaded all the bags into the back seat, then helped Katya into the truck. Now that I'd made her mine, Theo could technically come home, but I wanted a little more time with her first. She might accept that her father wouldn't want her back now, but it didn't mean she wouldn't try to sacrifice herself to save everyone else. If she thought for one moment that going to him would make the man leave me and Theo alone, I knew she'd take off in a heartbeat. I eyed her in the passenger seat and knew exactly how to make sure she stayed put, but she might not thank me for it.

As we pulled out onto the road, I noticed she was chewing at her lower lip and had her hands twisted in her lap. I reached over and untangled her fingers, lacing them with mine. She glanced my way, but I could see the uncertainty in her eyes. I knew the way the club worked was completely foreign to her, and she didn't understand when I said she was mine I meant it in the forever sense. I didn't know what to do in order to convince her.

I didn't know much about the Bratva, having never personally dealt with them, but it sounded like they only kept their women for as long as it was convenient, with marriages being more about power than anything else. Sounded like a miserable existence to me. I'd watched as each of my brothers fell for a woman. Torch might have agreed to claim Isabella as a way to save Ridley, but it was clear he adored her and their kids. I knew others had claimed their women in order to keep them safe, much like I was doing with Katya, except I really did want to keep her. Not just because she was in trouble, but because she completely fascinated me. I loved her spirit and the sweetness that came out when she let down her guard.

I could see the compound ahead and as I neared the gate, the Prospect opened it, letting us through. I went straight to the house, grateful not to see the kids out front. If Katya saw Theo, she'd use my son as a distraction, but there were some things we needed to discuss. After I filled the tub for her. The way she kept shifting in her seat, I knew she was still hurting.

"Come on, kitten. I'll bring all this in after I get you settled."

"I can help," she said.

I nodded. "I know, but right now I want to take care of you."

Her gaze went soft and a slight smile curved her lips. She followed me into the house, accepting my hand when I held it out for her. Maybe keeping her here would be easier than I thought. I just needed to show her that someone gave a shit, and prove to her that I wasn't a selfish asshole like the men she'd grown up around. Well, I *could* be a selfish asshole, especially when it came to keeping her, but I would also cherish her. Something I didn't think anyone had ever bothered to do. Even her sister had used her, which pissed me off. If Lily hadn't died, I'd be tempted to cuss her out for the way she'd treated Katya.

My sweet little kitten didn't even hold it against her. No, she'd wanted to make sure her nephew was safe, then she'd planned to take her sister's place. I didn't know too many people who would be willing to make that sort of sacrifice. She was a warrior, even if she didn't realize it.

I led her into the master bathroom and started the tub. Remembering that I'd added some bubble bath to the shopping cart at the store, I told her to undress and get in while I ran back outside. I snatched two handfuls of sacks and carried them inside, then stopped just inside the door to find the one with the bathroom items. When I got back to the bathroom, she'd sunk into the hot water and was skimming her hands across the surface. Her cheeks flushed when I entered the room, which was pretty fucking cute since I'd already gotten an up close look at her most intimate parts.

I added some of the bubble bath, made sure she had anything else she'd need, then finished bringing in the sacks from the truck. While she relaxed, I put the groceries away, then shifted my clothes around so she'd have room for her new things. I peeked into the bathroom and saw her eyes were closed, her breathing deep and even. Deciding to let her rest and relax, I kept an eye on her so she wouldn't slip under the water, but took care of a few things around the house.

"Dad!"

I cursed under my breath and went to the front door to find my daughter peering around the open door. A door I knew damn well I'd shut. I narrowed my eyes at her, but the little imp just grinned at me, then let herself all the way in. Knew I should have locked the damn thing, but I'd never had cause to in the past.

"Pepper, what the fuck?"

She batted her eyes at me at an exaggerated pace, and I couldn't do much other than sigh at her antics. I didn't know if her curiosity over my son was just too much for her to contain, or if she wanted to know more about Katya. Despite the fact I wanted alone time with my kitten, I didn't want to blow off my daughter either. After not meeting Pepper until she was fully grown, I tried to spend as much time with her as I could. The term making up for lost time was ridiculous. I could never replace all those lost years because her mother had been a selfish bitch. Had I known about Pepper, I'd have been part of her life long ago.

"What do you want?" I asked more directly.

"Well, I was just thinking…"

I ran a hand down my face. "Christ. Should I start running?"

"Funny, old man. No. It's just… I know the club has a way of making things happen. If you're determined to keep her, why not just ask Wire to legally marry the two of you? Or illegally. However that works."

It wasn't that I hadn't thought about getting Wire or Lavender to put their skills to use, but I didn't want to overwhelm Katya either. I'd thrown enough at her in a short amount of time. She'd come here with the intention of dropping off my kid and leaving, and now I'd taken her innocence and told her she was staying. I didn't know how she'd handle a "surprise we're married!" to go along with all that. As strong as she was, at some point, she was going to break.

"Let me handle Katya. Go take care of your brother."

Her nose wrinkled. "Do you know how fucked up it is that your son and your grandson are so close in age?"

"I'll let you tell Bull all about it and see how that goes." I smirked. "Hope you wear your running shoes because if he catches you it won't be pretty."

"Whatever," she muttered, then turned and let herself back out.

This time I locked the damn door. Lesson learned. I heard movement coming from the bedroom and went to check on Katya. She was standing in the middle of the room wrapped in a towel, and looking more than a little bit lost. Without a word, I went to her, pulling her against my chest and wrapping my arms around her.

She melted against me and sighed before rubbing her cheek on my shirt. "It's like you know just what I need when I need it."

"You don't get to be my age without learning to read people, kitten. But don't worry. Women will always be a mystery to men in the grand scheme of things."

"There's so much I don't know about you." She pulled away and looked up at me. "You're really not letting me go, are you?"

"Nope. You're here for good, kitten. I claimed you the second I took your innocence." In fact, I was about to remind her that she was mine. I reached for the top of her towel, working it loose until it fell to the floor. Her eyes went wide and her cheeks flushed a bright pink.

"What are you doing?" she asked.

"Going to make you scream my name again."

I stalked her, herding her closer to the bed, then I fisted her hair and kissed her hard. She whimpered and parted her lips, letting me in. My tongue tangled with hers. I placed my hand on her bare hip and gave her just enough of a shove that it broke our kiss and she toppled to the bed. I pulled off my boots, yanked my shirt over my head, and started removing the rest of my clothes. The way I'd taken her at Sensual Delights had been a jackass thing to do. She wasn't some club whore.

Her gaze scanned me and I saw her fingers twitch.

"You can touch me, kitten. You might be mine, but I'm yours too."

She blinked three times, opened and shut her mouth, then seemed to struggle a moment with what she wanted to say. "When you say you're mine... what exactly does that mean?"

"It means I won't be putting my dick into a pussy unless it's yours. Or putting it anywhere else for that matter. This may not be the most romantic thing you've ever dreamt about, but I promise that I will be faithful to you, Katya. I won't disrespect you by being with another woman."

"The Bratva doesn't care about such things. Women are to be used however the men see fit."

I nodded. "I'm getting that picture from what you've said, but this club doesn't work that way. Any guy here who has an ol' lady or wife will tell you that they don't want anyone else. Every last one of us faithful like a damn dog."

"Ol' lady?" she asked.

"Biker equivalent of a spouse is the best way I can describe it. I know in some clubs that doesn't mean as much as it does here. You'll get respect not just from my brothers, but by anyone who associates with this club. I just need to make it official with the club and get a property cut made for you."

She opened her mouth again, but I held up a hand to silence her. "Not to be an ass, but can we table this discussion?"

Her gaze dropped to my very hard cock and she snorted. "Yeah. My questions can wait."

"Get in the middle of the bed and spread those legs, kitten. Knees bent, feet flat on the mattress."

She scrambled to obey, but I could see the nervousness in her eyes. I needed to show her how our first time should have been. I got too fucking carried away when I spanked her at Sensual Delights. It was one thing to make her ass red and another to take her virginity in a damn sex toy shop. I'd felt that hot, wet, tight pussy and lost my damn mind. It wasn't like I never got laid, but shit. No one had ever turned me on the way Katya did, and apparently it made me do stupid shit.

She made a pretty picture, open and ready. Her hair fanned out across the bed. I took my time admiring her, and smiled as her cheeks flushed pink. She wouldn't quite hold my gaze, and that adorable blush worked its way down her neck to her breasts. Deciding to put her out of her misery, I settled between her splayed thighs, bracing my weight on my hands.

"Look at me, kitten."

She focused on me, quiet and waiting. The fact she listened in the bedroom was a big fucking turn-on. Now if I could just get her to do that when we weren't having sex, that would be amazing. I didn't think it would ever happen, though. She was too sassy for that, which I loved in all honesty.

"I'm sorry your first time wasn't as romantic as it should have been. That's on me. Will you let me make it up to you?"

She shut her eyes a moment, then I felt her body tremble. No. Not trembling. Her lips curved into a smile and I realized the little imp was laughing at me. If she weren't lying on her back, I'd smack her ass.

"You think that's funny?" I asked.

Katya laughed out loud and opened her eyes. "I think it's funny you think you need to make up for anything. While I was trying to do the reasonable thing and keep my distance, you didn't force me to do any of that, Lance. Was it a bit wild for my first time? Sure. Do I look like the type of woman who enjoys anything tame? I loved everything you did, and had I not been sore, I'd have gladly asked for more."

"So impertinent! You're just asking for another spanking."

She wagged her eyebrows up and down. "Promise? Because I rather liked it."

I leaned closer, brushing my nose against hers. "And what else would you like?"

"Anything you want to do to me," she said softly. "I trust you, even though I shouldn't. You're a stranger, even if you did fuck me. Somehow, I just know that you wouldn't do anything to hurt me."

I brushed her hair back, running my fingers through the silky strands. "You're right, kitten. I'd sooner cut off my arm than ever harm you. But just saying, *anything* leaves a lot of room. You sure you don't want to narrow that down a bit?"

She flung her hands over her head. "Do with me what you will!"

Ask and ye shall receive. I pulled back and flipped her over. She squeaked at the sudden move, but I wasn't done yet. I positioned her hands up by the top of the mattress and pulled her up onto her knees.

"Don't move." I swatted her ass as I got up and went to the closet. I'd never brought a woman to this house before, but it didn't mean I hadn't thought about it. Reaching into the top of the closet, I pulled out a long length of soft rope. I dropped to my knees beside the top of the bed and tossed one end toward the other side, then brought up the end I was holding to tie it around her wrist.

She stared at it, but didn't try to pull away. I got up and moved to the other side, securing that wrist as well. While I made sure the rope was snug, I also didn't want to hurt her. It was just loose enough that it wouldn't give her rope burn. Her gaze fastened on mine and the complete trust I saw in her eyes was humbling. I leaned closer and brushed my lips against hers before walking off. She peered at me over her shoulder as I moved to the end of the bed.

"Knees apart," I demanded.

She shifted to spread her legs more. Damn but that was a pretty sight. "You okay, kitten?"

"No. I hurt."

Everything in me tightened and I started toward her. I'd have sworn the ropes were loose enough. The last thing I wanted was to cause her pain. Not the bad kind anyway. Spanking her ass was different.

"I'm sorry, baby girl. I didn't realize I'd tied you down so tight."

She snorted. "Not that kind of hurting, Lance. You have me really turned on right now."

She lifted up a little and I saw that her nipples were hard little points. Well, that made all the difference. I grinned and reached for the closest breast, pinching the hard tip until she yelped. The way she bit her lip told me that she enjoyed it as much as the swats to her ass earlier. I went for the other one, giving it a tug that had her moaning.

"Never knew a virgin could like it rough," I said.

"I'm not one."

"Kitten, you were until earlier. This is still way above what I would expect of someone who had never been naked with a man before today." She practically purred as I pinched, twisted, and tugged on her nipples. It was giving me all sorts of ideas for another trip to Sensual Delights. One where I actually got a chance to purchase stuff. "What aren't you telling me?"

"I read dirty books, okay? And... I told you I'd seen porn before. Maybe once or twice at college."

"Once or twice?" I asked, then spanked her ass hard. Something told me it had been more often than that. "Just what kind did you watch?"

She gasped as I swatted her again. *Smack. Smack. Smack.* Her ass was turning a nice rosy hue, and as I slid my fingers down over her pussy, I felt how wet she was getting. I didn't know how I'd lucked out with such a wild woman in the bedroom, but I was going to savor every second.

"Three men and a woman." She buried her face in the mattress so the next two were muffled, but not enough I couldn't hear. "Anal play and some gay porn too."

"Two women?" I asked.

She snorted and glared at me. "Why is that every man's fantasy? Ever think that maybe a woman gets hot over seeing two men fuck each other?"

I paused. "You watched two men fucking?"

She nodded. "It was hot. Like really, really hot."

Hadn't expected that from her. I wouldn't be fulfilling that desire, no matter how turned on it made her. Men didn't do it for me. Never had and never would. I didn't begrudge anyone finding happiness with someone regardless of sex or race, but my cock wasn't going anywhere near another man's or his ass. Nope. Not happening.

I wet my fingers by sliding two into her tight channel, then brought them up to her ass. I circled the tight hole between her cheeks. "Anal play, huh? Like this?"

She went still. Almost too still. Then she spread herself open more and lifted her ass. "Not quite. It started like that."

I left her, which made her whine, but I only went as far as the bathroom. I came back with a bottle of lube and squirted some between her ass cheeks, then coated my fingers. If she was intrigued by having me play back here, then that's exactly what she'd get. I'd only fucked a woman there once, and it had been decades ago. But if Katya wanted to experiment, I'd be happy to try anything she wanted, as long as it was just the two of us involved. No threesomes, foursomes, or anything else. Just me and her.

I slowly worked my finger into her ass and reached for her pussy with my other hand. I toyed with her clit, wishing I had a damn vibrator. I'd gone into Sensual Delights for the express purpose of buying a small one just to use on her clit, but had come out empty-handed after she tried to run.

"You like that, kitten?" I murmured, going a little deeper as I worked on stretching her a little.

"Oh, God. Lance, it feels so good and so…" She moaned. "I-I-I… I don't know how to explain how it feels. It burns, but I like it."

I added a second finger, moving slow and shallow, then steadily going deeper. Every time she got close to coming, I'd back off her clit. I wanted her close, riding the edge, but not quite there yet.

"How much can you handle, kitten?" I asked. "Because I can keep it right like this and just fuck your pretty pussy. You tell me how far is too far."

"I want both. I want it all. Everything you can give me."

Damn. My dick got hard as granite at her words. It had been a while since I'd been able to come more than once close together, until this woman. If anyone could make it happen, it was Katya, and she proved that again and again. Her tight little pussy had felt like heaven earlier, and I probably could have gone again if I hadn't worried that she was in pain.

I kept sliding my fingers in and out as I positioned myself behind her. I lined my cock up with her wet pussy and eased inside. She was just as tight as earlier, and felt just as amazing. I fucked her slow, wanting to take my time. Last time, I'd lost my head and it had been over far too soon.

"I need more," she said, her voice a near whine.

"Kitten, I only have one dick. Not sure what you want me to do." Then I had an idea. She'd mentioned watching multiple men fuck a woman. While I wasn't about to let another man in here with us, didn't mean we couldn't pretend a little. "Close your eyes and don't open them. We're going to play a game of sorts."

Her eyes slid shut. "Game?"

"You want more?" I asked.

"Yes. So much more."

"Bet you'd like a man's face between your legs right now. Licking that hard clit while I fuck you." She whimpered and pressed back against me. Maybe this would work after all. "Can you feel his tongue? Feel it flick that little bud? Hear him moaning as he tastes you?"

"Oh, God. Don't stop."

"He's working that pussy, making you all hot and slick." Her hips jerked. "That's it, kitten. Ride his face. Take what you want."

I slammed into her harder, her pussy sucking me in. While I took her hard and fast, I added a third finger to her ass. Jesus! I was close to fucking exploding with the way she gripped me.

"He's tonguing your clit so good. Come, kitten. Come right the fuck now. Come all over his face." She screamed out as her release tore through her. Her pussy milked my cock, and I groaned with every thrust, emptying my balls and filling her with my cum. "That's it, baby girl. You want him to lick up all the mess I just left?"

"Yes! Yes, I want that."

I grinned. "Such a dirty girl. Let him lick that pussy clean, tease that clit some more too."

She whined and her body jerked again. I pulled out and my cock was still semi-hard. I stroked it as I watched my cum leak from her. Hottest fucking thing ever. My fingers were still stretching her out. I stopped long enough to add more lube and to slick my cock, even though her cream was still coating me. When I thought she was ready, and my dick was fully erect again, I pulled my fingers from her and placed the head of my cock between her ass cheeks.

"You ready, kitten? Ready for me to fuck this ass?"

"Please, Lance."

"Keep your eyes closed. You keep riding that guy's tongue." I had to be all kinds of fucked-up to even let her imagine another man in bed with us, but if it worked and made her happy, then I'd try it. Better than letting an actual man into bed with us. Besides, she hadn't had a chance to fulfill her fantasies. I'd already tried several of mine. Only seemed fair that she got a shot.

I worked my cock into her ass, trying to take it slow. I reached down between her legs and pinched her clit. Katya bucked and the next thing I knew I was balls-deep. *Shit!* "Damn, baby girl. Am I hurting you?"

"It stings, but don't stop. I want this."

I played with her pussy, wanting her to come while I was in her ass. She let out a loud keening sound and I felt the gush of her release against my hand. Her muscles clenched down on my dick and whatever patience I'd had evaporated.

I gripped her hips and drove into her, riding her hard and fast. My hips jerked as I slammed into her again and again, not stopping until I came. I felt spurt after spurt empty inside her, and when I had nothing left to give, I pulled out.

"Jesus Christ, woman. I think you about killed me."

She giggled, but her legs gave out and she collapsed onto her belly on the bed. She blinked at me, a sated look on her face. "We have to do that again."

"I really hope you don't mean right now because I'm too old for this shit."

She yanked at the ropes. "You're not old."

I lay down next to her, and kissed her cheek. "Kitten, I'm in my fifties. I'm far from being a spring chicken. But you're making me feel young at heart."

Katya yawned and I untied her wrists. She slipped from the bed and I followed her to the bathroom.

This time I didn't fill the tub and leave her. I ran the shower and pulled her in with me, then took my time cleaning her and exploring that sexy little body. Too many more days like this one and I might have a heart attack, but there were worse ways to go than death by sex.

Chapter Five

Katya

I felt like a zombie the next morning. Despite his fussing that he was too old, Sarge had found the stamina to make me scream his name twice more during the night. I ached, but in truly awesome ways. My ass was tender whenever I sat, but it was a small price to pay. My cheeks warmed as I thought about all the stuff I'd let him do, and all the things I had yet to try. At one point, he'd pulled up an online shop of sex toys and had me point out anything that looked intriguing.

When my father had insisted I marry a man in the Bratva, I'd known my sex life would be less than desirable because it would have never been about me. With Sarge, he wanted to fulfill my fantasies and make me come multiple times. Well, fulfill them without inviting others into the bedroom with us. I'd been surprised when he'd made me imagine another man in bed with us, but it had worked. I'd not only gotten off, but I could have sworn I actually felt someone's tongue on my clit. It had been amazing and I hoped he'd try that again at some point.

I was fine with it only being the two of us. Truthfully, I didn't think another man could ever compare to Sarge. It was one thing to pretend or imagine what it would be like, and another to actually follow through. I didn't see me ever desiring anyone else. If I'd lasted this long without having sex, then it was safe to say that I was picky about who put their dick inside me.

I sighed as I sipped at the coffee Sarge had brewed before he left, saying something about going for a run. I'd wondered how he kept in such great shape. Even though he'd told me multiple times he was in his fifties, I hadn't wanted to believe him. Not that I had a problem with him being older, but he just didn't *look* like an older man. Whatever he was doing, it was working. Maybe running kept him in shape. From the things he purchased at the grocery store, it was clear that he ate healthy, or relatively so.

"You the reason some jackass is at my gate bellowing about his daughter?" a deep voice said behind me.

I spun, my coffee sloshing over the rim of my mug. A silver fox stood in the kitchen doorway, his arms folded over his chest, and a stern look in his eyes. I skimmed him quickly, noting the black vest said *Torch -- President*. No, not a vest. Sarge had informed me it was called a cut. Shit. This was the man in charge.

"You going to answer me or just stare?" he asked.

"S-sorry. Um, what jackass is at the gate?"

He closed his eyes and shook his head, but I saw the smile play across his lips. "Damn. No wonder Sarge grabbed on and didn't let you go. All right, pretty girl. Let's try this a different way. I'm Torch and this is my club. There's a man at the gate, Russian, who claims we've taken his daughter."

I tried to process those words, but it was hard. My brain refused to accept my father could have found me. I'd been so careful, turned off any GPS that could have let him track me. It couldn't be him, right? Then again, what other Russian man would be at the gate asking for his daughter to be returned?

"Don't suppose you have another Russian woman here?" I asked.

"Nope. You're it."

I sighed and took a gulp of my coffee. Then another. I was starting to wish I'd spiked it. Now that Sarge had taken my virginity, and in the most spectacular way at that, there was no way I could go with my father unless I wanted to end up like my sister, and that was a fate I wasn't willing to accept.

"I turned off my GPS," I said. "It can't really be my father."

Even as I said it, I knew he was here. No other Russian would be looking for me, unless it was someone he'd sent. Either way, I wasn't leaving with them. No fucking way. I'd go down fighting. Assuming Sarge didn't just lock me up to protect me from the big bad wolf at the gate. That was a distinct possibility. Probably a good thing he wasn't here right now.

"One way to find out," Torch said, pulling out his phone. He tapped at the screen for a minute before putting it away again. "I'll have someone sweep your car. It's possible they put a tracker on it, one you couldn't just turn off and on."

What he said made sense. It was exactly the sort of thing my father would do. Either that, or microchip me like a damn dog. I really hoped that wasn't the case. I'd cut off my damn arm to get it out if need be. Thankfully, I didn't remember a time he'd have had the opportunity to do something like that. Not in the last six years anyway. Maybe when I was younger, but back then he'd only cared about Liliya and how she could advance his career. She'd always been the pretty, sweet, submissive one out of the two of us. Or at least she'd portrayed herself that way.

"Do you want any coffee?" I asked. "Sarge made it right before he left to go running."

"Already had two cups today. If I have another, my wife will nag me about being healthier. She's determined I'll live to the ripe old age of three hundred."

I snorted and took another swallow. "Does she realize that means you'll still be here after she's gone?"

He shrugged a shoulder and leaned against the doorframe. "She's younger than me. By quite a lot, actually. I'll be dying before her whether she likes it or not, but I don't plan to go anytime soon. I'm sixty-one so I have at least another ten or twenty years in me. Maybe more if I hand this club off to someone younger. I was hoping my son would take over one day, but I had daughters first."

"And girls can't run a club like this?" I asked.

"Considering they sent contract killers after my wife's stepmother, I wouldn't be surprised in the least if they tried to take over. Although, I'm not sure the world is ready for them to have that sort of power."

My eyes about bugged out of my head. His kids did what? Just what sort of children was he raising? Wolves? Grizzlies? Maybe we should put his daughters on the front lines for the next war. We might win within minutes.

"My oldest is thirteen now, but that happened several years ago. I'd like to say she learned her lesson, but if she keeps hanging out with my VP's kids, I can only imagine the horrors I'll be facing over the next five years," he said. "Venom's kids are... Well, they're hellions, pure and simple. Mariah is close to my Lyssa in age, but Farrah is sixteen. That one is pure trouble."

"How old is your son?" I asked.

"Hadrian is five, and completely different from my girls. He's very shy and laid back. Sweet boy. I only hope he stays that way, at least when it's needed. He'll have to be tough to be part of this club, but I want him to be fair."

"I still say you should hand the reins over to your daughter. She might surprise you. Not all women are weak and need to be protected."

He arched an eyebrow. "That so? Then by all means. Go see your daddy at the gate."

Did he just issue me a challenge? Did he expect me to back down? I threw my shoulders back, set my coffee down and brushed past him. When I got outside, I slid into my car and drove toward the gate with Torch following on his motorcycle. I stopped the vehicle at the edge of the clubhouse, where a line of bikes sat parked. Getting out, I gathered my courage and approached the gate and my father, who looked like he might explode at any moment. His face was nearly purple, his lips bracketed by tension lines, and his eyes snapping fire. Yeah, he was pissed he'd had to come after me.

"Did you think I'd not protect my assets after the stunt your sister pulled?" he asked as I stopped far enough away he couldn't reach through and grab me.

"I don't know how you found me, but I'm not going back with you. I'm staying here."

"*Nyet*. You're coming home to fulfill your obligations, Katya. You will not ruin this for me like your sister did."

I tipped my chin up a little and stared down my nose at him. It was a look I'd often used on handsy guys in college, but never before on my father. The tic in his jaw said he didn't appreciate my defiance, but too fucking bad.

"You don't own me. I'm not your property. I'm a living, breathing woman and I said I'm not going with you. That's final."

"*Suka*!"

"Call me all the names you want, *Father*. You can't get in here and I'm not coming out there. Not unless I'm armed, in which case you'd be better off in your bulletproof car because I *will* shoot your stupid ass."

He let loose a string of Russian that would have made me wince in the past, but Sarge had given me a newfound courage. I'd never been a coward before, but I had always obeyed my father. That time had come to an end, and I was more than happy to tell him exactly what I thought of him.

"I'm not yours to command. I was *never* yours." I screamed the last part, making him stop, his chest heaving and his eyes narrowed.

"When did she tell you?" he asked.

When did who tell me what? What did he ... Oh hell no. "Are you telling me that all this time you've demanded my obedience and you're not even my real father? I fucking hate you! You're nothing but a monster and I hope you choke and die."

I heard a crunching sound behind me and spun to find Flicker standing next to Torch, munching on popcorn of all damn things. I wanted to ask if he was enjoying the show, but the smirk he wore spoke volumes. When Torch reached over to grab a handful too, I nearly lost it and started laughing, but I held it together. Barely.

Facing the man I'd always thought was my father, I stared him down until he flinched. "Who is my real dad?"

"Could have been anyone," he said dismissively.

And that's when I knew. She hadn't cheated on him. He'd used her like a whore to get where he was today. And he was the reason she was gone. I'd always known that last part, but I'd never understood exactly what he'd done to her. I'd been a kid, but as an adult woman living in the Bratva world, I knew what he'd expected of her.

"How many?" I asked, my tone deceptively soft. "How many times did you whore her out around the time I would have been conceived? How many men did you let fuck her because it helped you in some way?"

"I let young Konstantin Bykov have her many times, as well as others. Until I realized she actually enjoyed being with him. Then I had to make an excuse for him to no longer have access to her." Voronin studied his hands. And yes, he was Boris Voronin now and never again would I think of him as my father.

I thought over his words and knew in my gut that Konstantin had likely fathered me. Our coloring was very close, and while I'd never seen pictures of him when he was younger, my sister had often commented that our noses and mouths held a similar shape. It wasn't until now that I realized she'd known all along. The way she'd said it, the sly looks… somehow, she'd known that Voronin wasn't my father.

I looked around, my gaze landing on a short length of pipe on the ground nearby. I went to pick it up, hefting the weight in my hands and assessing the best place to grip it. Swinging it a few times, I decided if the asshole wanted to come get me, I'd let him. And then I'd beat the shit out of him.

"Let him in," I said. "He wants me? He can come physically make me leave. If he dares. Just check him for weapons first. Boris Voronin never plays fair."

"Have you lost your fucking mind?" Torch asked from behind me. "Anything happens to you, so much as one scratch, and Sarge is going to come unglued."

I glanced at him. "You scared of your own man? One who doesn't even have a title in your club?"

His jaw tightened. "I'm more concerned for the damage he'll do to anyone and anything in his path if you get hurt. I've never known him to want to keep a woman before, which means you're special. Besides… you're not just his woman."

Flicker started laughing and then choked on his precious popcorn. Good. Served him right. "Oh, God. If you're going to tell her, at least let me go get some of the others. I can't wait to see how this plays out."

"You're a dick," I told him.

"Whatever you say… Mommy." He grinned and I growled at him. "That's right. You belong to Sarge, and since I'm married to his daughter…"

I flipped him off and focused on Voronin again, but I heard Flicker's laughter and his steps as he left. Only a moment later, there was a loud stomping of boots and I could have sworn a stampede was heading my way. A quick look assured me it was just Flicker and about four other bikers. Awesome. So glad I could be the entertainment for today.

"I'm going to charge admission," I told them.

When a handful of money landed at my feet, I couldn't hold it in anymore. I burst out laughing. My stomach hurt as I leaned over, trying to catch my breath, but my eyes were watering I was laughing so hard. These guys were too fucking much, but I was starting to like them. Even the ones I didn't yet know. If they were anything like Flicker, Sarge, and Torch, then I'd get along with them just fine.

"All right. We paid good money. Get to it," one of them said. "Let that pompous ass inside."

The man guarding the gate shrugged and opened it far enough for Voronin to step through, then he patted him down, removing two guns. It wouldn't surprise me if he had another weapon hidden somewhere, but I didn't plan to let him get the upper hand, and I had no doubt the men treating this like some big joke would stop him if he did try to hurt me. If for no other reason, then I was with Sarge. Whatever that meant.

"Your husband is going to go batshit crazy when he hears about this," Torch said.

Now that made me stop. I didn't dare turn my back on Voronin, but Torch definitely had my attention. "What husband?"

"Sarge. Flicker here decided to interfere and asked our resident hackers to handle it. Congratulations. You're officially part of the club because you're Sarge's whether you like it or not. Anyone who looks will find a very legit marriage license on file. Just don't tell Sarge yet. I plan to bust his balls a little." Torch came closer. "But by all means. Teach this fucker a lesson if you need to. We've got your back."

I heard more than one gun cock and glanced at the bikers long enough to see every last one had a weapon trained on Voronin. It was the first time I could remember that anyone had stood beside me. My eyes misted with tears for a moment. How fucked up was my life that the badass bikers at my back could make me cry because I was touched by their acceptance?

I stared down the man I'd call Father for so long. He sneered and lunged for me, but I swung the pipe, hitting his bicep with a loud *thwack*. Voronin howled and came for me again. I got in three more blows before he showed his true colors and yanked a knife from behind him. I had no idea where he'd hidden it, but it wasn't going to make me back down. I smiled, thinking of the old movie about the Australia guy visiting New York City. "That's not a knife," I muttered.

I heard someone snicker behind me. Voronin came at me again, and I gripped the pipe with both hands, slamming it against his wrist as he tried to jab me with the small blade. He dropped to his knees, and it was like the fury I'd contained the last six years bubbled up. Before I could second-guess myself, I brought the pipe down on his head. Not once. Not twice. Three times. Blood pooled under him, and as I stood panting, I realized I was shaking. I let the pipe go, and it clattered to the pavement at my feet.

"Oh God, oh God, oh God." I'd killed him. He wasn't moving, wasn't making any noise at all, and he didn't seem to be breathing. My knees gave out, but a strong arm around my waist, held me upright.

"Remind me not to piss her off," someone said.

I laughed and cried at the same time. I wiped at the moisture on my cheeks and one of the guys winked at me. I figured he must have said it. Looking up, I realized Flicker had me.

"Come on. I think I need to get you back home. Sarge is going to lose his shit when he hears about this." He led me over to the car and put me in the passenger seat. When he got in on the other side, he moved the seat all the way back and still looked uncomfortable. "If Sarge doesn't make you get rid of this car, I may accidentally set it on fire one night."

"What's wrong with my car?" I asked.

He looked at me with an *are you kidding me* expression. "It's a BMW. At a biker compound. What the fuck, Katya?"

He did have a point. "Fine. Someone can sell it or strip it for parts. However you get rid of cars you don't want. I only ask that at least part of the money goes to getting me a car I can drive safely with Theo in the back seat."

Flicker pulled away from the gate and just shook his head.

"Now what?" I asked.

"You really think you'll only need room for Theo? The walls around here aren't exactly soundproof. Stepped outside to sneak a cigarette last night and from what I heard, it wouldn't surprise me at all if you're knocked-up already."

I placed a hand against my belly. We hadn't used protection, and it honestly never crossed my mind. Damn. We hadn't even had the talk about previous partners. While I didn't have any, I knew Sarge hadn't been a monk. Did I need to go get tested? How could I have not even thought of that before now? So stupid! Then again, that hardly seemed pressing since I'd just murdered a man.

My heart slammed against my breastbone and I felt like I might pass out. What had I done? No one loved Boris Voronin, but the Bratva would never allow his death to go unpunished. They'd come for me. Make an example of me. I whimpered and curled against the door, resting my forehead against the window. I was so screwed. There was no way Viktor Petrov or Vadim Ivanov would let this one slide. My father's friends would demand justice be served. Or rather the man I'd thought was my father.

Wait. My father. Would Konstantin help me? Did he even know I existed? Or rather, did he know that I was his daughter? Girls were always a blessing to the Bratva men because we were bargaining chips. I couldn't imagine Konstantin not trying to take me after my mother died if he'd known. Then again, maybe I just hoped that he hadn't known because it meant that I hadn't been unwanted, only undiscovered.

"I need to make a call," I said.

"Sarge doesn't have a landline. You have a cell phone?" Flicker asked as he came to a stop in the driveway.

"Yes. I need to call Russia."

Flicker slowly turned to face me. "You need to do what now?"

"Call Russia. I need to speak with Konstantin Bykov. Assuming he'll even accept my call. If anyone can help me right now, it's him."

Flicker held up a hand. "Look, all kidding aside, you know we've got your back, right? That dick is going to disappear. No one will ever know what happened to him."

"That's sweet, but you don't understand. He'll have told people where he was going, possibly even brought some men with him. My guess is they're nearby. Close enough for him to call for backup, but far enough to give him privacy in case I embarrassed him."

"Not sure if I should be offended you think we can't handle those Bratva bastards, or admire the fact you want to resolve the issue yourself."

I opened the car door. "Go with option two."

Without waiting to hear anything else from him, I got out and went inside. Sarge wasn't back, but I had a feeling someone would find him and tell him everything. I didn't know if he'd be pissed, scared, or find it funny that itty bitty me bludgeoned a man to death. Only he would find humor in it, but he'd seemed amused over the way I handled the guy at the gate last night.

I grabbed my phone, made sure it had a decent charge, then took a breath to steady my nerves. I'd never called Konstantin Bykov before and didn't even know where to start. Except maybe Viktor Petrov. He'd want to know why I needed to speak with Bykov, but I'd come up with something. Even if it was at least the partial truth. I only had Viktor's number because I'd overheard my father say it once and I'd memorized it in case I ever needed to speak with him directly.

The phone rang a few times before the brigadier answered. "Petrov."

"Mr. Petrov, this is Katya…Voronin." I hoped the hesitation didn't cost me, but was I really a Voronin? I didn't share that man's blood. A call to Viktor Petrov wasn't something to take lightly. I'd heard tales about him all my life, and knew him to be a ruthless killer. I only hoped that maybe I'd catch him in a good mood and be able to get the information I needed.

"Miss Voronin, how may I help you?" he asked.

"I need to speak with Konstantin Bykov, but I'm uncertain how to reach him."

He made a noise that was almost a growl. "I'm not a directory, Miss Voronin. Ask your father for the number."

"Wait! Please don't hang up. It's important, Mr. Petrov, and I can't ask my father. The situation is a bit delicate."

"I'm listening."

"I recently learned my mother spent some time with Mr. Bykov. I need to speak with him about her, but I'm afraid it would anger my father if I mentioned it. Please, can you help me?"

He sighed. "Very well. I'll text his number to your phone. And, Miss Voronin, if I discover you've lied to me, I will be extremely upset." I heard a soft murmur in the background, but I couldn't hear his response. There was a scrape as if he'd covered the phone with something. "My wife informs me I'm being too harsh. If that's so, then I apologize. Just don't make me regret giving you that number."

"Thank you, Mr. Petrov."

He hung up before I could say anything else and I stared at my phone, waiting for the incoming text. When my phone beeped, I opened the message. My fingers were shaking as I pressed the number, bringing it up on the screen, then pushed "call" and waited as it rang.

It went to voicemail, and while I started to hang up, I decided to leave a brief message, explaining who I was and that I really needed to speak to him about something. I gave my number and then hung up. I hoped I hadn't just made a huge mistake, but I hadn't known what else to do.

The front door slammed into the wall and I turned to find Sarge barreling toward me. He didn't even slow down as he grabbed me, wrapping me tight in his arms until I feared I'd suffocate. I patted his back and squeaked.

"Can't. Breathe."

He set me down, but didn't release me. "What the fuck, kitten? I know you're all tough and shit, but what were you thinking?"

"Well, Torch practically dared me to go talk to Voronin, so…"

He held up a hand. "Wait. The Pres *dared* you to go talk to that man? And why are you calling him by his last name?"

"I guess they didn't tell you everything, then. It seems he's not really my father. He gave his wife out to other Bratva members whenever it would benefit him. I believe my birth father is Konstantin Bykov. He's the sovietnik and usually remains in Russia, but he does travel to the US on occasion."

"I have no idea what that title means, and I honestly don't give a shit right now. Are you okay? I saw Flicker outside. He was standing guard in the driveway, and seemed worried. He said you were shaken up by what happened. Although, the words badass and terrifying were also used." He smiled. "It seems you've made an impression."

I melted against him, letting him hold me. I hoped that my actions didn't blow back on the club. If anyone here got hurt because of me, I'd never forgive myself. Bringing Theo here hadn't turned out the way I'd hoped, but I was so grateful I'd met Sarge. Being with him was amazing, but I'd let my temper get the best of me, and now I'd possibly ruined what we had, and put everyone in danger.

Why did I keep fucking things up?

Chapter Six

Sarge

I'd found Tempest leaning over a dead body between the gate and the clubhouse, and I'd stopped to see what the fuck was going on. Hearing my woman had been the one to kill the man had been staggering. I'd known she was a fierce little thing, but I hadn't realized she was capable of taking a life. Considering the man had come to take her away, and then pulled a knife on her, she'd only been defending herself. I was proud that she'd taken the guy out on her own, but I'd worried about her mental state. Even a battle-hardened soldier struggled with killing the enemy. I could only imagine how my little kitten felt about taking out her own father.

The way she'd clung to me, and the confusing explanation of her father not really being her father, had left me reeling a bit. I'd expected to find her hysterical or at least crying. She'd been shaken, for certain, but was handling it far better than I'd have expected. It just proved how strong she was. Of course, that didn't mean I appreciated Torch throwing out a challenge and getting her to the gate. Which was why I was currently standing across from him at his home office.

I'd been thinking about what I wanted to say, and how to say it. Seeing the smug look on his face threw all those plans right out the window. In that moment, I didn't give a shit that he was the club Pres. I only cared that he'd put my woman at possible risk, and for what?

"Why the hell would you challenge her to go to the damn gate, knowing her father was there?" I asked.

Torch raised both eyebrows and his posture went from relaxed to stiff in a heartbeat. He pressed his hands to the desk and rose to his feet, staring me down.

"First off, mind your tongue when you speak to me. I may be getting old, but I'm not dead yet, and I still run this fucking club. If I wanted to throw her ass out, I could and would. Flicker spoke on your behalf to claim her, but you haven't asked in Church and I don't recall making anything official," he said. "She's not wearing a property cut and hasn't been inked."

"Well, seeing as how Wire and Lavender married us, either she stays or I go."

He thumped back down into his chair and sighed. "So I heard. I didn't give them permission for that shit either, but I can understand why they did it. They told me after the fact. It was amusing to see the look on Katya's face when she found out, but not so much when I discovered what they'd done. Some days I swear it's like the President patch on my cut is just a decoration. Did you know your wife suggested I leave the club to my daughter?"

No, she hadn't told me that, but it didn't surprise me. A woman like Katya could probably handle that sort of job. Not sure the Pres's little girl was up to it, though, not even when she was old enough. She was a hellion at times, but she tended to react before thinking things through. Of course, I didn't believe Katya had meant to kill Voronin so maybe she was just as hot-blooded.

"I'm sorry I lost my temper. At my age, I never thought I'd meet a woman I wanted to keep. Then I saw her stand up to the Prospect and land a punch to his ribs. Hottest fucking thing I've ever seen." I grinned. "Knew then she was a keeper."

"She's a scrappy little thing for sure. She's worried about the Bratva, isn't she?"

I nodded. She'd said something about calling Bykov, but I still didn't understand what she hoped to accomplish. What if the man didn't want a daughter? Or what if he only wanted to use her the way Voronin had? Something told me she was borrowing trouble by reaching out, but I hoped she proved me wrong. Until then, I knew Torch would have had someone handle Voronin's body and car.

"Found a tracker on her BMW," Torch said. "She told Flicker to take the car to a chop shop and use the money to buy her something sensible."

I opened my mouth, then snapped it shut. Yeah, I gave Flicker shit all the time since he was married to my daughter, but he was still an officer of the club. And Katya had *told* him what to do? Wonder how that had gone over. Then again, he seemed just as amused by her as I was, so he probably hadn't thought much of it. She had a lot of fire in her just like my Pepper did, so Flicker was probably used to it by now.

Torch tossed me a set of keys. "There's a silver Ford Explorer parked at the clubhouse. It's her new car, registered under the name Kat Reid. I also told Wire to go ahead and work on getting her documentation under that name. It won't erase Katya Voronin completely, but it's a step in removing her connection with the Bratva."

I stared at the keys in my hand. "What if she doesn't want to sever the connection? She just found out Voronin wasn't her father. The guy she thinks is her sperm donor is apparently higher up the ranks. She may want the chance to get to know him, if he isn't a first-class dick."

"Then we give her that chance… and invite the bastard here, where we can keep an eye on him. We already set up those guest apartments. We just make sure he's our only visitor during that time and put one of the Prospects next door to keep an eye on him. Those walls are a bit thin for a reason." Torch smiled. "I'm sure he's too smart to let us bug the place, but that doesn't mean the walls don't have ears."

"I'm keeping her," I said. "If I have to go into Church and make the request, fine, but either way, she's staying."

"Do you really think we wouldn't let you claim her?" he asked. "It's been a long-ass time since you were ever serious about someone. Since before this club if I remember right. The fact you took one look and knew that girl was yours is all the proof I need that she belongs here. Besides, I rather enjoyed watching her beat that piece of shit to death."

"You're a little fucked-up. You know that, right?" I asked.

He shrugged. "Didn't get to be at the top by being a pussy. I know things have calmed down a lot around here, especially with so many of us raising families, but we'll never completely walk the straight and narrow. I've pulled us back off a lot of bad shit over the last decade, but the fact remains we make a fuck ton off pot and guns, especially after Flicker put in that medicinal marijuana field and procured a license for it a year ago."

"I just don't want the ugliness in life to touch her. I know it's too late, that it's already had its hands on her, but is it wrong that I want to protect her?"

"Not wrong. Maybe not practical since she seems quite capable of taking care of herself, but it's certainly not wrong. If you'd fallen for a fellow soldier, would you have expected *her* to let you coddle her?"

"No," I said without hesitation.

"Then don't expect that of your wife. She may not have served our country, but she grew up in an environment that prepared her for a war of sorts. She's cunning and capable. You should be proud of her."

I sat in the chair across from him. "I *am* proud of her. Doesn't mean I wasn't scared shitless when I discovered the dead body was courtesy of my wife. Mostly, I was worried what state I'd find her in. But if that asshole really did have others lurking nearby, they may have seen her kill him. What then?"

"Then we handle it. When they get here -- and the Bratva *will* come to our gates -- I'll take care of it. I'll make sure I have Grimm with me." Torch leaned back in his chair, the leather creaking. "For now, go spend time with your woman. I'll call Church when I have more information on Voronin. You make your official request at that time, but that being said, I'm pretty sure Venom already ordered a property cut for your girl. You may get it before Church convenes."

"So it's just a formality?" I asked.

"Yep. We threw the rule book out long ago when it comes to our women. No point in enforcing that shit now. I was just busting your balls earlier. Just be warned that Pepper has already told the others about Katya. They'll be stopping by, most likely within a day or two. Everyone has tried to give the two of you some space to bond a bit more. Heard she was adamant about leaving."

"Not so much now. I think she's resigned herself to being stuck here, or maybe she even wants to stay. There's a longing in her eyes sometimes, and I don't think it has anything to do with where she came from, but the fact that she wants a home here and is just too afraid to grab on and not let go."

"Then go prove to her that her fears are unfounded," Torch said. "And for fuck's sake, get your kid's room ready for him! He can't take over Reed's space, not unless you revamp the place and make it *theirs*. Otherwise your son will feel like an interloper and Reed will feel like he's been replaced."

"I kind of forgot about that with everything else going on. I mean, I know I have a kid now, but there are times the dots don't all connect in my head. A little hard to wrap my brain around the fact my son and grandson are nearly the same age. Or that I have a son at all. Lily really fucked things up, didn't she? And she died because of it. I may not have wanted a family, but if she'd ever told me she was pregnant, then I'd have taken care of my kid."

"Of course you would have," Torch said. "And you'd also have never met Katya. Because if Lily hadn't been found by her family, if Katya hadn't needed to get Theo somewhere safe, then she would have remained with the Bratva and your paths would have never crossed."

He had a point. I didn't much like it, but he was right. Everything happened for a reason, and I knew that, but I hated missing out on so much of my son's life. Maybe Katya would want to help with the kids' room. We could make it Theo's and Reed's space. Put a bunk bed in there so they could have sleepovers. She knew my son better than I did, so I'd see what she thought about it.

"Go home, Sarge." Torch gave me a pointed look.

"Fine. I'm going." I hefted myself out of the chair and walked out. One of Isabella's favorite people, Saint, was coming up the walkway as I left so I tossed him the keys to the SUV. "When you go past the clubhouse on your way home, would you see that a Prospect brings the silver Explorer to my place?"

"You got it." He gave me a wave and went inside, most likely to visit with Isabella and the kids. I didn't see his daughter in tow, but that didn't mean much. The girl was attached to her stepmother from morning to night most days.

Getting on my Harley, I started the engine and revved it twice before backing down the driveway and heading for my house. It still amazed me sometimes how much our compound had grown over the years. Before Ridley showed up looking for Bull, we'd all been a bunch of bachelors, partying and living life to the fullest. Then Ridley hooked up with Venom, got pregnant, and one after another I watched my brothers take that same fall. At first, I'd been glad it wasn't me, but as time passed, I started to wonder if I'd ever find a woman to spend my life with. And now I had Katya. Or Kat as her new identification would say. I wasn't sure how she'd handle that.

Reed and Theo were out front playing in Flicker's yard when I pulled up. My grandson charged toward me with Theo following at a much slower pace. It made my chest ache that my own son wasn't that happy to see me, but I knew I was still a complete stranger to him. Other than handing him off to Flicker and introducing him to Pepper, I hadn't had time to get to know him better. I'd have to change that soon. Torch was right, though. The kid needed a room, or a space he could share with Reed where they could feel like it was theirs.

I got off the bike and swung Reed up into my arms, giving him a hug and kissing his cheek. "How's Grandpa's boy?"

"Good. We're playing trucks."

I smiled and looked from him to Theo. "I see that. Looks more like you're playing dirt dauber. You're both filthy."

Theo came closer and hesitantly wrapped his arm around my leg. I set Reed down and picked up my son. We stared at one another for a moment, then I hugged him tight to my chest. "I'm glad you're here, Theo. I only wish I'd known about you sooner. If your mom had ever told me about you, I'd have had you here with me every day."

He rested his head against me and put his arms around my neck. I had to make things right with him. If that meant giving him a kickass room, then that's where I'd start. But I also needed to explain why he wasn't living in my house yet. I didn't want him to feel left out, or like I didn't want him. Telling him was one thing, but I needed to show him that he was wanted.

"Hey, boyo," I said. "You're going to stay with Pepper and Flicker for another day or two while I get your room ready. Okay? I thought since you and Reed seem to get along so well, you might want me to make it a place where you could both hang out and play. Maybe put a bunk bed in there?"

Theo looked down at Reed. "Trucks?"

Reed nodded.

"I take it that means you both want trucks in the room. On the blankets too?" I asked.

Both boys grinned, which was answer enough. I hugged Theo once more and set him down. He ran off with Reed to play and I went in to tell Katya about her new name. I really hoped she took it well. Just in case, maybe I should make sure there weren't any bats, or other such objects nearby. The woman certainly knew how to do some damage, and I couldn't have been prouder of her. Scared shitless, but proud. I could have lost her, but I'd been assured she'd had backup if things had gone south. Didn't mean I liked her being put in that position to begin with.

"Kitten, where are you?" I called out as the front door shut behind me.

"Kitchen."

I followed her voice and found her standing on the counter, a chair pushed up to it that she'd probably used to get up there, pulling stuff off the top shelf of a cabinet. By the looks of things, she'd already done that to all the others. In fact, all the cabinet doors were open and none of them had a single item inside still, but every flat surface was covered from counters to the table and even the stove.

"What are you doing?" I asked.

"Reorganizing." She looked at me over her shoulder. "You don't mind, do you? I just thought if I was going to live here now, I'd make it feel more like… mine."

"Kitten, you can do whatever the hell you want. We can repaint. Buy new dishes. Just let me know, but I'd much prefer that you not climb on shit to reach things."

"I can climb a tree taller than your house. I think I'll be fine getting up on the counters, but thanks for worrying. As for paint…" She looked around. "I think the kitchen is fine, but I wouldn't mind painting our bedroom a different color. Maybe a nice tranquil green?"

"Anything you want."

She pulled the last of the items down, then backed down onto the chair, then the floor. She set the items on top of some other stuff nearby since she'd run out of room. As I looked over everything, I realized that I didn't even remember putting half that shit into the cabinets in the first place. It had either been there for years, or my daughter had been hoarding shit in my house. That last part wouldn't surprise me at all. She was constantly telling Flicker they needed more room.

"There's something we need to discuss," I said. "You know that Wire and Lavender worked their magic with the computer to make us legally -- or ill-legally -- married. I'm afraid that's not where they stopped."

She tipped her head to the side, just watching and waiting. At least she wasn't having a fit over the marriage thing. I'd take that as a good sign. And she didn't look ready to bludgeon me to death so there was that.

"They decided to change your name. I know the Bratva already knows you're here, but it would distance you a bit more from your Russian connections. I told Torch you might not appreciate that very much, since it's your heritage."

"So what did they call me?" she asked.

"Your new identification will say you're Kat Reid. I didn't ask, but I think that means they hacked into the DMV and you'll be getting a new driver's license in the mail. Hell, they probably went deeper than that. Who knows what sorts of shit they got into. Sometimes I think it's all a game for those two."

She placed her hand over her heart. "In here, I will always be Katya, but I don't mind everyone calling me Kat. Except you. I rather like the pet name you gave me. Now that I know you don't find me weak and pathetic."

I gave a bark of laughter. "Kitten, no one could ever think you're weak. Trust me. You've already made yourself a legend around here. The other ladies can't wait to meet you, but Torch thought we had a day or two before they descend on us. So I thought you could help me with something today."

Her gaze dropped to my cock, which started to harden under her appraisal. That wasn't what I'd had in mind, but she could certainly help with that too. By all rights, I should be worn the hell out from last night. I couldn't remember the last time I'd had sex that many times so close together. Hell, I barely touched the club whores most of the time. Getting laid wasn't as important now as it had seemed thirty years ago.

Shit. I didn't know if she knew about the girls at the clubhouse, or what went on up there at night. I knew I needed to tell her before she found out on her own, or before Ridley opened her damn mouth and said something, because that woman loved to stir up trouble, but I wasn't ready to get into all that just yet. Soon, though. Really soon.

"We can do that too," I said, drawing her gaze back up to my face. "But I need you to help me set up the room I've been using for Reed so that it will be good for both boys. Theo and Reed have both agreed to bunk beds and would like a truck theme."

She looked around. "Do we have time for me to put this all back?"

I snorted. "Kitten, it's going to take you hours to wade through all this shit. I'm betting part of it isn't even mine. Pepper has a tendency to stash things here when I'm not looking. Just leave it for now. We'll go shopping, then I'll work on the kids' room and you can organize all you want."

She nodded. "All right. Just need to get my shoes and purse."

"One more thing. Flicker already got a new car for you. Or new-ish. One of the Prospects will be dropping a silver Explorer by shortly. For now, we'll take the club truck that's still parked in the driveway. Might need it to haul some big shit."

She came closer, pausing to push up on her toes and press her lips to mine. Her gaze locked on mine and I wondered what she was searching for. Whatever it was, she seemed satisfied. Smiling, she kissed me once more, then walked out, leaving me to look at the chaos she'd made of the kitchen.

Living with a woman was going to be interesting.

Chapter Seven

Katya

Shopping had never been fun. I wasn't one of those girly types who enjoyed buying things. Probably because I'd learned the hard way that those purchases usually came with strings attached. With Sarge, it was different. He asked for my input on everything we looked at, from toys to bedding to furniture for Theo's room. It seemed my nephew had made fast friends with Sarge's grandson and they wanted a room that could be theirs. The theme of trucks wasn't as easy to accomplish as Sarge had thought, so we got creative.

It took multiple stores before we found comforters with a big firetruck on them. We opted for plain sheets after not finding any to match, but the walls were harder to decorate. Everything seemed too childish for Theo. Yes, he was still quite small, but he'd had to grow up quickly. I didn't think he'd appreciate the cartoon-looking decals we kept finding, so instead we stopped at a print shop and purchased framed prints of first responder vehicles to hang up.

Although, none of that was half as difficult as getting Sarge to not buy out the toy department in every store that had one. When he'd found a bunk bed set with two matching five-drawer chests, he'd bought them, then called a Prospect to come pick up the truck and furniture. They'd left my new SUV with us, and Sarge seemed intent to stuff it as much as possible with things the boys really didn't need. I eventually got him to stop buying toys, but then he went crazy getting clothes and shoes for Theo.

"Sarge, he's going to outgrow all that before he gets a chance to wear it. He doesn't need so many things right now," I said, putting back a handful of shirts and pants, then returned three shoe boxes to the shelf. "You don't have to buy him everything you see."

"I missed a lot of birthdays and Christmases," he said.

"And we'll make sure he knows that wasn't intentional. Anytime he's asked me about his daddy, I've told him that you lived far away. I didn't have the heart to say you didn't want him, and I'm glad that I never did. My sister was a selfish woman. She didn't deserve what happened to her, but she robbed you of time with your son, and stole Theo's chance at having a father all these years. All because she wanted you to marry her and settle down."

He reached over and took my hand, giving my fingers a squeeze. When he tugged me closer, I went willingly. I didn't care about the disapproving looks of some women nearby. He lowered his head and kissed me. It was soft and sweet, and just what I'd needed. Thinking about Liliya and how she'd fucked over all of us, including herself, just pissed me off. Part of it was that I felt hurt over her actions, and how little she'd obviously cared about me.

"Let's call it a day on buying stuff for the boys. We'll head over to that shop across the parking lot with all the containers stacked in the window. You'll be able to find the stuff you need for the kitchen," he said.

"So disgraceful," someone muttered nearby.

I turned and narrowed my gaze at the trio of women openly sneering at us. What the hell was their problem?

"Does your husband never kiss you when you're out together?" I asked. "Or do you have a particular problem with *my* husband?"

"He's old enough to be your father," one of the women said. "It's disgusting."

Her words rang with venom, but the look in her eyes told another story. I saw the hunger there, the way she practically salivated over Sarge. She wasn't upset about our age difference. Not exactly. I'd be willing to bet she was pissed that he'd chosen someone younger, which meant she'd have never had a shot with him.

I felt Sarge tense, and I tightened my hold on his hand. A quick glance was all I could spare him before facing the women again. I only hoped I could handle this before he decided he wouldn't remain silent anymore. I should have known better.

"You didn't think it was so disgusting when the younger woman was you," he said.

Now that had my attention. "You know her?"

He snorted. "Yeah. I know her. Never fucked her, but she sure did spread her legs willingly enough for anyone wearing a patch about twenty years ago. Do your friends know you were a club whore for the Dixie Reapers in your younger years? Because I don't recognize either of them, which means they weren't regulars like you."

I spun to face him, my jaw going tight. "Did you just call her a whore?"

"Not in the sense you're thinking," he said. "I'll explain later. I promise. Just know that she's only being so spiteful because she's jealous."

"I'd already figured that out, but I didn't know why. You're saying she used to hang out with your club?"

He nodded and his gaze shot over my head to the women again. When I turned, I realized the other two had taken a few steps away from the one now glaring at Sarge. Served her right. She'd opened her mouth and spewed her hatred instead of just leaving things alone. Her friends would have never known she'd once hung out with the club if she hadn't started this shit.

"Come on, kitten. Time to check out and finish our shopping elsewhere."

Sarge led me past the women and to the front of the store. After he paid and loaded the bags into the Explorer, he looked up at the sky a moment, then rolled his neck until it cracked twice. I had a feeling that whatever he needed to tell me wouldn't be something I liked. As long as he wasn't making money off selling women like the Bratva, then I didn't think it would be all that bad. Or maybe I just hoped that was the case.

We got into the car and he pulled over to the other store, but didn't turn off the engine and didn't move to get out. He just sat there. After a moment, he looked at me and I saw both determination and a hint of fear. I just didn't know why he'd be afraid to tell me whatever it was, unless I'd been wrong about them owning a brothel.

"The clubhouse gets rather wild at night, especially Friday and Saturday nights. Girls from the surrounding areas, usually under the age of twenty-six but never younger than eighteen, show up to party." He ran a hand across his jaw, his fingers rasping against his beard. "We call them club whores because they'll sleep with anyone in a Reapers cut. Some of them just want to have fun, but others are hoping to rope one of us into keeping them. They're there voluntarily."

I turned in my seat to get a better look at him. The guilt covering his face told me that he'd been with those women. Maybe not the one in the store, but he'd been with others. I'd known he wasn't a virgin by any means, especially since he had a daughter older than me and had Theo with my sister. Did I like that he'd participated in those types of events? No, but I hadn't known him then. So I only had one question for him.

"Will you still go to those parties? Still sleep with those women?"

"No! Fuck, no! Are you crazy, Katya?"

"No, I'm not crazy. It's a good question. We don't know each other that well. What if you go up there one night and some woman climbs onto your lap? You going to shove her to the floor, or are you going to decide to have some fun instead?"

He growled, but didn't say anything right away. "Listen. I've done a lot of fucked-up shit in my life, but I would never cheat on my wife. And since that's you, kitten, I hope you like my dick because you're the only one who will be seeing it. I don't want those women. Why would I? I have a beautiful, badass woman at home. None of them could ever compare to you."

My heart melted a little at his words. "All right."

"That's it? All that and you're just suddenly going to accept my word?"

I nodded. "Yes. Because no one has ever called me beautiful and meant it, and no one has ever seen me as being a badass."

He wrapped his hand around the back of my neck and pulled me closer, claiming my lips with his in a deep, hungry kiss. My toes curled in my shoes and I wished we were home. I felt my nipples harden and press against my bra, and my panties grew damp. If we weren't in a parking lot, or the windows were darker, I'd have crawled over to his side of the SUV and made both of our nights a lot better.

He pulled back and took my hand, pressing it down on his cock. "Feel what you do to me? That's all for you, kitten. Now and always."

I licked my lips and cast a quick look around. We were far enough away that no one could see *that* clearly into the car. Before I could talk myself out of it, I reached for his pants and unbuckled his belt, then slid his zipper down.

"Not that I'm complaining, but what are you doing?" he asked.

I freed his cock from his underwear and leaned over, licking the tip. He hissed in a breath and I decided to just show him instead of telling him. I took the head between my lips and sucked as much of him into my mouth as I could. It took a few strokes before I was able to take almost all of him. Placing my hand at the base of his cock, I used it stroke him while I bobbed my head up and down. I flicked my tongue against his shaft on every downstroke, and sucked hard every time I pulled back.

Sarge groaned and fisted my hair in his hand. "That's it, kitten. Show me how much you love that cock."

I hummed, and it seemed to release some beast inside him. Next thing I knew, he was thrusting up into my mouth while pushing me farther down. I gagged a little as he hit the back of my throat, but I let him guide me. When he started coming, he flooded my mouth and I tried to swallow. I managed to get most of it down, but some dribbled out the corners of my mouth. His cock twitched against my tongue and I pulled back. He released me and searched the car.

"Fuck. No napkins, kitten." He reached over and wiped his cum off my chin and I sucked his thumb into my mouth, cleaning it off. Sarge drew in a sharp breath and his eyes dilated. "My naughty girl. Can't wait to get you home."

"Then I guess we'd better hurry up."

He got out and I followed. In the store, I quickly found the things I'd need to organize the kitchen better. The checkout line wasn't that long, but the clerk was slow. Like sloth slow. By the time we were done and had everything loaded, I felt like I might combust if we didn't get home soon. I wanted him, so damn much. I'd gone from being a virgin who didn't care about being with a man to craving Sarge like a drug.

He pulled out onto the street and reached for me, unfastening my jeans and giving them a tug. "Take those off, kitten."

I hesitated only a moment before I worked them over my hips and down my legs. They were stuck around my ankles because of my shoes, but Sarge didn't seem to care. He slipped his hand inside my panties and stroked my pussy.

"Damn. Already wet, aren't you?"

I didn't think he needed an answer since he felt the evidence of my need. He stroked my clit and I tried to spread my legs, but while I could part my knees, it wasn't nearly far enough. Working his hand farther between my thighs, he plunged two fingers inside me and ground the heel of his hand against my clit.

"Ride, kitten. Take what you need."

I gripped the armrest for leverage and moved my hips, fucking myself on his hand. It felt good, but not nearly good enough. I strained for the release that was out of reach, twisting and turning, trying to get myself there. Before Sarge, I'd been able to get myself off in less than two minutes. Of course, now that I'd experienced the type of orgasms he could give me, I knew my self-pleasure ones hadn't been nearly as great as I'd thought.

"You got another fantasy, kitten?" he asked.

"I-I want someone to watch me."

"Watch you having sex?" he asked.

I nodded.

"All right. Close your eyes."

My eyes slid shut and I waited for his next instruction. I hoped it would be as amazing as what we'd done in the bedroom before.

"Imagine we're parked. There's a truck next to us with two guys. They're both looking at you, admiring how fucking beautiful you are."

I moaned and squirmed.

"Lift up your shirt, kitten."

My hands didn't want to work right, but I managed to tug my shirt up. I cupped my breasts, gasping at how sensitive my nipples felt.

"That's it. Pull the cups of your bra down. Let me see those pretty tits. Show those men what they're missing."

I did as he commanded, my nipples hardening more. Sarge pressed his hand tighter against my clit.

"Now ride my hand, kitten. Make those tits bounce and give them a show."

I worked my hips, rubbing my clit against his hand with every shift. It wasn't long before I was coming. I screamed out his name as I felt a rush of wetness slick my panties.

"You're so fucking pretty when you come, kitten. Open your eyes."

I opened them and realized he'd pulled down an isolated road. The car had stopped at some point and I hadn't even noticed. Sarge helped me right my clothes, but I couldn't keep my cheeks from burning. I couldn't believe I'd just done that.

"My little wild cat." He chuckled. "Don't worry, kitten. No one saw anything. You might fantasize about it, but I don't think it would be as awesome as you imagine."

"Thank you."

"For what? Making you come? Trust me. That was my pleasure."

I shook my head. "No, for finding a way to make my fantasies come true without actually involving other people. I like that it's just the two of us, but I've often wondered what it would be like to be with more than one guy, or have someone watch me have sex. I…"

"You what?"

"Sometimes when I was trying to get myself off, I'd imagine a man licking my pussy, another fucking my ass, and one fucking my mouth."

His eyebrows lifted. "Damn, kitten. You really are my little wild cat. And to think you were a pure, innocent virgin until I got my hands on you."

"Virgin, yes. Innocent, not so much." I smiled. "I'll have to show you some of the books I like to read."

"Maybe we can find a few scenes to reenact." He winked. "Now let's get home and put this shit away, then I plan on making you come even harder. Preferably with my cock inside you."

Yes, I wanted that. So much.

I liked that he didn't make me feel bad for wanting to experience new things. Or rather things some would consider deviant behavior, or too wild for an innocent like me. Sarge seemed to have just as much fun as I did when we played like this.

Who'd have ever known a blowjob in a parking lot could lead to me having an orgasm on the way home? If that was the response I got, I'd have to try that again. Maybe lots of times.

Unfortunately, we didn't get to play more when we got to the house. Utter chaos had erupted inside Sarge's home, well, my home now too it seemed. The Prospects he'd sent back with the truck and furniture had managed to put everything together, but for whatever reason, they'd also decided to paint the room. That would have been fine if they hadn't ended up with two buckets of different colored paint, which resulted in a shouting match between the two, and two women in the middle of it calling them both "fucking idiots."

Chapter Eight

Sarge

I pinched the bridge of my nose to stave off the headache I felt building behind my eyes. Walking into a screaming match between two Prospects, along with Pepper and Ridley, hadn't been part of my plans. At all. The fact they'd ruined the moment I'd shared with Katya, and had intended to continue when we reached the house, only served to piss me off more.

"One more time. You both decided to paint the room because…" I waved for someone to answer.

"Everyone knows you set up this room for Reed," Dalton said. "If you're changing it to your son's room, it only seemed right to paint it a different color."

"Uh-huh." I looked around the space. One wall was clearly a medium blue while the other was red. "Which genius decided red was an awesome color for a kid's room?"

Dalton snorted. "That one." He pointed to Hunter.

"It's called Gingersnap. The kid has red hair so I thought it was appropriate."

I hung my head and closed my eyes. "Pepper and Ridley are correct. You're both idiots. Neither of you thought to check with me first? Or hell, even go ask Theo what color room he'd like?"

"Told you," Ridley said.

"Not now." I glared at her. "Why the fuck are you even here? Does Venom know you slipped your leash?"

Ridley's back went ramrod straight. "Leash? Leash? Are you kidding me right now?"

"No, sadly, I'm not. Because he really should control you better. My daughter I can understand. She lives next door, and *she's my daughter*. I have no fucking clue why you're in my house, uninvited at that."

"Well, that's just rude," Ridley said, then huffed.

Pepper waved and I looked over my shoulder to see Katya taking in everything with wide eyes. She'd have to learn sooner or later that she'd just inherited a very fucked-up, dysfunctional family. And I didn't just mean my daughter, Flicker, and my grandson. The Reapers and their women were all my family in some way or another. We might not be related by blood, but I knew they had my back. I just wished the women didn't like to meddle so damn much.

"Kitten, come say hi to Pepper and Ridley, since I know the VP's woman is here simply because she's fucking nosy as shit."

Katya slipped her hand into mine and came to stand beside me. She surveyed the room and cocked her head to the side. After a moment, she focused on the two Prospects. One with a blue paint roller and the other still holding one covered in red paint.

"So finish painting that wall red and make the other three blue. It's an accent wall and we can use it for hanging the pictures and maybe put a few short bookshelves or some cube systems on that wall. Then it won't be quite so glaring, but the paint won't be wasted," Katya said.

I leaned over to brush a kiss on the top of her head. "Smart."

Ridley and Pepper looked from Katya to the wall, then stared at one another.

"Why didn't we think of that?" Ridley asked.

"Because we aren't as sophisticated as my new stepmom."

Katya made a choking sound, then burst out laughing. After a moment, she was wiping at tears streaking her cheeks and trying to catch her breath. I wasn't sure what amused her to that extent, but it was nice to see her look so happy.

"If you call me Mommie Dearest, I'm coming over to check your closet for wire hangers," Katya said.

Pepper's brow furrowed in confusion, but I snorted to hold back my own laughter. I caught the reference even if Pepper hadn't.

"Thank you both for stopping by to... what? Supervise? But I think we've got it handled. Get the fuck out," I told the two of them. Then switched my gaze to Hunter and Dalton. "And you two finish painting. Be sure to crack the windows so it airs out overnight."

"What are you going to do?" Pepper asked.

"Spend some time with my wife. Get going before I tell Flicker you're being a pest again."

Pepper rolled her eyes. "Oh, please. You love it when I come over. By the way, what happened to your kitchen?"

I looked down at Katya a moment. "Speaking of my kitchen, any of that shit that doesn't belong to me had better be gone. Otherwise, I'm letting your stepmother throw out anything we don't need or want."

Pepper gasped and took off running, with Ridley on her heels. I heard her rummaging through the glassware a moment later. Shaking my head, I led Katya to the living room. I knew we had a lot of shit to do, like finish Theo's room and get all the crap in the kitchen put away, but right now, we both needed a little downtime.

I handed Katya the remote and pressed a quick kiss to her lips. "Pick a movie. I'll grab some popcorn and drinks. It seems our plans are slightly delayed because I'm not kicking Dalton and Hunter out until that room is repainted. It can dry overnight, and then we can set it up tomorrow."

"Any movie?" she asked.

"Anything. I'll even watch one of those sappy romantic ones. As long as I'm watching it with you, nothing else matters."

Her gaze softened and she reached up to run her fingers over my beard. "You're making it hard."

"I thought that was my line."

She lightly smacked my cheek. Anyone else did that I'd rip them apart. But Katya wasn't anyone. She was my wife.

"I'm being serious. I tried to do the right thing and leave, but the second I heard your voice, when I saw you, it's like some part of me recognized you. Like…"

"Like we're supposed to be together?" I asked.

She nodded. "I didn't want to fall for you. For one, you were Lily's first. It seemed wrong to want the man who had been interested in my sister. There was also the plan for me to leave so the Bratva wouldn't come here. It's too late for the last part, and for the first… No matter how hard I've fought it, I think I'm starting to fall for you. That's what I meant. You make it really difficult to not fall in love with you."

I leaned down closer, caging her between my arms. "Then fall, kitten. I'll always be here to catch you."

"How do you know just the right thing to say?" she asked.

"Comics," Pepper yelled. "He reads comics."

Katya opened and shut her mouth, giving me an odd look. I sighed and knew I'd have to confess my secret obsession. Yes, I liked comics. A lot. As in, I owned about forty large comic storage boxes that were all full, and I still picked up new ones when I could.

"She's named after Pepper Potts," I said. "Her mother's idea, not mine, just to be clear."

"As in Iron Man's Pepper?" Katya asked.

"The very one," my daughter said as she stopped in the doorway, her arms full of all sorts of crap she'd been hoarding in my kitchen. "I'll be back in a minute. Don't throw anything out yet!"

She dashed away and I just shook my head. "You ready to be part of this craziness? Because it's a little late for you to back out."

"When she says you like comics…"

I pulled away, grabbed her hand, and hauled her off the couch. I led her past Theo's room and opened another door, one that I always kept shut. There was a massive shelving unit taking up one entire wall from floor to ceiling, where I'd put the various collectibles I'd picked up over the years. Although, the collection had grown since Pepper came into my life. She got a kick out of finding superheroes and giving them to me as gifts. I had a wide variety of action figures, statues, and even some miniature figures that came from mystery packs.

"Wow," Katya said. "But those aren't comics."

I slid open the closet door. It was a larger space than it seemed from the outside. Deep enough for three rows of boxes, and I'd removed the rod and shelf so I could stack them higher. It was long enough to fit five in that direction, so I had fifteen on the first layer. Although, there would come a time that I'd run out of room and need to figure out something else.

"Does this mean if I bought twenty pairs of shoes you won't tell me I have too many as long as I don't complain about your addiction to superheroes?" she asked.

"Kitten, if you can *fit* twenty pairs of shoes in our closet, more power to you."

She grinned. "Challenge accepted."

I couldn't help but laugh, and I had no doubt she'd find a way to pull it off. And I'd let her. Anything to see her smile like that. Maybe she wasn't the only one falling. I'd do anything for her already. The thought of losing her made my chest ache. I knew that sooner or later we'd have to deal with the repercussions of her killing Voronin, but until then, I'd enjoy each day with her and try to keep our minds focused elsewhere.

"Come on, kitten. Let's enjoy tonight. Movie and popcorn, then I'll help organize the kitchen." I tugged her closer. "And after Dalton and Hunter leave, I'll make you come again. Multiple times."

She leaned away and pushed the door. It shut with a soft *click* and she smiled up at me. "Or you could make me come now and show them you've still got it."

"Is this another thing on your list? Letting men hear you have sex?" I asked.

"Not really, but I figure it couldn't hurt your reputation, right? Is that still a thing? Men bragging about having stamina or making a woman come so hard she screams his name?" She tugged on my cut. "Or is that just in cheesy movies and books?"

"Oh, it's a real thing, but I wasn't planning to share any details of what happens between us. You're mine, and only mine. I'm not sure I like the idea of any of my brothers knowing what you sound like when you come. Flicker already said we were loud enough for him to hear us outside. But those two are right on the other side of that closet," I said tipping my head that way.

She slid down to her knees. "Then maybe I won't be the one screaming. Any objection to them hearing *you* coming?"

"Nope." I watched as she unbuckled my belt and unfastened my pants. She tugged them down my hips, then worked my underwear down too. My cock was hard and ready, and had been since the moment she'd shut the door and given me that look.

She nibbled on her lower lip and looked up at me. "Why don't you take control?"

I slid my hand into her hair, gripping it tight. "You liked it when I did that in the car? Made you take all of me?"

"Yeah. I did."

"Hands behind your back, kitten. And keep them there or I'll tie your wrists."

Her breath hitched and her eyes dilated. She quickly obeyed. Fuck but she was beautiful! I didn't know how I'd gotten so damn lucky.

"Part those pretty lips, kitten." She dropped her jaw a little and I gripped my cock, smearing pre-cum across her lips. "Lick it off."

Her tongue darted out to lap her upper lip, then her lower one. Jesus. That made me even harder.

"Open wider," I said, my voice getting gruff the more turned on I got. When she lowered her jaw more, I slid my cock between her lips. I used short, slow strokes, working my way deeper. Tipping her head back, it let me slide in even more. Soon I was bumping the back of her throat. "Ready to learn something new?"

She hummed around my cock.

"Relax your throat so you can take more of me." It took a few tries, but eventually she took all of me. I fucked her mouth, taking my time, drawing it out as much as I could. Thrusting deep, I held still. "Swallow, kitten."

She couldn't do it at first. Nor the second or third time she tried. Eventually, she managed, and it felt fan-fucking-tastic. It didn't take long before she caught on. I used fast, hard strokes, then slid deep and held still. She'd swallow each time I did that, then I'd start fucking her mouth again. When my balls drew up, I knew I was close. So fucking close.

"I'm gonna come, kitten. You going to be good and swallow like last time?"

She did that humming thing again and I couldn't hold back another second. I took what I wanted, what I needed, and unloaded jet after jet of cum into her mouth. She managed to swallow more of it this time, then licked up the mess when she was finished.

"Damn, baby girl. That was fucking hot."

She grinned, but still didn't move. Her hands were still behind her back. It thrust her breasts out and the hard peaks of her nipples were poking through her shirt. I reached down and pinched first one, then the other, making her moan.

There was a knock at the door and throat cleared. "Um, Sarge. Not to interrupt or anything, but there's a package that was just delivered. I didn't know where you wanted it, so I left it near the front door."

"That's fine. Finish painting that damn room, Dalton."

"On it!" I heard his steps move quickly back to Theo's room.

"It seems we're going to have a lot of fun after they're gone," I said. "But my kitten is hurting, aren't you?"

She nodded.

"Need to come?" I asked.

"Please." She licked her lips. "I want to come."

"Only one way you're coming right now." I pointed to my dick. "Get it hard again."

She eagerly took my cock back into her mouth, sucking and licking. It didn't take much for me to get hard again. I pulled free, then shoved my pants and underwear down past my knees before kneeling in front of her. Reaching for her, I unfastened her pants and worked them down as far as they could go in this position. Then I turned her around and pressed her chest down to the floor.

"Keep those hands behind your back." I gripped her wrists with one hand.

"I can't spread my legs," she said.

"Don't need you to." I teased her pussy, feeling how wet she was. It seemed she liked sucking my cock. I eased inside her, taking my time so I wouldn't hurt her. With her legs trapped by her pants and her thighs still together, she hugged my dick even tighter than before. "So fucking good, baby girl. You okay? Not hurting?"

"Don't stop," she begged.

I gripped her hip and thrust in hard and fast. "Like that, kitten? Tell me what you want?"

"I-I want… I want…"

"You want a hard fucking? You want it soft and sweet?"

"Hard. I want it hard!"

I chuckled and smacked her ass before taking hold of her hip again. "I was hoping you'd say that."

I drove into her, slamming my dick deep with each stroke. It was almost like I was possessed. It was a fucking, pure and simple. But more than that, I was going to fill her hot little pussy with as much cum as I could tonight. I might not have wanted a family, but the thought of Katya having my kid did things to me, brought out a beast I hadn't realized was buried inside.

"Oh, God! I'm going to come! Don't stop. Please, don't stop," she yelled.

I had no doubt the Prospects heard everything, and right then, I didn't give a shit. Let them listen. It wasn't like they were watching me fuck her.

"That's it, kitten. Take it. Take everything I give you."

I grunted as my cock twitched and jerked. Katya screamed out her release right about the same time I started filling her up. I ground against her ass, keeping my cock inside her, even after the last drops of cum had spurted into her wet pussy. I pushed deeper.

"This pussy mine?" I asked.

"Yes, only yours."

I ran my hand down the cheek of her ass. "And this ass?"

"Yours too. All of me is yours and only yours. I don't want anyone else."

"Good answer because you can't have anyone else. Another man puts his dick anywhere near you and I'll fucking kill him. Then I'll tie you down and fuck you until you remember that you're mine."

She glanced at me over her shoulder. "That's not exactly a deterrent. You realize that, right? Because that sounds like a good time to me. Well, not the killing part."

"You want to be tied up again?"

"I liked it."

"Good. Except this time, I'm tying your ankles too. You'll be spread open and unable to do a damn thing except come over and over."

Her gaze strayed to the wall. "Think they're done yet?"

"We're done!" Hunter yelled through the wall. "And we're leaving. Thirty seconds and you'll be the only ones here. Pepper came back, grabbed some stuff, heard way more than she liked, and took off like her ass was on fire. Doubt she's stopping back by tonight."

I heard the bedroom door to Theo's room shut and a moment later heard the front door open and close. It looked like the kitchen would have to wait because now I really wanted to open that damn box and have some fun. And anyone who disturbed us was going to incur my wrath.

Chapter Nine

Katya

Sarge hadn't been lying about tying me down. He had my wrists secured at either side of the mattress, and had spread my legs, tying my ankles as well. I was wide open and completely at his mercy. It wasn't fear that made my heart skip a beat, but anticipation. I didn't know what was in the box, but the heated look in his eyes told me enough. Whatever he'd bought, I was going to like it. A lot.

He held up a blindfold and arched an eyebrow, and I nodded. I'd read that it could heighten the senses when one was taken away. If I couldn't see what he was doing, maybe it would feel even more intense.

His lips brushed my cheek as he covered my eyes. "Trust me, kitten?"

"With my life."

"I do anything you don't like, you tell me. But for complete transparency, if you tell me to stop and I can tell you're close to coming, I'm going to make you come first. Pain is one thing, but I won't let you avoid pleasure, no matter how extreme it might be."

He shifted, moving away from me. He'd carried the box into the bathroom while I undressed and I'd heard him running the sink. When he'd come back, he'd told me that he'd washed and prepped everything. I still didn't have a clue what he'd bought, but I was more than ready to find out.

"You like me playing with your ass, didn't you? Liked getting fucked there?" he asked.

"You know I did."

I heard something *snick*, then felt something cold and wet on his fingers as he rubbed them down my pussy.

"Lift your hips, kitten."

I struggled to obey and was rewarded with him rubbing his fingers between my ass cheeks. He eased a finger into me, working it in and out a few times, before adding a second one. Then he pulled away. A moment later, something slightly large and freezing cold pressed there.

"Lance! It's cold!" I yelped as he pressed it inside me. "Wh-what is it?"

I heard a *click*, and then whatever it was started vibrating. I gasped and my back arched. *Holy shit!* It felt amazing. He never did tell me what he'd put inside me, but I'd told him that I trusted him, and I did. I heard something else that made a *whirring* noise, then something hard vibrated against my clit. "Oh, God! It's too much!"

"No, it's not. Remember what I said?" he asked.

"Th-that you'd only stop for pain, and not pleasure?"

"Right." He used his fingers to spread me open more, then worked the toy against the hard bud. I wanted to cry it felt so good and so... so... I yanked at the ropes, needing to move away while wanting to get closer. A sob welled in my throat and tears leaked from my eyes as I came so damn hard. And he didn't back off even a little. "That's it, kitten. Keep coming for me. Soak this fucking bed."

I was powerless to do anything but obey. I lost count of how many orgasms I had. Suddenly, the toy was gone and I felt Sarge shift away from me. Something circled my nipples and I thrust my breasts up. It was soft and almost tickled. He did it again, circling twice, then flicking whatever it was across the hard peaks, first one, then the other. I cried out, my pussy clenching with need.

"So responsive," he murmured.

He replaced the object with his mouth, sucking and licking, then rubbing his beard against my sensitive skin. While he teased my nipples, he put the other toy back against my clit. The sensations were incredible, and almost more than I could handle.

"Lance, please. I can't! I just... I can't."

"You seem to like using that mouth for all the wrong things, like saying you won't take the pleasure I'm giving you. Maybe I should give you something else to do with it?" I sucked in a breath. "I'd much rather come in your pussy, but keep it up and my dick is going back between those sassy lips."

"Oh, God. Lance, I... I need you."

"We have all night, kitten," he said softly. "All. Night."

I was both looking forward to it and dreading it. Would I survive? Was there such a thing as coming too much? I had a feeling I was going to find out.

"I'm going to fuck your pussy, come inside you, and then I'm going to get you off again and again. When you think you can't take any more, I'll fuck you again." He placed his lips by my ear. "There's a reason I wanted to tie you down."

"Why?" I asked.

He settled his body over mine and thrust deep with one stroke. I moaned at how amazing it felt to have him in my pussy and the toy in my ass. So full! He stroked in and out a few times, then kissed me hard.

"Why?" he asked. "Because I'm going to fuck every bit of cum into you that I can manage between now and morning."

I tried to process his words, but I was already coming again, and my brain was on overload. I felt the heat of his release, and noticed he hadn't gotten any softer. He started stroking in and out of me again.

"I'm going to fuck a baby into you, kitten. You're mine, this pussy is mine, your ass, all of you, remember? It's what you told me. And if you're mine, then I'm yours, and what better way to celebrate that than to create something together? A little part of you and a part of me?"

"Oh, Lance." I sighed. "You didn't have to tie me down for that."

"Want me to release you?"

"No. I didn't say I didn't *like* being tied down, just that I'd have agreed to have a baby with you. Ropes weren't required." I smiled. "They're just a bonus."

"Fuck it. I think I've already fallen, kitten. I love you. I don't give a shit that we've only known each other for two damn days. The second I saw you hit that Prospect, I knew."

"I want your baby, Lance. I want everything with you."

"Then you'll have it." He kissed me again, taking me harder and faster. We came at the same time, but he was far from done with me. By morning, I knew my pussy and ass would be sore, but I didn't care. It was a small price to pay for the wildest most incredible night of my life.

He spent the next two hours making me scream his name as he used one toy after another to make me come. He came inside me three times, his cum leaking down my thighs, before I told him I couldn't take much more. I really did need a break, and I knew he probably did too, even if he wouldn't admit it.

"One more, kitten."

"One more," I agreed.

He untied me and flipped me onto my stomach. Gently, he pulled the vibrator from my ass and switched it off. I still had my blindfold on and decided to leave it. I gripped the sheets and waited with bated breath for whatever he had in mind next. His hands gripped me, pulling my ass cheeks apart. I felt the head of his cock press against me, and then he was sinking into my ass.

I groaned and buried my face in the mattress. He slid a hand under my belly, lifting me higher and changing the angle. When he slid all the way in, tingles went down my spine. Using his fingers, he worked my clit while he stroked in and out. I didn't know if he could even come again, or if I could for that matter. I felt wrung out and exhausted.

"Come for me, kitten. Give me one more orgasm. Let me feel that ass squeeze my dick."

"I don't know if I can." My words were muffled against the bed, but he must have heard me. His fingers left my pussy and I heard one of the toys turn on again. He pressed it to my clit and I bucked and twisted beneath him. Sarge only laughed and took me harder.

"That's it, baby girl. Take it." He rubbed the toy faster against the hard bud and I came apart. I was crying I came so hard, and I felt his release as he thrust twice more. My body twitched and trembled. He moved the toy against my clit a few more times, and I came again even if it was just a small orgasm. He turned it off and I heard it thump on the mattress. Slowly, he pulled his cock from my ass and I groaned at how tender I was. My nipples, pussy, and ass felt very well used, but if he asked to do this again sometime, I'd agree in a second.

He tugged the blindfold off and smiled down at me. "Rest a minute, kitten. Going to run a bath for us."

Sarge got off the bed and I heard him walk into the bathroom. Then I heard the water running. When he returned for me, he lifted me into his arms and carried me to the tub. Instead of setting me down, he climbed over the side and sat, pulling me between his legs. I leaned back against his chest and closed my eyes, letting the hot water soothe me, but his presence did as well.

"Love you too," I said softly. "Even if that sounds crazy."

"I'm a Reaper, baby girl. Crazy is my specialty, especially when it comes to a pretty woman. Or rather the *right* woman. My brothers always said they knew when they met the only woman they'd want to fuck ever again. I hadn't believed them, until you."

"That's all it is?" I asked, my lips barely moving as I fought to stay awake.

"No. Not with you." He kissed my cheek. "Sometimes it's fucking. But sometimes it's making love. No reason we can't do both."

I hummed and placed my hand over his arm where he'd banded it across my waist. "For the record, if you knocked me up tonight and our kid one day asks where they came from, I'll let you figure out how to tell them you tied Mommy to a bed and fucked her nearly into a coma."

"I think we'll just say they were dropped off by a stork. Seems easier."

I snorted and smiled. I must have dozed off because the next time I opened my eyes, Sarge was lifting me from the tub and the water had cooled considerably. I stood on shaky legs while he dried me off, then dried himself. Even though I had pajamas now, I still preferred his shirts. I slipped one over my head, and decided to forgo panties. I was a bit too tender to want anything against my pussy right now.

We ordered pizza since the kitchen was still a wreck, watched some movies, and cuddled for hours. It was the best night of my life. Until my phone rang with a number I didn't recognize. My hand shook as I reached for it, and I dropped it twice. Sarge took it from me and answered. The fierce look on his face worried me.

"Speak English, fucker," Sarge said. His gaze shot to me. "What do you want with Katya?"

His expression cleared and he handed the phone to me. I held it to my ear, my heart hammering in my chest. "This is Katya."

"You have questions about your mother?" a deep voice asked in Russian.

And that's when I knew who had called. "Yes. This is Konstantin Bykov, isn't it?"

I kept my answers in English so that Sarge would have some idea of what was going on. He was pacing the room, tension lines bracketing his mouth, and his eyes clouded with worry for me.

"What do you want, Miss Voronin? It was many years ago that I knew your mother. I'm not sure how I can help you now."

I licked my lips. "Twenty-two years ago. Right?" There was a lengthy pause. So silent that I pulled the phone back to make sure he hadn't hung up. "Mr. Bykov?"

Still nothing. I took a breath and held Sarge's gaze. Did I dare?

"Father?" I asked, my voice soft and not as strong as I'd have liked.

There was some cursing on the other end of the line, then he cleared his throat. "Is that why you called, Katya? Did Voronin say something to make you think he's not your father?"

"He said he whored my mother out to his friends, let them use her to further his position with the Bratva." I swallowed hard. "He said you were with her for quite a while when you were younger. She became pregnant with me during that time. Please, I only want the truth. I want to know who I am."

"Your mother was nearly ten years older than me, but she was stunning. When she smiled, it lit up the entire room. When Voronin was present, she was like a meek little mouse. Timid. Scared. But when it was just the two of us? Ah... now those times I got to see the true woman I was falling for."

My throat tightened. "You were in love with my mother?"

"Yes, but she was already married. Voronin already had a daughter with her. I couldn't take her from him. It wouldn't have been fair to your sister." He paused again. "Where are you, Katya? I think we need to speak face-to-face."

"I'm in Alabama." I looked to Sarge for guidance. Was I permitted to give away my location? It wasn't like my father's men -- or the man I'd *thought* was my father -- didn't know he'd come here before he vanished. If they'd come looking for him, I hadn't heard of it. Then again, I doubted anyone would have necessarily shared that information with me. Sarge gave me a nod. "I'm at the Dixie Reapers compound."

Sarge held his hand out and I gave him the phone. He gave Bykov the address and then hung up. He crouched at my feet, reaching for my hands, lifting them and placing a kiss against my fingers.

"Whatever happens, I'm right here with you, kitten. You're mine. I'm yours. And no one is taking you from me."

I gave him a nod. I only hoped those words were true. Even if Konstantin Bykov *was* my father, the fact I killed Voronin put me in a sticky situation. The Bratva would demand justice, and I wasn't sure the Reapers would be able to stop them from taking me. For the first time since I was little, I prayed. If this was ever going to turn out okay, I was almost certain it would require divine intervention because the Bratva never backed down. They'd keep coming, sending more soldiers, until the Reapers were wiped out and I was firmly in their grasp. No one ever killed one of theirs and lived to tell the tale. I might have been born into that world, but I was a woman. Inferior. Only good for breeding and negotiations. And I'd killed one of their men.

Sarge sat and pulled me into his side, holding me as I tried to keep it together. I'd come this far. He called me his fierce kitten, and for him, I'd continue to fight. Whatever the outcome, I'd go down swinging.

Chapter Ten

Sarge

What had been an amazing night had turned to shit with one phone call. Katya had finally fallen asleep and I'd carried her to bed, then I'd gotten on the phone. Not only did Torch and Venom need to know we had company heading our way, but I wanted to see what Wire and Lavender could find on Bykov and anything that might be useful about the Bratva. After doing as much as I could, I went into Theo's room. The paint wasn't quite dry yet so I couldn't do a lot. I remembered Pepper washing any new clothes or bedding whenever I bought stuff for Reed, so I gathered up the stuff I'd purchased earlier and carried it to the laundry room.

As I dropped all the bags onto the floor, I realized the room was too damn small for someone with a family. It was one thing when Reed was only here to visit, but now I had a son who would be living with me, and a woman under my roof. She'd want more space in here. I looked around the area. I couldn't extend the width because Flicker's house was right across from the wall where the washer and dryer were hooked up, but the rear wall faced the backyard. The house had always been a strange shape instead of straight across the backside, but that worked in my favor right now.

I tapped on the wall in a few spots, trying to get a few ideas. One of the newer Prospects, Austin, had worked construction until an incident had cost him his job. It hadn't taken long for him to become our go-to for projects like this, even though he'd only been a Prospect for us about fifteen months. I didn't give a shit if he was sleeping or partying. Grabbing my phone, I called and kept calling until he picked up.

"Sarge?" he asked, his voice thick but not from sleep.

"You drink until you passed out? Or you still drinking?" I asked.

"Uh, maybe a bit of both?" He didn't sound certain, which told me he was pretty fucked-up right now. Great. "Get your ass to my house. I'll have coffee waiting. Once you're sobered up, I need to talk to you about something. And for fuck's sake, walk and don't try to ride your damn bike."

The line went dead and I just shook my head. I didn't know how long it would take for him to stumble his way here, but I hoped the fresh air would be a start to getting his head clear. The kitchen was still wrecked, but I could see that Pepper had taken quite a few things. I sifted through the stuff nearest the coffeemaker and realized most of it was probably hers too.

"My house isn't a damn storage unit," I mumbled. I kept a few boxes on hand and went to the carport to get one. There was a small room at the back that wasn't big enough for much of anything, but I kept about a half dozen boxes in there in case I ever needed them for something. I grabbed one, then took it to the kitchen and piled anything I didn't recognize into the box, then set it by the door for Pepper.

By the time I had coffee brewed, Austin came tumbling into the house. If he woke up Katya, I'd have to kick his ass, even if I did tell him to come here. I made him sit and got about three cups of coffee into him before he stopped slurring his words or looking about two seconds from passing out. When he was clearheaded and able to focus, I showed him the laundry room and explained what I wanted.

"Just expanding the laundry and nothing else?" he asked.

"What else would I need?"

He shrugged. "You have a woman now. Heard about your son. What if she wants more kids, or you do? Going to run out of rooms."

"I don't plan on having a dozen kids at my age."

"Just hear me out. I heard about Hunter and Dalton painting the room you were using for Reed to make a bedroom for Theo, and a place where Reed could still visit. What about making the room next to theirs a playroom?"

I was already shaking my head before he'd finished the sentence. Not only did I not want to give up that space because it was a pain in the ass to set all that shit up, but I wanted a buffer between my room and any space the kids would use. Katya wasn't exactly quiet when I was balls-deep inside her, and I planned on making her scream my name until I couldn't get it up anymore. And even then, that's what those little blue pills were for.

"You need more bedrooms," Austin said. "This house isn't designed for a large family in mind. Just listen. If you don't want me to do it, then tell me, but not until I've laid it all out. You have attic space upstairs, but it's not easily accessible right now. What if you made the master bedroom a bonus room and put in a staircase to the second floor? You could then renovate the attic and easily put the master bedroom up there and at least one or two other rooms."

I pinched the bridge of my nose. The kid was giving me a headache. "Austin, I appreciate your enthusiasm over the remodel, and your concern for how many kids I'll have, but I like the set up just fine. Except this room. I want a counter in here with cabinets underneath for storage. The extra space would also allow Katya to put the hampers in here all at one time and be able to move around without tripping over stuff."

Austin folded his arms. "How set are you on living next door to your daughter?"

Now he had my attention. I knew the Prospects didn't have their own homes, so he wasn't offering up his space. So what exactly did he plan to offer me? It wasn't like he had any say over things around here. Had Torch asked him to build something new? While most things went through Church, new houses had gone up or at least been started without any of us knowing until we heard the hammering.

"I like being near my grandson, and I think Theo wants to stay close to Reed." I leaned against the wall. "Why?"

"Since the club keeps growing, when we put in those small apartments for guests, Torch and Venom asked me to take on another project. At the time, I think it was more for Ridley's benefit."

"What the hell are you talking about?" I asked.

"Farther back, beyond the apartments, there's a cul-de-sac with four houses. Big ones. We're talking six bedrooms each, three full bathrooms, and a half bath downstairs in each. The yards aren't fenced separately out back, but instead it's one huge enclosed area. I was tasked with putting in play equipment, a pool with a wrought-iron fence and gate around it, sandbox, and a few picnic tables. It's nice. Really damn nice. No expense was spared on the inside either."

I waved a hand, wanting him to get to the damn point, although I always wanted to know how all that had been added without me knowing. Did Flicker know about it? Or anyone else?

"Venom and Bull are taking two of the houses. Ridley wanted to be closer to her dad, and she's gotten close to Darian too. The other two haven't been claimed. Since Flicker claimed your daughter, it's possible Torch would let you and Flicker take the other two houses. It would give you room to grow, keep you near your daughter and grandson, and it would give your woman three other Reapers ladies to lend a hand or keep her company when you're out on jobs."

Well, damn. The kid had really thought this one out. I didn't know how he'd gone from falling-down drunk less than hour ago to being this fucking logical. It made me think if he ever patched in, he'd be a damn good asset to the club, and someone I'd gladly call my brother. I knew he had his issues, but we all did.

Looking at the time, I knew it was risky to call Torch. The sun would be up in a few hours and I could check in then. I'd already pulled him from bed once, and this was hardly an emergency. Although…

"What's security like back there?" I asked. "Those homes easy to access without the club being aware of trouble? I didn't even know they were there. I won't ask Katya to move to a place that could leave her defenseless if our gates are breached."

Austin dropped his voice, even though we were the only ones awake in the house. "There's a bunker. It's not right by the houses, but about fifteen feet from the one Venom is taking. Torch plans to add another cul-de-sac on the other side of the bunker. It's big enough to hold maybe thirty or forty people. Not comfortably, but it would keep the women and kids safe if there was trouble. He's going to take one of the other homes. Tank, Rocky, and Gears will be offered the others."

Fucking hell. All the officers would have access to that bunker for their families. What about the rest of us? Sure, that meant Pepper and my grandson would be safe, but what about Theo and Katya? Or Zipper's family? Tex's and Wire's? What the fuck was going on around here?

I wanted that house if for no other reason than to make sure my family was safe. I just didn't like what it meant for everyone else. They were still near the front gates, and their families didn't have a safe place to hide if trouble came knocking. I didn't understand what Torch and Venom were thinking. We were brothers. We protected one another, including our women and kids.

My stomach knotted at the implication of what Austin had shared. I didn't think the kid even realized it yet. Those houses weren't the secret. It was the bunker. The rest was window dressing. Sure, someone would see them and ask questions, but if it was explained as a way for Bull and Ridley to stay close, or Torch and the other officers to be close to one another, no one would think anything of it. They'd never realize there was a secret room underground for those families.

"Thanks for coming by, Austin. I'll talk to Torch about the house."

He nodded and let himself out, but my heart was heavy. What was happening to the Dixie Reapers? And how had it all transpired without me even noticing? First Torch sending Katya to the gate to face who we thought was her father, and now this. As I thought over things, I realized there had been other risks over the years, ones that wouldn't have happened a decade ago.

I called Venom, not caring if he was asleep or not.

"What the fuck, Sarge? It's three in the damn morning."

"We need to talk. Now."

Venom growled. "Did you just issue me an order?"

I didn't even hesitate. "Yeah, I did. So get your ass to my house before I lose my shit. Learned some things tonight that don't make me very happy, and I doubt the others around here would like it either."

"Christ. I'll be there in ten. You better have coffee ready."

I hung up, brewed a fresh batch of coffee, and waited for the VP to arrive. I needed answers, preferably before Bykov showed up. If there was even a chance the club was changing in ways I wouldn't like, I needed to know before I entrusted them with keeping Katya safe. Once Bykov was inside the gates, all hell could break loose.

I heard Venom's bike but remained in the kitchen, leaning against the counter. There was already a fresh cup by the coffeemaker. Venom stomped into the house, went straight for the coffee, and took three gulps before he even looked at me.

"What the fuck is going on?" he asked.

"That's what I want to know. Learned about some houses at the back of the property, ones with a secret bunker for all the officers' families."

He sighed and closed his eyes. "I told Torch not to keep that shit to himself, but he said he wasn't ready yet. You know we had to make a deal when Renegade's sister got caught up in that mess a few years back. In order for our brothers to be released, Torch had to agree to let that asshole run trucks through here and let things fall off with no questions asked. He did the same thing with every club involved."

I motioned for him to keep going. I already knew all that shit. We all did.

"Well, Rocky decided to open one of those boxes before it was retrieved. We'd thought it was drugs. It's not. The guy is running guns and counterfeit cash. And I don't mean your average guns either. We're talking shit only the military should be able to access. Including a grenade launcher."

"And you think he's going to use those weapons against us?" I asked, not sure what that had to do with the bunker.

"It's possible, but if not him, then someone else could easily bring that shit to our gates. After what happened with Lavender, Torch decided enough was enough. He started on those homes and the bunker, but there's going to be more. Not more homes except for as we need them, but there's going to be two more bunkers, one on each end of the compound. He got the idea from Hades Abyss. Their Mississippi chapter has a pretty fucking sweet one, and while it was breached, it only showed us how to improve ours to keep that from happening."

"And it's just a coincidence the officers are getting access to the first one before anyone else knows it's there?" I asked.

"That was actually not my idea, or Torch's for that matter. You can thank Tank. He agreed to take one of the last homes going up, which construction is supposed to start in a few weeks on that set, but he said that we needed to make sure the officers' families were covered first. I guess he figured if anyone's kids would take over one day, it would be ours."

I still didn't like this shit. Then I had another thought. "The house next to Flicker. It was for Ryker and Laken, wasn't it?"

He nodded. "That was the plan, except Laken didn't want to be that close to her brother. She refused to take the house."

I folded my arms and thought about that a moment. Laken and Ryker knew, all the officers knew, but no one else. Well. Austin did, but he'd helped build them, which meant anyone else working on them knew about it too. How had they thought to keep this a secret? And why? What was the point in hiding the information until the bunkers were finished?

"I asked Austin to come over tonight. My laundry room looked too small now that I have a family, except he kept saying I needed more bedrooms."

Venom sighed. "And he told you about the houses. Bunker too?"

I nodded. "He did. I don't think he realized it was a secret, or his brain was still too pickled with alcohol for him to be thinking completely straight. He suggested I take the house next to Flicker so I could be near Pepper and my son could be next door to Reed."

Venom ran a hand down his beard. "Makes sense. I heard the two boys were getting along well. I also know Pepper likes being next door to you. After not having you in her life for so long, I think she's scared to go too far or you might vanish."

I hadn't thought of it that way before, but he was probably right. She was a tough girl and put on a brave face, but I knew that after finding me, she hadn't wanted to leave. The fact Flicker claimed her and already lived next door had just been a bonus. I hadn't thought of it as a bonus when I realized a man older than me was fucking my daughter, but she was a grown woman and could make her own choices. Besides, he treated her so damn well that I couldn't complain. Much.

"Why not just tell everyone the plan? It's not like we'd fight over getting to use the first bunker. As long as we know there's something be done to include all our families, that's all that matters. Right now, the officers would look guilty as hell of hiding something if this got out." I took a breath to calm myself down. "Look, I don't understand the reasoning behind it all, and I don't honestly give a rat's ass. Just fix it. If I found out, someone else will."

Venom nodded. "You're right. I'll talk to Torch. We'll add it to the list for Church later. He should be calling Church pretty early. We stayed up brainstorming for a while after your call. I'd just closed my eyes when you called again."

"Sorry, but I didn't feel like this could wait."

"I got here ready to knock the shit out of you. But you're right. It did look bad to keep that from the club. We'll fix it. Until then, if you want the house next to the one Flicker is supposed to take, you can have it. I don't even have to ask Torch about it." Venom drained his coffee and set the mug down. "Now, I'm going to go home and make another pot of coffee so I have a prayer of staying awake all day."

I started washing Theo's new things, then double-checked all the stuff scattered around the kitchen. I found more of Pepper's things and added them to the box by the door, then tried to regroup stuff so we could at least use the stove and a sliver of counter. I didn't want to leave all this for Katya, but maybe she could work on organizing this mess while I was in Church.

I sent a quick text to Pepper before checking on Katya. *Your shit is inside the front door. Come get it.*

My woman was still passed out, sleeping peacefully. I tugged the covers over her, pressed a kiss to her forehead, and let her get some rest. While she'd wanted to speak with Bykov and find out if he truly was her father, I could tell the thought of meeting him in person was freaking her out. I didn't know if she was worried he'd try to make her leave with him, or if it was more than that.

I hadn't wanted to put any more strain on her, but the men she'd claimed were with Voronin hadn't been found. One of the Prospects had noticed a black Lincoln drive by with blacked-out windows, more than once, but no one had approached the gates. If he really had brought men with him, then they knew this was the last place he'd said he was going. The fact they weren't asking questions made me think they already knew he hadn't walked out of here. Sooner or later, they'd make their move.

I thought about how much each Reaper loved their woman and kids. We all had blood on our hands, had walked on the wrong side of the law, but when it came down to it, we'd give our lives for our families. The Bratva didn't seem to give a shit about any of their women. Part of me hoped that Konstantin wasn't like the others. If he came here, thinking he'd use Katya in some way, then I'd quickly dissuade him. Even if it meant burying his ass six feet deep.

For Katya's sake, I hoped he was on her side and wanted what was best for her. She needed someone in her corner, someone other than me. I knew the Reapers would stand beside her as well, but I couldn't help feeling it was important to her to be accepted by her own people. If Konstantin Bykov could give that to her, then I'd welcome him with open arms. Hell, he could come to Thanksgiving dinner every fucking year.

Don't let her down, asshole, or I'll make you bleed.

Chapter Eleven

Katya

I'd woken to a note on the bed saying Sarge had gone to Church. I'd thought he meant the religious kind, but Pepper had stopped by and laughed until she'd cried when I was upset he hadn't taken me with him. She'd explained what Church meant to the Dixie Reapers, and then I'd understood why he'd left me home. Well, maybe a little. It bothered me they were possibly discussing me or the trouble I'd brought and I wasn't part of the conversation.

"You really going to sit here all meek and shit?" Pepper asked.

"You said women aren't allowed," I reminded her.

She nodded. "I did. Doesn't mean you have to listen. Technically, my dad hasn't told you shit about how all this works. This is your one chance to go in there, guns blazing, and get away with it by claiming ignorance."

She had a point. A flimsy one at best, but I could make it work. And she was right, sitting here worrying wasn't really my style. I was all about facing things head-on, or trying to find a solution to my own problems. While I loved that Sarge wanted to protect me, I didn't want to sit on the sidelines, not knowing what the hell was going on. I glanced down at my clothes. "Maybe I should change first."

I'd just slipped on some shorts and a shirt, thinking I'd tackle the kitchen. Then Pepper had shown up. While the outfit was fine, it didn't really scream that I belonged to a biker.

Pepper snorted. "You do look a bit like a cheerleader right now, with your hair up and that outfit. Then again, if you bent over, I bet your ass would stick out of those shorts. Might be an advantage. You could use it as a distraction."

I rolled my eyes and went to at least put on some jeans and a shirt that didn't have a cartoon character on it. When I got back to the kitchen, I had on my skinny jeans, Doc Martens, and a plain black shirt. Pepper gave me a thumbs-up, so I grabbed the keys to the SUV and left. When I got to the clubhouse, I saw the line of bikes and parked at the end. There were also a few cars that seemed out of place.

I got out and headed up the steps, my Docs thumping on the wood. Pushing open the clubhouse door, I blinked at the dim lighting and then cringed. There were a few mostly naked women running around. I remembered the woman from last night and Sarge calling her a club whore. This must have been what he meant. But he'd said they were here at night. I didn't see Sarge, or the others, but the guy I'd punched in the ribs was sprawled in a chair, one of the women sucking him off.

He leered at me. "You want to join in?"

I paused mid-step and only turned my head his way. I stared. Hard. I might not know a lot about how things worked around here, but after Sarge threatening to kill any man who tried to fuck me, I was pretty certain what he'd just said made him the dumbest guy on the planet.

I walked closer, and planted my hands on my hips. "What did you say to me?"

"I asked if you want to join in. Plenty of this to go around," he said, waving a hand down his torso.

I gave a sharp bark of laughter that made it clear what I thought about his *this*. I made sure to look long and hard at his cock, then smiled. "Doesn't look like enough to me."

"You bitch!" He shot up off the chair, knocking the woman over. She cried out as she fell backward. The asshole clenched his fists, but before he could make a move, I brought my knee up and nailed him right in the ribs with my Doc-shod foot. Same spot I'd punched him. He howled, then snarled at me.

I laughed as I danced out of reach, then kicked him again. He shifted and my foot glanced off his hip, but I'd take any hits I could get. The fact his dick was flopping around was almost too perfect. I aimed my fist right for it, but he moved again, and I caught him in the thigh.

"See, it's so small I couldn't even hit it," I taunted.

He launched himself at me, knocking me down. The air left my lungs in a *whoosh* and I gasped for breath, momentarily stunned as my head smacked the floor. I saw his hand go back, his fist aiming straight for my face, then I heard the bellow of rage that came from somewhere else.

"You're fucking dead!"

I smiled up at him. "You fucked up again."

Sarge yanked him off me and started in, hammering at him with his fists. Poor guy didn't stand a chance. Blood poured from his nose and mouth. When he fell to his knees, his face was already swelling and discolored. One eye was nearly shut, and I'd be willing to bet he had some broken ribs the way he was cradling them.

Torch came into my line of sight and stopped next to Sarge. "Wilson Peters, you're a disgrace to this club and to yourself."

Someone else approached and yanked the cut off his back. Two more came from behind me and grabbed him on either side, hauling him away. I didn't know what would happen to him, and I didn't much care right then. He was a dickhead who treated women like shit. The Bratva would have loved him.

A man knelt next to me, turning my chin one way, then the other. "You all right, *solnyshka*?"

I opened and shut my mouth twice.

He arched an eyebrow and seemed amused. His cut said *Grimm*. But what he said next was a complete surprise.

"He'll be handled. You're safe here," he said in Russian.

"Quit flirting with my woman, Grimm." Sarge shoved him aside and fell to his knees beside me. He yanked me into his arms and held me tight. "What the hell were you doing here? And what happened?"

"Pepper said that Church was held at the clubhouse. I came to find you. Then he asked if I wanted to join him and the woman sucking him off." I buried my face against him. "I might have said he had a small dick and there wasn't enough to share."

Sarge's body shook, and then he let out a loud guffaw. The other men surrounding us laughed as well. Something cool touched my arm and I turned my head to see Torch handing me a cut. I took it, not really understanding, until I read it. *Property of Sarge*.

"Wait. Property?" I pulled back. "Property? Are you kidding me right now?"

"Easy," Grimm said. "It's not like the Bratva. It only means you belong to Sarge, that you're his to protect, and therefore ours to protect as well. It shows you have a position of respect in this club."

"Unlike them," Torch said, nodding toward the barely dressed women.

"Oh." I clutched it to my chest. "Then that's okay."

Sarge laughed again, then kissed me. "I'm sorry I didn't explain things better, and I should have told you that Church is just for patched members and officers. Did you need something? Everything okay at home?"

I burrowed into him. "I felt left out."

He hugged me to his chest. "My fierce little kitten. You did a good job kicking that Prospect's ass. I'm only sorry it came down to that. The moment he tried to hit you when you showed up at the gates, I should have asked the club to take a vote and thrown his ass out."

Torch held up a hand. "Wait. He tried to hit her before? You'd said she punched him, but you left out *why* she'd hit him. I figured he'd just said some stupid shit. Why am I just now hearing about this?"

"She handled herself well that day. Impressed the hell out of me," Sarge said. "I made him scrub the toilets as punishment, and reminded him that women were to be protected."

"That worked well," Torch muttered.

I looked at the men closest to him. One had a cut that said *Venom* and the other said *Preacher*. I wondered how long it would take to learn all their names, and remember them. As I gazed around the room, I realized there were a lot of men in here. Just how big was the club?

"Tank has him," Venom said. "He'll be lucky if he's not pissing blood when he leaves."

"I think you mean *if* he leaves," another man said. I focused on his cut. *Rocky*. "He attacked Sarge's woman. You think Tank is going to let that slide?"

"Nope," said Preacher. "Kid fucked up. There's no coming back from what he did. I don't even want to imagine what he'd have done if we hadn't come out to investigate all the noise."

Flicker came over, arms folded across his chest. "So, Pepper told you where Church was held. She knows damn well there's no women allowed, which means she either told you that and you decided to come here anyway, or she left out that little tidbit, which is definitely going to earn her a spanking."

Sarge glared at him. "There are some things I *don't* need to hear, asshole."

"Yeah, because no one walking past your house in the last day or two has heard the two of you going at it. Pepper is scarred for life after going to your house last night for shit she hid over there. And yes, I knew she was hoarding stuff at your house, but we ran out of space," Flicker said.

"Which is why both of you are packing up your homes and moving to the new ones," Venom said. "I'll have my family ready to go by tonight. Prospects will be on furniture moving duty."

"Darian and I will be ready by tomorrow," said another guy.

We were moving? But they just painted Theo's room. Why did we have to go to a different house? Was there something wrong with ours? I looked at Sarge and wanted to ask, but he winked at me and I just cuddled against him again. I'd ask after we left the clubhouse.

Sarge stood and pulled me to my feet, then put his arm around my waist. "I'm taking her home. I'll come back for my bike later."

I let him lead me outside, then he helped me into the SUV. He was quiet on the drive home. Even as we pulled into the driveway, he didn't say a word. Except when he saw his daughter. Then he had plenty to say, and I hoped he didn't regret it later.

"Proud of yourself, Pepper?" he asked.

"I don't know what you're talking about."

He cracked his neck. "Sure you don't. You knew damn well she wouldn't be allowed into Church. Even worse, one of the Prospects decided to put his hands on her. If you hadn't sent her to the clubhouse, she wouldn't have been attacked."

Pepper gasped and her hand flew to her mouth. "What? Which Prospect?"

"Wilson. He's gone. Tank is handling the situation." Sarge shook his head. "I'm sorely disappointed in you right now, and I don't think Flicker is too happy either. Where exactly were my son and grandson while you were visiting my house this morning?"

"They were fine," Pepper said.

"Uh-huh. Be sure to tell Flicker that when he gets here. I'm sure he'll be relieved his kid was *fine* while you left him alone." Sarge took my hand and tugged me behind him. I shot Pepper a look, but she was staring at the ground, looking more than a little worried. Her husband wouldn't hurt her, would he? Were they even married?

In the house, Sarge led me into the living room, then sat on the couch, pulling me down next to him. He must have thought better of it because he picked me up and settled me on his lap. Sarge kissed my temple.

"I'm okay," I assured him. "You got to me before he could hurt me. I'm sorry I didn't stay here. I honestly didn't think anything bad would happen."

"We'll have to go over the rules for living here, but not right now. We need to pack up as much as we can in the next few hours. I'll have the furniture moved over, and all of Theo's new things, which are probably still in the washer or waiting to be cleaned. The stuff in my room will have to wait. I'll come back and pack stuff a little at a time. No one will need this house right away."

"I don't understand why we're moving," I said. "Is it because of me? Did I do something?"

"No, kitten. This house is just going to be too small for us. It was fine while it was just me, and occasionally my grandson, but now I have you, Theo, and Reed will still want to come over. And there's the part where I plan on knocking you up, if I haven't already. We need more space, more bedrooms. We'll still be next door to Flicker and Pepper, and Venom is going to move into a house that's right there too, as well as Bull and his woman, Darian. You'll have three women to hang out with, and Theo will have kids to play with." He brushed my hair back. "There's also a bunker near those homes. A place where you, Theo, and the other women and kids can go if trouble comes here."

I sighed. "So we're moving right now because my father is coming, my real father this time, and you're worried he might pose a threat to me."

He nodded. "That's part of it. We really do need more space. I also think you'll settle in better with Darian and Ridley right there. Especially Ridley. She was the first woman here. She's Bull's daughter. Came looking for him when she got into a tough spot, and ended up with Venom."

"She's the one who was here with Pepper last night?" I asked.

"That's the one. She's a bit of a firecracker, but I think you'll like her. She's fiercely loyal to her man and this club. Once we're settled, I'll talk to the others about getting all the ladies together so you can meet everyone and hopefully make some friends." He kissed my cheek. "I want you to feel like this place is your home, like you can go to anyone here if you need something."

"I guess we'd better get started. There's more stuff here than you probably realize. I don't see how the two of us can pack it all. Not fast enough to move by tonight."

There was a knock at the door and Sarge went to answer it. He came back a moment later with a woman at his heels. It only took me a second to realize it was the same woman who had been with the Prospect at the clubhouse, the one he'd knocked over when he charged me. She twisted her hands in front of her and seemed uncertain as she looked at me through her lashes.

"Katya, this is Candy. Against my better judgment, I agreed with her request to speak with you." Sarge glared at her. "You mind your manners or I'll personally toss you out on your ass."

She gave a jerky nod and waited for Sarge to leave before she approached me. Hesitantly, she held out her hand. I shook it, not really sure where this was going, or why she was here. She glanced around the space before returning her gaze to mine.

"You probably don't think very much of me," she said. "No one here does."

So she knew the guys looked down on her, possibly the other women too, and yet she still came to the compound. I didn't understand the motivation behind doing such a thing, but I wasn't going to judge her for it. She didn't say anything else for a few minutes, as if she were gathering her thoughts, or maybe her courage. I didn't think I was all that intimidating, but perhaps to her I was.

"It was pretty awesome the way you stood up for yourself against Wilson. He's pretty nasty to most of us, but we have to take it." She pulled her lower lip into her mouth, then released it with a *pop*. "I just wanted to say that I've never been with Sarge, and I know he's yours now so I won't try anything. And I wanted to thank you. Because of what you did, they threw Wilson out and he's not allowed to come back."

I moved closer to her. "Why do you care so much about him being gone if everyone here treats you like crap? What's different about him?"

She turned around and moved her hair to the side. I gasped when I saw the darkened bruises. It was clearly from a man gripping the back of her neck. She let her hair fall again. I wondered if she left it down specifically to hide the marks, and if she hadn't hidden them, would someone have stopped that jerk from hurting people long before now?

"I'm not the only one who will be grateful that he's gone," Candy said. "He's hurt Tessie and Anya before too. He got off on degrading us, forcing us to do stuff whether we wanted to or not. We were just too scared to say anything. They trusted him enough to let him prospect for the club, and we're just… pussy."

I reached out and took her hand. "You're more than that and don't let anyone tell you different, including my husband. If he was hurting you, why did you keep coming by? Why have the others? Don't you want to be around people who respect you? Or at the very least don't try to force your submission?"

"The three of us share an apartment in the not-so-great part of town. Honestly, it's a one-room hovel, but it beats being on the streets. When we're here, the guys tend to give us drinks and food. At least we come here by choice. On the streets near our place, the girls aren't given the option."

My stomach knotted at her words. I didn't know how to help her or the others, but I didn't like that they'd been backed into this particular corner. The way Sarge spoke to me and his reaction of what happened to my sister, I had to think if he knew about their plight that he would want to do something too. But would the others care? I didn't know enough about anyone here. I didn't think Sarge would purposefully hang out with guys like Wilson. Not with how pissed he'd been. Then again, I didn't know if he'd have reacted that same way if he'd known Wilson was hurting Candy instead of me.

"You come here every time they let you?" I asked.

"Yeah, all three of us do. I know some of the others are struggling too and come here to let off steam and just try to forget for a while. Then there are the ones who just want the thrill of being with these guys. It's just a temporary thing for me, a walk on the wild side or something."

I wasn't sure what I could do, but there was no damn way I was going to let her or the others suffer if I could stop it. I didn't have any power here. Not real power. Sure, they said I had a place of respect in the club because I belonged to Sarge, but it wasn't like I could make decisions for the club.

"Are you hungry?" I asked. "It seems we're moving. The fewer things in the fridge the less I have to box up. In fact, I think you'd be doing me a huge favor if you took a few things with you."

Her eyes teared and one lone tear slipped down her cheek. She hastily wiped it away. Before I realized her intentions, she'd thrown her arms around me and gave me the tightest hug. I patted her back, feeling completely at a loss as to how I should react. Sarge came into view, leaned against the doorframe, and just shook his head. But I saw the look in his eyes as he gazed at Candy clinging to me. He was worried. I wasn't sure if he was worried *for* her or *about* her. What exactly had he heard of our conversation?

"Come on. I'll make you a sandwich and we can see what's in there." I tugged her arms from around me. She wiped at her cheeks again where more tears had fallen and she followed me past Sarge.

He reached out to grab my hand. "Go on to the kitchen, Candy. She'll be there in a second."

I stayed with him, hoping he wasn't about to get angry that I'd offered to send her home with food. I wasn't about to let her or her friends go hungry, not if I could do something to help. While I didn't have any idea about Sarge's finances, I didn't think a few groceries would put us in a bind, but maybe I should have asked first.

"Are you mad?" I asked.

"That you're trying to help someone?"

"Yes. Well, that I'm trying to help one of your club whores." I winced. "I really don't like calling them that. She's not a whore, and it sounds like some of the others are only trying to survive the best they can."

"My soft-hearted kitten." He smiled and leaned down to kiss me. "I don't mind you helping her, but anything beyond feeding her will have to be discussed with the club. I think I'm learning how your mind works, and you don't want to stop here, do you?"

"Not really. It sounds like she's not in a safe place."

"All right. Go feed her, send food home with her, and we'll talk while we pack. Maybe I can come up with something to tell the club, a way to make it seem like a win-win situation not just for the girls but for my brothers too. They aren't a bad lot, but those women aren't exactly treated like more than a hole to fuck."

"Nice."

He shrugged. "Just telling you how it is, kitten. And yes, I was one of them for a while. Never really thought about their motivation for being here. I know several have tried to get pregnant over the years, hoping to snag one of us on a more permanent basis."

"Maybe it wasn't you they wanted and just stability," I pointed out.

He smacked my ass. "Stop trying to dent my ego. Otherwise you'll have to make it up to me later."

I pressed my lips to his. "I'm always happy to do that. Anytime. Maybe not any*where*, though. As hot as it is when we pretend someone is watching, I really don't think I'd like being on display in a room full of people."

"Good because I don't share. Now go help Candy and let's get to work."

I kissed him one last time, then went to the kitchen. Candy was leaning against the table, arms folded across her stomach. She looked both worried and scared. It occurred to me that she might think Sarge was reading me the riot act over offering to help her.

"I think we have both turkey and ham. Do you have a preference or do you want both?" I asked.

"You don't have to do this. No one else has ever cared."

I stopped and stared at her. "And that is exactly why I *should* do this. You're a person, Candy, not some toy they can play with, then toss away. If you need help, you should be able to tell someone. I'm not about to let you and your friends starve. There's plenty of food here, and I seriously don't want to box it all up to move it."

"Thank you," she said, her voice so soft I almost couldn't hear her.

I fed her, loaded down a box with canned goods, macaroni, pasta and some jars of sauce, then topped it off with some meat in the freezer. I knew it wouldn't last forever, but at least she and her friends could eat for the rest of the week and maybe a little beyond. She'd hugged me again, crying once more, and then left. My heart ached for her. Whatever it took, I'd make sure she was okay. It took guts to come here. I admired anyone who was strong, even if it wasn't a physical strength.

After she left, Sarge handed me a box, grabbed one for himself, and started packing up the living room. "Start talking. Tell me what you have in mind."

I glanced at him. "Well, I haven't really had a chance to come up with a complete plan or anything."

He gave me a look that clearly said he thought I was full of shit. I sighed and kept packing. I hadn't lied. Exactly. I really didn't have a plan, but it had occurred to me if they had space to build more homes, then maybe those women could share a house that was about to become vacant. Or if not one of these homes, maybe something could be built close to the clubhouse.

"You trust them enough to let them through the gates. Does the club trust them enough to give them free run of this place?"

Sarge seemed to contemplate my question. "I'm not sure how everyone would feel about that. Right now, there's a Prospect who watches them drive through the gates and stop at the clubhouse. They're watched while they're here, to some extent at any rate. There's shit that goes down inside the compound that we don't want just anyone to witness. We might not be as fucked-up as Voronin, but our hands aren't clean either, kitten."

"So maybe restrict them to the front part of the compound near the clubhouse? Are there any homes that way? Something empty I mean?"

"No, nothing empty. You thinking we should give them a house inside the gates?"

He didn't sound too thrilled over the idea. Which meant the rest of the club probably wouldn't like it either. For that matter, the other wives, girlfriends, or whatever they were might not like those women being here. Knowing how much Liliya had suffered, I couldn't just do nothing. Maybe that wasn't their life right now, but Candy had implied that was the fate that befell the women in her neighborhood. It felt wrong to just sit here and pretend it wasn't happening. I might not be able to save everyone, but if I could just help Candy and her two friends, then it was a start.

My head started to hurt the more I tried to figure it out. Then I remembered something. At the clubhouse, I'd seen a lot of doors beyond the main room. Were those rooms? Could they be made into bedrooms or small apartments? Then again, if the kids were ever permitted in the clubhouse, I didn't think their daddies would want those women hanging around.

Someone banged really hard on the front door, then I heard it open. I glanced in that direction and a man I hadn't yet met came into the room. Sarge stood, but didn't go any closer.

"Saint, something wrong?" Sarge asked.

"Candy was just bawling her eyes out at the gate. I thought something had happened so I decided to check it out. She kept calling your woman an angel, and blubbering a bunch of shit I couldn't even understand. Thought I'd come see what the hell was going on."

His name was Saint? With a name like that, maybe he'd help me. Or rather, help me help Candy. He'd stopped to talk to her when she was crying. That had to mean something, right?

"What do you know about Candy?" Sarge asked.

"She's from my old neighborhood, but obviously she was just a kid when I lived over there. She can't be more than eighteen or nineteen right now."

Sarge rubbed at his eyes. "Christ. Like you're so much older."

"She said it wasn't safe there," I said. "Is she in danger living there?"

Saint shrugged, then decided to take a seat. He braced his forearms on his knees and clasped his hands. "Truthfully, if one of the pimps hasn't picked her up yet, it's probably just a matter of time. Prostitution and drugs are pretty rampant over there. It's why I wanted my sister out of that shithole."

I folded my arms. "So you got your sister out, but no one is concerned that Candy and her two friends are living over there? Are they just expendable?

Just trash to kick out of the way when they aren't convenient?"

Sarge gripped my arm. "Easy, kitten. Calm the fuck down."

Saint looked from me to Sarge and back again. "What's this about?"

It wasn't my story to tell, but maybe if he knew, if they both knew, then the club would be more willing to help. I told them about the bruises, why she'd put up with it and kept coming back, and that she had two friends who came with her. I explained they were starving and grateful for a roof over their heads even in a shitty part of town. I made sure they both understood Candy hadn't asked for my help, that I was doing this completely on my own. I didn't want any backlash on her or anyone else.

Saint grimaced. "So we have some club whores who are only coming around so they don't starve, and they feel safer here than at home. That's just all kinds of awesome."

"Where does your sister live now? Maybe she could help?" I asked.

"Kayla is with Preacher, so she's here at the compound. But yeah, if she knew why Candy was coming around, she'd want to help. No one should feel they have to spread their legs just to have a meal. Fuck." He ran a hand over his mouth. "I haven't been with her, but it makes me sick to think any of the women I have been with might not have really wanted to be here."

"Hitting close to home?" Sarge asked.

Saint nodded. I must have looked as confused as I felt because he gave me a slight smile that quickly faded. "My wife lived in hell for years before she came here. Her father whored her out or let his men rape her as punishment when she didn't obey. I almost lost her because I was so fucking stubborn. If she knew about Candy and the others, she'd want to do something. Fuck, she'd expect *me* to do something."

"So, let's make a plan. The club would have to agree to help if we presented them with something solid, right?" I asked. "Or rather if the two of you did. I don't think they care what I have to say."

"You'd be surprised," Saint said. "I heard all about you kicking the shit out of Wilson. And there's some rumor about you beating a guy to death, but most aren't believing that actually happened. Still… The guys think you're pretty amazing."

"You going to stay and help us pack? We can talk it out," Sarge said.

Saint nodded. "You got it. Just need to call Sofia so she won't worry."

While he made his call, I smiled over at Sarge. He really was an incredible man. And lucky me, he was all mine.

Chapter Twelve

Sarge

We didn't get nearly as much packed as I'd have liked and we also didn't get to move into the new house like we'd planned. Konstantin Bykov arrived, as he'd said he would, demanding to see Katya. I'd been fighting a headache for hours and I was ready to punch something. Bykov seemed like a good enough target. I met him in front of the clubhouse, without Katya, which only seemed to piss him off.

"Is there a reason Katya isn't with you?" he asked. "I came here to meet her."

"You think I'm letting my wife get anywhere near you without knowing your intentions? I'm not giving you the chance to hurt her. Voronin tried to kill her, and he was the one who raised her. Far as I'm concerned, that makes you even more of a threat since she's just a name to you."

His expression cleared. "I see. You love her."

"Yes, I do, and I will do whatever is necessary to keep her happy and safe. If that means I end your life here and now, so be it. Plenty of places to bury the pieces."

Bykov smiled. "I think we'll get along just fine."

My gaze traced his features and I had to admit that I could see the resemblance. If he wasn't Katya's father, then I'd be surprised. Would he demand a paternity test? Or would he see what I did and just decide to accept her? I still wasn't sure what that would entail, but I knew she wasn't fucking leaving with him.

"I've heard that Voronin seems to have disappeared," Bykov said. "Is that your doing? If he tried to kill your wife, it's understandable. To me, anyway. The Bratva not so much. Voronin was not of high rank, but every position is important."

"He didn't kill Voronin. I did."

I cursed and turned to glare at my wife. She tipped her chin up, giving me that defiant sassy look that made me want to spank her ass.

"Kitten, we discussed this. You're supposed to wait at the house while I make sure it's safe for you to be here."

She stopped beside me, her gaze on the man who had likely sired her. "And let you take the fall for what I did? Not going to happen, but I love you for trying to protect me. I won't let him punish you or the club for something I did."

Bykov's gaze softened as he stared at Katya. I'd have even sworn his eyes looked glassy for a moment, as if he might cry. Instead, his posture stiffened and so did his jaw. "Katya Voronin?"

"Not Voronin. I was never a Voronin, despite what my birth certificate says. I go by Kat Reid now."

"Actually, I think Wire made that birth certificate vanish," I said quietly.

"Good. I never want to be associated with that monster." She stared at Bykov. "Are you a monster too? Am I going to regret meeting you?"

"No." He moved closer and reached for her. I tensed, but he only smoothed her hair from her face. "I'd like to show you something."

Slowly, he reached into his pocket and pulled out his wallet. He took out a photo and held it out to Katya. She gasped when she saw the image and I had to admit, there was an uncanny resemblance between her and the woman in the picture.

"Who is she?" Katya asked.

"Your grandmother. A younger version at any rate. She passed nearly twelve years ago, but she would have been very happy to meet you." He smiled, and reached for her again. "I have a daughter."

Katya let him hug her, and her eyes closed after a moment. I hadn't realized until right then just how much she needed this, needed a parent who gave a shit about her. I hoped that would be Bykov. So far, he seemed happy to have met her. That could all change, and there was the issue of Voronin's death to deal with.

"You said the Bratva wasn't happy about Voronin vanishing. You know damn well he was last seen here because his goons have stopped by multiple times, or driven past, searching for him."

Katya turned wide eyes toward me. "You never said anything."

"I didn't want you to worry, kitten."

Bykov rubbed the back of his neck. "If I claim Katya as my daughter, there will be certain expectations. Of you. As her husband, you and this club will have obligations to the Bratva."

"No," Katya said. "I won't let you pull them into any of that nastiness. I know about the brothels. My sister died in one. I refuse to let you drag Sarge into that crap."

Bykov shook his head. "I'm sorry for what happened with Liliya. She knew the risk when she ran. However, not all of us are monsters, as you put it. I'd have never punished you that way. I can protect you, Katya, even keep you from paying the price for Voronin's death, but only if you can be beneficial in some other way to the Bratva."

I sighed. "Let's take this inside. My President and VP are in the clubhouse. I can't make any promises on behalf of the Dixie Reapers, not without their okay. Lay out whatever plan you have, and we'll go from there. Katya won't be leaving here, and anyone who tries to take her or hurt her will end up dead. I'll do whatever it takes to keep her safe, even try my best to wipe the Bratva from the US."

"Bold words," Bykov said. "I knew I liked you."

They weren't just words. I might not be able to take on a big crime organization on my own, but the club had enough connections that I could at least hurt them. He didn't need to know that the club, or Torch specifically, had a tie to Casper VanHorne. The man had been the deadliest assassin until he'd retired in recent years. Even if Casper wasn't active, he knew enough people to still be of help to us on occasion. These days, he stuck close to his young wife. After nearly losing her, I couldn't blame him.

Inside the clubhouse, I pulled out a chair at the table where Torch and Venom were already seated, and I tugged Katya down onto my lap. I kicked out another chair and Bykov sat. The man was wearing a suit that probably cost more than most people paid a month on rent, but he didn't even stop to see if the seat was clean. It seemed he didn't mind getting dirty, which was always a good thing to know about a man, especially one with his sort of connections. I still didn't know what his position in the Bratva meant, but if I were a betting man, I'd say he probably did a good bit of the dirty work himself.

"Thank you, gentlemen, for keeping my daughter safe," Bykov said.

Torch started laughing. "That girl doesn't need anyone to keep her safe. She can handle herself."

"Her mouth might get her into trouble, though," Venom said. "Told a Prospect he had a tiny dick."

Bykov remained impassive. He looked at his daughter, then back at Torch. "Well, did he have a tiny dick?"

At least Katya came by it honestly. It seemed she got that sassy mouth from her father's side of the family. I had a feeling if the two had a chance to spend some time together, they would become rather close. Or as close as his position would permit. For her sake, I hoped he found a way.

"Let's get down to business, shall we?" Bykov asked. "It seems my Katya took a life, one that belonged to the Bratva. It puts me in a precarious position. Of course, I don't want to see my daughter come to harm, especially having just met her. However, there's a price to pay."

"What sort of price?" Torch asked.

"That depends on the Vor, but I'll need some assurances before I can negotiate. We don't typically have dealings this far south, or at least not in your state. Should that change, I'll need to know that you'll look the other way, or lend assistance if it's needed." Bykov steepled his fingers in front of him. "My daughter has already said no to anything pertaining to brothels, so be assured it wouldn't include that sort of business."

Venom cracked his neck. "Just what sort of business would it include?"

Bykov waved a hand. "Hard to say. Maybe a few extra men for certain, shall we say, business deals? Assistance cleaning some cash? A blind eye when it comes to Bratva authorized dealers in your town? Perhaps those sorts of things."

"No," Katya said, going stiff in my arms. "I'll take the punishment. You're not involving them in your dirty dealings. They have families. Sarge and I have a family. I won't put them at risk. I avoided everything to do with the Bratva for as long as I could. I won't let you drag them into it, and me along with them."

Bykov smiled at her. "I see why he calls you kitten. Sheath your claws, daughter. This is between the men."

And that's where he went wrong and proved he knew nothing of his daughter. The man didn't do his homework, and obviously hadn't been listening. I didn't even try to contain her. Torch and Venom leaned back, looking like they were ready to enjoy the show. I'd heard Flicker brought popcorn when she beat the shit out of Voronin. I half expected someone to show up with some this time too.

Katya shot off my lap, hands balled at her sides, and glared at her father. She bared her teeth and snarled at him, right before she launched herself straight for him. The chair went over with Katya straddling Bykov. She fisted his shirt and leaned down close.

"You may be related by blood, but you're *not* my father. I don't have one. Certainly not a criminal like you. So much for not being a monster. Just where do you think those drugs go? Into the hands of children!" She yanked on his shirt. "I won't stand by and let you murder the children of this town."

Bykov showed no emotion as his daughter yelled at him. He merely stayed in the chair, on the floor, and let her have her say. When Katya ran out of steam, she deflated, her shoulders drooping and her head hanging. I got up and lifted her into my arms, cradling her close. She buried her face in my neck and clung to me.

"I want to go home," she said. "I never should have called him. He's just as bad as the others. They're all murdering bastards who care for no one but themselves. I wanted a father, but I'll never have one."

Bykov got up, dusted himself off, and heaved a sigh. "So much spirit. I'll be sorry to see it broken."

I met his gaze and let him see exactly what would happen if he tried to hurt my wife. I'd been in the military, and had served this club since getting out. There was blood on my hands. A lot of it. Adding his to it wouldn't faze me even a little. No one would ever break Katya. I wouldn't let them. If he thought for one moment I would let him take her, or anyone else for that matter, then he must not have taken my threat seriously. But I'd meant every damn word.

"The only one here who will break, is you, Mr. Bykov. Don't come near my wife again. Any of your men try to get to her and I'll fucking kill them without a second of hesitation. Do I make myself clear?" I asked.

Bykov looked at Torch and Venom. "And you agree with him? Your club is ready to go to war over Katya?"

"She's one of us," Torch said. "We protect our women and children, unlike the Bratva. If Sarge says he'll kill your men if they come for her, I'd believe him. And if he doesn't get the job done, the rest of us will."

"So you won't assist the Bratva when we call, and you refuse to hand over Katya for punishment. Is that correct?" Bykov asked.

"Damn right," Venom said. "I'd suggest you leave while you still can."

Bykov pulled a phone from his pocket. "Did you get all that?"

I froze and stared at the phone. He'd made a call? When? Had he been talking to them all this time? And who the fuck was he talking to? Had we just put Katya in more danger?

"It seems your daughter is well-liked and protected, Konstantin," said a voice on the other end. "Gentleman, and Katya, my name is Vadim Ivanov."

"The Vor," Katya whispered.

"I apologize if Konstantin seemed a bit… cruel to his daughter. We had to be sure she was in good hands. If you'd agreed, then we'd have known you were weak. And if you had handed Katya over to avoid trouble, then Konstantin would have gladly taken his daughter with him, but your club would have had a string of bad luck for the foreseeable future."

"You mean all that was horse shit?" Torch asked.

"I'm afraid so. It was my decision to test the lot of you, especially Katya's husband. We had to ensure that she was safe," Ivanov said.

"Finding out I had a daughter was a gift," Bykov said. "If I had known that Katya was mine all these years, I'd have found a way to have her by my side. She'd have been treated like a princess."

"And Voronin?" Venom asked. "The penalty for his death. Is that something we need to be worried about?"

"There are those who will continue to question his absence," Ivanov said. "It's a problem."

Katya tugged on my beard, drawing my attention to her. She pressed her lips near my ear and whispered so no one else would hear. "What about the man who married us? If he can do that, could he do something about Voronin too?"

- 158 -

Smart girl. I'd actually thought of that before, but with Voronin's men lurking, it didn't seem like something that would actually work. They'd been determined to come in and search for him, or his body. We'd held them off, and now the higher-ups were involved. If the Vor and Bykov both agreed to let Wire lay a false trail, then maybe we could make it work.

"Voronin's men keep coming by, asking about him. They know he came here, and I think they may know he never left," I said. "But if the two of you tell your people that he's left the country, perhaps they'll listen. We have someone who could make it look like Voronin really did skip town. Wire could send those goons on a wild goose chase."

"And you haven't done this until now, why?" Ivanov asked.

"One of them claims to have seen Voronin come in here and never leave. He's been hard to dissuade," Torch said.

"Have your man plant the false information," Ivanov said. "I'll handle it from this end. Katya, I hope to meet you one day. You're very fierce and loyal, two traits I admire. Please forgive your father for his deception. It was necessary."

"Does that mean you're staying for a bit, Bykov?" Venom asked. "We set up guest quarters for you. Just a small apartment, but it would give you privacy when you're not visiting your daughter. I'm sure she'd like a chance to know you better."

Bykov nodded. "Yes. I'll stay for a few days."

"Konstantin, I'll handle things here for a while. Stay longer than a few days," Ivanov said. "You have memories to make with your daughter."

"Thank you," Bykov said.

He ended the call and stared at Katya with longing. I eased her down, and once I knew she was steady on her feet, I released her. She took a cautious step toward Bykov. When he opened his arms, she flung herself at him, hugging him.

Bykov ran a hand down her hair. "My daughter. My beautiful, strong, amazing daughter."

I looked at Torch and Venom, who each gave me a nod. We walked off a short ways, keeping Katya in my view, but getting out of range for whatever conversation they were about to have. She needed this time with her father. I only hoped that he'd finally told the truth and he wouldn't break her heart.

Torch called Wire and placed the order to make it seem as if Voronin had left the country, and Venom went to get us a few beers. We chose another table and sat while Katya and Bykov got acquainted. I still had a shit ton of packing to do and wanted in the new house tonight. It was past time to bring Theo home. As much as I'd loved the time I'd had with my wife, I needed my son to know that I wanted him, and that he had a place in my life and Katya's.

"Why don't you get your boy?" Torch asked. "You can take him, Katya, and your father-in-law out for the day. Maybe any lingering Bratva would see you have the support of Bykov and keep their distance. I'll send Dalton, Sam, and Lief over to your place to finish packing. Except your special room."

I flipped him off. He was always giving me shit about my comics and collectibles. As I liked to remind him, I'd been a geek long before I'd been a biker. I couldn't argue about spending time with my family, though. I sent a text to Flicker and then sat back to finish my beer while I waited on my son to join us. I wasn't sure what Bykov would think of Theo. He wasn't technically the boy's grandfather, but since Katya was now Theo's stepmother, I was hoping he'd be willing to take on that role.

"Shit." I pulled out my phone and stared at it.

"What?" Venom asked.

"I haven't told my parents they're grandparents. Again. My mom is going to fucking flip when she finds out I had yet another kid without knowing about him."

Torch grinned. "Does this mean she's going to start sending you those large envelopes full of condoms again?"

I groaned. "Probably. Although, once she finds out I'm married, maybe not. I'll definitely get chewed up and spit out for not having a wedding she could attend. Maybe Katya will want to exchange vows."

"How fast can your parents get here?" Venom asked.

"Why?"

He held out his hand. "Let me see your phone."

I hesitated a minute, then gave it to him. He scrolled through my contacts and the next thing I knew he was talking to my mother and inviting my parents to the clubhouse for a special event tonight. I didn't know what the fuck he was up to, but something told me to just roll with it. I only hoped that decision didn't come back to bite me in the ass.

Chapter Thirteen

Katya

I'd been kidnapped. Well, maybe not kidnapped *exactly*. Pepper was watching Theo and Reed, and Venom had left with Sarge. Which left me shopping on Main Street with Ridley, and two other ladies I'd just met -- Darian and Kalani. I just didn't understand why they insisted we go into some fancy dress shop. The place looked like it cost a small fortune for even something off the clearance rack. While I'd been told not to worry about cost, I couldn't help it.

"Why are we here?" I asked.

Ridley planted her hands on her hips. "You're going to ruin the surprise. Just go with it, okay? My man had an idea and I'm helping him carry it out."

"And you two?" I asked Kalani and Darian.

"We're here in case you make a run for it," Darian said. "Ridley's words, not mine."

Part of me wanted to enjoy the day. The crisis with the Bratva was over, and I'd been informed our belongings were being moved into our new home today. I was getting a fresh start, but I felt like I should be spending it with Sarge and Theo. The man hadn't even had a chance to get to know his son yet, and I missed Theo terribly. Kalani must have read the look on my face. She placed a hand on my shoulder and gave it a slight squeeze.

"We'll tackle this one task, and then maybe you can have Sarge and Theo meet you at the park. It's not far from here and will get you away from the compound for a bit. We have a playground there too, but I think the three of you need some family time," she said.

"The park sounds nice. I still don't know why we're at this store."

"What size do you wear?" Ridley asked, eyeing me up and down.

"It depends on the cut and design. I've worn anything from an eight to a twelve." Her eyebrows arched as a look of disbelief crossed her face. "I'm not as small as I look. My hips and ass require extra material."

Darian snorted. "Yeah, because you're just so huge."

I waved a hand. "Not what I meant. It's just that my sister wore fours and sixes. She was always fine-boned and delicate looking. I'm not."

Kalani nudged me with her elbow. "I think that's a good thing. Sarge seems to like you just the way you are. If he'd wanted your sister, then he'd have kept her."

I nodded, knowing she was right. I let Ridley grab an armful of dresses, then she shoved me into a fitting room with orders to come out so they could see each one. I started to notice a theme by the third pale-colored dress. Each was either white, ivory, cream, or a pink so pale it was nearly white. What were they up to? And what was up with all these washed-out colors? They looked horrible on me.

"I need color," I said. "I look like an albino in these."

Darian snickered. "She's not wrong."

Kalani came over with a lavender dress draped over her arm and a pale aqua one in her hand. "Try these."

"But…" Ridley snapped her mouth shut. "Fine."

After trying both dresses, and modeling for the ladies, it was decided the aqua suited me the best.

Darian added a pair of strappy silver sandals, making sure they were my size, and Ridley shooed me from the shop while she paid for everything. I'd have to find out how much it all cost so I could pay her back. When I stepped outside, Sarge was leaning against my SUV with Theo in his arms. They looked so much alike, I had to just stop and admire them a moment. My heart felt full to bursting.

"I've been told you'd like some family time at the park," Sarge said.

"You haven't had a chance to spend any time with Theo. And I've missed him." Theo held out his arms, and I took him, hugging him tight.

"He said I can call you Momma now." His soft voice, and the way he cuddled against me, nearly made me cry. I didn't want him to forget his real mother, but hearing him call me that was one of the happiest moments of my life.

Sarge came closer, putting his arm around my waist. "Come on, kitten. Let's take our boy to the park and have a little fun."

We put Theo into his booster seat, then drove down to the park in town. The moment he was released from the car, he took off for the slide. Sarge pulled a blanket from the back floorboard and spread it on the ground not far from the play area. He tugged me down next to him, and we watched our son play. It felt right, thinking of Theo as mine. I'd taken care of him more than Liliya ever had, even if that hadn't been her choice.

"We need to discuss a few things," Sarge said. "For one, the club is working on a solution for Candy and the others. Torch isn't too thrilled about having them here full-time, especially around the kids, but he agreed that we couldn't leave them in a dangerous situation either."

"If they can't stay at the compound, then where?"

"There's an old motel a little past the compound. It's actually just outside the town limits. Been abandoned for years. It's going to need a shit ton of work, but the club is going to fix it into studio apartments. A few will be left vacant for people coming in to visit, ones that Torch doesn't trust to remain inside our gates. The others will be rented to Candy and women like her who need a hand up. The rent will be cheap, but part of the deal is that anyone staying there helps keep the grounds and vacant rooms clean."

That didn't sound like a bad deal to me. I wondered if they'd already discussed it with Candy and her friends. But I didn't understand what would keep the less savory types of people from trying to lure those women away. If they weren't near the club, and weren't in the town limits, weren't they still vulnerable? I asked as much and Sarge kissed my cheek.

"Such a soft-hearted woman. Don't worry about them, kitten. We'll make sure someone rides by frequently enough, and never on an exact schedule, so that anyone watching won't know when to expect one of us. Torch also mentioned assigning one of the Prospects as a contact for the women in case of an emergency." He cuddled me closer. "They'll be taken care of, kitten."

"If they could barely afford a studio apartment in a bad area, and were starving, how is charging them rent going to help?" I asked.

"It won't start right away. For one, we still have to renovate the building. Torch put the extra houses at the compound on hold to get that tackled first. He'll give them a few months to get back on their feet before the rent kicks in."

"They're going to have kitchens?"

"Sort of. They'll have a cooktop with two burners, a microwave, coffeepot, smaller-size fridge with freezer, and a sink. Or that's what we discussed. Dalton may see the space and tell us that won't work."

I hadn't been in a lot of motel rooms, but I remembered them all being on the small side. I couldn't picture them being turned into a studio apartment. Not without making the living space even tinier. The women would probably just be grateful to be safe, but it didn't mean they couldn't be comfortable too.

"What about making one of the rooms into a full kitchen with at least two tables where they could have meals? Then the rooms could remain about the same and maybe just update them a little? You'd have less work to do overall. And…" I clamped my mouth shut. I'd already said more than I probably should have. I might be Sarge's and therefore a part of the club, but I'd already learned I had no say in how things were done.

"What else, kitten?" he asked.

"All motels have an office, right? Why not change it into an apartment or something where one of the guys could stay full-time? Even if your Prospects took turns crashing there, just having a man there twenty-four hours could cut down on any trouble."

"Smart. Sexy. Sassy. I got the whole package with you, didn't I?" He smiled. "I'll run it by Torch and Venom. With us losing Wilson, we'll need to think about accepting another Prospect, maybe two. Might be a good trial to put any new ones out there. Set up the bedroom bunk style or something. We'll figure it out."

Theo came running for us, collapsing on the blanket. I reached out and ran my fingers through his sweaty hair. He grinned at me, then reached for Sarge, who instantly picked him up. He might not have wanted kids, but he seemed to be pretty great with them. I'd noticed right off how much his grandson adored him, and Theo seemed to as well.

Abandoning our blanket, we went to push Theo on the swings, listening to him chatter about all the fun he'd had with Reed. It seemed the time with Pepper and Flicker had been good for him. I didn't remember ever hearing him so excited. Nor had he ever had a friend his age before. It broke my heart at the same time that I was so damn happy he had a family now, other than just me.

"Flicker made this cool fort," Theo said. "And Reed said we could hide in there, so Pepper gave us cookies and milk and we stayed in there forever and ever."

Sarge chuckled. "Is that right? Maybe our new house can have a fort out back. The kind you don't have to take down."

Theo's eyes went comically wide. "Reed said we were moving, but I told him he was wrong. Mom promised when we came here I wouldn't have to move again, that I was going to have a real home."

"Theo, you're still going to have a real home," Sarge said. "Just a bigger one. Flicker, Pepper, and Reed are moving too. You'll still be next door to them. And there are going to be other kids to play with too." Sarge watched his son. "There are actually a lot of kids close to your age. Torch and Saint both have sons who are five. Wire has a son who's four. There are a few girls close to your age too."

"So you all had kids around the same time?" I asked.

"Not all, but we've noticed the kids do seem to come in sets. In Preacher's case, his woman was pregnant with twins right off. Kalani and Tex had a boy around that same time. Bull and Rocky had boys close together too. Then there's Tank."

"What about him?" I asked.

"He had triplets. Girls. The club is still having fun with that one. You should see him if any of the boys even look at his girls. They're six, but it's like he's scared they'll start dating any moment."

"That's actually kinda cute. I only met him once, but he seemed so intimidating. I can only imagine how he is around a bunch of little girls."

Sarge gave me a mock glare. "You're not allowed to get that sappy look on your face while talking about another man."

I smiled at him, moved in closer, then pressed my lips to his. "I promise. You're the only one who makes all the right parts tingle. I can think it's cute some big guy is growly over his daughters without wanting to jump in bed with him."

Sarge wrapped an arm around my waist and kissed me harder. Deeper. A throat cleared and my face burned as a stern-looking mom glared at us.

"There are kids present. What is wrong with you?"

Sarge stared her down. "Not a damn thing. Last time I checked, this is the start of how you make *more* kids. Maybe yours were dropped off by a stork, though, because I'm damn sure you've never --" I slapped my hand over his mouth to muffle the rest. "--Screamed a man's name while he was balls-deep."

Thankfully, while the mom heard the last of it, the kids seemed oblivious. The woman gasped in outrage, grabbed her kid, and hustled away. I wasn't sure if I should be amused or embarrassed. Would every family outing be like this one?

"You're so bad," I said.

He wagged his eyebrows. "And I'll be happy to show you exactly how bad I am later tonight."

I knew my face had to be about four shades of red in that moment, but I didn't care. It was the happiest I'd ever been. I had a father in my life who actually seemed to care, a man I adored, and a little boy who'd stolen my heart the moment he'd been born. I didn't know how anything could make my life any better.

"Time to head back," Sarge said. "The club planned something special and you'll need time to get ready. We both will."

"Get ready? Wait, is that what the dress was for? What are they up to?"

"You'll see. I'm supposed to drop you off at Torch's house. I'll get ready at home and meet you at the clubhouse. Torch and Isabella are going to stay with you. Kalani offered to watch the kids until it's time for the... event."

Cryptic much? I'd go with it, but I was both excited and nervous to see what they'd planned. Sarge scooped Theo into his arms and we walked back to the SUV. Sarge drove carefully, glancing in the rearview mirror every few minutes. At first, I'd thought he was worried about someone following us, until I'd realized he was watching Theo. My heart warmed. I could tell he was going to be a wonderful father.

He dropped me in front of one of the large homes in the compound. A woman was waiting outside, and I knew she must be Isabella. I hadn't had a chance to meet her yet, but the smile she aimed my way set me at ease immediately. I shouldn't have been surprised she was so much younger than her husband. She easily looked like she could have been his daughter. Maybe even his granddaughter.

"I'm so glad Sarge finally found someone," she said, tugging me into the house. "I'm Isabella and I belong to Torch. I know you already met him, and I heard all about how that turned out the first time. If you'd gotten hurt, I would have cut him off for a month."

"Watch it, woman!" I heard bellowed from the other room.

Isabella rolled her eyes and dropped her voice. "Like everyone hasn't already figured out that he'd do anything for me. If I told him no, then he'd not push the issue. He wouldn't like it, but he'd never hurt me."

"I'm getting that vibe from all the guys here."

She nodded. "They're a tough bunch, but once they fall, that's it. They'll never notice another woman, or ever touch one."

"What exactly am I walking into?" I asked.

Isabella hugged me. "You'll see. Now come on. Your stuff is upstairs in my room, and I had Pepper raid Sarge's house for your bathroom stuff. She said you didn't have any makeup, and no one else here is quite as fair as you, so Darian and Kalani picked out a few things. If they don't work, then we won't worry about it."

Makeup? And a fancy dress? At a biker compound? I was getting more and more confused, but Sarge seemed happy about whatever was going on, so

I'd trust him. He hadn't given me a reason not to so far. I took a shower in Isabella's bathroom, using the products from Sarge's house, then she helped me dry my hair. When she pulled out a curling iron, I laughed.

"You're not going to curl my hair."

Her brow creased. "Why not?"

"I didn't mean I wouldn't let you, but even professionals have tried before. My hair won't hold a curl. It just falls straight even right after it's been around the curling iron. Nothing works."

"An updo?" she asked.

I shook my head again. "I can pull it back, but little pieces will fall here and there. It doesn't stay neat for more than an hour. Not without about two bottles of hairspray and lots of pins."

She tipped her head one way, then the other as she studied me. "Well, you're marrying a biker. I heard you showed up in combat-type boots. Seems to me you're a little more rock and roll than classical. Let's play that up."

I didn't know what she meant, but I pulled on a bra and panties I knew I hadn't purchased, then shimmied into the dress. I got it mostly zipped, but Isabella had to finish it. Then I put on the sandals. I saw what was in her hand and couldn't contain my laughter.

"Hair chalk?" I asked.

"It's my daughter's, but she never uses it." Isabella put two streaks of aqua in my hair on the right side of my face, then added a streak of pink between them. She left that side down, then found some pins with crystal flowers to pin back the other side. I had to admit it looked amazing. "Now just a touch of makeup."

The powder the others had picked up was too dark, so she wiped it off, then started over. She ended up doing a light blush on my cheeks, a shimmery eyeshadow, and some mascara. I didn't know who had picked out the soft mauve lip stain, but it was perfect. She had me top it with a pale pink shimmer gloss. I couldn't remember ever looking this beautiful before, and I nearly cried as I stared at my reflection.

"Come on. I know Sarge can't wait to see you," Isabella said. She led me to the living room, where Torch was waiting with two teen girls who were dressed up. He made quick introductions while Isabella disappeared, only to return fifteen minutes later in a dress and heels.

No one would tell me what was going on, but I went with them to the clubhouse, and my jaw dropped when I stepped inside. The tables had been pushed to the walls and the chairs flanked a long, purple runner. Sarge stood at the end along with Preacher, who was holding a Bible.

"I don't understand," I said.

"It's your wedding," Torch said. "You're already married, but Sarge mentioned that you might like to exchange vows. Have an actual ceremony."

My eyes misted with tears and my throat grew tight. He was so damn sweet. My dad seemed to materialize out of nowhere, holding out his arm. I placed my hand in the crook of his elbow and he led me down to Sarge. I saw Theo on the front row with Pepper, Flicker, and Reed. But it was the older couple who made my steps falter. I knew they had to be Sarge's parents. He looked just like them.

My gaze met Sarge's and he gave me a wink. When we made it all the way to the front, he took my hands and just stared at me. So many emotions played across his face. Lust. Happiness. Awe. And I knew each one was just for me. I'd never felt so special in my life.

"Love you, kitten."

"I love you too."

Preacher cleared his throat. "The two of you ready?"

I nodded. "Would you mind if we didn't do the traditional wedding stuff?"

Preacher waved a hand. I stared at Sarge and wasn't quite sure where to start. "When I came here, I thought I was dropping off your son with you and leaving. I was going to face a life that would eventually kill me. Instead, I found a man who intrigued me more than anyone ever had before. The way you refused to let me leave, then insisted I was yours..." My throat got tight again. "I wanted to stay, so badly, but I was scared you'd get hurt. You and Theo. I think I knew even then that I'd come to love you if given the chance. You're everything I ever wanted and thought I'd never have."

Sarge squeezed my hands. "First time I saw you, I was pissed. Not at you, but at the Prospect who'd dare to try and hit you. Then I saw you duck and punch him back. I knew right then and there I wasn't letting you leave. I didn't know who you were or what you wanted, but I wanted you to be mine. You were this cute little pixie, but you had enough sass to try and take on men twice your size. I was in awe of you, and I still am. You're the best thing that ever happened to me, other than my kids. I love you, kitten, and I will until my dying day."

"Do you have the rings?" Preacher asked.

Sarge reached out a hand and someone placed a ring on his palm. I didn't give it more than a glance because I didn't care what it looked like. Only thing that mattered to me was that he was giving it to me because he wanted me. Forever.

"With this ring, I thee wed," Sarge said, sliding the ring onto my finger.

Someone nudged me and I turned to see Ridley. She smiled and handed me a wedding band. I slid it onto Sarge's finger, repeating his words.

"Congratulations. You're now husband and wife. Again."

Everyone laughed, except us. I could feel the heat of Sarge's gaze all the way to my toes. He leaned in closer and kissed me. It started as a soft peck, but soon his arm banded across my lower back, and his lips devoured mine. My head was spinning when he pulled back.

"*Now* can I meet my daughter-in-law?" a woman asked.

I blinked and looked at Sarge's mom. She gave me a warm smile and practically yanked me out of her son's arms, hugging me so tight I could barely breathe.

"I'm so happy he has you now," she said. "And thank you for my grandson. I can't wait to get to know him better."

His father stepped up next to us. "But that doesn't mean we wouldn't mind a few more."

"Dad," Sarge said, a warning in his tone.

Pepper joined us with Flicker, Theo, and Reed in tow. "Oh, please. Like you haven't already been trying to give me another sibling."

"Better hurry if you want them to be close in age to our kid," Flicker said. "I know Theo and Reed were a fluke, so maybe you can plan this one."

Sarge's mother squealed and turned to Pepper, hugging her. "You're pregnant? When? How?"

Flicker grinned and I knew whatever came out of his mouth would be scandalous. "Well, you see, the last two months I've spent every possible second…"

Pepper glared. "You finish that sentence and this morning will have been the last time *ever* that you do that."

"I didn't need to hear that," Sarge muttered, running a hand down his face. "Didn't. Really, really didn't."

"It's the perfect time," Ridley said. "Preacher already knocked-up Kayla, and it seems Zipper and Delphine are pregnant too. You know we have to have babies in groups. Instant playmates."

I leaned against Sarge and placed a hand over my belly. As often as he'd tried to get me pregnant, it was possible I was, but it was too soon to know. If he wanted another baby, I'd gladly give him one. Or two. I had the family I'd always wanted and thought I'd never have, and it seemed to be growing already.

I spent the rest of the night getting to know my in-laws and the other Reapers. My feet ached by the time we called it a night. I'd either danced or stood talking with people for what felt like hours. I wouldn't have traded a moment of it. I knew these memories would stay with me for a long time, and I'd always think back on this day fondly. Thanks to Wire, we may have already been married, but now I had a special memory to go with it. And pictures! Every time we'd turned around, someone was taking our picture either with an actual camera or their phone. I'd been promised lots of pictures in the upcoming week.

I rested my cheek against Sarge's chest. "Thank you."

"For what?"

"You. Everything. I went from living a lonely, cold life full of fear to having everything I've ever wanted. You're all I need to be happy."

"Same goes, kitten. Love you more than anything."

He kissed me in the middle of the clubhouse, our friends and family celebrating with us, and I knew that my happily-ever-after was only just beginning.

Dragon (Devil's Fury MC 3)

Lilian -- I may have survived my time with the Colombian cartel, but it nearly broke me. Even now, I can't stand to be touched by men. But there's one man who makes me feel safe. Dragon. He's intrigued me for so long. I never counted on things getting heated between us, or me ending up pregnant. He made it clear he doesn't want me, or a baby, so I ran. I thought I'd found sanctuary with the Reckless Kings, but it only put me in the crosshairs of a lunatic intent on revenge.

Dragon -- I knew Lilian was still skittish with men. When she asked for my help in learning self-defense, I'd been surprised. I never counted on those lessons bringing us closer together, or that she'd ask the unthinkable of me. Now she's carrying my kid, and I f***d up six ways to Sunday. When she's kidnapped, I realize it's time to bring her home. My home. Whatever it takes, I'll make sure Lilian knows she's mine. Even if I have to grovel a little.

Prologue

Dragon

Lilian stretched, bending over to touch her toes, ass in the air, and fuck if I didn't start getting hard. Well, hard-er. My dick was always at attention around her. I'd known when she asked that this was a bad fucking idea. For six months I'd been helping her with no one the wiser, but I knew my control wouldn't last much longer.

"This is our last session," I said.

She stood and turned to face me. "What? Why?"

"Lil, you know this is all kinds of wrong. What would Grizzly say if he knew you were here with me right now? Alone."

Her lips thinned and she refused to answer, but we both knew how he'd feel about it. He'd adopted her after she'd been rescued from Colombia, little more than a whore for an underground fighting ring. Lilian had jumped at shadows when she'd come here, and even years later still had trouble being around men. I couldn't blame her, not after all she'd suffered. I didn't know why she'd chosen me for this particular request, but I'd been both honored and horrified. If my Pres knew that I was here with her, and sporting wood, he'd string me up from the nearest fucking tree.

He might have mellowed a little with the birth of his first grandchild, but not by much. He adored Gunner, Badger's son, but the rest of us were still fair game when we fucked up. I wasn't sure even putting the kid between us would save me once I crossed that line, and I was seriously fucking close. Lilian had no clue just how much she tempted me.

When she'd asked me to teach her how to defend herself, I'd known it could go sideways in a moment.

But she'd looked at me with those big brown eyes and I'd been unable to say no. There really wasn't much more I could teach her, and being this close to her, not to mention alone, was starting to fuck with my head. I didn't see her as some scared little rabbit anymore. She was all woman. Every time she bent over to stick that sweet ass up in the air, it was all I could do not to walk up behind her and show her exactly how she was affecting me.

"You know how to defend yourself now," I said, trying to keep my tone calm. She still startled if anyone raised their voice or moved too fast. "You don't need to keep meeting with me."

"But why --"

I lifted a hand to stop her. "Because I'm a man, you're an attractive woman, and my body didn't get the memo that you're hands-off. So this is our last session because I honestly can't be this close to you anymore without wanting to fuck you."

She flinched slightly at the word "fuck," but she didn't back down. If anything, she came closer. Her tongue slid across her lower lip, teasing me.

"Maybe that wouldn't be so bad," she said.

What the hell? Did she seriously just say that to me? The heat in her eyes confirmed my ears weren't malfunctioning, but I didn't fucking get it. She'd not gone out with a single guy since coming here, and I knew she damn sure hadn't been sleeping with anyone. At least no one at the clubhouse, and she seldom ventured out unless Grizzly was with her.

"Lilian, I'm not the type of guy to be all gentle and shit when it comes to sex. I'm the last person you need in that capacity."

She came closer still, not stopping until she slid a hand up my chest to my shoulder and pressed her curves against me. She was more than a handful, but still tiny compared to me. I liked the fact her thighs jiggled a little and that her belly was slightly rounded. She was cute as fuck.

With her this close, I could smell the scent of her perfume. It made me want to bury my face in the crook of her neck and just breathe her in. She always smelled amazing. I couldn't remember ever getting turned-on just from the scent of a woman, until now. Six months was too damn long for this kind of torture. I'd tried using the club whores, but after the first few times, I'd given up. I was left unsatisfied, and oddly ashamed of myself. It wasn't like Lilian and I were a thing, and we never would be, but it had felt like I was cheating on her.

"If I can't handle having sex with someone I've spent so much time with, someone I trust completely, then I'll never get over my fears and all of this was pointless."

My dick jerked in my pants, completely onboard. Thankfully, my brain was still mostly in control. Otherwise, I'd have already bent her over and I'd be balls deep right now. Then we'd both be fucked and not in a fun way because the Pres really would fucking kill me if I touched her.

"Lil, you don't know what you're saying."

She nodded. "I do. I really, truly do. I want you to be my first."

I blinked at her choice of words. I knew her story. We all did. So when she said her first, it wasn't her virginity she was giving me, but it didn't change the fact it would make me the first man to take her willingly. I had to wonder if this was just a knee-jerk reaction to what I'd said. Would she wake up tomorrow and regret it?

"Lilian. I..."

She reached behind my neck, tugging me down, then pressed her lips against mine. I groaned as her watermelon lip balm smeared against my mouth. Unable to resist just the tiniest taste, I flicked my tongue across her lips. When she opened to me, I knew I was a goner. I threaded my fingers in her hair and held her tight as I ravaged her mouth. She didn't struggle or pull away. If anything, she melted against me, a soft little sigh escaping her, as if she'd wanted this all along.

I released her and staggered back. "You need to leave. Now."

She shook her head and came toward me, but I backed up farther.

"I mean it, Lilian. Leave! Fucking leave!" I screamed at her, knowing that if she asked me again that I'd fuck her without a second thought. She deserved better than that. Better than me.

"No," she said. "I want it to be you."

I snarled and advanced, gripping her tight before ripping her shirt over her head. A sports bra contained her breasts, but they nearly overflowed, the stretchy material not enough to hold them in. I tugged it over her breasts, letting them bounce free. She didn't stop me, didn't shy away. Her gaze held mine boldly, as if challenging me to take what I wanted, but the slight tremor in her body belied her nerves.

"Is this what you want? Because it won't be soft or sweet. I'll strip you bare, bend you over, and fuck you."

She drew in a shuddering breath, then released it, not saying a word, but turning to give me her back. She pushed at the waistband of her leggings, shimmying a little to work them down her thighs. I didn't even give her a chance to pull them all the way off. I took her to the floor, snapped the fabric of her panties, tearing them from her body, and bent her over.

I waited, my breath sawing in and out of my lungs, knowing at any moment she'd start crying or try to run. But she didn't. If anything, she just wagged her ass at me. I reached between her thighs and groaned when my fingers slid against her smooth, wet pussy. Working a finger inside her, I realized she was soaked.

"Damn, Lil."

"I've been wanting you," she said, "but I didn't know how to ask."

I took a shuddering breath, so fucking close to losing it. I'd had no idea she felt that way. It didn't change things, not long-term. Grizzly still would have a shit fit if a brother so much as thought of claiming her, and I damn well knew it. So did she, even if she wasn't thinking straight right now. She had to know this was dangerous.

"This is a one-time thing. After this, we keep our distance from each other." I drove my finger in deeper. "Understand?"

"Yes! God, yes! Just… don't stop."

I added a second finger, working her pussy, stretching her to take me. I might not be the biggest guy, but I wasn't exactly small either, and I knew Lilian hadn't had sex since she'd come here six years ago. Hell, she'd been a kid back then. None of us would have touched her, and if any of the little punks around town had even tried, we would have ended them.

"You ever come before, Lil?" I asked, my voice nearly a growl from my need for her.

"No." She whimpered. "Please, Dragon."

"Call me Dane. Just this once. After today, it's Dragon again." I had to be fucked in the head to even let her use my name this one time.

"Dane. I need it! Need you!"

I pressed my chest to her back, and adjusted my hand so that I could rub her clit with my thumb as my fingers stroked in and out. It didn't take much to set her off. She screamed out my name, her pussy clenching down as she soaked my hand with her release. But it was hearing my name on her lips as she found her pleasure that snapped the last of my control.

I unfastened my belt and jeans, pulled out my cock, and without a moment's hesitation, I thrust hard and deep, filling her up. My eyes shut at how fucking perfect she felt. With a hand gripping her waist, I drove into her. I was so far gone, the first flutter of another climax, her pussy tightening even just a little, was enough to make me come. I growled as I thrust faster. It wasn't until I'd emptied my balls and pulled free, that I realized I'd been a complete dumbass and taken her bare.

"Shit," I muttered.

"What's wrong?" she asked, looking at me over her shoulder.

"Didn't use a condom."

I sat back on my heels, shoving my dick back into my pants and fastening them. She stood on shaky legs and looked down at me. The sight of my cum sliding down her inner thigh made my cock twitch, and I wished I could fuck her again. Hell, I'd take her over and over. It would be a death sentence if I even tried. The second Griz found out I'd been with Lilian, he'd fucking gut me.

No matter how much I wanted her again, I'd said once and I meant it. She was too much of a temptation for me, and far too good for a biker.

"I don't think I can get pregnant," she said. She twisted her hands. "I never did before, and…"

She didn't have to say more. I understood. The men who had fucked her in Colombia hadn't cared about her one way or another. I knew she'd been tested when she was brought here, and Grizzly had been so damn relieved she was clean that he'd told everyone during Church one day. It had weighed on him. She had enough bad memories to deal with and hadn't needed the extra burden.

"Better take the morning after pill just in case." I stood and clenched my fists so I wouldn't reach for her. Watching her cover up all that dusky skin was painful. If things were different, I'd keep her in bed, naked, for days.

I wanted to say more, to make sure she was okay, reassure her or something, but the way she was looking at me, that small spark of hope in her eyes changed everything. I knew what I had to do, even if it made me the biggest asshole. And a fucking liar. Hurting Lilian would be like kicking a puppy, but it was necessary.

"Look, you should probably get tested. I go once a month, and I always wrap my dick, but you don't want to take any chances." Her breath hitched and her eyes went a little wider. Yeah, I was going to hell for this one. I rubbed my beard. "You know how club pussy is. They could be carrying something and we'd never know. The blonde chick from last night looked like she probably got around. Should have wrapped it twice just to be safe, but I wasn't exactly thinking clear. Woman sucked dick like a pro."

Lilian stepped back, looking for all the world like I'd just taken out my gun and shot her. I hated myself right then, but it had to be done. She was smart. Really fucking smart, and way too good for me or anyone else around here. She needed to get the hell away from me and never look back. It was for the best. Not just for her, but for me. I rather liked my balls attached, and her papa bear was fierce when it came to his girls. Didn't matter he wasn't their biological dad. As far as Grizzly was concerned, they were his daughters, and no one fucked with them.

"See you around, Lilian."

Before I could stop myself, or change my mind, I walked out. The door hadn't even shut behind me before I heard the first of her sobs, and my heart fucking broke in half. I'd done that, made her cry, but I knew it was for the best. Grizzly would never let her be with me. He'd paid for her to get her nursing degree, and I knew the Pres wanted his daughter to end up with some college grad or at least someone who stayed on the legal side of things.

One thing was for certain. If I hadn't been going to hell before, I certainly was now. I'd just sealed my fate, and if Griz ever found out I'd fucked his daughter, I'd be going there a lot sooner by way of a painful death and a shallow grave.

Chapter One

Lilian
Five Months Later

My stomach rolled and it felt like my lunch was about to come up. I cast a furtive glance around the room and saw Dr. Larkin eyeing me. *Shit*. It wouldn't take him long to figure it out, then I'd be in trouble for sure. Not that my little secret was going away. If anything, my life would just get more complicated as the days wore on. My baby sister already knew, but only because I'd told her. I'd hated keeping the news to myself, and she'd been worried when she'd noticed I kept getting sick.

I shouldn't have said anything to her. Should have kept it completely to myself a little while longer. I didn't have a clue what I was going to do. My clothes had already gotten tight and while I hadn't picked up maternity clothes, I had bought stretchy things in larger sizes. It was the best I could do for the moment. I hadn't even told the father, and I wasn't sure I was going to. Common sense said I'd eventually have no choice, but I was dragging it out as long as possible. He wouldn't be happy. Especially since he'd told me to get the morning after pill.

It had gone against everything I believed in to take that pill, so I hadn't gone to pick one up. Besides, even if Dragon had only thought of me as a quick fuck, I'd been head over heels for him. Having his child filled me with joy, or it would have if I weren't scared shitless. It wasn't just his reaction I worried about, but my father's as well. For that matter, the entire club wouldn't be too happy about it.

"Everything okay, Lilian?" Dr. Larkin asked. "You look a little green. Hope you aren't catching that virus going around."

Virus. Right. Only if it lasts about nine months and then lives with you for another eighteen years. I could lie and say I was sick, but sooner or later, Dr. Larkin would start putting the pieces together. I'd managed to hide my morning sickness so far. Or rather my all damn day sickness. Not to mention that telling him I was sick would only get me sent home, and then when I got sick the next time, he'd either figure it out or run blood tests to make sure I wouldn't infect his staff and patients with anything.

"I-I think maybe my lunch just didn't hit me right. Maybe the meat spoiled."

I'd no sooner uttered the words than I bolted for the bathroom, not even stopping to lock it. The door swung shut as I hit my knees in front of the toilet and threw up everything I'd eaten or drunk for the day. My throat burned and my eyes watered. I blew my nose, flushed the toilet, and stood up. After rinsing my mouth and splashing cool water on my face, I figured I was as presentable as I'd get without a mint or some gum. I should probably put a toothbrush and toothpaste in my bag just to have for emergencies like this.

I opened the door and nearly collided with Dr. Larkin. He reached out to steady me, his hands gentle, then he released me quickly. Since he catered to the club, he knew about my past and what triggered me. Except for one man, I couldn't stand for any man to touch me. Even now, if Grizzly gave me a hug, I'd sometimes tense up, and he treated me like I was his own flesh and blood and not just adopted.

"Sorry," I muttered.

His gaze was kind as he studied me. My reflection had already told me I looked like hell. He likely saw the same thing I had. I was paler than usual, and my face was puffy. Of course, that was from the pregnancy, but he didn't know that, and I wasn't enlightening him just yet.

"Maybe you should head home. If you're not feeling better in the morning, give me a call. I'll make sure your shift is covered."

"I'm off the next two days," I said. Only because I needed to see an OBGYN as far from this place as possible. I'd managed to arrange my schedule so I could get there and back without drawing suspicion. I'd already told Grizzly I was going on a shopping trip in another town.

"Good, then use the time to rest, and I'll see you when you get back."

I thanked him and hurried to the break room. After I gathered my things, I rushed out to the car the club had given me for my eighteenth birthday. It had been used even then, but the ten-year-old Honda ran like a dream and still had a glossy finish. I loved it, and once my secret wasn't such a secret anymore, I'd be thankful for the spacious backseat.

Driving home, I wondered if Grizzly was there, or Shella. Our dad had given her the option of attending college, but she'd taken a few classes, then asked to take some time off and figure out what she wanted to do with her life. I'd known for years that I wanted to be a nurse, and while I had only gotten my two-year degree and certification, it would help me provide a home for my little one.

I pressed a hand to my belly as I came to a stoplight. "I promise I will give you the best life I can. No one will ever hurt you."

Maybe it was stupid. My parents hadn't been able to protect me any more than I could keep this child out of the wrong hands. Sometimes Fate just liked to fuck you over. I didn't remember a lot about my parents, and my memories had become fuzzy over the years. I didn't know if they'd handed me to the cartel, or if I'd been taken without their knowledge. When I'd been rescued, I'd been offered the chance to go home, but I couldn't face my parents. They were devout Catholics, and even though I'd been violated and not given up my virginity freely, I hadn't been certain they'd have seen the difference. To them, I still would have sinned.

So I'd come home with the Devil's Boneyard and Grizzly, a friend from another club, had taken me into his home. He'd shown me papers that said I was legally his adopted daughter, and he'd had my name changed from Lilian Sanchez to Lilian Moore. He'd offered to let me change my first name, but I'd kept it as a reminder of where I'd come from, and what I'd survived.

A horn honked behind me and I startled, realizing the light had changed at some point. I eased through the intersection and headed for the clubhouse. The Prospect at the gate waved me through and I went straight home. My sister's car was in the driveway and I was reluctant to go inside. I loved Shella, but there were times she could be a bit trying. All I'd wanted was to shower, change into something comfortable, and relax for a while. Now that didn't seem likely.

I walked inside and shut the door, only to frown when I heard Shella talking to someone. I hadn't seen our dad's bike out front, or anyone else's, so who did she have over? Creeping closer to the sound of her voice, I stopped when I realized she was on the phone.

"I don't know why she didn't tell you, Daddy, but I thought you needed to know."

She was quiet a moment, and I had a sinking suspicion she was discussing me. What exactly had she told Grizzly while I was gone? And then I heard it. The one name that made it very clear what she was doing.

"Dragon. She said it was Dragon."

Motherfucker!

I could hear my dad roaring on the other end of the line before Shella hung up. Her eyes were wide when she stared at me.

"What did you do?" I demanded.

"I had to tell him! He needs to know that someone hurt you," she said, her eyes filling with tears.

Sweet baby Jesus. "Shella, I told you I wasn't hurt. No one forced me. Dragon tried really hard to walk away, but I wouldn't let him."

She hadn't believed me when I'd told her, but I'd thought I made her understand. It seemed I'd been wrong, and now Grizzly knew one of his patched members had knocked up his daughter. This wasn't going to end well. There was only one thing I could think to do. Leave. If I wasn't here, then he couldn't take his fury out on Dragon. Out of sight, out of mind, right?

I raced upstairs and started tossing things into a bag. I didn't know where I'd go, or what I'd do, but I needed to get out of here before he came home, and I knew I had precious little time. If he was somewhere inside the compound, he could be here any second. Shella was babbling something at me from the hall, but I shoved past her and went back to my car, tossing my bag into the backseat. After I retrieved my purse and keys from the house, I got in and started the engine, checking the gas gauge. Half a tank. That would get me far enough for the moment.

I slammed my foot on the gas, reversing out of the driveway, then shot forward toward the gates. I didn't see my dad as I neared the front entrance, and didn't even try to slow down. The poor Prospect rushed to open the gates before I barreled through them, hitting the road that would lead me out of town and to the highway. My heart was racing and my palms were damp.

What the fuck did you just do?

There wasn't time to second-guess myself. I'd run, and now I needed to see it through. I'd drive for a while, until I needed a break, and see where I ended up. I didn't dare go south into Florida. The Devil's Boneyard were too close going that direction, so I went north. I knew my dad was friends with another club up that way, or at least he'd mentioned them in passing and didn't seem to hate them. For Grizzly that was as good as a stamp of approval.

My fingers twitched on the steering wheel, and I wondered if I should warn Dragon. I'd never told him I was pregnant, and he'd be completely blindsided when my dad confronted him. *If* Dad went to him. With me no longer there, and I knew Shella had seen my overstuffed bag, maybe he'd be more focused on finding me than chewing out Dragon. The man had only done what I'd asked, and it hardly seemed fair that he pay for that now.

I kept one eye on the rearview and the other on the road ahead, hoping no one followed me. I knew the Prospect would tell my dad which way I'd gone, but I didn't plan for that to be of much help. I cut through Atlanta and kept going north. I stopped for gas and food, but that was it. It wasn't until I'd crossed the state line into Tennessee that some of the tension eased from my shoulders. If they hadn't caught up to me yet, then maybe they couldn't find my trail.

I was exhausted, but I didn't want to use what little money was in my account to stop at a motel. I pulled over for another break and used my phone to look up the Reckless Kings, hoping there would be some mention of exactly where they were located, or at least which town. When my phone rang, I nearly dropped it. *Outlaw*.

Oh hell. Did that mean he knew where I was? Would he tell my dad? Of course he would. Outlaw was nothing if not loyal to the club, which meant he was loyal to Grizzly. I answered, dread filling me.

"Hi, Outlaw."

"Lilian, you are in so much fucking trouble right now. Why the fuck are you in Tennessee?"

I did drop the phone that time, and scrambled to pick it back up. "What? I-I'm not."

"Yeah, darlin', you are. I can trace your phone and your car. Didn't tell anyone shit just yet, though. Needed to talk to you and make sure you were okay. Want to tell me what's going on?" he asked.

"I'm pregnant, Outlaw. Shella told Dad and I could hear through the phone how pissed he was. I left because I didn't want..." I stopped, not knowing if everyone knew about Dragon now.

"You didn't want Dragon to get into trouble with the Pres?" he asked.

"Right."

"Too late. Griz ripped him a new one, then started pounding on him, until he discovered you were missing. When Shella called to tell him you'd taken off, it scared the piss out of him. Everyone's been out searching. Told them you must have shut off your phone because I couldn't find you. No one knows I can track your car except me, or that I lied about your phone being off."

I swallowed the knot in my throat. "How angry is Dragon?"

"I'm not sure angry is the word. He yelled something about a morning after pill to Griz, and then your dad hit him. I think he's more shocked than anything." Outlaw sighed. "Look, I get it. Running seemed like the best option, but you need to come home. Grizzly is losing his damn mind."

"Please don't tell him where I am, Outlaw. I need some time. I was trying to find the Reckless Kings, hoping they'd let me stay there a few days at least. Maybe my dad will cool off by then, and it will give Dragon time to…" I wasn't sure what it would give him time to do. He'd told me to get that pill. I'd known he didn't want me to end up pregnant, even when I'd said I didn't think I could. Well, it seemed that I *could* and I *did*. If he didn't want kids, then I wouldn't force him to be part of my child's life, but I wouldn't give up my baby.

"You're putting me in a sticky spot, Lilian."

"I know, and I'm sorry. I'm not ready to face either of them. I know my dad is mad because Shella made it seem like Dragon forced himself on me, but he didn't. When he gets angry, he doesn't always listen, and I need him to hear me when I talk to him." Or I could just keep running and never go back.

"I'll text you the location of the Reckless Kings, but their Pres is probably going to call Griz the second you get there. I'm not sure how much of a safe haven it will be for you."

"Thank you, Outlaw."

The call disconnected and I waited for the address. When I entered it into the map on my phone, it gave me directions. I didn't stop again until I'd pulled up to the Reckless Kings' gate. They had a Prospect standing guard, and he tapped on my window. I rolled it down, hoping I could stay awake long enough to get through this. It was so late and I was beyond exhausted.

"You need to turn around," he said.

"Please, I need to speak with your President. It's important."

"Sure it is, doll. You're not getting in."

I opened my door and nearly fell out of the car. My legs didn't want to cooperate from driving for so long. I placed a hand over my belly, cradling my unborn child, as I tried to straighten. Everything spun, and I knew I was close to passing out. I fought it, tried to keep my gaze focused, but the Prospect's face started to blur.

I heard a muttered "shit" before he yelled out for help. His arms went around me as my body started to slump. I was still conscious, but barely. A deep growly voice asked what was going on.

"Lilian," I said, my name nearly slurring. "Moore."

"Lilian Moore?" the man asked.

"Grizzly." That was all I could manage. I was passed off to someone else, a large, strong man who smelled like pine or something woodsy. I felt him carry me, and it wasn't long before I was spread out on something soft.

"Sweetheart, are you trying to tell me you belong to Grizzly? You're Devil's Fury property?"

My mouth didn't want to work right. I was just too damn tired. Even my brain felt fuzzy.

The man cursed. "Anyone heard from Devil's Fury? They missing a woman?"

"Got a call from Outlaw," someone said. "He mentioned Griz had a daughter on the run. It seems her daddy just found out she's pregnant, and instead of staying to talk to him, she took off."

"Well, shit." The big man huffed, then smoothed my hair back. "All right, little chick. You can stay for tonight, but in the morning, I want some answers."

I murmured a thank-you, but I didn't know if he'd heard me. Sleep pulled me under fast and hard.

Chapter Two

Dragon

Lilian was pregnant? What the fuck?

I alternated between holding the ice-cold beer bottle to my aching jaw and draining the contents of said bottle. Grizzly had knocked the fuck out of me before I even knew why. The worst part was him thinking I'd forced Lilian. My stomach twisted. Why would she have told him that? I knew I'd hurt her feelings by walking out the way I had, and the nasty things I'd said really had been horrible, but was she trying to get me killed?

I drained another beer, then went to stand, only to have a hand shove me back down onto the stool. I glanced up at Grizzly, and tried to prepare myself for whatever he'd say next. Was I going to be tossed out? That was probably the best-case scenario. It was more likely he'd have me hauled out and shot by my brothers. I still couldn't wrap my brain around the fact he thought I was capable of raping Lilian, or any woman.

"We need to talk, boy," he said, claiming the spot next to me.

"I didn't take advantage of Lil. I asked her several times if she was sure. Even told her it would just be the one time because I knew you didn't want her with someone like me."

Grizzly stared at me. Hard. "Like you?"

"A biker. She deserves better."

He grunted. "That she does, but as much as I hate to admit it, she's a grown woman and can make her own decisions. The fact she let you get that close tells me more than you'd probably like."

I shifted on the stool. Was he about to say he was angry that I'd pushed her away? It wasn't like he'd have given his blessing. Even if he was being all calm and cool now, the reaction he'd had earlier would have been what I'd gotten if I'd tried to claim Lilian. Fuck but I would have loved that. I'd had my eye on her since she'd turned eighteen. Even before that, I'd admired how pretty she was. It wasn't until I'd started spending so much time with her that I'd known I was in trouble.

"I've tried to do right by those girls," Grizzly said. "Wanted them to have a good life. Opportunities. Never occurred to me they might fall for any of you."

"She didn't fall for me," I said.

"That alone tells me you're a dumbass. Lilian wouldn't have let you get that close if she didn't feel something for you. Question is whether or not you have feelings for her."

I opened and shut my mouth. I didn't really know what I felt for Lilian. Knew I wanted her in my bed every night. Didn't mean I was in love with her. Admiring her was one thing. But love? I didn't know shit about love.

"She's gone," Grizzly said.

My head jerked his way. "What? What do you mean she's gone?"

"She overheard Shella telling me about the two of you."

Shella. Not Lilian. My woman hadn't sold me out. Shit. *Not your woman, asshole.* Maybe not, but I wanted her to be. Had for a while. I just didn't have the balls to go up against the Pres to claim her.

I held up a hand. "What do you mean Shella told you? I thought Lilian had talked to you." I'd been pissed as hell that Lilian had claimed I'd forced her, and all this time, she hadn't even been the one to tell Grizzly? Had she told anyone? Maybe Shella had jumped to conclusions, but how had she known Lilian was pregnant when no one else had? I'd noticed she was a bit curvier lately, but I hadn't realized it was because there was a baby in her.

He shook his head. "Never said a word. Shella said you'd taken advantage of Lilian and she was pregnant. I lost it, and I can admit that I should have talked to Lilian before I went after you like that. Now she's run off. She got scared or pissed that Shella had run her mouth, packed a bag, and left. I have no idea where she is or where she's going. Outlaw said he couldn't track her."

I stood so fast the stool tipped over. Lilian was gone? If she was carrying my kid, why hadn't she just come to talk to me? Was I that big of an asshole that she'd thought I would be pissed? Then I'd remembered all the things I'd told her that day. Yeah, she probably did think I was an asshole. And I'd told her to take the morning after pill. The fact she was carrying my kid told me she hadn't listened. Either she really hadn't thought she could get pregnant, or… No, I didn't want to think about that.

"You really don't know where she went?" I asked.

"Not a fucking clue. Prospect said she was heading for the highway when she flew through the gates. Keep your phone charged in case she reaches out. I just have to hope she doesn't wreck the damn car. If she was that upset when she left, she's not thinking clearly, and her reaction time might be off."

My stomach knotted. If she did wreck, she could lose the baby. I might have told her to take the morning after pill, but now that I knew she was carrying my kid, I had to admit I rather liked the idea. I'd bet she'd be cute as hell with a baby belly. Where would she go? Heading to the highway didn't really narrow anything down. We had clubs we considered friends, and one we called family. Would she have gone to any of them?

"Did you check with Devil's Boneyard?" I asked. They'd not only been there the day of Lilian's rescue, but Dingo was related to their Sergeant-at-Arms' ol' lady. Jordan and Havoc had been here several times since Lilian came to live with Grizzly. I didn't know how close she was to Jordan, but maybe she'd reached out.

"You think she'd go there?" he asked.

"I have no fucking clue where she'd go, but it's worth a shot. If not them, who's the next closest? She doesn't know anyone outside of the clubs. It's possible she's going it alone, but I think she'd try to take refuge somewhere. She's still too fucked-up over what happened to trust just anyone."

"No club we call an ally would take her in without calling us." Grizzly folded his arms and leaned them on the bar top. "Unless she turned those big brown eyes on them and begged for some time. Which sounds like something she'd do."

"Tell me which direction to go, and I'll hit the road now. I'll bring her home."

I'd even drive one of the fucking trucks if I had to. No way was she getting on my bike while she was carrying my kid. I'd do anything to bring her back. If I hadn't been such an ass, she'd have never left. We could have faced Grizzly together, and she'd be safe right now.

He gave me a faint smile. "Home, huh? And just whose home would you be taking her to once you got her back here? Mine or yours?"

With any other woman, I'd flat out tell her she was coming to my house, moving in, taking my protection. Lilian wasn't just any woman. She'd been through hell, and I wasn't sure how she'd react if I did that with her, especially after the way we'd left things. Or rather, the vile shit I'd said to push her away. Looked like I'd done a bang-up job, since she hadn't even told me she was pregnant with my kid. I'd fucked this up enough already.

"I'll let her decide," I said. "Anyone else, I'd just fucking tell her she was coming home with me, but…"

"But you're worried Lilian might not do so well with orders," Grizzly said.

"Right."

Griz rubbed a hand along his beard. He was quiet for a few minutes. I wasn't sure if that was a good silence, or an I needed to get my ass as far from him as possible type of silence. When he finally spoke, it wasn't what I'd expected. At all.

"Let me ask you something, and you don't have to answer me, just think about it. The times you spent with Lilian, did she seem to ever shy away when you told her to do something? Ever shrink from you in fear? Give you any indication that she didn't trust you completely?"

Only when I'd been a dick after I fucked her. Until then, she'd leaned into my touch, hadn't flinched away after the first session or two. We'd grown close while I'd taught her to defend herself. During those hours, I'd gotten to see a side of Lilian I didn't think she showed anyone else. The answer must have shown on my face because Grizzly was nodding. He pointed a finger at me, then got up and walked off. So, maybe Lilian wouldn't freak the hell out if I demanded she come home with me. I just had to find her first.

Griz said that no one knew where she was, and Outlaw claimed her phone was off. That didn't seem like something a pregnant woman would do. Wouldn't she want to keep it charged and nearby in case she needed help? And I knew which phone Lil had. It took that fucking thing a good thirty to sixty seconds to boot up once she turned it on, and in an emergency, every second counted. No, my money was on her phone being on, which would mean Outlaw had lied to the Pres. I just didn't know why, but I was going to find out.

I finished my beer and left the clubhouse. Getting on my bike, I started her up and headed for Outlaw's house. The fucker was going to talk, no matter what it took. I'd threaten to take a baseball bat to his precious computers. I pulled into his driveway and hadn't even turned off the bike before he stepped out, leaning against a porch post. He shoved his hands into his pockets.

"I'm not telling you shit," he said.

Fucker. Like I'd thought this would be easy? Yeah, right. I'd come prepared to threaten what he held dear. Until Elena, Outlaw hadn't loved anyone. His computers, however, were his babies.

"Yeah, that's what I figured." I shut off the bike and made my way over to him. "But if I threaten your precious babies I figured you'd start singing like a canary."

Outlaw rolled his eyes. "Have you been watching old gangster movies? What the fuck, Dragon? Besides, I don't hack much these days. Just the basics."

He pulled his hand from his pocket and flexed it, reminding me of the hell he'd been through all to save Wire's woman. It made me feel a little like a dick, but I needed to know where Lilian was, or at least if she was safe.

"I'm not fucking around, Outlaw. I know damn well you know exactly where Lilian is. There's no way she'd shut off her phone, and since you can track it, you know where she went."

"Maybe she doesn't want to be found," he said. "She seems to think you'll be angry that she's pregnant, that you need time to adjust to the idea."

What. The. Fuck. "So you did talk to her. Is she safe? Is she… Just tell me she's okay."

Outlaw relaxed and sighed, shaking his head. "Should have seen this shit coming. I knew damn well if you went there it had to mean something. No one would do this shit and incur Grizzly's wrath over a piece of ass. Why does she think you don't want her? Or the baby?"

I rubbed the back of my neck and tried to think of a way to tell him without coming off as a complete asshole, but truthfully, I *had* been an ass to her. I decided to come clean and told him about the one and only time I'd fucked Lilian, or rather how I acted afterward. The scowl he sent my way would have scared a lesser man. What he didn't have in bulk, he had in brains, and I knew it wouldn't take much for him to wipe out my entire existence with his damn computer. Or my bank account for that matter. He didn't need fast fingers for that sort of thing, which he'd proven several times.

"I was trying to push her away because I knew Grizzly wouldn't want her with a biker. She went to college, and she's really fucking smart, Outlaw. Lil could have had any guy out there, even a doctor. What the hell does she want with a biker like me?" I asked.

He smirked and stared me down. It was creepy as fuck, but I didn't back off. I just waited him out. Sooner or later, he'd tell me what the hell that smile meant.

"You're missing a key part to what you just said. She could have any man she wants, but she *chose* you. I have no fucking idea why, but she must have trusted you. I used past tense because after what you did, you'll probably have to do some major groveling to get her back."

Well, that wasn't a "no" to him helping me. Did that mean he'd tell me where she was? He just stared at me, and I started to feel a little twitchy. "Are you going to help me or not?"

"Come back tomorrow. I want to talk to Lilian and see what she has to say. If she doesn't want your ass anywhere near her, then I'll give her a few more days. Just know that she's safe. And if you tell Grizzly I know where she is, I'll be sure he knows exactly what you did to her."

Shit. That wasn't something I ever wanted the Pres to find out. He might be okay with me going after Lilian and making her mine, but if he heard the crap I'd said to her, he'd gut me like a damn fish. No, I'd be dressed-out like a fucking deer, and he'd probably leave my carcass hanging near the gate as a warning to anyone else. I was so fucked.

"Fine. I'll be back tomorrow. But, Outlaw, when you talk to her, let her know I asked about her? I don't like that she's out there somewhere alone, and pregnant with my kid. I wish like hell she'd come to me. I fucked up, and I know it, but I was trying to do the right thing. She deserves better than me."

"On that I think everyone will agree," Outlaw said. "But she chose you, Dragon, and she's the only opinion that should have fucking mattered."

I hung my head, knowing he was right. I only hoped she gave me a chance to explain. I should have grown a set and told her she was mine that day. Faced Griz like a man. But no, I'd pushed her away, and look how that had worked out. I'd known she deserved better than me, but now I felt like she deserved better because I was a fucking pussy.

"Just tell her I'm sorry." I didn't give him a chance to say anything else. I got on my bike and hauled ass out of there. When I got to my house, I stared at it and wondered if Lilian would like living in it. Since I was lower down on the totem pole around here, I'd gotten a smaller home. It was still three bedrooms and two bathrooms, but they weren't spacious rooms. She was used to living with Grizzly in his big-ass fucking house.

I went inside, tossing my keys onto the coffee table. My furniture was comfortable, and while it wasn't what I'd consider stylish, it was still nice. The walls were all the same damn color in every room. It was a bachelor pad. If Lil moved in, she could change whatever she wanted. I wasn't loaded, but I had enough for her to pick out some paint and maybe change up a few smaller things. Any major overhauls would have to be put on the back burner, especially since we had a kid on the way.

A baby. Fuck. I didn't know what the hell to do with a kid. I pulled out my phone and started searching for articles on how to care for a kid. Then I researched the best way to care for a pregnant woman. One thing became clear, I had a lot to learn, and if I wanted any painting done, it needed to happen before

Lil came here. Every damn thing I pulled up said paint fumes were bad while she was pregnant.

I knew that Dingo and Mei were new to the parenting thing. Which meant neither of them were sleeping much. No fucking way I'd call over there and take a chance on waking up the baby Wen. Adalia and Badger had just had a kid too, but I wasn't taking a chance on Badger killing me if I woke up Gunner. Which left Outlaw and Elena. He wasn't too happy with me right now, and might very well ignore my call. Or hang up on me. I called and promised I'd hang up after four rings if no one answered.

"What the hell do you want?" Outlaw asked when he picked up.

"So, uh… I wanted to set up a nursery, but I don't know what color to paint it, or what type of shit I need. Figured since you're going through this right now, you could point me in the right direction."

"Fucking hell," Outlaw muttered. "Yellow or green walls if you want it to be neutral. Why are you setting up a nursery if she's on the run?"

"Because I'm going to go get her. Maybe not today, or tomorrow. But soon. She can't run forever, Outlaw. That kid is mine, and so is she."

He snorted. "Does *she* know that?"

"Not yet, but she will."

Chapter Three

Lilian

The smell of coffee and bacon woke me. *Dad must be up. Shella can't cook.*

Then everything hit me. I wasn't at home. Shella had run her mouth to Dad about me being pregnant and I'd left. Oh, God. What had I done? I pressed a hand to my mouth and bolted from the bed. I didn't know where the bathroom was, but thankfully found it before I threw up. After I flushed the toilet and stood, my gaze caught a reflection in the mirror. A big beast of a man stood in the doorway, his tattooed forearms exposed, and a steaming coffee cup clutched in his huge hand.

"There's extra toothbrushes in the drawer to the right of the sink. I'm Beast. Come to the kitchen when you're ready." He turned and walked off, leaving me feeling a bit shaken.

Not long on words. I wasn't sure if that was a good thing or a bad thing. I'd thought he looked like a beast. Figured that would be his actual name. Or rather, his road name. I brushed my teeth, splashed some water on my face, then went back to the room where I'd woken. My bag was on the floor and I pulled out a change of clothes and my toiletries. He'd said to meet him when I was ready. I hoped that meant he was okay with me taking a shower first.

I didn't linger, but the warm water made me feel more human. I saturated my hair with conditioner, then combed it through. By the time I'd rinsed, gotten out, and dried off, I was thinking a little clearer. I knew that I'd need to call Dad and at least get him off Dragon's back. Regardless of what Shella had told him, Dragon hadn't forced me. I'd wanted him, and even though he'd only offered the one time, I'd taken it. Anything had to be better than nothing, or so I'd told myself. Except now I knew what I was missing, and it had kept me awake at night for months.

I made my way to the kitchen, finding it after a few minutes, and Beast kicked a chair out from the table. I sat and he slid a coffee cup over to me, except it wasn't coffee. My nose wrinkled at the scent of cinnamon and apples. "This isn't coffee."

"No shit. It's herbal tea. Not my first rodeo. No caffeine, little chick."

I sighed and took a sip, surprised I actually liked it, and my stomach wasn't revolting. Next, he gave me some toast and eggs, all of which stayed down. I was feeling more like myself once I was full, and the hot tea was easing the tension in my body. Although, it made me wonder what he'd meant. He made it sound like he'd been around pregnant women before, but I hadn't seen signs of a woman living here, or a kid.

"Thank you. And thank you for not turning me away last night."

He tapped the table. "About that. I don't mind you staying a bit, but you need to call Grizzly. At least let him know that you're safe. If you don't want to disclose your location, I'll give you a few days, but, little chick, this is just a rest stop. You know damn well you need to go back home."

"I know. I'm just not ready yet." Or possibly ever. Just because he told me to leave didn't mean I'd go back to the Devil's Fury. I could only imagine how awkward things would be with Dragon if I were to go back.

He studied me, and I couldn't help but squirm under his intense gaze. "That baby in your belly also property of Devil's Fury? And I don't mean in the way that you're carrying it and *you're* Devil's Fury property. Who's the daddy?"

My stomach started to churn and I twisted my hands in my lap. *Shit*. I didn't know if he knew Dragon or not. What if they were friends and he got pissed that I'd taken off the way I had? It was risky, but he didn't seem like the type of man to back down. Beast had alpha written all over him, and I'd been around domineering bikers long enough to know when they wanted something, they got it. Whether it was given freely or not.

"It's Dragon's baby, and before you ask, no, I didn't tell him." I blew out a breath and stared at the table. "It was just the one time and he told me to take the morning after pill. Obviously, I didn't. I'm sure he's pissed at me."

Beast just stared, not saying a word. He pulled a phone from his pocket and dialed a number. Then he put it on speaker. My stomach clenched again and I worried I would throw up my breakfast. Was he calling Grizzly?

When the call connected and I heard Outlaw's voice, I felt every muscle in my body relax. Since he knew where I was already, it should be safe to talk to him. Unless he'd told Dad, or worse, Dragon.

"How is she?" Outlaw asked.

"The little chick is fine, and she's right here. You're on speaker," Beast said.

"Lilian, you can rest a day or two, but you need to come back. Things aren't as bad you feared. Grizzly is worried, but he's not bellowing in rage anymore. Hell, he had a civil conversation with Dragon yesterday from what I heard."

"Dragon doesn't want me, or this baby," I said, fighting back the despair that welled up inside me.

"Dragon isn't pissed, Lilian. Shocked. But not pissed," Outlaw said. "He's worried about you too. When he heard how you took off, I think he got scared you'd end up hurting yourself by driving off the road. He came here. Asking if I knew where you were."

"But you'd already told everyone you didn't," I said.

Beast arched an eyebrow and I wondered if he'd known that part. He must have if he realized Grizzly didn't know my location, but Outlaw had already spoken to someone here. Unless his club was keeping things from him. I was just mucking things up left and right, not just for me but for everyone involved.

"Dragon isn't stupid, Lilian. He knew you'd keep your phone on, which meant I could track it. He doesn't know I can track your car too. That's still just between us. And now Beast."

Beast grunted. "She can rest a day or two, but her man needs to come get her."

I gasped and shot to my feet. "I'm not *his*."

Beast gave a pointed look at my stomach. "Little chick, the babe in your belly says otherwise. Whether you like it or not, you're Dragon's. Just a matter of whether or not he's man enough to claim you."

"I'll give you twenty-four hours, Lilian. Then I'm telling them where you are." Outlaw sighed. "Running isn't the answer."

Easy for him to say. He wasn't the one knocked-up from a one-day stand, by a man who'd insisted I take the morning after pill, after he'd made sure I knew he'd been with the women at the clubhouse just the night before. Bile rose in my throat and I felt the blood drain from my face as I remembered his words. I pressed a hand to my mouth and ran from the room, finding the nearest bathroom. I dropped to my knees and threw up.

Beast found me a moment later. "Something you're not saying?"

I slumped against the wall and looked up at him through blurry eyes. A tear slipped down my cheek and I hastily dashed it away. What would it hurt to tell him? He didn't seem like a complete asshole. The tears fell faster and soon I didn't bother wiping them off my cheeks.

Beast hunkered down in front of me, running a finger along my jaw. "Little chick, I can't help if I don't know what's going on. Did Dragon do something he shouldn't? You said it was just the one time, but did he maybe push you into something you didn't really want?"

Why did everyone think Dragon was capable of such a thing? The guy might be a dick, but he wasn't a rapist. I shook my head. "It wasn't that."

"Then what. Help me understand."

"He… he said it was just the one time and that it couldn't be more. Told me to keep my distance after. He warned me before anything happened." I drew in a shuddering breath. "It was after that everything fell apart."

Beast stood, then leaned down and lifted me into his arms. As I settled against his chest, I realized it had been his scent last night. He'd been the one to carry me through the gates. He took me back to the room I'd woken in earlier and eased me down onto the bed. Smoothing my hair back, he studied me a moment.

"What did he do after?" Beast asked.

"Told me I should get tested since the club whore he'd been with the night before might have been carrying something, but that she'd…" It still hurt to think about it, but I made myself continue. "But that she'd sucked his cock real good. Told me to get the morning after pill. So, you see, you're wrong. You and Outlaw both. Dragon doesn't want me. He made that abundantly clear when he made me feel like trash before he walked out that day."

Beast cursed and started pacing the room. His body was tensed, and I could have sworn I heard him grind his teeth. I didn't know if this changed things or not. Would he still make me leave tomorrow? Did he still think I belonged to Dragon? Anger practically radiated off him and I didn't understand why. I was no one to him.

He came to a halt beside the bed and reached down to squeeze my hand. "I'm sorry the man is a dick. I'm not going to make you go back to him. In fact, I think it's best you remain here a little while. You can take some time to figure things out. Just call your dad so he knows you're safe."

"Thank you, Beast."

"No thanks needed, little chick. I might be an asshole, but I'd never turn away a woman in trouble. Get some rest. When you're up for it, I'll see what I have in the kitchen that might settle your stomach. You need to eat."

"Gingersnaps help a little," I said. "Sometimes crackers."

He nodded. "I'll send out a Prospect to get both, along with a few other things we can try. Just close your eyes and try not to worry so much. Everything will work out one way or another."

I shut my eyes and drew in a deep breath, trying to calm my nerves. I heard him walk out and pull the door shut behind them, then I stared up at the ceiling. I didn't want to talk to my dad yet, but Beast was right.

It was wrong to make Grizzly worry. He'd been a wonderful parent, even if he hadn't been my sperm donor. There was no reason he had to take me in when the Devil's Boneyard had found me in Colombia, but he had, and he'd done everything he could for me. He'd paid for me to go to college, made sure I had a car to drive. And most importantly, he'd made sure I was safe.

I grabbed my phone and placed the call, no matter how many knots my belly was in. When he answered, I could hear the worry in his voice.

"Lilian! Where are you? I'll come right now."

"Dad, I'm fine. I'm safe, and you don't need to worry about me."

He growled softly. "Like I'm ever going to stop worrying? Was it so scary to tell me about the baby that you felt you had to run?"

I took a breath and tried to find the right words. "I knew you'd be disappointed in me, and I wasn't sure how you'd react with Dragon. I heard what Shella said. She made it sound like he'd forced me, but he didn't. It was my choice. He's the only man I've willingly been with, and it was something I needed to do. Getting pregnant just wasn't part of the plan."

"So why didn't you stay to talk to me?" he asked. "Were you afraid I'd hurt you?"

I could hear how much it cost him to ask that. Bile rose in my throat but I forced it down. "No, Dad. I never thought you'd hurt me. I worried you'd go after Dragon, and I thought maybe if I wasn't there, then you'd leave him alone. I'm sorry. I never meant to scare you. I need some time to work through everything in my head."

"Will you tell me where you are?" he asked.

"Not yet. But I'm with friends, and they'll keep me safe. Nothing is going to happen to me."

He cleared his throat. "Do you know how far along you are? Or what you're having?"

"I'm about five months. I had an appointment scheduled a few towns over, but I missed it because of all this. They were going to tell me more and do an ultrasound. I'm sorry I kept it from you for so long. I was just scared. All that time in Colombia and I never got pregnant, and one time with Dragon and I'm suddenly having a baby."

"You need to come home, Lilian. He'll do right by you."

I snorted. "I don't want you to force him to have anything to do with me or the baby. We'll be fine without him. He made it perfectly clear he didn't want a kid."

"He said something about the morning after pill," Grizzly muttered.

"I didn't get one. I didn't think there was a chance in hell I'd get pregnant. Guess I was wrong. While this wasn't what I'd planned, I will love this baby until my dying breath. Being a mom is a little frightening. I don't exactly have a role model for this sort of thing. Mei and Adalia are both new to motherhood, and while I'm sure they'll have some tips for me, they're still figuring shit out too."

He laughed a little. "You're right there."

"I'll keep my phone on so you can reach me, but please don't ask Outlaw to trace it. I need you to trust me. I'm a big girl now, with a baby on the way. I don't know where I'll go when I leave here. Maybe I'll come home, or maybe it's time for me to try making a life somewhere else. Someplace away from Dragon."

Grizzly sighed. "Why are you so adamant about avoiding him? So he told you to take the morning after pill. You didn't and now you're having a baby. He'll get over it. It's possible he already has."

I chewed on my lip, knowing that he'd be furious if I told him what Dragon had said or done. The last thing I wanted was for him to go kill the guy. Yeah, he'd been an ass, but it didn't mean I wanted him dead. If things were different, I'd gladly become Dragon's. There was nothing I'd have wanted more, before the words he'd spoken after he was done that day. Now I just wanted to move on. Or at least try to deal with him as little as possible. I didn't know that I'd ever want another man. It had taken a while before I'd trusted Dragon enough to go that far.

Oddly, whenever Beast came near me, I didn't flinch or get an anxiety spike. As huge as he was, I should have been scared out of my mind. Instead, he had a calming presence. Maybe it was because my dad was a big guy too. He'd said I could stay a little while, and I was going to take him up on the offer. I knew I couldn't live here indefinitely. Sooner or later, I needed to figure my shit out. For now, I just wanted to rest a day or two, maybe find out if there was an OBGYN nearby who had an opening, and just go from there.

"Lilian, you got quiet."

I gave myself a mental shake, having forgotten my dad was on the phone still. "Sorry. Just thinking. I'm going to stay here at least a few days. I'll call when I know what my next move will be. Love you, Dad."

"Love you too. Don't do anything foolish."

Famous last words. I'd always been cautious, until now. I disconnected the call and sat up. There was no way I could sleep right now. Beast hadn't said I was confined to this room, so I went to explore a little. I didn't make it far before I stopped, slinking back into the shadows.

Beast was staring down at a woman, a very pregnant one, a scowl on his face. "Why are you here?" he asked.

"Don't be like that. You know my brother would have never let us be together."

Beast snorted. "I'm his President. He'd have done whatever the fuck I said he should. I held back out of respect for your brother, and because it's what you wanted. If you'd made it clear I was the only guy for you, then things would have been different. You made your decision, Charlotte. Stop coming here."

She sighed and gave a slight nod. "I only came to tell you I'm moving."

She turned and walked out, with Beast watching her go. I felt like I'd interrupted something I shouldn't have, or rather eavesdropped. Did I need to alert him to my presence? Or just head back to my room. I went to take a step back, but he turned and looked right at me.

"Might as well come out. She's gone."

I winced as I moved closer. "I didn't mean to overhear that. I couldn't sleep and thought I'd learn the layout of your house, in case you're willing to let me stay a little while. I know you said I didn't have to leave, but that didn't mean I'd be in this particular house either."

"You can stay as long as you want," he said. "Don't tell anyone about what you just heard. Her brother doesn't know that I have feelings for her. Not that it matters anymore. She moved on."

"She did, but you didn't?" I asked.

"Something like that. She was never mine to claim."

I reached out and placed my hand on his cheek, a bold move for me. "She was lucky to have someone like you in her life, in any capacity. I'm sorry things didn't work out between you."

He gave me a faint smile, reached up for my hand and gave it a squeeze before taking a step back. Right. Message received. Don't get too close.

"Come on, little chick. You can tell me what you want from the store."

I followed him to the kitchen, where he'd left a pad and pen, and a partially written grocery list. I sat down and told him the things I liked, and what I'd been craving lately. By the time he was finished, a Prospect was at the door. He handed off the list, then seemed at a loss as to what to do next.

"You don't have to stay here and babysit," I said. "I'll just use the Internet on my phone to find a doctor."

He tensed and his gaze locked on me. "You're hurt? Is something wrong with the baby?"

"No, nothing like that. I had an appointment scheduled for this morning that I missed. I need an ultrasound and the baby needs to be checked in general. Just make sure everything is still good. I'm not familiar with the doctors in this area."

"Prospero's brother is the club doctor. He might know of someone, or might be able to handle it himself. I'll just give him a call."

While Beast made arrangements for me to see a doctor, I studied what I could see of his house. It was comfortable, but also quality. From what I'd seen, I'd be willing to bet the Reckless Kings had more money coming in than my dad's club. I wondered how they did so well, and then decided I didn't really want to know. If it was illegal, it was better for me to remain in the dark.

"You're in luck, little chick. You have an appointment in three hours. So whatever you need to do between now and then, get to it. I'll drive you over in my SUV."

I decided that meant I was dismissed and went back to the room I'd woken in first thing today. Not knowing how long I'd be here, there was no point in unpacking. Instead, I decided to stretch out on the bed and read a book on my phone. It felt like butterflies were swooping around in my belly. I hoped I'd get to see my baby today, or at least get a good report.

I placed a hand on my belly. "I will do everything I can to make sure you're safe and loved. No matter the cost."

I only hoped that it didn't leave me with a broken heart along the way. Dragon had already left a huge crack in it. I didn't think it could handle much more.

Chapter Four

Dragon

I'd stayed up all damn night, and it was now going on thirty-six hours since I'd last slept. Didn't matter. I had shit to do. The baby's room was painted a pale green that was nearly white. I'd even repainted the trim and doors. A quick trip to a baby store twenty minutes down the highway and now I was staring at shit that made me feel like I'd entered another world.

I found the furniture section easy enough, but I didn't know the difference between one set and another. A sales lady rushed over, a smile on her face, and a gleam in her eyes. Except, this wasn't the gleam I was used to, the I-want-in-your-pants one. No, this one said, *Open your wallet*. As pricey as this stuff was, I had a feeling I'd be making a big dent in my account, but my kid was worth it. Assuming I ever got Lil back home where she belonged. One step at a time.

"First baby?" the lady asked.

"Yep. Can't decide which set I like more." I rubbed a hand along my jaw. "Don't see a lot of difference other than style and color."

"Some are heavier than others and better made," the lady said. "Did your wife not tell you a preference?"

I just shook my head. I wasn't going down that rabbit hole. If everyone wanted to assume I was married, then so be it. If I had my way, Lil would be wearing my name *and* my ring soon enough. Of course, I had to find her first, and Outlaw didn't seem ready to tell me her location. As pissed as I'd been, I'd also liked that he was trying to do right by her. She'd wanted space, so he was giving it to her. I just didn't like that she wanted space from me.

"Do you know if it's a boy or girl?" the lady asked.

"Don't know yet." Did Lilian know? Had I missed all the doctor appointments and shit that Badger and Dingo had both been to with their women? I felt a little cheated right now, but it was my own fucking fault.

"Well, let's find something that would be appropriate for either. Since this is your first, you'll want something that lasts. That way you can use it again with the next one." She smiled and I tried like hell not to fucking run. Next one? Shit. I was still wrapping my head around the fact I was having a kid, and now she was adding more.

I felt a little dazed as we narrowed down the selection, and somehow ended up buying the most expensive set in the store. Bed, changing table, dresser, and even a rocking chair that while pretty awesome looking didn't seem like it would be very comfortable. I'd have to remember to get Lil a cushion or something. She also loaded a bedding set into my cart with little owls on it, and four extra sheets. Before she could dump more shit in there, I thanked her, told her I'd be up front to pay for the furniture when I was done, then ran like hell.

I hated fucking shopping. And baby shopping was now at the top of my *never want to do this again* list. There were two women in the section with bath stuff so I looked over the items, and from the corner of my eye, I watched to see what they bought. After they walked off, I selected a few of the items they'd grabbed and added them to my cart. I knew bibs were important. Or I assumed they were since Dingo and Badger both had a shit ton at their homes.

Not knowing if Lil was having a boy or girl limited my choices, but I found a few that seemed gender neutral. Any kid could wear the white one with little yellow ducks, right? Or the yellow one with giraffes. One of each went into the cart, and then I moved on to the toy section, and holy shit. So many colors, textures, and types. Some made noise, and some didn't. My head was starting to pound, and my chest ached.

"First baby?" a female voice asked.

I glanced to my left and saw a blonde who was bouncing on her toes. She was cute in a cheerleader type of way, and looked too fucking young to be buying baby shit, but her cart contained two packs of diapers. Not that I would judge her for having a kid young, but I wondered if she knew what she was in for. Seeing Badger look like he'd last slept a year ago was enough to make most of the guys want to run the other way. I had a feeling the stock on condoms was about to go up.

"Yeah. You?"

She giggled. "Oh, these are for my sister. She had a baby two months ago, but didn't want to leave the house just yet. If you want a good first toy, try one of the stuffed animals. The eyes are stitched so they can't pull anything off."

I glanced at the animals. "They can't put it in their mouths or against their faces and suffocate or choke?"

"Well, you could always leave it out of the crib until the baby is older," she said, still smiling. And what the fuck? Was she batting her eyes while twirling her hair? This chick wasn't seriously flirting in a baby store, was she?

"Thanks." I reached for a brown bear and added it to the cart. Before I could move, she'd placed her hand on my forearm.

"Need help with anything else? And I mean *anything*."

Fuck my life. "Look, you're a pretty girl, but hitting on fathers in a baby store is not going to end the way you want it to. I have a woman who's carrying that baby, and I'm not going to cheat on her."

Shit. My chest got even tighter. Had I cheated on Lilian? Fucking hell. We weren't anything, hadn't been anything but a one-time deal. As disgusted as I'd been with myself, I hadn't touched a woman for weeks after that. Eventually, I'd groped a few club sluts, but other than grabbing some tits and ass, I hadn't done anything else. Even though it hadn't gone beyond that, it still felt like I'd done something wrong. I suddenly thought I might throw up. When Lilian asked me who I'd been with, I'd have to tell her the truth. I might not have had sex with those women, or kissed them, but I'd still touched them.

The way she'd sobbed the day I'd walked out still damn near gutted me. I didn't know if I could do that to her again. Lying to her wasn't right either. I'd have to hope if I was honest with her, she'd forgive me. I'd given the club whores a wide berth the last four and a half months. It had only taken a few times of holding them on my lap, touching them, to realize they weren't what I wanted.

I hadn't even realized the girl had wandered off. I rubbed at my chest wondering if I was about to have a heart attack, then decided it was just guilt. Finishing up my shopping, I paid for everything, then loaded it all into the club truck I'd borrowed. I remembered all the cussing Badger had done when he'd tried to put the crib together for Gunner. I'd done okay with the entertainment center in my living room, and I didn't think baby furniture would be all that different.

When I pulled up to the gates, Carver stepped up to the truck. I rolled down the window to see what the hell he wanted. Fucker should have opened the gate when he saw me coming. He eyed the shit in the truck bed before looking at me again.

"You need help unloading? I'm off the gate in another ten. I could swing by."

Huh. The Prospects we had were decent enough, but not many volunteered themselves for work. They'd jump to do anything we asked, but I'd planned on hauling all this shit into the house myself. "You any good at putting shit together?" I asked.

"Somewhat. Two sets of hands will still be better than one."

I nodded. "All right. When you're done, stop by. You can help me unload the furniture. I want the baby's room done before I go get Lilian."

His eyebrows shot up. "I thought no one knew where she was."

"Outlaw knows. He just won't tell me. But he will. Eventually."

The Prospect opened the gates and I pulled through, giving him a wave as I turned toward my house. I pulled into my driveway a few minutes later and carried in the bags of various baby items, leaving the heavy furniture for Carver. If he wanted to help and try to earn his patch, then I'd let him. I set the bags inside the closet in the nursery and put the packages of diapers under the window.

I didn't know what Lilian would think of the baby's room. It was my hope she'd see the effort I'd put in and realize I wasn't running from her and our baby. I wanted that kid, as much as I wanted her. No, it hadn't been in my plans to start a family right now, but maybe Fate knew more than I did. Lilian wouldn't have gotten pregnant unless there was a reason, other than she didn't get that damn pill I told her to take. She'd been right, though. What were the odds she'd conceive now when she never had before? I didn't kid myself and think I had super sperm, which meant for whatever reason, this baby was meant to be.

I'd spectacularly fucked this up, but I'd fix it. I just had to convince her to give me a chance first. Or rather, I had to find her location and bring her home. Outlaw couldn't keep her hidden forever. Eventually, the Pres would demand to know the location of his daughter and unborn grandkid. Since Griz didn't seem so pissed at me anymore, I was about ninety percent certain he'd share the information with me when he found out.

A knock at the door told me Carver had arrived. I went to let him in, only to be greeted by the large box containing the crib. I stepped aside and he carried it into the house. After telling him which room was the nursery, I went to get the changing table box. It only took another few minutes to get the other box into the nursery along with the rocker, and then we both stared at the three.

"Maybe crib first." It seemed logical. The kid needed a bed more than the other things, right?

"On it," Carver said. "If there's something else you need to do, I can handle this. I can at least get it all together, then you can put it wherever you want it."

If he was offering, I wouldn't say no. I gave him a nod and walked out. My phone alerted me to a message and I quickly checked it.

Church in ten.

Looked like I was about to be busy anyway. I'd left my bike at the clubhouse when I'd picked up the truck for my shopping earlier. Taking the truck back to the front of the compound, I parked it and then went inside the clubhouse, putting the keys back on the hook for whoever needed it next. I saw Dingo, Wolf, and Scorpion stepping through the doors of Church and followed. After I took my seat, I realized everyone was here.

"This may bring up unpleasant memories for some of you," Grizzly said, looking at me, "but Julio Ramirez isn't just dropping packages in our area anymore. It looks like he's mobilizing his own crew."

I digested that news a moment. The bastard had someone torture me so the Pres would agree to let him hide shipments in our territory as a way to slowly overthrow his boss. It seemed that time had come. As much as I hated the bastard, I knew it was just business. He hadn't singled me out. I hadn't signed up for this life thinking it would be a cake walk. "His crew in our territory?" I asked.

"From what I can see, it looks like they're unloading the crates they have stashed in town. The question is where they'll be taking them," Grizzly said. "Now that we have kids here, I don't want to take the risks we have in the past."

Demon snorted. "We've always had kids here. You keep taking in strays."

Grizzly flipped him off. "Leave my girls out of this."

"Technically, Demon is right, and you put them in this by bringing up kids," Slash said. "But that's neither here nor there. We need to find out what Ramirez is up to. If he's making his move to take down his boss, I don't want that shit happening here in our town."

"Agreed," said Hot Shot. "This fucker blindsided us once. I'll be damned if he gets to do it twice."

"Anyone doing recon?" I asked.

"I tracked them a little ways, but I lost them partway through town. I don't know if he's just changing the location of his merchandise, or if he's taking it out of the area," Wolf said.

"Basically, we've got a whole lot of nothing," Grizzly said. "And I don't fucking like it. Dragon, I know you've got other shit to worry about, but you were with Ramirez and his men. If anyone knows how these fuckers work, it's you. I need you to see what you can find out."

"What about Lilian?" I asked.

Outlaw cleared his throat. "She's fine, and when she's ready, she told me to disclose her location. To Grizzly. Sorry, Dragon. The way you handled things has her convinced you don't want her or the baby. She needs time. Focus on this right now. Lilian is okay."

"Fine. Tell me where to go and I'll head out now." I didn't like it, but Outlaw was right. I'd fucked up shit with Lilian and no matter how much I wanted to bring her home, maybe she needed some time away. At least if she wasn't around Ramirez, I knew she'd be safe.

Wolf gave me the last location he'd seen Ramirez's men, along with the location of the crates he'd been storing. With that information in hand, I walked out and decided to do what I did best. Focus on club shit. Women were too damn complicated. There was a reason I'd remained single all this time. A wife and kids hadn't been on my radar, at least not for another decade, if ever. Now I didn't have a choice, at least on the kid part.

I got on my bike and pulled through the gate. I decided to scout the storage facility first, and it was a legit storage place. All this time, I'd thought Ramirez would have some secret warehouse or something, but no. He'd rented a set of storage lockers at the local spot. I idled my bike across the street, sticking to the shadows. The goons in suits had to be part of Ramirez's crew. No one else around here wore shit like that unless there was a funeral. And even then, half the people would still be in jeans, or what Adalia had once called country chic. Whatever the hell that was.

The men loaded wooden crates into the back of an SUV, then pulled out. I waited a moment, keeping them in my sights. Just as I was about to follow, another black SUV pulled up, identical to the other. Deciding to see if they were more of Ramirez's men, I hung back. Three men in suits got out. I didn't know why they weren't pulling inside to load up. Made more sense to me. Unless…

I eyed the storage facility and saw cameras posted at various places behind the gate. Each time one of the men passed one, they looked the other way. It seemed they were camera shy, and probably didn't want their plates on video. That told me the plates were probably legit. After they'd loaded several crates and pulled off, I discreetly snapped a pic of the car tag with my phone, then sent it off to Outlaw. Even though he didn't do a lot of computer work these days, he'd get someone to help if he couldn't handle it.

This time, I decided to wait and see if any others came through. After ten minutes of no more SUVs, I decided to call it a day. I didn't know if the plate would tell us anything, but I'd ask Outlaw to pull the footage from the storage facility as well. Maybe we'd catch a break and get this shit figured out. Grizzly was right to worry. If Ramirez came after our women the way his men had gone after Ashes' woman, I knew there would be hell to pay. Lilian might not officially be mine, but I'd die to protect her, and I knew Dingo and Outlaw felt the same about their women. Blades and Mei's mom were unofficially together, and there was no fucking way he'd let someone get their hands on her.

Not that he didn't want to claim her, but after the hell she'd been through, I could understand him giving her space. They lived together, and he doted on her, but she wasn't ready to officially belong to anyone. I admired that he was able to hold back on what he wanted in order to ensure she had what she needed. Probably should have learned something from him before I fucked shit up with Lil.

I'd no sooner pulled through the gate at the compound than Slash approached. His expression was grim, and I could hear Grizzly roaring from somewhere nearby. My heart kicked against my ribs and my stomach knotted.

"What happened?" I asked. "Where is she?"

Slash shook his head. "We don't know. Someone took her."

Motherfucker. This was the last damn time I listened to everyone. If I'd found a way to track her and gone after Lilian, then she'd be safe right now. But no, I'd given her space.

"Reckless Kings called," he said. "She was staying with Beast. He's tearing the place apart searching for her, but… there's no ransom note. Nothing. She's just gone."

"I'm going to need a truck."

Slash nodded. "Already having one gassed up for you. Go get your shit. Wolf said he's going with you, and I'm sure several others will too. Griz wants to go, but Shella needs him here. We've got your back."

I snorted. "Right. Now that she's gone you have my back. When I wanted to go get her, everyone told me to just wait, that she'd come home when she was ready. How did that fucking work out?"

"You're right. Outlaw should have told you where she was. Maybe she'd be safe right now. Or maybe whoever has her would have found a way to get to her anyway. We don't know if this is related to the Reckless Kings, to us, or she's a random victim. Meet back here in fifteen minutes." Slash stepped back. "Whatever you need to get her back, you've got it. Pay the fuckers off if you need to. Just find her. Not only for you, but for Griz too. He's losing it."

I nodded and revved the engine on my bike, heading for the house. A few changes of clothes, and every fucking gun I owned would be packed in record time. Then my ass was out of here, whether the others were ready or not.

Hold on, Lil. I'm coming for you.

Chapter Five

Lilian

I'd never felt so stupid in my entire life. Not even when I'd given myself to Dragon and he'd stomped all over my heart. Or when I'd run after hearing Shella talking to our dad. Nope. This topped the damn list. Beast had said he'd take me to the appointment, but then he'd gotten a call. While he'd been busy, I'd watched the minutes tick by. I hadn't wanted to miss seeing the doctor, so I'd grabbed the address he'd written down, programmed it into my phone, then decided to drive myself.

Being a grown-ass woman, that shouldn't have been an issue. I just forgot for a moment that I was staying with bikers, and there was a reason they lived in a damn fortress. Because shit on *this* side of the gate wasn't safe. Maybe I'd gotten complacent since I'd been safe ever since I went to live with Grizzly. He'd always cautioned me that the club still had enemies and I'd be seen as an easy target. I just hadn't thought I'd get snatched when I wasn't anywhere near home, which made me think this had to do with the Reckless Kings.

"Stupid bitch couldn't do even the simplest thing," my captor muttered as he paced. He'd tied me to a chair, but other than a headache from whatever he'd used to knock me out, he hadn't hurt me. Scared the crap out of me, but he hadn't done any permanent harm that I could tell.

"What was I supposed to have done?" I asked. If he was referring to me as the incompetent bitch, then it would at least be nice to know why I'd been snatched from my car. I hadn't even made it very far from the compound before I'd had a flat and pulled over. Idiot that I am, I got out to see the damage, only to get grabbed from behind.

"Not you. Charlotte." He spat on the floor. "Took time to lure that bitch in. I knew Beast had a thing for her. Everyone knows it. What happens? She gets knocked-up and now she doesn't want anything to do with him. Fucking useless."

I had a feeling he was talking about the woman I'd seen with Beast, but I couldn't remember if he'd shared her name. My head was pounding. I knew if it didn't abate soon, I'd end up throwing up all over myself. As much as I'd love to douse the guy with puke, I didn't think that would earn me any favors. He seemed a teensy bit unhinged, and I wasn't sure how he'd react. "So this has to do with Beast?" I asked.

He snarled at me. "Of course! Why else would I take you? Obviously, I picked the wrong woman. If I hadn't seen you in his house, I'd have never realized my mistake."

Wait. *He'd seen me in Beast's house*? How? It was far enough back from the gate or even the fence line I didn't think anyone could see in the windows, unless they were *inside* the compound. If that was the case, had this man been let in voluntarily, or did the compound have a weak spot no one had discovered? I wanted to tell him that I didn't belong to Beast, but if he thought I was useless to him, he might decide I was expendable. "What do you need with Beast?" I asked.

"It's his fault. All his fault."

Well, that answered… nothing. "What's his fault?"

The man flung his arm out, his eyes wide and crazy. "Everything! She should have been mine. No, if he hadn't interfered, she *would* have been mine."

I was starting to feel a little like I was talking to the March Hare. Not a damn word he said made any sort of sense. The more information he gave me, the less I understood. He obviously felt Beast had wronged him somehow. And it seemed to have something to do with a woman, but... not Charlotte?

If I'd even somewhat followed his craziness, he'd been using her to get closer to Beast. Since it hadn't worked out, I was a little worried about where Charlotte might be right now. Had he hurt her?

"But you're his, and carrying his kid. He'll care about that. Just need to send the right message, then all this will be over. He can have you back, and I'll have what I need."

Oh, shit. No, I wasn't Beast's, and my baby certainly wasn't either. If the guy had been keeping tabs on the club, wouldn't he have noticed I just showed up the other day? Although, when he started mumbling to himself, things became a little clearer. Well, in the fact I now understood the level of crazy I was facing, not so much that he actually made sense.

His voice rose an octave. "I told you the woman was useless, but you insisted he favored her. Now look at this mess!"

"I know! I know I screwed up, but I'm fixing it. I have the right woman now," he said in his normal voice. Or the voice he'd used with me up to this point.

"Always such a screwup," he said, in yet another tone. "Never could do shit right. Useless. Fucking useless. Should have been drowned at birth."

Anger lit his eyes and his body tensed. "Not useless!" he shouted in the voice of... person one? I might not have gotten a degree in psychology, but I'd taken enough of those courses to be almost certain I was dealing with someone who had multiple personalities. I only hoped none of them were homicidal.

I began working my wrists, trying to loosen the rope. He hadn't bothered tying my legs, and since I hadn't kicked at him, he must have thought I was adequately subdued. I wasn't about to dissuade him of that notion. Not until I thought I might actually have a chance of escaping.

Sure, Lilian. Run away from home. What's the worst that could happen? Well, getting kidnapped by a crazy person was at the top of that list now. Normally I would have never been so callous as to even think of a mentally ill person as crazy, but when that person had kidnapped me, tied me to a chair, and planned to use me as bait or something, then crazy seemed to fit. Sadly, if he'd ever been medicated for his illness, it seemed he'd stopped taking the pills. Or his doctor was an incompetent idiot.

Whatever the case, I was well and truly fucked. For now. I kept working at the ropes, hoping I could slip one of my hands free. I could feel the rough fibers tearing at the skin and I had no doubt I'd be bleeding before I was done. Being free would be worth it. I'd been a victim for too long, and then a survivor, to deal with this shit now. Not to mention, I really needed to pee. Dragon's kid had to be sitting directly on my bladder.

The man continued to pace, having an argument with the various people in his head, or however that worked. Right now, I needed to focus on getting free. I kept an eye on him, in case he came closer or seemed like he might hurt me, but otherwise I did my damnedest to get my wrists free. I didn't know if I could pull off some of the self-defense moves I'd learned, since I was now five months pregnant, but I was going to try my hardest to get out of here. I didn't even know where *here* was, but I'd figure it out once I'd put my kidnapper far behind me.

I wondered if anyone had found my car yet. Beast had to know I was missing, which meant my father likely did as well. I'd be lucky if I was permitted outside the gates after this. Goodbye job and freedom. Grizzly had always been protective, but something told me he was about to up his game about a million percent. I'd have felt sorry for what that meant for Shella too, but since her treacherous mouth is why I'd left to begin with, it served her right if she was put on lockdown.

I could admit I was still a little bitter over what felt like a betrayal. She might have been trying to do what she felt was right, but she'd fucked up. When I told her I hadn't been forced, she should have listened. But no, she heard what she wanted, saw what she wanted, and then acted how she'd wanted. It was past time for her to grow the hell up. Either that, or someone just needed to turn her over their knee and paddle her ass. From what I'd seen, Dagger would be happy to handle it, or rather handle Shella.

Dad might have wanted more for us than pairing off with bikers in his club, or any club, but he should just get used to the fact we felt safe with men like him. Adalia and Badger were happy, and if Dragon hadn't been an asshole, I'd have been over the moon to be his. It was only a matter of time before Dagger made a move and claimed Shella. At least, that was my prediction.

My breath stalled in my lungs when I managed to pull one of my hands free. My wrist throbbed and I felt blood trickle down my palm. I closed my fist so it wouldn't drip onto the floor, then watched the man pace in front of me some more. I counted his steps, watched for a pattern, and when he seemed to be deep enough in an argument with one of his selves, I made my move.

I might not have been quite as quick as before, and I'd been stuck in that chair for who knew how long, but I was desperate. Shooting to my feet, I used the element of surprise to nail him right between the legs. His eyes went comically wide and his jaw dropped as he fell to the floor, hitting his knees and cupping his crotch. His eyes watered. Ignoring his accusations and ranting, I ran for the door on the far side of the building. Daylight streamed through the grimy windows along that wall, so it was my hope it led outside.

As I burst through it, it occurred to me he might have had help. I cast a furtive glance around, but we seemed to be in a warehouse district, and not another soul was within sight. I didn't know where I was or how to get back to the Reckless Kings, but I wasn't stopping until I found a way to call for help. Even if that meant calling my dad.

My stomach cramped and my vision blurred as I ran, my breath coming out in pants. This was the most running I'd done… Well, ever. I didn't know how much farther I could go. I could see a busy street not too far ahead, and I pushed myself harder. I might have made it, if I hadn't tripped and fallen.

I cradled my stomach, hoping I hadn't injured my baby. As I struggled to stand, hands gripped me tightly from behind and I screamed, only to have a fist smash into the side of my head. I sucked in a breath as stars danced across my vision. The man lifted me into his arms and carried me back the way I'd come.

When he put me back on the wooden chair, I groaned and shook my head. "Bathroom. Please."

"Bitch! I don't care if you piss yourself." The tone suggested it was one of the other voices I was dealing with this time. "Told him you were a stupid cunt, but he didn't listen."

My arms were wrenched behind me and secured once more. Not only with rope this time, but he wrapped duct tape around my wrists too. Then he fastened my ankles to the chair legs. I wanted to cry, but tears wouldn't get me anywhere. I'd escaped once, which meant maybe I could do it again. I seriously needed to pee, though. The thought of wetting myself made me wince, but eventually my bladder would demand that I go. Even if that meant going while I was tied up in this chair. Dammit.

"Where's Charlotte?" I asked.

"You need to worry about you right now," the man said in the second voice I'd heard before. "Need to get a message to Beast, but it must be the right one."

He eyed me and my skin crawled. What was he going to do? When he approached, I leaned as far back as I could, but it was no use. The ropes and chair held me immobile. He lifted my hair, bringing it to his nose and breathing in my scent. His eyes shut and he smiled faintly.

"What are you going to do with me?" I asked.

"Such a pretty little whore. First, I need to make sure that stupid oaf knows you're missing. I think a lock of your hair might send the right message." He pulled out a knife, grabbed a handful of my hair, and sawed off nearly six inches.

I'd held it together so far, and I refused to break down over my hair of all things. So I'd cut it. No big deal. It would grow back. I shut my eyes and remembered the way Dragon would often stare at my hair, the way it had felt the few times he'd touched it. I knew he loved my long locks, and I had too. But it was just hair and it would grow back. As long as I stayed breathing at any rate.

"Don't worry, pretty. I'll be back." He gave me a smile that made him look more than a little demented, then he skipped out of the warehouse. Fucking. Skipped.

I looked around and tried to see anything I might be able to use, if I could get free again. My wrists were throbbing and still bleeding, but I worked at the ropes and tape just the same. A doctor could patch me up later, but I had to get out of here first. No matter how much I twisted, turned, or tugged, I couldn't break free.

When Mr. Psycho returned, there was a gleam in his eyes I didn't like. He looked exceedingly pleased with himself. What had he done? The lunatic actually rubbed his hands together like a cartoon villain when he got closer. "Now I'll get everything I want. It's all falling into place."

I wasn't about to ask what he meant. I was too worried about the answer. As long as there was hope he'd let me go at some point, then I could remain somewhat calm. He walked a circle around me. Twice. When he stopped in front of me again, he looked like he was shaking. From excitement? Had he taken drugs and was coming down? I didn't know what the hell was going on, or how I'd make it through this. I hadn't survived those years in Colombia to be taken down by this guy now.

"We're going to make sure he knows I mean business. But first, a gift for the pretty." He pulled out the duct tape, ripped a piece off, then slapped it over my mouth. My eyes went wide and my heart slammed against my ribs. "Now we can play!"

Play? What the fuck kind of playing did he have in mind? I had a feeling it was the sort that would make me scream, and he'd just effectively silenced me. Thanks to my hands being tied, I hadn't had a chance to shove him away. My feet being secured meant kicking wouldn't help either.

My kidnapper pulled out a pocketknife, flicked open the blade, then came even closer. I couldn't stop the tears this time as they slipped down my cheeks. Whatever he was about to do, I was completely helpless. He'd made sure I couldn't attack him again. The one chance I'd had to escape and I'd been captured again.

He grabbed the neckline of my shirt with his hand, pulled it away from my body, then sliced the material until it exposed my breasts. Everything in me went cold. My mind started to drift, and I prepared to shut down like I had before. It had been the only way to survive then, and I worried I'd have to go to that quiet place again. I braced myself for him to touch me, but he didn't. Instead, he sliced the top of one breast with the knife. A shallow cut, but it still throbbed.

"Hmm. This knife just won't do at all. Don't worry, pretty. I have just what we need." He scurried off. I watched as he approached a dark corner of the warehouse. A flash of something gleamed in the shadows, then he returned with a larger, much sharper-looking knife. Before I could react, he began slicing my pants off my body, leaving me in my panties. "Oh. You had to go to the bathroom, didn't you?"

I nodded frantically, hoping he might release me. If he led me to a bathroom, maybe there was a chance I could escape again. Instead, he reached out, gripped my panties, then sliced them off me.

"There! Now you won't have wet nasty fabric against you."

I recoiled, wanting to close my legs. He pulled a phone from his pocket, then waved it front of my face. I eyed it, wondering what he would do next. Was he going to call Beast? With my mouth taped shut, I couldn't scream for help, or tell him what was happening. I couldn't give him a clue to my location.

I yanked my wrists again, but the rope and tape still held tight. I hadn't even loosened it a little, which made my spirits plummet. I had to face reality. Unless this man let me go, or someone came for me, I wasn't leaving until he was ready for me to go. I could only hope when that time came that I was still breathing and wasn't leaving by way of a body bag.

The creep snapped a picture of my face, then backed up and took a full body shot. Humiliation burned through me. He was going to send that to Beast, wasn't he?

A man I barely knew was about to see me nearly naked, exposed and vulnerable. I hated it. Hated this man who was doing these vile things to me. And maybe I hated myself a little too. If I hadn't tried to go to the appointment on my own, then there was a chance I'd still be safe right now.

You're an idiot, Lilian. A big fucking idiot.

"Now. All we have to do is wait for him to ask for my demands. Then the fun begins." The man laughed, but it sounded like something you'd hear in a horror movie.

That's because you're living in one. Again.

Whatever happened, if I made it out of this in one piece, I wanted to make this asshole pay. Any sympathy I might have felt for him, any lenience I'd have given due to him being ill, was now gone. I wanted him to suffer.

Chapter Six

Dragon

"What the fuck do you mean you still can't find her?" I demanded. Okay, so I was on thin ice. You didn't go into someone else's territory, then yell at their Pres. It just wasn't done. Not if you wanted to keep breathing. "I'm sorry. I just… We have to find her."

Beast growled. Literally growled. I wondered if that was why he'd gotten the name *Beast*. If it had anything to do with the bedroom, I really didn't want to know. The thought of Lilian taking shelter with him still lit a fire inside me.

"You're a fucking idiot, Dragon. You had someone sweet like Lilian give herself to you, and you threw it away. Threw *her* away. I'm looking for her. Not for you, but for her. As far as I'm concerned, you can go fuck yourself," Beast said.

"Pres," said a voice at the doorway. I turned and saw a Prospect with a package in his hand. "This just arrived at the gate. Kid said he was paid to drop it off."

"Is he still here?" Beast asked.

"Yep. He's waiting at the gate. Gave him a soda as a bribe."

Beast took the package and opened it. A phone fell out. Had the kidnapper sent it? Were they going to call? If we just knew what they wanted, then maybe I could get Lilian back. Beast pulled a bandana from his back pocket and used it to pick up the phone. He unlocked the screen with a quick swipe, and I watched as the blood drained from his face.

"Motherfucker," he muttered. Then he roared it. "Where's that kid? Find out who paid him. I want to know everything. Where they were, what the person looked like. Every. Fucking. Detail."

The Prospect nodded and took off.

I moved closer, but Beast moved the phone so that I couldn't see anything. "Is that about Lilian?"

"You know damn well it is," he said. "And don't even ask to see it."

"I have a right to know what's being done to the mother of my child." I had a feeling if I called Lilian my woman, he'd try to take my head off. I didn't know what was going on between them, but it was obvious he felt protective of her. I hoped like hell that's all it was. I hadn't even realized she knew the President of the Reckless Kings until now.

Beast looked toward the doorway and bellowed, "Get me Shield!"

Shield. The name was familiar. Then I remembered. Shield was the hacker for the Reckless Kings, and one of the men Outlaw relied on when his hands wouldn't cooperate. I didn't know what a hacker could do with the phone, but if the man could find Lilian, I didn't care how he did it.

Another Prospect came to the door. "Shield isn't at the clubhouse. Do you want me to get him? Or take something to his place?"

Beast slid the phone back into the package, careful not to let me see the screen. Then he handed it to the Prospect. "See if he can trace where this phone came from. I didn't touch it, so if there are prints, they should belong to the man who has Lilian. I want this asshole found. Now."

The guy grabbed the package and left. I studied the President, noting that he looked like he hadn't slept in days. As much as I wanted to be a dick and remind him Lilian was mine and not his, I also knew I needed his help. And it was clear he cared about her well-being.

"You in love with my woman?" I asked, then silently cursed myself. Not what I'd meant to say. Aloud at any rate. I wasn't sure how he'd react to me claiming Lil, especially if he felt something for her.

"No. I'm not in love with Lilian, but I give a shit what happens to her. She was taken on my watch, and it pisses me off." He shuffled some papers around on his desk, and a lock of hair fell from a plain white envelope.

Everything in me went still. "That's Lilian's hair."

He nodded. "I suspected as much. It arrived this morning. Now the phone. I'm a little worried about what he'll send next."

Shit. This guy was escalating fast. I didn't like it.

"You look like hell. There are some empty rooms upstairs. I'll have a Prospect show you and your brothers where to go. Get some rest. If I hear anything, I'll send someone to get you."

"You think I can sleep right now?" I asked.

"No. But I don't want you in the way either. You're emotional and not thinking clearly. I get it. She's yours and that's your kid in her belly. Although you have a shit way of showing you care. Just go chill for a while. Take a shower. Something. Anything that gets you the fuck away from me so I can figure this shit out. They keep sending their clues to me, which makes me think this has to do with my club or me personally. I just can't fit everything together in my head."

"Fine. I'll give you some space and some time. But every second she's gone makes it less likely I'm getting her back."

He stared at me. "I'm aware."

I walked out of his office, caught the attention of a Prospect, and said Beast wanted me to have an empty room. The kid led me upstairs and showed me where I could crash. My brothers could find their own rooms when they were ready. Right now, Wolf was MIA, Colorado was at the bar nursing a beer and chatting with a Reckless King, and Cobra was at a table with three other Reckless Kings.

I went to the truck and grabbed my bags, then carried them to the room. After I shut and locked the door, I pulled out a fresh set of clothes and decided a shower might clear my head. I sure the fuck hoped these rooms came with shampoo and shit because I hadn't thought to pack anything like that. I did have my toothbrush and some deodorant, but I'd damn near left those behind too. It wasn't like I'd been packing for a vacation. The only thought on my mind had been getting to Lilian and bringing her home.

The bathroom was small, but it had a shower stall, sink, and toilet. That's all I needed. I started the water, letting it warm, then checked the cabinet under the sink. I pulled out one of the two towels under there, and found a bottle of shampoo and several bars of soap. The mirrored cabinet over the sink had a few unopened travel-sized toothpastes and four new toothbrushes. Nice to know they took care of their guests.

I grabbed a bar of soap, unwrapped it, then placed it in the shower. There wasn't a shelf or rack where I could place the shampoo, so I just set it in the corner on the floor. There was a shelf over the toilet, so I set the towel up there. A small mat was already next to the shower stall. Since everything else seemed new or clean, and the place smelled like citrus cleanser, I figured the mat was clean too. Not that I was squeamish about that sort of thing.

Stripping out of my clothes, I set my cut on the foot of the bed and dumped the rest on the floor. I shook my head over the wood flooring, and cast a glance around the room. Everything seemed to be of decent quality. There was even a TV hanging on the wall over the dresser. But then the Reckless Kings weren't hurting for money. I kicked my pile of clothes out of the way, then went back to the bathroom. The water had warmed considerably, so I stepped under the spray and slid the frosted door shut.

I used the shampoo to scrub my hair and beard, then let the hot water beat against my neck and shoulders as I braced a hand on the wall. Whoever had Lilian had cut her fucking hair, and I didn't know what the fuck was on that damn phone, but it had to have been bad. If they had hurt her, I'd make them all pay. I'd tear them the fuck apart, then show them why I was called Dragon.

Closing my eyes, I pictured Lilian the way she'd been that last day we'd been together. She'd smiled and been so damn sweet. When she'd asked me to fuck her... shit. I couldn't remember ever wanting something more. She'd been tight. Wet. So fucking perfect. If I could go back and do that day over, I'd have taken her a different way. It would have been amazing to slide into her sweet pussy, then watch her gorgeous tits bounce as I fucked her. With all those generous curves, she'd been well blessed in the tits and ass department. Something I'd noticed the moment I'd realized she was an adult.

I felt like an asshole when my dick started to get hard, but it did that every time I remembered that day. Up to the point where I'd fucked up. But before that had been amazing. I reached for the soap and slicked my palm before grabbing my cock. The way she'd bent over, showing me that luscious ass, and giving me a glimpse of paradise was a sight I saw every night when I closed my eyes. Remembering what it had felt like to slide inside her, I yanked my dick, each stroke harder and faster than the first.

I'd taken her like a man possessed, and maybe I had been. Her scent had filled my nose, the softness of her skin had been a temptation I'd never forget. She'd been dripping wet when I'd taken her. I should have been slow and tender, but I'd lost control, slamming into her. I groaned as cum sprayed over my hand and hit the wall. I kept tugging until the last drops left my balls.

Opening my eyes, I stared at the mess I'd made. It wasn't the first time I'd jerked off to thoughts of Lilian. Shame burned inside me, though. This time was different. She was missing. Possibly hurt, and here I was getting off to memories of our one time together. It made me a sick bastard.

I cleaned up, finished washing, then got out. Once I'd dried off and pulled on fresh clothes, I stretched out on the bed and tried to clear my mind. The release in the shower had served to ease a little of my tension, but I was still no closer to figuring out who had Lilian or where she was. Beast wanted me out of the way, but I wanted answers. I ran a hand over the faded scars over my side and lower abdomen. Ramirez's men had given them to me, and I'd come here fully expecting that bastard had somehow gotten to Lil. If that wasn't the case, then things were even worse.

At least with Ramirez, I'd known what demon I was fighting. I couldn't fight a monster if I didn't know who they were, or why they'd taken my woman. On the way here, I'd learned her purse and phone had been left in her car on the side of the road. Someone had sabotaged her tire. From what the Reckless Kings had seen, it looked like someone had placed spikes across the road, then removed them when they ran off with Lilian. The tire had multiple punctures, and the dirt at the edge of the road had been disturbed, like something had slid through it. She'd been targeted for whatever reason, and they'd counted on her getting out to inspect her tire.

Either she'd frozen despite the self-defense lessons, or they'd knocked her out somehow. Outlaw may have placed a tracker on her phone and car, but that didn't do us a damn bit of good when she didn't have either one with her. When all this was over, I'd be sorely tempted to chip her ass like a puppy, even though I knew it would piss her the hell off. I'd rather her furious and safe, than lose her again. Was she hurting? Had they touched her? Even though she'd survived that before, I didn't know what it would do to her if she had to live through that hell again.

"Where are you, Lil?" I murmured, wishing for some divine intervention. Anything to point me in the right direction. If I had even a clue as to where I should go, I'd barge in there, guns blazing, and get her back to safety.

But I didn't. I was lost, wandering in the dark, with no fucking clue how to get her home. My phone rang and I realized I'd left it in my pants pocket. I got up and dug it out, frowning when I saw Grizzly's name. If he wanted an update, or some good news, I didn't have shit for him.

"Hey, Pres."

"Why is it quiet where you are?" he demanded.

"Because Beast said I was in the fucking way and sent me to my room." I snorted. If he weren't the Pres for this club, I'd have told him to fuck off and stayed where I was. "They don't know shit, Griz. No fucking clue who has her, where they've taken her, what they want. They're just sitting here like dumbasses waiting for clues to fall into their hands."

He growled but remained quiet. I could hear him pacing and wondered if he was in his office at the clubhouse, or the one in his home. With Shella still there, and likely upset over the latest turn of events, I'd be willing to bet he was at his house, trying to keep her calm.

"They sent a chunk of her hair," I said softly. "Looked like they hacked it off with a knife. And a phone, but Beast wouldn't show me what was on it. Whatever the fuck it was, it had to be bad. He lost a few shades of color."

"Her hair and a phone. Jesus. If they start sending pieces of her body, and I find out this has anything to do with the Reckless Kings and not us, I may very well rip Beast apart with my bare hands."

I knew the feeling. Except Grizzly was our President, which meant he could go toe to toe with Beast and still keep the man's respect. If I tried that shit, the entire Reckless Kings would be down my throat and beating my ass, or trying to. The more I thought about this, the more I knew this had to be about the Reckless Kings and not Devil's Fury. No one had known Lil was here. The kidnapper had to have snatched her, having seen her at this compound. He probably believed she belonged to someone here. The fact the items were being delivered to Beast made me think the idiot thought Lil was the Pres' ol' lady, or at least his girlfriend.

"This isn't on us," I said. "In my gut, I know it ties to Beast. I just don't know how or why."

"I'll have Outlaw reach out to Shield and see if he can find out something for us. Any news I get, I'll pass on to you, but if you hear so much as a word about Lilian, you call me. Understood?"

"Yes, Pres." My throat was tight. "You know I'll do everything I can to get her back. Even trade myself if that's what it takes."

"I know. Just get her back in one piece, Dragon. I'm not ready to lose my daughter."

I heard the part he didn't say. If he hadn't lost his temper over her being pregnant, then she wouldn't have run. She'd left because she worried that I'd get hurt, which made my stomach feel like acid was bubbling inside it. I was every bit as much to blame for this shit, and I could own up to it.

I only hoped I got the chance to apologize to her in person.

A little while later, my phone chimed. When I checked the message from Outlaw, I wished I hadn't. Shield must have shared the picture from the phone Beast had received. It was an image of Lil that I knew I'd never unsee. The fucker had stripped her. Cut her. Tied her to a damn chair with her legs splayed and every part of her on display. I gripped my phone so hard I heard the case crack.

Whoever this fucker was, he was dead. No one did this shit to my woman and got away with it. Fuck giving in to his demands. If he finally sent a message that asked for something, I'd be happy to respond. I'd torture the shit out of him, then shove a stick of dynamite up his ass. He'd picked the wrong woman to kidnap and abuse.

I could feel the flames of my anger flickering in my veins, bubbling under my skin, ready to burst free. This asshole was mine even if he didn't know it yet. His time was coming. And if he hurt Lil more than he already had, if the worst happened, I'd make him scream for days. Weeks. It would be the lullaby I heard before I drifted to sleep at night, knowing that he was paying for his sins.

"I'm coming for you and nothing can save you," I vowed, looking at the image on my phone one more time. I was sending this fucker straight to hell.

Chapter Seven

Lilian

I'd pissed myself. Anger and humiliation filled me at the indignity I'd had to suffer at the hands of the crazy man pacing the warehouse. I didn't know how long I'd been here, but since I'd woken that first time the sun had risen twice. So, at least two days. Maybe longer. He hadn't fed me. Had grudgingly gave me some sips of water here and there, but that was it. No food. No bathroom. And when I did manage to sleep, it was while I was tied to the damn chair.

No, I didn't pity him anymore. Didn't wish that he'd get help for whatever illness he had. Now I just wanted him dead, but first I wanted him to experience everything he'd done to me, and then some. I'd never been a vindictive person. Until now.

I'd never stopped fighting. My wrists were so swollen and bloody I worried an infection was going to set in. This place was disgusting. But I'd finally loosened my bonds again. Enough that I managed to slip a hand free. I kept my arms pinned behind my back, not wanting the man to discover I was close to escaping. He muttered to himself in four different voices as he walked the length of the warehouse.

Suddenly, he came to a stop and stared at me. "They need a better message. That's all. I didn't make it clear enough."

The hairs on my nape prickled. He'd hacked off my hair. Taken a picture of me splayed and naked. What the fuck was he going to do now? He came closer, his eyes wild and feverish. My body tensed, but he leaned down and picked up the panties he'd cut off me. When I realized what he was going to do, I slammed my eyes shut, but I could still hear him. The sound of him yanking his dick made me want to throw up.

He laughed maniacally. "There. A nice little present for your Beast. I'll just have this delivered and see what happens. Surely he can't ignore this!"

I didn't think Beast would have ignored anything he'd sent so far, which made me wonder... had the idiot even given him a way to respond? I knew the man was unhinged, but this was getting ridiculous. He shoved the soiled panties into an envelope, and raced to the door, only pausing a moment to waggle his fingers at me.

"Back soon, pretty."

The door shut behind him and I immediately relaxed. I pulled my arms from behind me and tried not to scream in agony. My fingers felt cold and numb, and painful prickles raced from my shoulders to my hands. I managed to pull the tape from my mouth, then worked to get my ankles free.

I was now fully naked and my clothes were sliced to pieces. I had nothing to wear, and running outside as I was could be risky. But if I stayed, I had no doubt that he'd eventually hurt me far worse. Maybe even kill me if he didn't get what he wanted. Standing nearly took me to my knees, but I managed to stagger my way to the door. I eased it open, wincing as the metal hinges creaked, but a quick glance outside didn't show a single person within viewing distance.

I crept outside, moving slow at first. When no one jumped out at me, and the crazy man seemed to truly be gone, I moved faster. As quick as my aching limbs would carry me. I saw the street again, the one I'd tried to reach before. My heart raced as I wondered if I'd make it this time. I eventually broke free of the warehouses and turned down the street. This area of town didn't look like it was the best, but I'd take my chances. If anything, maybe a cop would drive by and stop to arrest me for public indecency. There was a gas station on the corner and I ran inside, hoping whoever worked there might be nice enough to let me make a call. And maybe get a drink and some food. Clothes would be nice too.

I gasped for breath when I collapsed against the counter, the clerk not looking even slightly fazed. Then again, judging the rough neighborhood, this probably wasn't the worst thing she'd ever seen. The woman popped her gum and watched me, waiting. When I finally thought I could talk without passing out, I asked for the phone.

"Please. I need to call for help," I said.

Her gaze skimmed me up and down. "You running from a man?"

Did she get naked women in here all the time who were bleeding all over the floor? What the hell kind of place was this?

I nodded. "Yes, but not mine. He snatched me when my car got a flat. I need to call my dad."

Her eyebrow arched. "Yours or the baby's?"

I glanced down at my stomach and cradled my baby. "Mine. He'll tell everyone else whatever they need to know. Just, please… I need to call before the man comes looking for me. He's completely crazy."

She sighed and pulled a cordless phone from behind her, then slid it across the counter. "Better be a local call."

Shit. It wasn't. "Um. Change of plan. Do you by any chance know how to reach the Reckless Kings?"

Now that got a reaction. She paled a little and stopped chewing her gum. Her hand trembled as she took the phone back, dialed a number, and handed it over. I knew the club wasn't out doing good deeds left and right, they were outlaws just like my dad's club, but her reaction seemed a little extreme. It was also curious she knew their number by heart. Just what sort of reputation did Beast and his men have around here? And what was their connection to her or the town in general?

"You make sure they know I helped you," she said.

Confusing, but whatever. If she had a problem with them, that was on her. I just needed to get the hell out of here. And fast. The sixth ring someone answered.

"What the hell do you want?" a man asked.

"I need to speak to Beast."

"Yeah, right. Sure you do. Look, you probably suck cock like a pro, but he's busy."

"Wait!" I yelled, hoping he wouldn't hang up. "This is Lilian. Grizzly's daughter."

I heard a muttered *shit*. "Where are you?"

I looked at the clerk. "What's the address of this place?"

She reached over and took the phone from me. After rattling off the address, she told them to hurry up and get me. Then she hung up on whoever had answered. If she was scared of them, that probably hadn't been a way to endear herself to the club. If I'd learned anything it was that big, growly, alpha bikers didn't like it when you hung up on them. I'd done it more than once since living with the Devil's Fury. It was still the fastest way to piss off my dad.

She eyed me again, then heaved a sigh. Walking around the counter, she went over to a display and dug through a pile of cheap T-shirts. Yanking one off the shelf, she handed it to me. I gratefully pulled it over my head, happy it went down to mid-thigh. When she handed me a bottle of cold water, I nearly cried. I tried to sip it slowly so I wouldn't get sick, but it was the best thing I'd tasted in days.

While I waited, I tried to keep away from the windows and yet still keep the street within view. I didn't want Mr. Crazy Kidnapper to find me. If he did, I wasn't sure if the store clerk would let me hide in the back or not. She didn't seem overly sympathetic to my plight. For all I knew, she got women in here weekly claiming to have been kidnapped.

I heard the pipes before I saw the first bike. Beast pulled into the lot with three other Reckless Kings, a big truck, and... My heart gave a hard thump when I saw several cuts from Devil's Fury. When had Outlaw shared my location? I'd told Dad I was okay, but I hadn't said where I was staying because I'd known he would send someone after me. I wondered if the Reckless Kings had called when I'd gone missing. If that was the case, I knew my dad had to be frantic.

Beast was the first one through the door. "Little chick, where are you?" I hurried over and he quickly wrapped me in a hug. "Thank fuck. Scared ten years off my damn life."

"I'm fine."

"No, she's not," said another voice. I looked over and eyed the Reckless King with *Copper* stitched on his cut. "She's bleeding."

Oh. Right. I hadn't even noticed the pain in my wrists until he'd brought it up. Now they throbbed and hurt like a bitch. Beast set me back and looked me over, taking my hands in his, he studied the wounds on my wrists. "Were you tied up with ropes or tape?" he asked.

"Both. I managed to work free of the ropes, then kicked my kidnapper in the balls and ran like hell. He caught me the first time. I didn't give up, though. This time I waited until he left, got myself free, and ran here."

He gave a snort that turned into full out laughter. "Good job, little chick. You remember where you were held?"

I described the area as best I could and Beast sent his men to check it out. The Devil's Fury members came forward, and when I saw Dragon was with them, I fought damn hard not to cry. I wouldn't show weakness! He'd already ripped out my heart and stomped on it. I'd be damned before I let him know how much I liked seeing him right now, knowing that he'd come for me.

"Lil," he said, holding out a hand. "You okay?"

I gave a short nod. "I'll be fine."

"We'll let a doctor decide that," Beast said. "I'll call the place you were supposed to go three days ago and have them work you in."

"Wait." I looked from him to the setting sun outside and back again. "Three days? I've been gone for *three* days?"

Beast hesitated a moment. "Little chick, I think you need to start talking. What happened? How do you not know how much time has passed? You've been gone over seventy-two hours."

And that's all it took before my bladder decided it was in a state of emergency. I squeaked and ran for the hall with the bathroom sign.

"You need a key," yelled out the clerk.

"Then give me one!" I screamed. "I need it ten minutes ago!"

It was Beast who came after me, key in hand. He unlocked the bathroom, surveyed the area, then stepped back and let me inside. I nearly gagged as I looked the place over. By some miracle I managed to squat over the toilet without touching it, then used some toilet paper to push the handle down to flush. After I washed my hands, I tapped the door with my toe because there was no damn way I was touching that door handle. Hell, just knowing my bare feet were touching the floor was enough to make me want to throw up.

"Let's get you out of here, then we'll talk," he said.

I let him lead me outside, but he took me over to a truck that was all too familiar. I hadn't recognized it when it had first pulled in. With Dragon in the driver's seat. "Beast, I..." His grip tightened. "Fine. I'll go with him, but I won't like it."

Beast chuckled. "Don't have to like it, little chick. But he'll keep you safe, and you're sure as hell not riding on a bike while you're pregnant. Not to mention nearly naked. Now give me the condensed version of what happened so I can figure out our next step."

I explained about my tire going flat and getting snatched off the road. How I'd woken up in a warehouse, tied to a chair. I tried to describe the man who had taken me, and told him he'd used Charlotte to get to Beast.

"He didn't make any sense," I said. "But it seems he blames you for something that cost him *her*. I don't think the *her* was in reference to Charlotte."

Beast nodded. "We'll figure it out. I'll text Dragon the address of the doctor. He technically has an office inside the clubhouse, but he's had back-to-back appointments at his place in town. Plus he mentioned something about an ultrasound, and he doesn't keep that type of equipment at the compound. You get checked out, then head back. In the meantime, my crew will find the asshole who took you and we'll get some answers."

"Good luck. I think he's suffering either from multiple personality disorder, or he's had some sort of mental breakdown." Possibly both.

Beast shut the door, then thumped the top of the truck. Once I was buckled, Dragon pulled out of the parking space and out onto the road. His phone chirped and he tossed it to me. "Passcode is 7894."

I glanced at him as I input the numbers. I read off the address of the doctor's office, then set his phone to give him directions. When I tried to hand it back, he shook his head.

"You want me to hold it while you drive?" I asked.

"No. I want you to go through all the texts and pictures."

What the hell was he up to? I opened the messages first, noting that most were from other club members. Some were from names I didn't recognize, but not a single one was from a woman. Didn't mean anything. He could have deleted all the booty call texts before he got here. But it was the pictures that made me cry.

"Is this... a nursery?" I asked, flipping through the images.

"Yep. For our baby." My gaze met his, but he quickly looked back at the road. "I know I fucked up. I never should have said what I did, and I've felt sick over it ever since. It was wrong, but I was trying to do the right thing. For you. Lil, you deserve so much better than me."

"You said all that to push me away?" I asked slowly. "It wasn't true?"

"No, it wasn't true. I hadn't been with a woman recently when I..." His cheeks flushed a little and he cleared his throat. "Anyway, I lied so that you wouldn't try to hold onto me. Not because I didn't want you, but because I wasn't worthy of you. I'm still not."

My throat felt tight and I tried to swallow. "And now? Have there been women since then?"

His features tightened, and I dreaded his response. I shouldn't have asked, not if I wasn't prepared for the answer. I wanted to hear that he'd not touched another woman, hadn't wanted anyone else. It was foolish to think that. Dragon was attractive, single, and he'd never lacked for female company. I'd heard all about the many women he had in a night. Just not recently.

"I let some club whores sit on my lap now and then, at least those first few weeks. I felt them up a little." He glanced at me. "But I didn't fuck them. My dick hasn't been inside anyone but you since that day."

"Not even their mouths?" I asked, remembering his cruel words about getting sucked off the night before we were together.

He winced. "I deserved that. And no, not even their mouths. Only action my dick has seen in months is my own hand. Saying those things to you was the hardest fucking thing I've ever done, but I saw the way you looked at me after." *How I'd looked at him*? I must have appeared as confused as I felt because he answered my unspoken question. "You had hope etched all over your face, like you expected me to go tell your dad I wanted to keep you. I knew that wouldn't be a good thing for either of us, but especially you."

I was twenty-two and everyone thought they knew what was best for me. Grizzly had pushed me to get a college degree, and while he'd been right about that, it irked me that he hadn't given me the time to figure it out for myself. Maybe if I'd been louder about it, like Shella, things would have been different. I hadn't had that much fight in me at the time. Dragon pushed me away because it was in my best interest. Outlaw tracked my damn car so he'd know where I was, and therefore my father would too, every second of the day.

"When do I get to decide what's best for me?" I asked quietly. "When I'm twenty-five? Thirty? Or will I die never having been given the choice of making my own decisions without some man telling me he knows what's best for me? You. My dad. Hell, probably every Devil's Fury officer, member, and even the Prospects think they know what's best for me."

"Damn," he muttered. "I wasn't trying to treat you like a child, Lil."

I knew he hadn't done it on purpose. None of them did. They wanted to protect me, keep me safe. I loved that, to an extent, but I could be sheltered by their strength and still be able to make decisions about my future. If I'd wanted to be with Dragon, and he'd wanted me in return, why was that a bad thing? Yes, I was glad I'd gone to college, even if it was only for two years, but it would have been nice to decide that for myself and not feel pushed into going.

"In all the time I've been with the Devil's Fury, I've never wanted to be touched by a man. Even when Grizzly hugs me, there are times I tense up and my mind goes back to Colombia. It was different with you.

When you touched me, even just during our lessons, I burned for more. I wanted you to kiss me, to make love to me. I just wanted you and only you." I sighed. "I may never be able to stand having another man touch me for the rest of my life, Dane. You made me feel safe. Special. Until you didn't."

We came to a stop in the doctor's office parking lot and he shut off the engine. When I reached for my door handle, he placed a hand on my arm to stop me. The look in his eyes nearly ripped my heart in half. Before I knew it, I was sobbing and being pulled against his chest. His hand ran through my hair.

"I'm so fucking sorry, Lil. If I'd just grown a set and admitted I felt something for you, that I wanted more, then none of this would have happened. You ran off and got hurt because I was weak. I'm sorry, baby. I'm sorry." He just kept murmuring *I'm sorry* over and over.

Eventually my tears subsided and I drew back enough to hold his gaze. I reached up and placed my hand on his cheek. "I forgive you, as long you try to never hurt me like that again. Your rejection was the most painful thing I've ever experienced."

He blanched and gave a quick nod. "Promise, Lil. I'll do better. Just give me a chance."

"All right. Come on. Let's go see if our baby is okay."

He pressed a kiss to my forehead, then got out of the truck and walked around to my side. I'd opened the door, but he was there to help me down. He carried me into the clinic, his arm pinning the shirt beneath my ass cheeks so I didn't flash anyone, and we were immediately ushered into the back. Not before I saw a few startled looks cast my way, and I realized I must look like hell. I only hoped they didn't think Dragon was responsible.

A nurse took my vitals and asked some basic questions, then left a gown on the padded table. After she left, Dragon helped me change, and then we waited. I only wished I'd had time to take a shower. I was filthy, smelled horrible, and still had pee on me from being in the chair for so long.

Chapter Eight

Dragon

Seeing her battered wrists, the dirt smudging her skin, the slice across her breast, and the tangled state of her hair made me realize that I was damn lucky right now. Not only was she okay, but she'd not been afraid when she was taken. This time she'd fought back, and she'd escaped on her own. Twice, apparently. I was so fucking proud of her.

The doctor had tended to her wounds and bandaged them, and thankfully hadn't said a damn word about her needing a shower. If they'd had one in this place, I'd have demanded they let her use it to clean up. I knew it bothered her. I could see it in her eyes and the way she held herself.

But right now I wasn't looking at Lil. I was staring at a very tiny human on a computer screen. No, not just one. Two tiny humans. My Lil was having twins. I had two babies on the way. The baby currently on the screen kept moving, not letting us get too long a look before shifting again. It felt like my heart swelled as I looked at the little face, hands, and feet.

"Ah ha!" the doctor said, freezing the image on the screen and zooming in. "Congratulations, Baby A is a girl."

A daughter? *Holy shit!* Forget a second crib, I needed to go buy more ammo and guns. I stared in awe at the little human on the screen. Whatever it took, I'd keep her safe. And hopefully do a better job than I'd done with Lilian.

"And Baby B," the doctor said, pressing on Lil's stomach to reposition the other baby, "is a boy! One of each! Aren't the two of you lucky?"

"Yeah," I said. "At least I'll have some help keeping the boys away from my daughter. Just have to train her brother young."

Lilian squeezed my hand and the doctor laughed. He wiped the goop off Lil's stomach, then I helped her sit up.

"Everything looks good," the doctor said. "Find an OBGYN close to your home and stick with them through this. I can make a few recommendations if you'd like, or if you already have one picked out, just make sure you schedule an appointment soon. Call my office with their information and we'll send over a report from today's visit."

"Thank you, Dr. Cooper," I said, reaching out to shake his hand.

"I would recommend that you give her a day or two of rest before you make that long drive back home. She needs to rehydrate as well, and eat a few balanced meals. After what she's been through, it's a miracle she didn't lose the babies. Once you get back home, no more road trips. And by that I mean, try to keep travel to within an hour of your residence, and keep her as stress free as possible, and good luck dealing with pregnancy hormones. I have four kids and I swear my normally docile wife turned into a barracuda with each pregnancy."

Lil glared at him and I had no doubt she was contemplating giving him a kick on his wife's behalf, but thankfully she refrained. I helped her off the table, and once the doctor left, she removed the gown and put the T-shirt back on. Clenching my hands at my sides, I had to fight the urge to reach over and place my hand on her belly. Two babies. Seeing them on the screen made it all more real. I led her out to the front. The receptionist said the bill was covered, which meant

I owed the Reckless Kings yet another debt, but since it was for Lilian, I'd take it.

I didn't know where we'd stay the next day or two, but I'd figure it out back at the Reckless Kings' compound. Beast had let Lilian stay at his house, but I wasn't so sure he'd welcome both of us. I hoped they had some guest quarters somewhere, but if not, I'd find the most secure hotel in the area.

I handed my phone back to Lilian. "Call your dad."

She found him in my contacts, then put the phone on speaker while it rang. When Grizzly answered, he sounded tired as hell.

"How is she?" he asked.

"I'm fine, Dad," Lilian said. "But I hope you plan to have a big room set up at your house for your grandchildren."

"Why is that?" he asked.

"Because there are two," she said. "I'm having twins. A girl and a boy."

Griz cleared his throat. "That's amazing, Lilian. Is Dragon with you?"

"I'm right here," I said. "The doctor said she needed to rest a day or two before we head back. She's dehydrated and hungry as well. I'm going to see if Beast has a place we can stay. If not, I'll find a hotel. The doc said no more road trips once we're home."

"Just get my girl home safe. That's all I ask. And, Lilian?"

"Yeah, Dad?" she asked.

"If you weren't pregnant, I'd tan your hide for running off like that. You could have died. What if someone had forced you back into the life you had before? Please don't leave town again without an escort," Grizzly said.

I was impressed he'd said please. I knew he wouldn't really give her a choice. He'd have her shadowed even if she didn't like it, but at least he made it sound like she had the option of going on her own. Hell, after this, I might not let her out of my sight for a solid week. Nothing had ever scared me as much as hearing that she was missing. It had been bad enough not knowing where she'd run off to, but she'd been safe. Supposedly.

"We'll be home soon, Dad."

Lilian ended the call and I inwardly winced. Griz wouldn't be too happy about that. Then again, he doted on his girls, so if anyone could get away with hanging up on him, it would be Lilian. As we neared the gates of the Reckless Kings' compound, a Prospect opened the gate and let us through. I stopped in front of the clubhouse, unsure where to go.

"My things are at Beast's house," Lilian said.

As if I needed a reminder she'd gone to him for help, instead of coming to tell me she was pregnant. Yes, I'd dug my own hole when it came to her, but it still hurt. I let her point the way to the President's house, and I stopped in his driveway. The man must have been expecting us because he leaned against a porch post, waiting. Lilian got up and went up to him, giving him a quick hug before disappearing inside.

What the fuck? I hadn't gotten a fucking hug until she'd fallen apart in the damn truck.

I got out slower, and stopped at the foot of the steps. "The doc said she can't travel for a day or two."

"She's got a room here already."

I shoved my hands into my pockets. "Realize that. Where am I staying?"

"Heard what you said to her. That was a fucking dick move. Then I saw the way you looked at her. She know you love her?"

Whoa. I never said a damn thing about loving her. I cared about her, didn't want to lose her, but... *Shit*. I did love her. Beast just shook his head and went inside, motioning for me to follow. He led me to a small guest room, and I saw Lilian sitting on the edge of the bed.

"The two of you can stay here. But just saying, no sex in my house. If I'm not getting any, neither are you," he said, then walked off.

Lilian's cheeks pinked. I gave her a reassuring smile and moved farther into the room. I'd packed my shit expecting to track her down and shoot some people, among other things. Instead, I only needed my clothes. Although... I did wonder if Beast's men had found her kidnapper and what would happen to him. As much as I wanted to tear that fucker apart, right now, Lilian needed me.

She stood and came closer, reaching up to put her hand on my cheek. "Go ask him."

"Ask what?"

She rolled her eyes. "You know damn well what. It's written all over your face. You want to know if they found the guy, and quite frankly, so do I. But you can skip any gory details if they're going to hurt him. I just want to know if he's been picked up, or I won't feel safe. I'll get cleaned up while you do that."

I kissed her softly, then went in search of Beast. I found him in the kitchen, sipping a cup of what smelled like coffee.

"Did you find who did this?" I asked.

"Yep. His name is Warren Bruce. He used to be part of a rival club, until he got too crazy even for them. They kicked his ass out, stripped his colors, and apparently he's even more batshit crazy than before."

All right. So that gave me the who, but that wasn't enough. I didn't have any idea who Warren Bruce was, or why he'd chosen Lilian as his victim. I just knew I was fucking pissed about it.

"Why did he do it?" I asked.

Beast sighed. "My fault. Sort of. During a negotiation with the Pres of Bruce's club, I caught the eye of the VP's sister. I never encouraged her, but I guess she had it in her head that she could have me. Shot her down. Multiple times. I heard the VP finally married the bitch off to some other club as a way to cement their alliance. Only an officer would do, so she's with their Sergeant-at-Arms."

"And this guy blames you for… What exactly?" I asked, feeling really damn confused.

"He loved her. Honestly, the guy seems to have about six people inside his head. Possibly more. I have no idea what he was thinking, or why he blamed me. He wanted her, and when she was given to another club, he decided he wanted revenge. Who knows if she even knew this asshole's name?"

I knew that love could make people do stupid shit, but this was taking it too far. Lilian had thought he was mentally ill, and maybe he was. Didn't mean he had the right to go around hurting other people. He still needed to be held accountable.

"Where is he?" I asked.

"My boys were going to play with him a little, but I couldn't do it. Charlotte never saw this side of him. There's no way she would have let him get her pregnant, much less planned to leave the area with him, if she'd known he was this unhinged. Somehow, he managed to hide his other personalities when he was around her. She's pregnant and doesn't need the stress."

"You have *seen* Charlotte since all this happened, right?" I asked, a weird feeling twisting my gut. If this guy was going to use Lil as bait, and thought Charlotte was useless to him, would he have kept her around? After the things he'd done to Lilian, I could only imagine what he would do to Charlotte once he determined he didn't need her anymore.

Beast froze. He pulled his phone from his pocket and dialed a number. After a few moments, he ended the call and dialed again. He did that a dozen times before he started cursing. "Brick is going to fucking lose it. She's his baby sister, which is why I never went there. Or part of the reason, anyway. If Charlotte had wanted me to fight for her, then I'd have told Brick to shut the fuck up. But she moved on easily enough."

"I hope you find her."

Beast charged out of the house and I heard the pipes of his bike as he took off. If they found Charlotte, I hoped she was in good health. I also worried for her baby. If it didn't belong to Beast and it belonged to the kidnapper, would it have mental health issues at some point too? That wasn't a road I wished any parent to travel. Or the kid.

I turned to find Lilian behind me, her face pale and her eyes filled with sadness. Her hair was still wet from her shower, and I saw the section that was shorter than the rest. "She's gone, isn't she?"

"Don't know that, baby. Beast is going to find her. Right now, I need you to rest. Remember what the doctor said? You need to try and remain as stress free as possible. Worrying over Charlotte is doing the opposite. Are you hungry? Thirsty?"

"Maybe a little of both."

"I'll get Wolf to find a place with soup and sandwiches. Sound good? If you went a few days without nourishment, I'm worried anything greasy or too rich would just come back up." She sank onto a kitchen chair and held out her hand. I took it, kneeling next to her. "What is it, Lil?"

"I'm sorry I didn't tell you I was pregnant," she said. "If I had, if I'd given you a chance, then maybe none of this would have happened. Maybe the Reckless Kings would have kept Charlotte safe."

"Or they may not have known anything was wrong until it was too late." I leaned closer and pressed my lips to hers. "Don't blame yourself, baby. No one does. Least of all me. Am I upset you didn't tell me? Sure. I also take responsibility for my part in all this. I pushed you away when I shouldn't have."

"No more secrets?" she asked.

"No more. Unless it's club business. I'm still not telling you that no matter how much you pester me."

Lilian leaned into me, wrapping her arms around my neck. "I love you, Dane. You broke my heart that day, but I still loved you. It's why I left. I thought if I was gone maybe my dad wouldn't hurt you for getting me pregnant. I didn't want anything to happen to you."

I tightened my hold on her. I knew now that she'd loved me the day she'd given herself to me, and I'd treated her like shit. Even if I spent the rest of my life treating her like a damn queen, it wouldn't be enough. "I love you too, Lil. So much. Why don't I find some scissors and I can try to even out your hair?"

She gave me a slight smile. I knew how much pride she'd taken in her hair. I couldn't remove what she'd been through with a quick trim, but at least I could take away one of the visible reminders. Her hair would be shorter all the way around, but maybe she could pretend she'd just gotten a haircut and not that it had been cut from necessity. It had to be better than a huge chunk being so much shorter than the rest, especially since the ass had taken it off near the front.

"It won't be perfect," I warned, "but it should be close to even until you can get to a salon. Or wherever you go to have your hair done."

I ran my fingers through her hair. Probably best to cut it while it was still wet. It felt wrong digging through shit in Beast's house, but I eventually found some scissors that seemed sharp enough. Lil brought me her brush and I did the best I could. Seeing her hair fall on the floor made my stomach twist. She'd been growing it for so long, and I had to admit I loved her hair. I knew it would grow back, but it felt like just another way I'd failed her. If I hadn't been a dick, none of this would have happened. Didn't matter what she said. She might not blame me, but I did.

When I was finished, I swept up the mess, and tried to assess Lil. She was quiet. Almost too quiet. I noticed she fingered the ends of her hair, but her eyes were vacant. I fucking hated what this asshole had done to her. She'd been doing so much better. At least, she'd seemed better. She had a job, family, friends. Now it seemed like she was retreating into herself the way she'd done when we'd first brought her home.

I knelt at her feet, taking her hands in mine. I squeezed, slowly applying pressure until she looked at me. "Lil, it's over. You're safe. And as soon as you can travel, we'll go home."

"It's over for me, but what about Charlotte?" she asked.

I shook my head, not knowing how to answer that. I really wanted to rip apart the fucker who had taken her, but if Charlotte meant something to Beast, which it seemed she did, then I knew he'd probably squeeze the life from the guy before I even had a chance to get in the room. I wanted vengeance for all she'd suffered. Having her see that side of me was another matter. She knew I was capable of doing bad things, but she'd never witnessed it. Even if she wasn't in the room with me, she'd know that I hurt him. Maybe even killed him. I didn't want her to see me differently, not in that way.

"What do you need, Lil? Whatever it is, I'll make it happen. Just say the word."

She took a shaky breath and held my gaze. "I want him to pay. Make him pay, Dane."

Holy shit. That was the last thing I'd expected my sweet woman to say. "Babe, are you sure? Do you know what you're asking?"

She nodded. "I know what you do. I've heard the whispers, even when I wasn't supposed to be listening. Don't let him ever hurt anyone else. I want him to hurt. To be humiliated. And I want him to die."

If that's what she wanted, what she needed, then I'd give it to her. I studied her face, looking for any signs that she was just talking out her ass and didn't really want this, but I saw determination in her gaze. She really wanted me to hurt the fucker. Kill him.

"When Wolf gets here, I'll have him stay with you and I'll see where they put this asshole. I'm not leaving you alone, though. Don't even fucking ask that of me."

She reached out and ran her fingers through my beard. Leaning in closer, I brushed my lips over hers. I tried to go slow. Be gentle. One taste and I knew I'd made a mistake. I thrust my tongue between her lips and ravaged her mouth, making sure she damn well knew she was mine. I might not be able to claim her the way I wanted right now, but this would do. It would give her something to think about at the least.

Whatever it took, I'd make sure she felt safe again.

Chapter Nine

Lilian

My lips still tingled from kissing Dragon. The man was lethal, and not just in the killing kind of way. Although, I had no doubt he'd keep his word and make sure my kidnapper paid in blood. It was wrong of me to ask that of him, but I'd lived with bikers long enough to know he didn't mind getting his hands dirty. Maybe it would put a stain on my soul to request a man's death, but I had to hope that by ending his life I was saving others. In some way, I felt it would balance the scales. One bad soul to keep countless good souls safe.

Beast hadn't returned yet, and I worried that something really bad had happened to Charlotte. I hoped they found her safe somewhere, but with the way the crazy person had been ranting, I didn't think that was likely. I felt useless. I hadn't learned anything that would help them. I couldn't go out and help look for her. I might have gotten away, but now what? Just sit here? I couldn't keep my mind clear of everything I'd been through, and wondering if Charlotte had been through worse.

"You're too tense, Lil," Dragon said as he tried to tug me closer. We'd settled in to watch a movie while we waited on Wolf to arrive with food. I didn't know what was taking so long, and the more time that passed, the less chance Dragon had to do what needed to be done.

I knew what would ease my *tension*, not to mention pass the time and get me out of my head, but I also knew he'd never go for it. Dragon had been so careful with me since we'd left the doctor's office. Honestly, it was a side of him I'd never seen. Before the day it had all gone wrong, he'd been careful in a different way. Trying not to touch me for fear of scaring me, yet making sure I knew how to defend myself if I got into trouble or had some handsy asshole bothering me.

If anyone else had been here with me, I'd have been putting some space between us. Even though I'd hugged Beast earlier, I hadn't felt as at ease as I had previously. The man who had taken me hadn't just scared me and humiliated me, he'd stolen what little confidence I'd gained. Men had still made me uncomfortable, but not as much as before. I'd gotten better over the years. Until now.

And yet, having Dragon pressed against me, having him touch me didn't send me running. If anything, I wanted to lean in closer. I needed more than just his arm around me. The way he'd kissed me in the kitchen, everything inside me had warmed and my body had craved his touch. Then he'd pulled back and I knew he wouldn't be repeating it anytime soon. He was treating me as if I were broken. Maybe I was. A little. But I knew that only Dragon could put me back together. He'd been the one to do it before, and he could do it again.

"Do you regret kissing me in the kitchen?" I asked.

His body tensed and slowly turned his head toward me. "Why would you ask that?"

"I could feel you retreating afterward. And your arm is around me, but it's… it's more like a friend is holding me than the man who claims to love me."

He shut his eyes and I felt his body shake, then I realized he was laughing at me. I smacked his chest with the back of my hand. It wasn't funny. Not even a little. At least, to me it wasn't.

Dragon took my hand and pressed it over the zipper of his jeans. "Babe, does that feel even a little like I think of you as a friend?"

His cock twitched under my touch and my heart kicked in my chest. "No. But I don't understand."

He lifted me onto his lap, his arms around me. If only he'd held me like this before. It's what I'd wanted, what I'd hoped for when he'd taken me that day. He'd been rough and demanding, but it hadn't scared me. I'd wanted him, and still did. I'd felt so embarrassed when even weeks later I tried to get myself off to thoughts of how he'd felt inside me, believing he'd just used me and didn't want to make me his.

"Lil, the doctor said you need to rest. Do you really think he'd give the green light for sex right now?"

I chewed on my lip. "You could be gentle."

Dragon arched his eyebrows. Okay. Maybe he couldn't be gentle. I'd gotten off on how alpha he'd been the one and only time we'd been together, and I got wet just thinking about it. But he was right. The doctor probably wouldn't think it was a good idea. It didn't make me want him any less, or ease the ache that was now starting to build between my thighs. My clit pulsed and under Dragon's intense gaze, I felt my nipples harden.

"Beast said no sex in his house," Dragon reminded me.

I wanted to scream, *But he's not here*! He tipped his head, then tapped my thigh. I stood up and he rose from the couch. Taking my hand, he led me back to the bedroom I'd used previously. Dragon shut the door and twisted the lock, then leaned against it, arms folded.

"Strip," he said. "Everything off. Right the fuck now."

My pulse raced and my fingers trembled as I hastened to comply. If it had been anyone other than Dragon, I'd have balked and tried to run. But this was *my* Dragon, my Dane. The only man I'd ever love or ever want.

He jerked his chin toward the bed behind me and I sat on the edge. Under his steely gaze, I hastened to the center of the bed. Dragon pulled off his boots, then stood at the end of the bed. He tapped my ankle.

"Knees up and spread. Feet flat on the bed," he said.

My heart raced as I complied.

"Hands over your head, Lil. You don't fucking touch me. Got it? You reach for me, and I'll use my belt to tie your hands down."

I sucked in a sharp breath and stared at him. Was he serious? Yeah. The heated look he gave me was confirmation enough. He'd not only do it, but he'd get off on it. I lifted my hands over my head and gripped the headboard. Dragon put his knee on the bed, then crawled a little closer. The fact I was completely bare and he was still fully clothed added a hint of naughtiness to the moment.

Dragon dragged a finger down my pussy and I tried hard not to whimper and beg. He parted the lips, then blew on my clit. "So pretty. And mine. Say it, Lil."

"Yours."

"What's mine?" he asked.

"I… I'm yours."

He held my gaze. "And?"

I didn't know what else he wanted. He tapped my clit and I gasped. "And my pussy is yours?"

"Is that a question?"

I frantically shook my head. "No. I'm yours and my pussy is yours."

"Damn right. Any man touches this but me, I'll fucking kill him." He rubbed my clit with such a soft touch that I wanted to cry. It felt good but not enough to make me come. "I'm the one who filled up this pretty pussy with cum. The one who put not one but two babies in you. This is mine, Lil. *You're* mine."

His words might have offended some women, but for someone who had always wanted to belong, to be loved, it only made me want to hear more. He spread the lips wide, then leaned down and dragged his tongue the length of my pussy, giving my clit a hard flick before he started again.

"Dane, please!"

"Been without this pretty pussy for months. You get to come when I say you can." He licked me again. "Didn't get to play like this before. Need to make sure you know you're mine. Only I can make you feel this good, Lil."

"Only you," I murmured. As if I'd want anyone else to touch me.

"Good girl." He licked and sucked at my pussy until I wanted to cry from frustration. He'd get me so close to coming, then back off again. I wanted more. Needed more.

"Dane. I need it. Let me come. Please."

"My pretty girl wants to come?" he asked before licking my clit again. I nodded frantically. "You want a good fucking?"

"You know I do."

He sank a finger into me, stroking it in and out a few times before adding a second one. It wasn't as good as his cock would have been, but when he went back to torturing me with his mouth, I knew I was close to coming.

"Dane, I'm so close."

He growled and drove his fingers into me faster. "Come, Lil. Now."

He gently bit my clit, and I came so hard I soaked the bed and screamed out his name. Even then, he didn't stop. Dragon kept teasing me, making little shockwaves of pleasure flow through me. When I had nothing left to give, he withdrew and licked his fingers clean.

"Good girl."

"Arf."

He smirked. "If you weren't recovering, I'd turn you over my knee and spank you for that sass."

Was it wrong that the idea kind of turned me on? I'd heard the stories about him when no one thought I was listening. The women who hung around the club gushed over how dominant he was, how powerful. I'd not really understood, or thought I'd like someone like that, until now.

I saw the hard length of his cock pressing against his pants. He hadn't told me I could move yet. Slowly, I straightened my legs and closed them. His eyebrow shot up, but he didn't say anything. I pulled my hands back down by my sides, seeing what he'd do. Still nothing. Rolling to my knees, I moved closer and reached out to cup him through the denim of his pants.

Dragon growled and grabbed my wrist. "Lil, no."

"I can make you feel good without us actually having sex." I blinked up at him. "Don't you want my mouth on you?"

He cursed and tried to put some distance between us.

"Dane?"

He stood, shaking his head. "No. Nope. Not fucking happening, Lil. I don't have enough control for that. I'd end up fucking your mouth, using you. That's not what you need."

"Or maybe it's exactly what I need." He was doing it again. Thinking he knew what was best for me.

I got off the bed and sank to my knees in front of him, placing my hands in my lap. I stared up at him, hoping he'd see how much I trusted him. "Use me, Dane. I'm yours. You said so."

"Yes, you're mine. That means I take care of you, and using you like a whore after everything you've suffered the last few days, is doing the exact opposite. You think it's what you want, but it's not. I'm not a gentle guy, Lil. What you experienced before? That was nothing. Just the tip of the iceberg."

I reached for him, placing my hand on his thigh, but he backed away. It hurt. He might think he was doing the right thing, but if he wasn't going to take his pleasure from me, did that mean he'd get it somewhere else? He claimed to have only touched the club whores back home a few times and not gone any further. As much as I wanted to believe him, I had to wonder if he would stray at some point.

"Stop," he said, his voice harsh and cold. "Stop that right the fuck now."

"I didn't do anything."

"Yeah, you fucking did. I can see it all over your face. You think I'm going to walk out of here and go fuck some woman up at the clubhouse? You doubt me when I say I don't want anyone but you?"

"Dane, I..." I clamped my lips shut. Was that it? Did I doubt that he would stay with me? That I would be enough?

I was just a whore. Maybe not by choice, but it's what that awful man in Colombia had made me. I was dirty. Dragon might have fucked me once before, but would he be content with me the rest of his life? I knew Dingo had accepted Mei, even after what she'd suffered, but they didn't have the past I had with Dragon. Dingo hadn't walked out after being with Mei, he hadn't pushed her away. With Dragon, everything was different.

He came closer, gripping the back of my neck. I looked up, not sure what I'd find, but there was tenderness in his eyes. "Babe, I don't want anyone else. When I say you're mine, it means I'm also yours."

"But you don't want me," I said softly.

His grip tightened a moment. "Unbuckle my belt."

I reached up and obeyed, my fingers shaking a little.

"Unfasten my pants and take out my cock." I did as he demanded. "Now lick it."

I flicked my tongue out and gathered the pre-cum before working my way down his shaft. He tugged me closer and I opened, taking all of him into my mouth. Dragon dragged me down his length until my nose pressed against him. I relaxed my throat, then swallowed, pulling a groan from him.

"Fuck, babe. So good."

Dragon used his hold on me to control my motions. I felt his cock get even harder and knew he had to be close. When he gripped my head with both hands and started driving into my mouth hard and deep, I felt a flutter of excitement.

"That's it. Take everything I give you," he murmured. "Suck me dry, baby girl."

The hot spurts of his cum hit my tongue and the back of my throat. I swallowed it all. When he slipped from my mouth, I noticed his eyes were darker and his chest rose and fell rapidly. Dragon helped me to my feet, then kissed me hard.

"No more, Lil. I mean it. Not until we're home and a doctor has checked you over. I want to fuck you, so damn bad, but not at the risk of hurting you."

There was someone banging on the front door and I scrambled to get my clothes back on. Dragon tucked himself back into his pants, zipped up, then walked out as he fastened his belt. I heard the murmur of voices and wondered if the food had finally arrived, and if that was Wolf, did that mean Dragon was about to leave? I'd asked him to handle the man who'd snatched me, and I knew he would… assuming the Reckless Kings let him.

I went to the kitchen and found Dragon fixing a plate and a glass of sweet tea. He set them both down and gave me a nod. "Eat, Lil. Wolf will stay here with you while I'm gone."

"Aren't you hungry?" I asked.

"It can wait." He leaned down and pressed his lips to mine in a quick kiss. "I made you a promise, and I'm going to keep it. Rest. Do what Wolf says, and don't leave this fucking house for anything. Unless it's on fire."

Watching him leave, I had mixed feelings. Part of me wanted to ask him to stay with me, but I needed him to go take care of Mr. Crazypants. I ate my food with Wolf watching my every move. When I glanced his way, I found a slight smile curving his lips.

"What?" I asked.

He shook his head. "Never thought I'd see the day the mighty Dragon was brought to heel by a woman."

I snorted. "You really think anyone can tame him?"

"Didn't say he was tamed. But it's clear he's in love with you. He damn near lost it when he heard you were missing. I don't know what happened between the two of you, and I don't need to. Just know that he'd do anything for you, Lilian. That man would lay down his life for you."

"I know," I said softly. "I didn't before, but I do now."

He gave a nod and went back to silently watching me. I'd never known quite what to make of Wolf. He never talked much, but I'd seen him laugh with the other guys. And yet, there was always something lurking in his eyes. Like he was haunted. I'd heard he was in the military, and there were rumors he was missing a leg, even though he seemed to have two. If he wore a prosthesis, I couldn't tell.

Whatever demons he wrestled, I hoped he managed to find happiness along the way. If someone could accept me with my past, then I knew there had to be a woman out there for Wolf. Maybe I'd work on finding him someone when I got back home. All the guys needed someone. If they settled down, then the club pussy would go away. I knew Mei and Adalia would be fine with that. So would China and Elena.

I fought not to smile. Maybe I'd enlist their help. We could call it Project Matchmaker. Watching the guys fall would be entertaining as hell, and I knew that none of them would know what hit them.

Chapter Ten

Dragon

Warren Bruce wasn't at all what I'd expected. Already battered and bruised from the Reckless Kings taking their pound of flesh, he seemed rather sad and pathetic. Until he looked at you. I could see the madness in his eyes, and I knew that Lil was right. If this man went free, he'd hurt someone else. Even getting him help wasn't a guarantee. If she needed this man in the ground in order to feel safe, then I'd make it happen.

"He hasn't given us Charlotte's location," said Hawk, the Reckless Kings' VP. "Beast is out looking, but he's chasing his tail at this point."

"I'll see what I can get out of him."

Hawk sighed. "You don't intend to leave him breathing, do you?"

"Nope. Lil needs this, needs him gone." I glanced his way. "If you're squeamish, better head out. This is going to get messy."

"Fuck," Hawk muttered. "I heard the rumors, but I didn't know they were true. That really how you got your name?"

I nodded and nudged the bag at my feet. "I don't have all my stuff, but I brought enough, and ran to a store so I could improvise a little. I'm about to strip this fucker down. Leave him naked and tied down like he did to my woman."

"*Your* woman?" Bruce asked. "Yours? The pregnant bitch didn't belong to Beast?"

"Nope. You snatched my woman, terrorized her. Now you're going to pay the price." I unzipped my bag and pulled out a large knife. The man alternated between whimpering and laughing like a lunatic as I sliced through his clothes, leaving him bare-assed in the chair. "Anything you want to say before we get started?"

"Wanted to hurt Beast," the man muttered. "This was all to get to Beast. Bitch lied. She was supposed to be important. Fucking cunt."

I narrowed my eyes. "Lilian told you she was important to Beast?"

"Not the pregnant whore. The other. Charlotte." He said her name and sneered. "Fucking useless."

I leaned down into his space. "And what did you do with the useless woman?"

He cackled and whipped his head from side to side. "She's gone! Gone, gone, gone."

I could feel Hawk behind me, knew he wanted answers. "Is she alive? Or did you kill her?"

The man smiled, but it was like watching the Joker smile. "She's alive. For now."

He giggled, then started cackling again. Fucking lunatic. I used my knife to make a shallow cut across his chest, like he'd done to Lil's breast. He screamed and thrashed against the bonds tying him down.

"Where is Charlotte?" I asked.

He giggled. "I'll never tell. Never. Never. Never tell."

"He's batshit fucking crazy," Hawk muttered. "And this is just one version. Wait until you meet the others."

Others. Now there was an idea. Exactly how did I draw those out? The cut hadn't done the trick. Threatening him hadn't worked. Maybe I hadn't threatened the right person? "Too bad about his woman," I said, looking at Hawk and hoping the VP would play along.

"What?" the man asked, his voice and tone completely different from before. "What did you do to her? If you've harmed her, I'll fuck up your stupid whore."

Bingo! I winked at Hawk, then turned to face the man. I blanked my expression, trying to look as bored as possible. Any emotion and I could tip my hand. "Oh, not me. I haven't done anything." I slid my cut from my shoulders and handed it to Hawk, knowing things would get messy soon. "But those guys upstairs? Oh, they're having a good time with her."

Bruce screamed and yanked at the duct tape holding him down.

"Talk about a whore," Hawk said. "She loves getting fucked by multiple men. Begs for it."

"Lies!" the man screamed and thrashed some more, spit flying from his mouth. "She'd never do that! She was supposed to be mine!"

I looked at Hawk, an idea forming. "Maybe he needs proof. A visual. He was nice enough to send one of my woman stripped and tied down."

"No! No, no, no." Bruce shook his head, his eyes wide and his chest heaving. I'd struck a nerve. Good.

I nodded to Hawk and we moved out of range so the psycho couldn't hear us. "Find out the description of the woman he wanted. See if you have a club whore who would look close enough if we leave her face out of it. Then get her stripped, tied down, and take a few photos of her getting fucked. We'll break this bastard."

Hawk nodded and left me alone with Warren Bruce. The man was going to pay for what he'd done to Lilian. I knew Beast would want a piece of him if Charlotte had been hurt, but I didn't plan on leaving anything. The man had taken my woman and I wasn't going to let that slide. She wanted justice, and I was damn well going to give it to her.

While Hawk handled the proof we needed, I decided to work on Bruce a little more. I added a few shallow cuts to his arms, his thighs. Even scraped the blade along his pubic bone, letting it trail down to his pathetic dick. No wonder the woman hadn't wanted him. I didn't think she'd have noticed if he fucked her. I'd seen babies with bigger dicks.

"Maybe your woman just couldn't be satisfied with someone like you," I said, smacking his dick with the flat of the blade. "She needed someone bigger. Stronger."

He hurled curses at me, his voice changing several times during his tirade. Yeah, I had this fucker where I wanted him. That bitch of his was the key to everything. Beast had known it, to some extent, but he hadn't thought to use it to get what he needed. I'd get this ass to talk one way or another. Break him. Get Charlotte's location, then I'd do what I did best and make him scream.

By the time Hawk returned, I'd removed the man's fingernails, toenails, and had even snipped off the tip of his pinky. He'd cried, screamed, begged. But he hadn't broken. Yet. Hawk gave me a lift of his chin and held out his phone, and I knew he'd gotten what we needed. I only hoped it was good enough to fool this piece of shit.

I turned the screen so Bruce could see a woman with her hands tied behind her, a gag clearly tied around her mouth and knotted in her hair. They'd bent her over and had men holding her legs open. I hoped they compensated the woman for this shit, unless she actually liked it, then getting fucked was compensation enough.

I showed Bruce four different Reckless Kings fucking the woman, and he came unglued. "Here's your precious whore. Look at her! She loves getting tied up and fucked. Loves being held down and forced to take those big dicks."

I swiped the screen again. "Oh-ho! I bet she really loved this one."

I showed him the image of the biggest cock in the shots taking her ass. And that's when I knew he'd give me what I wanted. He cried. Tears ran down his cheeks, snot covered his upper lip, and he looked utterly crushed.

"No." He whimpered. "She wouldn't. She's not like that."

"Oh, she is. She's up there getting fucked by every guy here, and she loves it. Can't get enough. In her cunt, her ass. I bet she'd take three men at once and swallow some dick too."

Bruce sobbed and went boneless.

"Where the fuck is Charlotte?" I asked. "Next time I have to ask, I'm cutting off your dick and showing it to your whore so she can laugh at how pathetic it is while she's up there having fun with real men."

He blubbered and babbled, but I eventually got her location. Hawk gave me a nod and took off, and I knew he'd get the info to Beast.

"You made a grave error when you took Lilian," I said, reaching into my bag. I pulled out the tools I needed, then started a fire in the metal barrel nearby. Once the flames were nice and hot, I knew it was time to begin. "You're going to scream. Beg. Cry. You'll want me to end it and let you die, and you will. But only when I'm ready. You fucked up, Warren Bruce, and you took my woman. The mother of my children. And now you're going to pay the price."

There was no fight left in him, which took a little of the excitement out of it. Yeah, I was a sadistic fucker. I got off on causing pain to assholes like this one. I'd never harm an innocent, but anyone who fucked over the club or came after Lil was fair game.

I toyed with him, dragging things out. I gave the Reckless Kings enough time to verify the intel was good. Once I knew this fucker hadn't lied, I stopped holding back. One nod from Hawk, and I let loose.

After I ripped his balls off, I knew I didn't have long before he'd bleed out, so I put the metal poker into the flames until the end glowed red, then I used it to cauterize the wound. His screams only made me smile. Poor fool didn't realize we were only getting started.

By the time I'd finished with him, half his body was scorched until the skin had blackened. I'd used the hot poker several times to burn through layers of flesh, or rammed it straight through parts of his body. The floor was soaked in his blood and waste, and I held his heart in my hand, crushing it. I tossed the useless organ into the burn barrel.

"We'll get rid of the body," Hawk said. "Beast called. When he found Charlotte, she was unconscious and her pulse was weak, but she made it to the hospital. We're hoping she'll make a full recovery. Baby's gone, though. Beast said it looked like she'd miscarried."

"Might be a good thing, if this fucker was the father," I said.

Hawk nodded. "That's how we feel too, but Charlotte... I'm not sure how she'll handle all this. Mentally, I mean."

"Women are stronger than we give them credit for," I said, thinking of all Lilian had been through.

"You're not going back to yours looking like that, are you?" he asked.

I looked down at my blood-soaked clothes and boots. Fuck. I'd really loved these boots too. I wasn't sure the blood and gore could be scrubbed from them, but I'd get a Prospect to do his best. "She'll want to know I did what I'd promised."

Hawk's brow furrowed. "She made you promise to kill him?"

I held his gaze. "No. She made me promise to do what I do best." I waved a hand at what was left of Bruce, letting him know that Lil knew of this side of me and it was what she'd wanted.

He gave me a nod. I used a rag to clean my hands off. I'd need my tools cleaned and returned to me, but I'd handle that later. I grabbed my cut, then walked out, but his voice halted me. "You can't go into Beast's home like that. Use the room at the clubhouse. I'll have Lilian brought to you."

I walked out and went to the room I'd been given that first day, then stood there, waiting for Lilian to arrive. When she came through the door with Wolf at her back, she took in my appearance. She didn't look sick, or get pale. Her gaze scanned me head to toe, and when she looked into my eyes, I saw acceptance and relief.

"Shower and I'll burn that shit," Wolf said.

"Get someone to clean the boots."

He looked at them and snorted. "Yeah. Right. I'll do that, but I'll also make sure you have another pair because there's no fucking way all that's coming out of the leather."

I removed the boots and tossed them into the hall, then stripped off my clothes, Wolf gathered them and left, leaving me alone with Lilian. I got the shower as hot as I could stand it, then scrubbed the shit out of my hair, beard, and body. I didn't want a single trace of that asshole's blood on me when I took Lil into my arms.

"They found Charlotte," I told her through the open shower door. I didn't give a shit if the floor was getting wet. Right now, I needed to see Lil because she was the only reason I had a grip on my humanity.

"You made him talk," she said.

"Yeah. He gave up her location, but Hawk said she lost the baby. Said it looked like she'd had a miscarriage."

Lil cradled her own belly. I knew she was trying to put herself in Charlotte's position, but I didn't want her going there. Our babies were fine, and so was she. And I'd make damn sure it stayed that way.

When the water ran clear, I got out and dried off. Lilian rummaged through my things and handed me some boxer briefs and a pair of jeans. I pulled them on, then gathered her into my arms. She stared up at me, full of trust and love. My heart warmed, knowing that the darkness inside me hadn't scared her. Then again, she'd been with men worse than me. Maybe to her I wasn't all that dark and fell more into the shades of gray. I wasn't good, but I wasn't completely evil either. "You okay, baby?" I asked.

She nodded. "Thank you."

I pressed my lips to hers, kissing her soft and slow. "I'll always give what you need, and try to give you what you want. I knew you needed him in the ground, and you wanted him to suffer first. It's done. Just don't ask about the details."

"Was he humiliated?" she asked.

I grinned. "Stripped him naked while he was tied to the chair. Made fun of his tiny dick, then made him think the woman he wanted was getting off on being tied up while multiple men fucked her. Even found a way to give him visual proof. And Hawk seemed to make sure every damn one was well-endowed just to make the shit feel even worse."

"Good."

"You know, your dad and I both thought you'd be better off with a doctor, lawyer, or just some regular guy with a normal job. Someone safe. We were wrong, weren't we? That's not what you need at all."

She slowly shook her head.

"You need someone with a little monster inside, a darkness that can be used to keep you safe when necessary." I ran my nose down the length of hers. "Someone to make you obey, tell you what to do, and punish you when you don't listen. Isn't that right, baby?"

"Yes, Dane. That's what I need. I think it's been you since the moment I saw you. Even then, when I was terrified and broken, there was something between us. I could feel it. Whenever you were nearby, I watched you, felt drawn to you like a magnet. It's why I asked you to help me."

"I don't like the thought of you here with all these men so close, but do you want to stay here until we leave? If Beast found Charlotte, he may want the extra space at his house. I'd imagine he'll try to take her home with him when she's released from the hospital."

She glanced around the room. "This is fine. It's just a few days, right?"

"Right. Then we're going home. And no, I'm not leaving you with Grizzly. When I say we're going home, I mean you're going *home*."

"To your house?" she asked.

"No, babe. To *our* house. You can change whatever you want. Make it into a home. But your shit had better be hanging next to mine in the closet, and if you go to Grizzly's it had damn well better only be for a short visit. Your ass will be in our bed every fucking night. Naked."

She smiled. "I can live with that."

"Damn right you can." I kissed her again, needing to taste her. Feel her. Remind myself that she was mine, and I was hers. And maybe remind her too.

Chapter Eleven

Lilian
One week later

The Reckless Kings had been nice, and hospitable, but when it was time to go, I could tell they'd been happy to see us leave. Honestly, I thought Dragon might have scared them a little. I'd heard whispers about what he'd done to the man who'd kidnapped me, and the way they said it, the overall tone, left no doubt they were a little worried about my man and what he was capable of doing.

Charlotte had still been in the hospital, but Beast had called the clubhouse to let everyone know she'd pull through. I wondered if maybe this time he'd claim her and ignore the little voice telling him she deserved someone better. If nothing else, I hoped the scariness we'd all survived had taught him that life was too short to not take what he wanted. And I'd been able to clearly see how much he wanted Charlotte, enough to give her up if he thought she'd be better off with another man. He might have spouted some nonsense about Charlotte's brother, but if the man had eyes, then he'd already known that Beast cared for her. Hell, the psycho who planned all this shit had noticed it. The entire club had to know how their Pres felt. Idiot.

Being home felt… strange. Everyone looked at me differently, even though the men still kept their distance. If anything, they gave me even more space. Dragon thought they were worried I was going to break after my ordeal, but they were wrong. Being with Dragon made me feel stronger. I still wasn't too thrilled about other men getting close or touching me, but I didn't feel as terrified as I had in the past. I wasn't going to voluntarily leave the compound without at least one Devil's Fury member or Prospect with me anytime soon, but I liked to think that was just me being cautious and not too chicken to live my life.

I'd moved into Dragon's house, or as he called it *our* house, and surprisingly my dad hadn't even grumbled a little. He had hugged me so hard I thought he might crack some ribs when I'd first gotten back, but he seemed to accept that I was with Dragon. I even had a property cut to prove I was his. Wearing it gave me the biggest thrill, even if he didn't allow me on his bike right now. He was convinced it wasn't safe while I was pregnant, and he was so cute in overprotective mode that I hadn't argued. Yet.

I'd made dinner and ended up eating alone. He'd barely left my side since he'd found me, keeping a close watch on me since we'd been back, only leaving when duty called. Until now. Until tonight. And while I'd felt smothered, now that I was home alone it just felt… cold. Lonely. I didn't like it.

Looking at the screen on my phone, I tried to decide what to do. I had a feeling that whatever I decided would be a turning point of sorts. The fucker was at a party at the clubhouse, and I knew damn well there was club pussy all over the place. He might say he was mine and I was his, but I knew damn well those skanks up there didn't give a shit. If they thought they could get into his pants, they'd try.

The text he'd sent twenty minutes ago mocked me.

Be home late. Don't wait up.

What the absolute fuck? Don't wait up? I was supposed to just sit here, alone, while he partied with everyone? Uh-uh. No, I wasn't going to sit here like some sweet, mild-mannered little housewife -- who wasn't even his damn wife -- while he sat up there with naked women draped over him. Not happening.

I looked down at the maternity shorts I had on, knowing how much he hated me leaving the house in them, claiming they were too short and showed off my ass. My maternity top was just a plain tee, but it hugged my curves and my baby bump. I thought I looked rather cute. And if Dragon got pissed, well… I smiled. He'd just have to punish me.

I grabbed my property cut and slipped on canvas shoes. I'd have gone with flip- flops, but I knew how disgusting the clubhouse could get on a night like this. No way in hell was I going in there nearly barefoot. I'd probably need every shot known to man if I did that, and could still end up catching something. It was a long walk to the front, and my car hadn't made it here. I found it strange that it had *accidentally* been lost between the Reckless Kings' place and home.

Dragon had said he was getting me a small SUV so I'd have room for the babies, but we hadn't gone car shopping yet. It was warm outside, nearly too warm, as I trudged my way to the clubhouse. The houses were all dark and quiet, except for Dingo's place. I saw the flicker of the TV through their living room window, and I wondered if he was there with Mei or at the party too. Considering how much he adored her, I doubted he was tossing back shots with club whores right now. I knew Badger would be home with my sister, Adalia. They'd been together long before I was adopted by Grizzly, but I'd heard more than once that he hardly ever went to parties these days. It seemed everything he wanted was already at home.

It just made me snarl and stomp a little harder as I made my way to the front of the compound. All that *I'm sorry* bullshit, *I love you*, and me being all he wanted. If that was the case, his ass would be home with me tonight and not drinking with the others and the women at the clubhouse. By the time I reached the steps, I was beyond livid. If I'd been a cartoon character, steam would have been pouring from my ears and whistles would be blowing like a damn tea kettle on the stove.

Savage was on the porch and took a step back as I drew closer to the door. "Shit. Hey, Lilian, I don't think you really want to go in there."

I stopped, foot still lifted to take my next step and only turned my head his way. I could nearly hear him gulp as he backed up farther, hands held out. With a growl, I shoved open the door and went inside. The smoke was so thick it burned my eyes and nose, and I was fairly sure I wasn't just breathing in nasty cigarette smoke. I covered my nose, hoping I didn't inhale anything that would hurt my babies, and scanned the room for Dragon.

My gaze narrowed as I spotted him across the room at a table with Colorado and Cobra. I shoved my way through the crowd, the men parting like the Red Sea and the women giving me dirty looks. When I stopped in front of Dragon, I eyed the naked woman shoving her tits in his face. I didn't say a word, just waited. Cobra noticed me first, his eyes going wide. Dragon was the last to detect my presence, and the smile slipped from his face immediately. His gaze jerked to the woman practically sticking her nipples in his mouth and back to me.

I still didn't say anything. I just grabbed a handful of platinum hair and started to drag her ass across the floor.

"Let me go, you bitch!" she screamed as she kicked and flailed.

"Shut up, whore! I hope you get splinters in your ass." I kept going, not stopping until I met a wall of leather cuts. I glared at each and every one of them, then released the woman, only to turn around and straddle her body. I gripped her hair and slammed her head onto the floor several times, until she was crying and trying to shove me away.

"Fuck, Dragon took an ol' lady," one of the other women said. "She's pissed as hell too."

"Thought everyone knew," another woman said softly.

I snarled at them. "You even look in his direction and you're next."

Dragon shoved his way through and hunkered next to me. There was remorse in his gaze, and a hint of guilt as he glanced at the woman I was trying to knock unconscious. "Hey, Lil. Let's go home, okay?"

I stood up, shaking from the anger coursing through my veins, then closed my eyes and took a breath. When I opened them, I looked right through him, giving him the most blank stare I could manage with all that I was feeling.

"No. You wanted to party? Stay and party. Play with all the tits and pussy you want." I shrugged the cut off my shoulders and threw it at his face. "They're all yours but I'm not."

I shoved past everyone and went outside, feeling like I was seconds from bursting into tears. I walked to the gate, wanting to get far from the noise, but not knowing where the hell to go. Beau was on duty and gave me a wary look. I was done. Finished with men who lied to me, used me, and didn't think about my feelings at all. I motioned for him to open the gates, and while it seemed like he wouldn't at first, he eventually let me through.

I walked toward town, not really having a destination in mind. I just needed to clear my head, and figure out what the hell I was going to do next. I had no doubt that when Dragon found me, I'd get some stupid reason he hadn't shoved her away. It made me wonder, though, had he been lying when he'd said he only touched them after that first time with us? After what I'd just witnessed, could I trust that he hadn't gone further?

No. What I should be asking myself was whether or not I wanted to be with a man who thought his behavior tonight was all right. He'd said I was his, and he was mine. That hadn't looked like a guy thinking of his pregnant woman at home. He'd probably enjoyed that club whore shoving her tits in his face. My hands fisted at my sides as anger surged through me again. Instead of beating the shit out of that woman, I should have gone after Dragon, except then he'd have to make an example of me. As it was, I'd probably embarrassed him by throwing the property cut back at him. I had no doubt I'd pay for that later.

As I neared town, I heard the pipes on several bikes heading my way. I recognized the guys that flew past me, and stopped, heaving a sigh, when I heard one of them turn around. Demon slowed and came to a stop next to me.

"There a reason you're walking this late at night?" he asked. "Shouldn't you be at home?"

"Nope. I can go wherever the fuck I want." I folded my arms and stared at him.

"Uh-huh," he muttered. "What did Dragon do this time?"

I rolled my eyes and started walking. He kept pace with me, walking the bike forward for each of my steps. It seemed he wasn't going to leave until I told him something. Even that wouldn't guarantee he'd leave me alone.

"Caught him with a naked club whore at the clubhouse," I said.

"And you were at the clubhouse because..." Demon arched a brow. "You know damn well you aren't allowed in there, Lilian."

I stopped again and glared. "Why? Why am I not allowed? Worried I'll see something I shouldn't? Like the father of my babies looking at a woman's tits while she practically feeds them to him? I'm supposed to sit at home, let him roll in whenever after he's done who knows what with those club whores, and just pretend everything is fine?"

He shrugged. "Well, yeah. It's what you signed on for when you agreed to be his."

"Well, I take it back. I'm not Dragon's. I won't belong to anyone who acts like that and sees nothing wrong with it. If I even looked at another man in appreciation, he'd lose his shit and you damn well know it."

"You know. This is the most you've ever said to me," he said. "And you're not shaking, or running in fear. Exactly what happened in Tennessee?"

"I learned I'm stronger than I thought, and that I deserve happiness. No, what I deserve is an honorable man who will stand next to me and show me some respect."

Demon cracked his neck. "And Dragon isn't respecting you."

I waved a hand back toward the direction of the Devil's Fury compound. "If that's the way he shows that he respects his woman, then someone else can have him. Know who I didn't see there? Badger.

Dingo. Shit, even Blades wasn't there and China isn't officially his."

Demon opened his mouth, but I held up a hand to stop him. I lowered my voice, my throat aching with unshed tears. "Every single guy who claims to love a woman was at home, except Dragon. How can he love me and do that? How can…"

I broke. Tears streaked my cheeks as I sobbed. I tried to wrap my arms around my waist and hold myself together, but it wasn't working. Demon cursed, shut off his bike, and then I found myself in his embrace. He rubbed my back, even if he was awkward as fuck about it, and murmured words of comfort.

"Lilian, I can't tell you what Dragon's thinking because I don't know. But if you're going to track him down every time he decides to party with the club, then the two of you are going to have constant problems."

I pulled back and wiped my face with my hands. "If he'd told me ahead of time he'd be gone most of the night, then I'd have made my own plans. I just don't think I can trust him after what I saw, Demon. If you don't have trust in a relationship, then you've got nothing."

"Come on. I'll take you home."

I shook my head. I didn't want to go back.

Demon led me over to his bike, then he got on and held out his hand. I reluctantly took it, and he helped me onto the back before he started it up again. He drove slow as he headed back toward the Devil's Fury, and as we pulled through the gates, he came to a stop, bracing his feet on the pavement.

I looked over his shoulder and saw Dragon on the steps of the clubhouse, his head in his hands. He looked up and took in the scene of me riding with the club's Sergeant-at-Arms, then slowly stood and came toward us. I tensed, not knowing what to expect from him. The property cut I'd thrown at his head was gripped in his hand.

"Did you lose something?" Demon asked.

Dragon stared at me, not saying anything. I gripped Demon's waist tighter, not sure what I should do. I decided to wait and see what Dragon would do. He seemed to be struggling, but eventually came closer.

"There a reason my pregnant woman is on your bike?" he asked Demon.

Demon placed his hand on my calf. "Is she? Yours? Don't see a property cut or ink on her. Seems to me she's available."

My breath froze in my lungs. What the hell was he doing? He gently squeezed my leg, and I took that to mean I needed to stay quiet. Whatever he'd planned, I hoped it worked the way he wanted. Dragon looked pissed.

Dragon snarled and stormed over, gripping my arm and hauling me off Demon's bike. I stumbled into him, but he only put me behind him, keeping his hand on my waist.

"You know damn well she's mine, Demon. Every fucker here knows it."

Demon chuckled darkly. "Really? Do *you* know it? Are you sure *she* knows it?"

Dragon cursed, turning to face me. He forced the property cut back over my shoulders, then started pushing me toward his bike. Before I had a chance to balk, he lifted me and placed me on the back before getting on. When I tried to dismount the bike, he gripped my hip and growled at me. The fury flashing in his eyes made my heart race, and kept my ass planted on his bike. He started it up, walked it back out of the parking space, then took off toward the house. I held on tight, worried I'd tumble off.

Dragon came to a stop in the driveway and shut off the bike. I got off, my legs trembling. He swung his leg over the seat and stood, then stalked toward me. I could see the anger rolling off him and I backed up a step, but I didn't get far. He gripped my wrist, then swung me up into his arms and carried me inside. After he kicked the door shut, he kept going, not stopping again until we reached the bedroom.

He walked us over to the mirror hanging on the closet door and pointed at our reflection. "Do you see this?"

I wasn't sure what I was supposed to see so I kept quiet.

He placed his hand on my belly. "These are my babies, Lil. Mine."

I swallowed hard and gave a jerky nod. Then he slid his hand down and worked it between my thighs.

"This pussy is *mine*. Understood?"

I nodded again, my breath coming out faster and harder as my heart pounded.

He turned me and pushed my chin until I looked over my shoulder. "That's my fucking name on your back, Lil. Why? Because you're mine. *You're fucking mine!*"

My gaze met his in the mirror. "Was that woman yours too? Did you want her to be? Is that why you were there, letting her put her tits in your face, instead of being here with me? Do you prefer blondes? Skinny women?"

He muttered a curse and turned me to face him. "Babe, I barely even noticed her. I'd already pushed her away four times, or it might have been another woman. I wasn't really looking."

"Your eyes were glued to what she so clearly offered."

He shook his head. "Lil, I didn't want any of them even when you weren't here in my house. Why would I want them now?"

I dropped my gaze. "They don't have thighs that jiggle. I was chubby before I got pregnant, and now that I'm having twins, I'm going to be huge."

"Babe." He gripped my chin and forced me to look at him. "I fucking love that your thighs jiggle. I love your thick thighs, round ass, and your soft belly. And your tits? Fuck, Lil. Better than anything those girls at the clubhouse have, even if they tried to pay for it. I've wanted you since you turned eighteen. Now that you're mine, do you really think I'd want any of those bitches?"

"You didn't come home," I said softly. "You said… you told me not to wait up." I hated feeling like this. All insecure and broken. This wasn't who I was, but apparently it was the new me filled with pregnancy hormones. I cried at the drop of a hat. When I'd burned the macaroni for lunch yesterday, I'd bawled my eyes out, feeling like the world had ended.

"I didn't even text you, Lil. What the hell are you talking about?" he asked.

I sniffled and pulled away, going to get my phone. I found it on the bed, where I'd dropped it when I'd come to get my shoes and cut. Unlocking the screen, I pulled up the message from him and showed him. "I'm not making it up. That's what I got and I got mad. I wanted to go tell you to come home."

He narrowed his gaze at the screen, then reached into his pocket for his phone. He patted all his pockets, then cursed. "I don't even have my damn phone. Someone is fucking with us, Lil. I don't know if it's one my brothers, or if one of the damn whores got her hands on my phone. And I sure the fuck don't know how they unlocked it, but either way, I didn't send that shit. I'd planned to finish my beer, maybe have one more, then I was going to come home."

"I'm sorry if I embarrassed you in front of the club."

"Oh, hell no, babe. That's not going to cut it." He grinned. "I might not have laid that trap, but you still landed in it, then threw your cut at my face. In front of everyone. What did I tell you before? What happens when you don't listen?"

I bit my lip. "I get punished."

He nodded, then walked over to the bed and sat on the edge. He crooked a finger at me, and I went, my heart racing.

Chapter Twelve

Dragon

I'd figure out who had my phone in a little while, and handle that shit, but first I needed to make sure Lil remembered she was mine. I felt her tremble as I pulled her over my lap, making sure our babies weren't pressed against my thighs. It wouldn't be much longer before I couldn't do this anymore. At least, not until after the babies got here. I'd left her dressed, but I worked her shorts and panties over her ass and down to her knees, then pulled them all the way off.

"Spread those legs, Lil. Show me what's mine."

She parted her thighs and I saw she was already wet. *Fuck*. It was hard to punish her when she got off on it. Made my dick hard as a rock. I rubbed her ass cheeks, then brought my hand down hard, leaving a red handprint on one side. She squeaked and jerked, but I put my arm across her upper back and held her still.

"You have a lesson to learn, Lil. I think you've earned at least ten spankings."

Her breath hitched, and I wasn't sure if it was from excitement or apprehension. Seeing how soaked she was, I was going with option one. I had a feeling my night was about to get a lot more interesting.

I brought my hand down on the other cheek with a loud *crack*. She yelped, but didn't try to get away. I spanked her ass, one side, then the other, three more times. Her ass was red and I could feel the heat from her abused flesh. I brought my hand down on the backs of her thighs, one swat on each, hard enough to turn the skin pink.

"How many is that, babe?" I asked.

"Seven."

I gave a humorless chuckle. "No, babe. That's six. The first one happened before I said you'd earned ten. You've got four more to go. Every time you sit tomorrow, you'll remember what happens when you disobey, or jump to conclusions."

"Dragon, please. It hurts."

"It's supposed to." I brought my hand down twice more on her ass cheeks. "Spread those thighs more."

She struggled but managed to part them farther.

The final swat went on her pussy, and she yelped as she tried to scramble off my lap. I held firm, not letting her go. She struggled, but the second I parted the lips of her pussy and brushed my fingers over her clit, she went completely still.

I swiped it again. "This feels awfully hard, Lil. I think you enjoyed getting your ass paddled. Maybe even liked the spanking on your pussy too."

I could hear her breathing hard, and could almost feel the embarrassment burning through her. And that just wouldn't do. What we did in our home was just between us. There was no reason for her to feel ashamed if she liked what I did to her.

I helped her stand up, then removed the rest of her clothes. "Middle of the bed. Hands and knees."

She crawled onto the bed and did as I'd demanded. I went to the closet and pulled down a different bag. It looked similar to the kit I used when I let the darkness take over, but this one had a different set of tools inside. Ones I'd purchased specifically with Lilian in mind.

I dropped it onto the bed and pulled out a length of rope. I'd made sure to get the softest kind I could, but strong enough to hold her. She stared at me, and I could see her pulse pounding. I knew what she'd been through in Colombia. What Outlaw, Wire, and the others had found on the women rescued from that bastard had been shared among the clubs, so we'd know what we were dealing with. Which meant I knew damn well they'd tied her up so she couldn't fight back.

"I need you to trust me, Lil, and right now I don't think you do." She eyed the rope as I pulled it through my hand. "I'm tying you up, babe. Then I'm going to fuck you."

Her gaze lifted to mine. I saw her fear, but I also saw that she needed this. Giving herself to me had been a huge step for her, and I admired her courage, but it was time to break down more of those walls, wash away some of those memories. I wanted her to heal completely, even if it meant facing her fears head on.

"Hands by the headboard."

She put them over her head, stretching so that her breasts pressed to the mattress. I wrapped the rope around her wrists, making sure it was snug enough she couldn't break free, then I slipped it down past the mattress and tied it to the bedframe. A headboard with spindles or something would have been easier, but she might have broken it. If we were going to play like this again, I'd have to come up with something.

Lil pulled at the rope, but couldn't get free. I could see her starting to panic and knew I needed to ground her. I smacked her ass hard enough my hand stung. She sucked in a breath and froze, her body locked tight.

"You're safe, Lilian. I've got you." I leaned down until her gaze fastened on mine. "Babe, it's just you and me here. Did you freak like this when you were kidnapped?"

She shook her head. "But I was tied to a chair. It was different."

"Because beds are for fucking?" I asked.

She nodded.

"When those assholes in Colombia tied you up, did they always fuck you on a bed?"

She stared at me. Hard.

"Yeah, babe. I know everything that happened there." A tear slipped down her cheek, and I wiped it away, pressing my lips to hers. "Love you, Lil. You're mine. No one else's. Just you and me here. You're my strong, brave, fierce woman."

She gave me a quick nod and I knew she'd be fine.

"I promised to always give you what you *need*, Lil. Even if you don't want to acknowledge it, you need this. I'm going to restrain your legs, babe. Spread you open. You're at my mercy." I leaned in closer, my lips brushing her ear. "I can fuck you. Spank you. Do anything I want."

"Dane." Her voice was so soft I nearly didn't hear her.

"Trust me, Lil. You get too scared, you tell me. If this is too soon, we'll stop and try again some other time." I smoothed her hair back from her face. "That what you want? You want to wait?"

She hesitated a moment, looked at the ropes holding her to the bed, then shook her head. I pressed a kiss to her temple, then moved behind her. Reaching into my bag, I pulled out a spreader bar. I buckled the leather cuffs around her ankles, leaving her no choice but to remain open and vulnerable. If anyone who knew her history saw me right now, they'd call me a monster, an asshole, a heartless dick. But I wasn't. I had a darker side, and those desires did appear in the bedroom at times, but if she could handle the demon inside that I let loose on men like Warren Bruce, then I knew she could handle me in the bedroom too. I just needed her to see that.

"So fucking beautiful, babe. Love seeing you like this." I ran my hand over her ass cheek, then gave it another swat. I slipped my hand between her thighs and brushed my fingers over her pussy. Despite her uncertainty, she was still wet. I stroked her clit, hoping to put her at ease and make her beg for release.

She whimpered and wiggled, but her mind was no longer on the restraints holding her down. I reached into the bag and pulled out a small vibrator. It was only an inch around and five inches long, nowhere near the size of my cock, but I didn't plan on putting it in her pussy. I turned it on low, then used it to tease her clit. It didn't take much to make her come that first time. Her release rolled down her inner thighs, and I turned the toy up another notch, making her come twice more.

I grabbed some lube and slicked the toy, then spread her ass cheeks and squeezed more onto her tight hole. She shrieked and tensed, making me spank her ass again. Three hard slaps had her gasping and holding still.

Slowly, I worked the vibrator into her ass until I was fucking her with it. Lil moaned and arched, sticking her ass up farther. Knew my baby would like this, although I'd expected it to take a few times before she warmed up.

While I worked her ass with the toy, I rubbed and pinched her clit, rolling it between my fingers until she was screaming out her release. She soaked her thighs and the bed she came so fucking hard, and I made sure she kept coming. When I couldn't take my own torture anymore, I lined my cock up with her pussy and thrust hard and deep, making her take every inch.

"Oh, God! Dane!"

"That's it, baby."

I pushed the toy all the way into her ass and held it there as I rode her hard, my cock slamming into her. The loud keening sound that slipped past her lips was all the warning I got before she came, nearly breaking my dick when her inner muscles clamped down. I drove into her, not stopping until I'd filled her with my cum. My cock twitched, and I wished I could stay like this a while longer. Pulling out, I groaned at the sight of my release coating her pussy.

"You okay, Lil?" I asked softly.

"I'm good."

I ran my hand down her back, giving the vibrator a slight twist. I eased it from her body and contemplated fucking her ass, but decided to save that for another time. I'd already put her through hell tonight, and pushed her boundaries. I undid the restraints on the spreader bar and pushed it aside, then worked on freeing her wrists.

"I wasn't too rough?" I asked.

"My ass hurts, but other than that I'm okay."

I kissed the tip of her nose. "It's supposed to hurt."

She curled against me, and even though I needed to clean up the toys and put everything away, I held her close and stretched out on the bed.

"How did you know all that stuff?" she asked. "What happened in Colombia, I mean."

I wasn't sure how she'd handle what I was about to say, but she needed to know. It was time. "We all know, Lil. Outlaw, Wire, and the others pulled whatever they could from your time there. Not just info on you, but on every woman we brought home. He shared it with the club so we'd know how to act around you, what might trigger you."

She buried her face in my chest. "Everyone knows? All of it? How I was… used?"

"Yeah, babe. We all knew since the first week you were here. The way you reacted that first time we were together, it gave me some ideas. I hoped what we just did would help you heal in some way."

"Did you have to spank me so hard?" she asked.

I tipped her chin up and pressed my lips to hers. "Babe, seeing your ass all red and swollen from your spanking was hot as fuck. Considering how wet you were, you didn't mind it too much. Next time, it will be harder. And you'll like it."

She shivered, but I noticed she didn't deny she'd enjoyed getting spanked. It might take time, but I'd teach her how to embrace the darkness that simmered under her skin. I'd seen it, felt it the day she'd let me take her that first time. She needed someone to take control, give her pleasure, and maybe a little pain mixed in. There was no shame in it.

"Love you, babe," I said.

"Love you too, Dane." She lifted her gaze to mine. "You're the only one I've ever trusted this much. It hurt when I thought you wanted that other woman. I didn't think I'd be able to ever trust you again. I… I'm still not…"

I put a finger over her lips. "Hush, babe. I get it. My past reactions combined with what you saw made you think the worst. We'll get there. In the meantime,

I'll find out who took my phone, how they accessed it, and deal with it."

She clutched at me. "Don't go!"

"I'm not. Not far anyway. Need to clean up the toys, and I'm going to run you a hot bath. I'll leave the bathroom door open."

I got out of bed and carried the vibrator into the bathroom. While I washed it off, I let the tub fill with hot water and added some bubbles I'd picked up just for her. I shut off the water when the level was just right, then helped her into the tub. She watched my every move, until I walked out of the bathroom. I wiped down the spreader bar and cuffs, then put everything away.

"Lil, I'm borrowing your phone a minute," I called out.

"Okay. Don't be long."

I smiled and dialed Demon's number. But the smile quickly slipped from my face when I found out exactly why my phone was missing and who had sent that message. The bitch was dead if I got my hands on her. I'd wring her fucking neck. It seemed that Lilian was right to be worried about the whore who'd been trying to get my attention.

"Where is she?" I asked the Sergeant-at-Arms.

"I'll handle it."

"Demon, that bitch nearly cost me Lil. She thought the worst because of that conniving cunt. Not to mention my phone was locked. How the fuck did she get past the code?"

"I'll find out everything we need to know, and she'll pay," Demon said. "You need to focus on your woman and babies. Let me take care of the whore. I'll make an example of her so no one fucks with us again.

They're starting to get too bold, thinking they can do whatever the fuck they want."

"Make it public, Demon. And make every one of those bitches watch."

I could hear the smile in his voice. "Oh, I will."

I put Lil's phone on the charger, then went into the bathroom to check on her. She'd craned her neck, and watched as I walked back into the room. I could see the curiosity in her eyes and knew she'd likely heard just enough to want to know what was going on. While I wouldn't discuss club business with her, this time it involved her too.

"The woman you pulled off me managed to get my phone and send that text. Demon said he'd handle it. Make sure the others don't try that shit."

She nodded, then held out her hand. "Come join me?"

I eyed her, licking my lips as I looked at the swells of her breast and the way her nipples peeked through the bubbles. "If I get in there, I'm going to fuck you. Right now, you need to relax. Not sure you can handle another round tonight."

"I can handle it, Dragon."

I arched an eyebrow.

"Dane," she corrected. "I don't want you to hold back with me."

"Worried I'll go elsewhere if you can't take it?" I asked.

She didn't answer, but I could see that's clearly what she'd thought. "If your ass wasn't already cherry red from your spankings, I'd give you more for thinking that."

Fuck if her nipples didn't get harder, and the way she shifted told me the thought of me putting her over my knee turned her on. She was my match made in fucking heaven. But she was also the mother of my kids, and I didn't want her pushing herself too hard right now.

"Babe, everything we did tonight was a little intense. I'm not trying to break you."

She studied me a moment, apparently gathering her courage. "If I weren't pregnant, would things be different? What would you do to me right now?"

I snorted. "But you *are* pregnant."

"Still… what would you do? What do you want right now?"

I ran a hand over my beard and wondered if I should give her the truth. "You want to know what I'd do right now? With you being all mouthy and shit?"

She nodded.

"I'd fuck your mouth, make you take my cock and swallow my cum. Then I'd make you bend over and grab your ankles, ass in the air. I'd use a wooden paddle and spank that ass. And no, I wouldn't be holding back and be gentle and shit. You'd be hurting for days every time you sat. Then with your ass throbbing, I'd make you hold that position while I fucked you. A good, hard fucking that showed you that you were mine and I was in charge."

Her eyes had dilated, and her lips had parted as she hung on my every word. *Shit*! I wasn't supposed to be turning her on! I needed her worried, a little fearful, and not all ready for that kind of thing. It was something we'd work up to, but it seemed she was eager to try anything and everything with me.

"No, Lil. Not tonight. One day, but not right now."

"Were you always into this stuff?" she asked.

I shrugged. "I've always been a dominant asshole. If you're asking if I kept a dungeon and wore leather while wielding a whip, the answer is no. I like to play, and I play hard. But the greatest pleasure I get is when you scream while you come all over yourself, just knowing that you want my cock and only get it when I say you can have it."

"Dane, I…" Her cheeks got pink as she shifted in the tub again.

"My baby need to come again?"

She nodded. "I'm always so… so… I mean, only with you, but… I'm …"

"Horny." I laughed. "Yeah, I did some reading and it seems that pregnancy can do that to you. Let's get you dried off, then I'll eat that pretty pussy until you come. Then it's time for bed. You're exhausted. I can see it in your eyes, so don't even try to argue with me."

I helped her from the tub, drained the water, and used a soft towel to dry her off. Then I made good on my promise and let her come three times before I tucked her into bed next to me.

If I'd have known that having her in bed with me would be this amazing, I might have not only faced Griz when I took her that first time, but I'd have done it sooner. Who'd have ever guessed that sweet, shy, timid Lilian had such fire in her veins? And she was all mine.

Chapter Thirteen

Lilian

I glanced around the people gathered out back of the clubhouse and felt incredibly out of place. The only other women present were club whores, the regulars who were here all the damn time. Other than that, it was a sea of Devil's Fury cuts. Dragon stood next to me, holding my hand. I didn't know if he was worried I'd run, or if he was making it clear I belonged to him. The cut I was wearing should have been good enough, but I wouldn't put it past him to try and pee on my leg.

"I called all of you here for a reason," Grizzly said. "You see this woman strung up from the tree?"

There were murmurs, and I eyed the blonde from the night before. Someone had bound her hands and hung her over a tree limb with her feet dangling off the ground. She was alive, and looked scared shitless. As much as I'd wanted to beat her ass, and had done an adequate job -- or so I'd thought -- I didn't know what my dad and Demon had planned, and I was a little scared to watch.

"She's a traitorous bitch. She stole Dragon's phone, then sent a message to his pregnant woman -- *my daughter* -- that worried her enough she came to the clubhouse. A place she's never willingly ventured before." My dad eyed the crowd, especially the women. "This stupid cunt tried to take Dragon from my daughter. While Lilian gave her a good ass-whooping, the lying whore then tried to hide what she'd done. Not only that, but she's been spying on every brother here. She accessed Dragon's phone because she'd watched him unlock it before. Sneaky bitch was just waiting for the opportunity to get to one of us."

Demon stepped forward. "As Sergeant-at-Arms for the Devil's Fury, it's my job to make sure everyone in this club is protected. And that sure the fuck includes the ol' ladies, and our kids. Let this be a lesson to anyone who even thinks of fucking us over. Cheri is going to be branded a traitor forever, and if I ever see her lying face here again, I'll fucking kill her."

My blood chilled in my veins. I could tell he meant every word. What the hell did he mean she was going to be... My eyes went wide when I saw the burn barrel dragged closer. Holy shit. He meant he was literally going to brand her? I placed a hand over my stomach, not sure I wouldn't throw up. Demon picked up a branding iron, showing it to the crowd. It was just a simple "X" but I knew if he stuck that in the flames that were now shooting up from the barrel, then pressed it to her skin, it would be pure agony.

"Dragon." I tugged on his hand. "I don't think I can stomach this."

He glanced down at me. "I was covered in blood and gore from your kidnapper. You can and will watch this, Lil. Be fierce."

I gave a short nod and took a breath, trying to find my courage. Was I pissed at the woman? Yes. But I felt that what I'd already done to her was enough. It seemed Dragon, my dad, and Demon had other ideas.

Demon placed the branding iron into the flames, holding it until the metal glowed orange it was so damn hot. I squeezed Dragon's hand and forced myself not to flinch when Demon pressed the X to the skin of her lower belly. Cheri screamed and thrashed. Even though he didn't hold it there long, I could tell the pain wouldn't fade anytime soon.

"She wanted to use her body to lure Dragon away from his woman," Demon said. "So now any man who fucks her, will see that she's been branded. Every club within four hundred miles will be told of her treachery."

The women in the crowd were whispering to one another and shifting about nervously. I couldn't blame them. It seemed extreme, even for Demon. What the hell had gotten into him? To all of them! They were supposed to protect women, not hurt them. Tears stung my eyes and I wanted to turn away, or demand answers. Instead, I stood there. Watching. Waiting. Just like everyone else.

Dragon lifted my hand to his lips and kissed my fingers, then led me over to Demon and my father. I didn't want to go, but I wasn't about to balk and embarrass him again. My dad gave me a quick hug and Demon even smiled at me.

"For those who think this was too harsh a punishment, it wasn't," Demon said. "After Cheri's stunt, I found Lilian wandering the streets. At night. Alone. What you don't know is that she's suffered horribly during her life. She was used by the Colombian cartel, even when she was just a kid. She's been kidnapped and tortured. But she's a survivor. Watching what Cheri did nearly break Lilian made me realize that the punishment needed to be severe. If you don't agree with my methods, you know where the gate is. Get the fuck out and don't come back. Any whore who lies and steals as a way to separate a brother from his woman will face dire consequences."

Demon turned and I thought he was going to cut her down, but he unzipped his pants. I jerked my gaze up to Dragon's and he winked at me before whispering in my ear. "Glad you didn't try to sneak a peek at Demon's junk. I'd have paddled your ass later."

My cheeks heated, but I just kept watching Dragon. I heard Demon zip his pants.

"No," Demon said, zipping his pants back up. "She's not even worth pissing on."

Before I could tear my gaze from my man's, he released me and walked over to Cheri. Every man in the club walked up there, and Cheri was left sobbing as she hung from the tree. They didn't pee on, like Demon had threatened, but several spat at her. As much as I'd hated her last night, I felt sorry for her. I didn't know why she'd done what she had, but this was so wrong. I gazed at my dad and hoped he understood what I was feeling right then. I wasn't happy with any of them, but I was especially upset with him and Demon.

My dad came closer and bent his head to mine. "Don't you fucking feel sorry for her. You hear me, Lilian? She's not worth it. We have enemies outside these gates. When you left here, if Demon hadn't found you, do you know what could have happened?"

"Dad, I'm fine."

"Yeah, because my Sergeant-at-Arms hauled your ass back here." He took a breath, scanned the crowd, then focused on me again. "There was a body found this morning. Three blocks from where Demon picked you up. She was raped, tortured, and then gutted. We don't know who fucking did it, or why, but it could have been you, Lilian. They're estimating her time of death within two hours of your little walk. I know you think this was cruel and over the top, but it wasn't. These bitches need to know their place, and if they can't accept that they're only here to spread their legs, they can leave."

I'd never heard him speak like that before and I realized that he was truly frightened. Not in all the time I'd been here had I ever seen my dad scared.

Dragon looped an arm around my waist and pulled me back against chest. I leaned into him.

"Lil, we protect our own," Dragon said. "You're mine, and you're the daughter of our Pres. Whether you like it or not, that makes you special, puts you above other women except Adalia. Even Shella is one step below you. This was harsh, but it needed to be done. I won't risk your life because some stupid cunt is on a power trip. You hear me?"

I nodded. "I understand. I don't like it, but I understand."

Dragon pointed at Cheri, as Demon cut her down. "That woman made a choice. A conscious decision to do something she knew would hurt you. She knew it was fucking wrong when she did it. There are clubs out there who would have done far worse to her. She'd have been beaten. Tortured. And eventually killed."

My dad cupped my cheek. "Love you, Lilian. Doesn't matter that you're not from my loins, you're my daughter just the same. I will do whatever it takes to keep you safe. If that means I have to string someone up, or let these streets flow with blood, then I'll do it."

I saw two Prospects carry the woman away and Demon joined us. The crowd had dispersed, and I noticed the other women practically ran for their vehicles and took off as fast as they could. I wondered if any of them would be back, or if Demon had just ensured the club was without pussy for the foreseeable future. I could only imagine how well that would go over.

"No one disrespects you in your own house," Demon said. "Griz adopting you made you club royalty. You may not walk the walk or talk the talk, but you're a motherfucking badass princess and you need to own that shit. Don't let Dragon's name be the thing that sends fear into those bitches, or the Devil's Fury property cut on your back. You make them scared to even look in your direction, or his. You got me?"

I nodded. "I understand. I thought…"

"You thought that little display last night was good enough," Dragon said.

"Yeah. I've never lost my temper like that before. Never hurt anyone on purpose except for when I tried to escape being hurt myself."

Dragon rubbed his beard against my neck. "That's because you're my sweet girl, but you need to let that darkness out sometimes, babe. And it's okay to do that, especially here. Consider us your safety net. Bottling up all that anger, pain, fear. It's not good."

"Just maybe hold off on the ass kicking until my grandkids are born," Grizzly said. "You named them yet?"

"No," Dragon said.

"Actually, I kind of did pick two names." My man narrowed his eyes at me, but didn't say anything. I had a feeling I'd pay for it later, in a pleasurable way. "Ronan for our son and Mila for our daughter."

"I like it," my dad said, smiling widely. "Can't wait to hold my grandbabies."

"Dad, you have Gunner. It's not like you don't have a grandkid already."

He waved a hand. "Badger hogs the boy. I slip over there and hold him when I can, but I know Dragon won't keep the kids from me."

"Why are you so sure of that?" Dragon asked.

My dad stared at him a moment. "Because if I hadn't told you to get off your ass, you never would have gone after Lilian, or prepped that damn nursery. You owe me."

I snickered. He'd done a nice job getting the room ready for what he'd thought was his one and only baby. Now we needed a second crib and would have to rearrange the room, and get a few extra toys. But since we knew what we were having, we could get whatever colors we wanted. I was looking forward to a little baby shopping, but apparently the last trip had scarred Dragon for life and he wasn't too anxious to go back.

My dad eyed Dragon, then winked at me. "Ronan and Mila Moore. Has a nice ring to it."

"Now wait one fucking minute. Why are my kids taking *your* last name?" Dragon asked.

Griz shrugged. "Because you haven't married their momma. Grow a pair and ask her already. Do I have to do everything for you?"

Dragon growled and I pushed back against him until he'd taken a step, then another. He obviously needed a little distance from my dad. Shella came around the corner of the clubhouse and I saw Dagger stiffen out of the corner of my eye. She marched up to Dad, then wrinkled her nose.

"Why does it smell like burned meat?" she asked.

I gagged and tried not to think about what I'd seen.

"Little girls should be at home where they belong," Dagger said. "Not at the clubhouse causing problems."

Shella rolled her eyes, then looked at our dad. "I have a date. We're going to a movie, dinner, and possibly dancing at that under twenty-one club a few towns over. I'll be home late."

As my sister skipped off, I saw a vein pulsing in Dagger's head. I smiled, turning away only to freeze. I blinked, thinking my eyes were playing tricks on me, but no. One of the Prospects, Jared, was eyeing both Dagger *and* my sister with longing. Holy shit! I watched another moment, saw the second Dagger felt someone staring at him. He unerringly found Jared nearby, and from the sparks shooting between them, I had to wonder if something wasn't going on there. I just wasn't sure what that meant for my sister.

Shella was something of a wild child, but I didn't see her trying to take on two bikers at once. If she was smart, she'd elope with one of her prissy pretty boys she hung around. Her smart mouth wouldn't fare too well with men like Dagger. I rubbed at my own ass, remembering my punishment. Shella was far worse than me. I could only imagine what would happen to her if she mouthed off to either of those men.

I should still be angry with her, but I wasn't. At least, not entirely. If she hadn't run her mouth, then I wouldn't have run off. I still couldn't lay everything at her feet, though. She was younger than me, and hadn't seen nearly as much. Shella might be a little imp, but I knew she'd truly believed she was doing the right thing at the time. I just wasn't ready to completely forgive her.

"You got tense," Dragon murmured in my ear.

"Just thinking."

"About what?"

"Wondering if Shella knows both Dagger and Jared have a thing for her."

Dragon made a humming sound, then put his lips near my ear and whispered, "What you should be wondering is how long before they both try to make her submit. Those two wouldn't mind sharing."

Well, that was more than I ever wanted to know about the men in this club. And I certainly didn't want to think about them with my little sister. Honestly, Shella was a brat. They would be better off with someone else. Someone sweeter. Innocent. I didn't doubt they *thought* she was innocent, but I'd heard her talking on the phone with her friends. My sister was braver than me when it came to guys, and she'd taken charge of her sex life. Instead of hiding from it like I had -- until Dragon. "So they're bisexual?" I asked.

He nodded. "Club doesn't care as long as they aren't flaunting it, I guess. Doesn't bother me either way, but some wouldn't handle it well."

"I'll find them someone," I said. "Shella's not right for them. She likes boys who let her be in charge. If those two tried to take control, she'd probably flip out."

"Guess we'll just have to wait and see." My stomach rumbled and I felt Dragon's hold tighten on me. "But it looks like what I need to do right now is get my woman and kids some food. You want to eat out?"

"I'd like that. Maybe somewhere that has a lot of options?" I asked. My cravings had been insane lately.

"I'll get the keys to a club truck and we'll head out."

He threaded our fingers together and led me around the front of the clubhouse. I stood next to one of the trucks while I waited for him. When he returned, Dragon opened my door and lifted me into the truck. He pressed a kiss to my cheek before buckling me in, then going around to the driver's side. Ever since he'd come for me, he was always taking care of me. To some it might seem overbearing, but I loved it. Mostly.

As he drove past the main part of town, and all my favorite restaurants, I cast a glance his way. Dragon didn't so much as look at me, just kept driving. It wasn't until we'd left town that I realized where we were going. Three towns over, and a good hour drive, was a place I'd always wanted to try, but I'd never been. There was a courtyard with plenty of seating, which was surrounded on all sides by different restaurants. Not the type where you ordered and ate there, but spots where you could walk up, order, and then take your food to a table in the courtyard. They weren't fast food, which is why they only offered certain dishes on particular days.

I practically bounced in my seat as he parked, then helped me out of the truck. We stopped at the Mexican place and I ordered three different types of tacos. Then I got a bowl of shrimp fried rice from the Chinese place. The Greek restaurant had my nose twitching and my mouth watering. I ordered two lamb gyros with peppers and onions. And I topped it all off with a decadent piece of pecan pie from the southern style café on the corner.

Dragon helped me carry everything to a table, then he went to get something for himself while I dug in. I was so intent on my food, I didn't notice the whispers at first. Until the voices got louder.

Wonder why he's with a fatty like her.

Oh my God. Is all that food for her? No wonder her ass is so wide.

I nearly choked as I tried to swallow my bite of chicken taco. My eyes watered, and I sucked down some sweet tea, and pretended I didn't hear the catty bitches. But the more they mocked me, the worse I felt. It only took Dragon a second when he returned to tell something was wrong.

"Babe, why aren't you eating? Is it not good? Want something else?"

Like she needs anything else.

I hoped he hadn't heard the remark, but the way his brows lowered and his jaw tensed, I knew he had. He scanned the area and found the women a few tables over. Before I could stop him, he'd stood and stomped over there. The giggling stopped as he glowered at them. "Do you have a problem?" he demanded.

"Yeah. Her fat ass is making me lose my appetite. I can't believe you'd fuck that."

I closed my eyes, not wanting to see if he took a swing at her. When a hand gripped my arm, I jolted, but saw it was only Dragon. He hauled me over to their table. Putting me in front of him, he wrapped his arms around me, placing his hands on my belly.

"I not only fuck her, as often as I can, but I planted two babies in her. She's sexy, passionate, and she's *mine*. If you have a problem with her, you can get the hell out of here." I could feel Dragon practically vibrating in anger.

A security guard ambled over, looking like he was just this side of sixty but still fit. He was nearly as tall as Dragon, even if he wasn't as bulky. His gaze took in the scene as he approached. "What's the problem here? You scaring these women?"

Dragon snarled. "Am I scaring them? I sure the fuck hope so after they insulted my pregnant girlfriend. They called her fat and said she was disgusting."

The guard frowned and looked at the two women. They tried batting their eyes at him and acting all innocent. The man didn't seem fooled. "Perhaps the two of you should take your meal to go. Nothing wrong with a woman having a healthy appetite."

The two flounced off, leaving their trash behind. The guard shook his head.

"Thank you," I said. "They were making me uncomfortable."

The guard smiled. "Just doing my job, ma'am. You've got a good one there, looking out for you. Don't let catty women like those two get you down. Congratulations to you both."

Dragon led me back to our table, and I managed to finish my food, including the pie. Then wished I hadn't. It was a good thing I was pregnant. If I didn't already have a baby bump, my tummy would have been sticking out for sure just from the sheer amount of food I'd consumed. Sadly, I knew I'd be hungry again in about an hour. I had a feeling these kids were going to be huge.

"All right. I've fed my baby-momma. Now what do you want to do?" he asked.

"Whatever it takes for you to never call me that again?"

He smiled and winked, which told me I'd be hearing it even more now. Sometimes, I would swear that Dragon was still a kid. He reminded me of those boys in movies that teased and tormented the girls they liked. I'd told Griz they were immature and asked when boys grew up. He'd said never, and I hadn't believed him. Until Dragon.

We walked out of the courtyard and he led me down the strip of shops that lined the street. Stopping in front of a jewelry store, he wrapped an arm around my waist. "You want a different title than baby-momma? I'm afraid you'll have to make an honest man of me."

I looked up at him. "I don't think anyone could ever make you honest. You must have mistaken me for a genie in a bottle."

He swatted my ass. "Smartass. You'll pay for that later."

"Are you being serious right now?" I asked, gesturing to the shop.

He nodded. "Yeah. Your dad is right. I love you, Lilian. You're mine, in every other way. I want to make it legal too. Get you a ring, let you plan a wedding."

I held up a hand. "Stop right there. I'm preparing to have two babies at one time. I'm *not* planning a wedding. You want to marry me? Fine. We can go to the Justice of the Peace, or just ask Outlaw to handle it."

Dragon rocked back on his heels. "You don't want an actual wedding?"

"Don't need one."

"Okay, so you don't *need* one, but do you want one? Don't all women want that kind of thing when they settle down? Flowers, dresses, and all that shit?"

I tipped my head back and looked up at him. "Do I look like the type of woman who cares about any of that? After everything I've been through, I don't need all that silly stuff. It sounds like a headache."

He pulled out his phone, then hesitated. "You're sure? Like, one hundred fifty percent certain that you don't want an actual wedding of any sort?"

I reached out and snatched his phone, pulling up a message to Outlaw. *Marry us already.*

I tossed the phone back to him, watched as he read what I'd sent, then a big grin spread across his lips. He held me close and kissed the hell out of me, not seeming to care that we were in the middle of a sidewalk or that we were surrounded by strangers. And I let him because despite the hell he'd put me through, I loved him. Maybe some would see me as weak, but I deserved some happiness, and Dragon gave that to me, and so much more.

I didn't argue when he dragged me into the jewelry store. He kept trying to get me a flashy ring, but that's not what I needed. I just wanted a plain band. He eyed a black band the salesman said was made of something called tungsten carbide. It surprised me that he'd be willing to wear a wedding ring, so I opted to get one that matched, just a much smaller one. The band I chose was thin and light.

We walked out wearing our rings, and even though I'd said I didn't need to be married to him, I liked having that ring on my finger. Even more, I liked that he was wearing one. Even when he wasn't at the clubhouse, women would know he was taken. Some wouldn't care and might make a play for him anyway, but I'd have to learn to trust him. I did trust him with my life, but trusting him with my heart was difficult after he'd broken it. Granted, the last time hadn't been Dragon but the club whore. My stomach clenched as I remembered what Demon had done to her.

"Let's go home," he said, lifting my hand to kiss my fingers.

Chapter Fourteen

Dragon
One Month Later

I glanced at the time, hating that I was stuck in Church when Lil was getting off work. Dr. Larkin had taken her back after she'd explained what happened, but he'd reduced her hours since she was carrying twins. I had a feeling it wouldn't be long before he suggested she stay home. I damn well knew he'd replaced her already and her part-time hours were just a courtesy. My woman didn't need to work, but if she wanted to, I'd try to understand. I'd much rather have her home with our kids.

"Ramirez reached out," Grizzly said. "The man he answered to has been toppled from the throne, and Ramirez is stepping in. While he no longer needs to hide shipments in our town, or any other, he said he does have one last favor."

"Thought he planned to call for us at some point," Demon said. "Does this favor include firepower? Blowing shit up? Killing innocents?"

Grizzly shook his head. "None of the above, but I'd have preferred any of those."

"Then what the fuck is it?" Dagger asked.

"Women. It seems the big boss had a few sweatshops up in New York. He brought the women up from South America and Mexico. They were trying to earn passage and citizenship for their families here in the US." Grizzly sat back. "Ramirez apparently draws the line at using women. He's emptying out the sweatshops, but he doesn't have a place to put all of them."

"Shit," I muttered. "We're supposed to keep them here?"

"Some of them," Grizzly said. "He's calling on the other clubs he manipulated before. I don't know the total number of women he's trying to place, but I do know we're getting four of them. From what I've heard, they're skittish and I'd honestly be surprised if all this hadn't made them scared shitless. I doubt they're going to trust any of us."

"Don't even think of asking Adalia to help," Badger said. "I'm not putting my woman and kid at risk."

"Neither am I," said Dingo.

I was shaking my head already when the Pres looked my way. Nope. Lilian wasn't going anywhere near those women until I knew it was safe. She still had a few months to go before she delivered Ronan and Mila. I wasn't taking any chances with her or the babies. If those women were scared, they would possibly lash out.

Blades cleared his throat. "I can talk to China. She may be sympathetic enough to try and guide them. Can't make any promises."

"Shella is too young, and too damn wild to be of any help," Grizzly said.

"This shit right here is why you need a woman, Pres," Scorpion said.

Griz was already shaking his head. I knew damn well he'd never claim another woman. His wife had been his one and only. Losing her to cancer had just about killed him. If it hadn't been for Adalia, I didn't think he'd have pulled through. Even though he didn't have May anymore, I seldom saw him with a club whore. After, he always looked guilty as hell, like he'd cheated on his woman. The single guys couldn't get it, but the rest of us understood. If something happened to Lil, I wouldn't want another woman in my house or my bed. Ever. She was it for me.

"Where are we putting them?" I asked. "They can't exactly stay at the clubhouse. Do we have any homes to spare?"

"We'll have to use the duplexes where we put guests. I'm not sure how long they'll be here," Grizzly said. "It's possible Ramirez just needs a resting spot for them while he figures shit out. If they'll be here longer than a few weeks, then I'll come up with something else."

"How long did it take us to put those up?" I asked. Half the club called them duplexes, some called them townhomes. It was three small apartments, all one level, and attached across. They weren't that big.

"Think we need another three?" Grizzly asked.

"I was thinking four if there are four women, but even if they don't stay for more than a few weeks or a few months, we could always use them for something later. Things haven't been that bad around here, but if we ever go to war with another club, or another cartel, having extra sleeping spots for anyone willing to help wouldn't be a bad idea," I said.

"If we used the same plans and made two more sets of those little apartments, three across just like the current one, we could set it up like a little community of sorts and have plenty of space for whatever we might need in the future," Cobra said.

"Henry headed up that project," Grizzly said. "We'll see how long it would take him to build more. Whatever crew or equipment he needs, see that he gets it. I have no fucking clue who will ride herd on those women if China isn't up for the task, but we'll figure that shit out when we have to."

"Wonder what else Ramirez will want?" Demon asked. "This seems like more of a fluff kind of job than anything hard-hitting. Even though he's taking over, I get the feeling he likes us in his pocket."

"So we play along for now," Wolf said. "If things get out of hand, or he wants something we aren't willing to give, then we push back. Until then... is the club getting paid for our help?"

"Ramirez promised a bag of cash to offset any expenses we incur from having the women here," Grizzly said. "He didn't give an exact amount, and I was still pissed over the fact he's dropping women on our doorstep. Not sure how long it will take him to get them here from New York."

There was a knock on the door, which had the Pres scowling fiercely. Wolf got up to answer, murmured to whoever was outside, then opened the door to let Beau inside. The Prospect looked about two seconds from bolting out of the room.

"Interrupting Church isn't the way to earn your patch," Griz said.

"Sorry, Pres. There's, um... there are bunch of... females at the gate."

Females? Had we been dropped into a sci-fi movie? Why not just call them women? Griz stood and strode from the room with the rest of us following. When we reached the front gate, I understood exactly why Beau had phrased it that way. Fucking hell. One glance at the Pres and I knew he was going to go nuclear if Ramirez showed his face. Not only did we have more than four, but two of them certainly weren't women. Yet.

"How old are you?" Griz asked the smallest.

"Thirteen," she mumbled.

"And you?" Griz asked the girl next to her.

"Fifteen." She tipped her chin up, but I noticed her hands trembled. Poor thing was trying to be brave.

"Who brought you here?" Demon asked one of the older women in the group, who couldn't have been more than early twenties.

"Mr. Ramirez had his men leave us down the street. We were told to walk to your gates and ask to see Grizzly." She licked her lips and glanced at the other women. "We've been traveling a while. Could we have some water? The younger ones are hungry."

Demon's gaze softened. "What's your name?"

"Rosa. Rosa Perez."

"We don't have a spot ready for you since we just learned you would be coming here. The clubhouse isn't the cleanest, but you can rest and have something to drink and bite to eat," Demon said. He held out his hand, and she slowly eased her palm into his.

As he walked off, I stared after them, feeling as if I'd just stepped into an alternate reality. Since when was our big bad Sergeant-at-Arms all soft and sweet with a woman? Lilian, Shella, and Adalia were different. They were the Pres' daughters. But this woman? We didn't know shit about her, including whether or not she'd told us the truth.

"Francisca," said another woman, lifting her fingers in a slight wave. "But call me Franny."

Her voice wasn't as heavily accented as the others who had spoken. It made me wonder if she'd been in our country longer, even though she looked really damn young. Probably close to Shella's age, if not younger.

"Come on, Franny," Wolf said, leading her away. "Anyone else who is hungry, thirsty, or needs to use the bathroom better head with us to the clubhouse. We'll figure out where to put you after that."

I stepped back as they followed Wolf and Demon. Grizzly came to stand next to me, his arms folded over his chest, but I noticed he watched the younger ones. I had a feeling the Pres would be opening up his home to more strays. It was just his way. He and May had always wanted kids, but never been blessed with any of their own. They'd taken in Adalia when she needed help, then later Grizzly did the same for Lilian and Shella. I had a feeling he'd keep adopting kids until the day he died. Maybe it was his way of honoring his wife's memory. Filling the house with the kids they always wanted.

"What now, Pres?" I asked.

"Now I get to tell Adalia and Lilian they don't have rooms at my house anymore. The two younger ones will need them. Then I get to wait for Shella to have a fit that I'm bringing someone into our home."

"You really should have turned that one over your knee long ago," I said. "No offense, Pres, but your daughter is a brat."

"I've let her run wild," he said. "I shouldn't have, but what's done is done. Might be time to push that chick from the nest."

My eyebrows rose at that. Griz would have let Lilian live with him indefinitely, and she was older than Shella. I'd heard about Shella drinking and partying in town with the college friends she'd made, and knew she'd gotten into some trouble in high school. Was the Pres really going to toss her out? Kid didn't have anywhere to go that I knew of. She'd had boyfriends, if you could call those pretty bastards boys, but I didn't know if she was seeing someone right now.

"You know, if you toss her out, Lilian will try to bring her to our house. No matter what happened between them, they're sisters." I looked at him. "That's not happening. Not now, not ever."

"I'll handle it. Maybe Irish is ready for a visit. Shella could see her baby sister."

He was going to set that hellion loose on the Devil's Boneyard? Part of me wanted to call and warn them, but then I decided to just sit back and see how it played out. No one here would ever tame Shella, even though it looked like Dagger and Jared might have liked trying. I damn well knew that wouldn't have ended in anything but heartache and a screaming match.

I clapped the Pres on the back. "You do that. Let's go figure out where all these women are staying. You think those two are the only young ones? Everyone else seemed older. Hopefully, old enough to stay on their own. Even if we have to put more than one into an apartment, they could have a place to stay for tonight. Just need to make sure those units are cleaned and stocked."

Beau cleared his throat, having remained nearby. "I could do it. Maybe get Carver and Simon to make a run to the store for groceries, but I can make sure there's new soap, shampoo, clean towels and all that shit ready for the women. I know how to run a vacuum if I need to."

Griz snorted. "All right. Which one is it?"

Beau opened and shut his mouth. "Um, which one is what?"

"Which of those women caught your eye? And don't you fucking say it's one of the younger ones or I'll string you up by your balls." Griz glared at him.

"None of them! I just want to help. If we don't have a place for them, where are they going to go? Out on the streets? I don't want..." He clamped his mouth shut, but I knew what he was going to say. He didn't want them to end up like Dingo's woman, Meiling, who happened to be friends with Beau long before she came here.

"Go," Griz said. "I'll assign a few men to buy groceries. I've bought shit for my girls enough to know what else to add to the list. We'll make sure they have enough basics to get them settled for a few days."

Everyone walked off, leaving me alone with the Pres. He eyed the clubhouse thoughtfully, rubbing a hand over his beard. I didn't know what he was thinking, but when a slight smile curved his lips, I knew it couldn't be anything good. He was scheming, and I had a feeling it had to do with those women and all the single men at the compound. Never before had I been more thankful that Lilian was mine. It would save me from his matchmaking.

"If you don't need me, I'm out. Lilian should be coming home any minute."

The words no sooner left my mouth than the SUV I'd bought her a few weeks ago came through the gate. She stopped and rolled down her window, eyeing me and her dad. "Should I be worried?"

Griz jerked his chin at me. "Go with her. Keep her home if you must, but tell her what's going on. Then you'll likely have to tie her down to keep her in your house. She'll want to help."

Yeah, he wasn't telling me anything I didn't already know. Dammit. I motioned for Lil to head to the house and I went to get my bike from in front of the clubhouse. As I backed out and started to pull forward, a blacked-out car caught my attention. The window rolled down and I tensed, half expecting a gun to appear, but instead a large duffle was thrown out the window on the drive near our gate.

Griz walked over and unzipped it, then stood, lifting it. The way he'd approached, all confident, told me he'd had an idea of who was throwing shit at our gates. I waited until he'd gotten closer to find out what the hell was going on. When he showed me the large amount of cash inside, I knew it was from Ramirez, and had no doubt he'd just bought those women far more than a few weeks. Something told me they were here to stay until we could make other arrangements for them.

"Well, Pres. Now if you try to pair those ladies up with our brothers, you'll be a pimp, seeing as how Ramirez just paid you a fuck ton of money."

Grizzly flipped me off and went into the clubhouse. I had no doubt he'd still try to pair them off with someone, even if it was just temporary. The guy wouldn't hesitate to make someone bleed, would walk through hell for those he considered family, but under all that was a soft heart where women and kids were concerned.

I didn't know what our future held, but I had a feeling that things were about to change.

Epilogue

Lilian
Three Months Later

"So help me God, if you put your dick anywhere near me after this, I'm going to cut it off!" I screamed as another contraction hit. The medical staff laughed, but Dragon winced and reached down to place a hand over his crotch.

"Push, Mrs. Starke. Almost there."

"Don't you fucking lie to me. I know damn well there's another one in there." Why had I thought having kids was going to be amazing? I'd been so excited the last several months, but now I was rethinking everything.

"One more push and the head will be out," the doctor said.

I gritted my teeth and pushed, trying not to scream. Dragon's kids were fucking huge and I was convinced they were going to rip me in half. A few more pushes, and I collapsed back on my pillows.

"Congratulations, Mom and Dad. Baby Ronan is here."

Dragon smirked. "Good. He can protect his little sister when the time comes."

I gave him a half-hearted slap on the chest. I was exhausted. Another contraction gripped me, and soon I was trying to push out our daughter. It didn't seem to hurt as much as her brother had, but hearing her cry was the sweetest sound. I smiled, my eyes closed, as I tried to find some energy to inspect my kids.

The murmuring caught my attention, then I felt Dragon gripping my hand tighter. I opened my eyes to find the nurses surrounding the babies, and my heart gave a kick. Was something wrong? I'd heard her cry. That meant she was fine, didn't it?

"We'll get the babies cleaned up and be back soon," said a nurse, before my children were whisked from the room. The doctor remained to deliver the afterbirth, then a nurse helped clean me up.

"Where are the babies?" I asked.

She gave me a sympathetic look, then hurried from the room. I looked up at my husband with tears in my eyes. What was going on? Why wouldn't they tell us if something was wrong?

"Dane. My babies!"

He smoothed my hair back. "I'm sure they'll bring them right back."

Dragon was right about our babies coming back to the room, but I didn't think the look on the doctor's face bode well. I reached for my children, and they placed Ronan in my arms first, swaddled in a blue blanket. He blinked up at me, and my heart melted. He was precious. Perfect.

"Hello, Ronan. I'm your mommy." I stroked his soft cheek and pressed a kiss to his head.

They handed Mila to Dragon, and he stared at her. His gaze cut over to me, and I wondered what that meant. I lifted a hand, wanting him to show my daughter to me, but he seemed to tuck her closer to his chest and turn away a little. My brow furrowed as I tried to puzzle out his odd behavior.

"Mr. and Mrs. Starke, you have two beautiful, healthy babies. As Mr. Starke has probably noticed, Mila is a little different from her brother."

"Different how?" I asked the doctor.

"She has congenital cataracts. It's more common than you think, and there's no need to panic. She'll need an operation to remove the cataracts, and the sooner the better. We can get it scheduled as early as next week."

"Surgery?" My heart rate spiked at the thought of my precious baby needing surgery.

"It requires anesthesia, and there is some risk involved. I believe Mila will pull through beautifully. Once the cataracts are removed, then she'll need contacts to help focus her vision. I can have the surgeon stop by and speak with you. He'll be able to answer your questions and explain things a little more."

"Thank you, Doctor," Dragon said.

"Your son weighed seven pounds three ounces," the nurse said. "Baby Mila was only six pounds four ounces. Even though she's smaller, she's a scrappy thing with a good set of lungs. Most twins we see aren't quite as large as yours. You must have been feeding them all the right things."

Ronan started to fuss and turn his face toward me. I panicked, not knowing what to do.

"He wants to eat," the nurse said. "Do you plan to breastfeed?"

I nodded. She helped me get Ronan situated, and helped him latch on the first time. It was an odd sensation, and my breasts were aching. After he had his fill, I fed Mila. My precious babies were beautiful.

"Most of the club is in the waiting room," Dragon said. "Your dad is especially antsy to come see his grandkids. Let me know when you want to bring him back."

"Not just yet. I'm so tired." I yawned, my jaw cracking. Dragon took Mila from me, placed our babies into the little hospital cribs, then came back to hold my hand. My stomach rumbled from hunger, but I didn't care. Giving birth had exhausted me.

"You did so good, babe." He kissed my forehead. "They're beautiful, and perfect."

"Never doing that again," I mumbled. My contractions had started a good eight hours before Ronan made his appearance. I'd tried to come to the hospital when I felt the first ones, but they'd sent me home, saying it was too soon. Those evil bitches! By the time Dragon had brought me back, and they'd admitted me, I'd been informed my contractions were too close together for an epidural.

"Lil, unless one of us gets fixed, we'll have more kids. I'm not using a condom to fuck my wife."

I opened one eye to glare at him. "I just pushed out two giant humans from a very sensitive place. I'm not getting fixed. You can get neutered."

He winced. "Uh, yeah. We'll discuss it in a few weeks. Remember, the doc said it would be about six weeks before you could have sex again anyway. Maybe longer since you had twins."

Like I needed the reminder! My body no longer felt like my own. Even though I didn't look like there was a basketball under my hospital gown, my belly still felt strange. The skin was looser and rounder than it had been pre-pregnancy. I didn't know if I'd ever slim down again. Not that I'd been skinny to begin with.

"I hope you meant what you said about liking me all soft and curvy," I said.

"Why's that?"

"Because I'm pretty sure your kids just added another few inches to my waist. Permanently."

Dragon kissed me softly on the lips, then rubbed his beard against my cheek. "Babe, I love you exactly as you are. Curves. Stretch marks. This beautiful body gave me those precious babies over there, and there is no one I find sexier than you. Only thing that changed is that I love you more than I did before."

I smiled a little. "I love you too, Dane. Now let me sleep. Wake me if the babies need to eat."

I didn't know what tomorrow would bring, or the next month. For now, I had my husband, my babies, and an unconventional family I adored. I knew that Dragon and the other Devil's Fury would do anything to keep me and the children safe. I might not agree with their methods, but I couldn't deny they were effective. After Demon had branded the club whore, I'd been told no one had so much as looked at Dragon, and the amount of trouble from those women had dropped considerably. Dragon said a few had left, but some remained. And I knew there would always be new ones.

My life wasn't perfect, but it was mine. I'd survived so much to get to this point. But knowing what I did now, that I'd end up with an amazing guy like Dragon and two beautiful children, I'd do it again. Even after all I'd suffered, I knew that it had made me into the person I was today. If the Devil's Boneyard hadn't found me in Colombia when they rescued their man, I never would have come to this country, much less been adopted by Grizzly. I didn't pretend to understand why horrible things had to happen, but I did know something wonderful had come from all the pain and suffering.

I'd never known the love of a man, until Dragon. Never known pleasure, until Dragon. And I'd never wanted to give complete control to a man, until Dragon. He was my everything, and I knew I meant everything to him. Two halves of a whole.

Whatever the future had in store for us, I knew we'd face it together.

Harley Wylde

Harley Wylde is the International Bestselling Author of the Dixie Reapers MC, Devil's Boneyard MC, and Hades Abyss MC series.

When Harley's writing, her motto is the hotter the better -- off the charts sex, commanding men, and the women who can't deny them. If you want men who talk dirty, are sexy as hell, and take what they want, then you've come to the right place. She doesn't shy away from the dangers and nastiness in the world, bringing those realities to the pages of her books, but always gives her characters a happily-ever-after and makes sure the bad guys get what they deserve.

The times Harley isn't writing, she's thinking up naughty things to do to her husband, drinking copious amounts of Starbucks, and reading. She loves to read and devours a book a day, sometimes more. She's also fond of TV shows and movies from the 1980's, as well as paranormal shows from the 1990's to today, even though she'd much rather be reading or writing.

You can find out more about Harley or enter her monthly giveaway on her website. Be sure to join her newsletter while you're there to learn more about discounts, signing events, and other goodies!

Harley at Changeling: changelingpress.com/harley-wylde-a-196

Changeling Press E-Books

More Sci-Fi, Fantasy, Paranormal, and BDSM adventures available in e-book format for immediate download at ChangelingPress.com -- Werewolves, Vampires, Dragons, Shapeshifters and more -- Erotic Tales from the edge of your imagination.

What are E-Books?

E-books, or electronic books, are books designed to be read in digital format -- on your desktop or laptop computer, notebook, tablet, Smart Phone, or any electronic e-book reader.

Where can I get Changeling Press E-Books?

Changeling Press e-books are available at ChangelingPress.com, Amazon, Apple Books, Barnes & Noble, and Kobo/Walmart.

ChangelingPress.com

Printed in Great Britain
by Amazon